CW01475522

The Cat AND THE CHRISTMAS Kidnapper

By L T Shearer

L T SHEARER

The Cat AND THE CHRISTMAS Kidnapper

MACMILLAN

First published 2025 by Macmillan
an imprint of Pan Macmillan
The Smithson, 6 Briset Street, London EC1M 5NR
EU representative: Macmillan Publishers Ireland Ltd, 1st Floor,
The Liffey Trust Centre, 117–126 Sheriff Street Upper,
Dublin 1 D01 YC43
Associated companies throughout the world

ISBN 978-1-0350-4384-2 HB
ISBN 978-1-0350-4385-9 TPB

1 3 5 7 9 8 6 4 2

A CIP catalogue record for this book is available from the British Library.

Typeset by Palimpsest Book Production Ltd, Falkirk, Stirlingshire
Printed and bound in the UK using 100% Renewable Electricity
by CPI Group (UK) Ltd

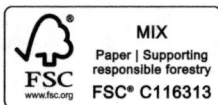

MIX
Paper | Supporting
responsible forestry
FSC® C116313
FSC
www.fsc.org

Visit **www.panmacmillan.com** to read more about
all our books and to buy them.

The Cat AND THE CHRISTMAS Kidnapper

1

'Are you hungry?' asked Conrad. 'The reason I ask is that I am definitely getting peckish.' He looked up at Lulu, who was holding the tiller of her narrowboat, *The Lark*, as it phut-phut-phutted its way along the Kennet and Avon Canal, heading towards Bath.

Conrad was sitting on the metal seat at the stern, the cold December wind ruffling his fur. He was a good-looking cat, of that there was no question. The right side of his head was mainly black with an uneven white patch around the nose and mouth, and the left side was brown and white. His eyes were a vibrant green and his mouth seemed to form a sly smile, as if he'd just heard something that amused him. His front legs and chest were white, his body and tail were thick stripes of black and brown and his rear legs had white socks. He was a typical calico cat in many respects, but it was his ability to talk that set him apart from all other cats.

Lulu had been shocked the first time Conrad had spoken to her, after he'd jumped onto *The Lark* at her mooring in Little Venice – so shocked that she'd thought she was either dreaming or losing her mind. Neither was the case. Conrad really could talk, but he had made it clear from the outset that he would only talk to her. Lulu had no idea why Conrad had chosen her, but no one else who came across him received anything more communicative than a 'meow' or, if he was in a particularly good mood, a throaty purr.

'I think lunch would be a very good idea,' said Lulu. She was wearing a heavy sheepskin jacket over a thick pullover, blue jeans tucked into Caterpillar boots, and wool fingerless gloves, but she was still feeling the cold. It had taken *The Lark* just over a week to travel the eighty-odd miles from Reading. It was a picturesque journey with almost a hundred locks to be opened and closed along the way. Dealing with locks single-handedly in the winter was challenging, but not over difficult, and Lulu had become adept at opening and closing the gates, opening the sluices and using the centre line to keep *The Lark* in the middle of the chamber as the water rose or fell. Truth be told, operating the locks kept her warm, while standing next to the tiller meant she had no choice but to face the bitter wind that blew along the canal.

She took her iPhone from her jacket pocket and used her left hand to scroll through the app she was using to keep track of their journey. 'There's a cafe about a mile ahead of us,' she said.

'Is it cat friendly?' asked Conrad.

'There's a terrace at the side of the canal, so I assume so,' said Lulu, putting the phone back into her pocket.

'So where are we?' asked Conrad, narrowing his eyes against the wind.

'We're coming up to Bradford-on-Avon,' said Lulu. 'It's about nine miles from Bath.'

Bath was their ultimate destination, and Lulu hoped to get there before dark. *The Lark*'s top speed was about four miles an hour, but generally Lulu kept to about three miles an hour, even slower whenever she passed moored boats. Considerate boaters always slowed down to pass moored boats; there was nothing worse than being tossed up and down by the wake of a speeding narrowboat.

The canal was clear, so she didn't have to slow down as they headed towards the cafe. They passed a couple of boats coming the other way, and like her the owners were well wrapped up against the winter wind. The first owner was a middle-aged man with a flat cap and a red and white scarf wrapped around his neck. He gave a cheery wave and shouted hello as he went by. Five minutes later they passed a compact narrowboat that couldn't have been more than thirty feet long, about half the length of *The Lark*. The boat was in lovely condition, dark blue with brass portholes and a roof decked out with brightly painted planters filled with small conifers. The boater was, like Lulu, a woman in her sixties, wrapped up against the cold with a padded coat and a white fleece beanie pulled low over her ears. She was holding the tiller with her right hand and had a steaming mug of something hot in her left. The woman raised her mug in salute, and Lulu waved.

A young boy on a bicycle passed by on the towpath, travelling at probably three times *The Lark*'s pace. Narrowboats weren't built for speed, and it wasn't unusual for Lulu to be overtaken by joggers or even fast walkers. Like most boaters, she appreciated the journey as much as the arrival. Getting to wherever she was going was half the fun. Probably more than half, to be honest – although on this occasion she was very much looking forward to spending Christmas in Bath with her goddaughter, Amanda, and her family.

Conrad jumped up onto the roof of *The Lark*. 'Is that it?' he asked, gazing ahead.

Lulu narrowed her eyes as she peered into the wind. 'Yes,

I think so,' she said. There was a stone building at the side of the canal with a roofed terrace. Three narrowboats were moored close by. 'You have such good eyesight.'

'Actually, humans have better long vision than cats,' said Conrad. 'Everything gets a bit blurry for me beyond about twenty feet, but you humans can see clearly up to more than two hundred feet.'

'So how did you see the cafe?'

'I can smell the food,' said Conrad.

'Ah yes, of course,' said Lulu. 'Didn't you tell me that your sense of smell is fifteen times better than mine?'

'Fourteen,' said Conrad. 'Cats have more than two hundred million odour sensors in their noses; humans have just five million.'

'And how does the food smell?' asked Lulu, easing back on the throttle.

'Pretty good,' said Conrad.

Lulu went slowly past the moored narrowboats before pulling in and reversing back. She put the engine to idle, grabbed the stern line, stepped off onto the towpath and used the line to gently ease *The Lark* into place. Then she secured the line, tied the bow and centre lines and climbed back onto the rear deck to kill the engine.

'You always make that look so easy,' said Conrad.

'It's the advantage of opposable thumbs,' said Lulu. The cafe overlooked *The Lark*, so she didn't bother locking up. Conrad jumped up onto her shoulders and Lulu stepped back onto the towpath.

'I am so hungry,' said Conrad.

'Yes, you said.'

The Lock Inn was a beautiful stone cottage with an

outdoor terrace under a roof made from plastic sheeting. Lulu peered through a window and saw that most of the tables inside were occupied. A decorated Christmas tree with flashing fairy lights stood in the corner of the room. There were only two men out on the terrace, and they were standing up to leave. The terrace was shielded from the wind, so Lulu decided she would sit outside.

'Lovely day for it,' said one of the men. He was in his fifties with a bushy grey beard and a captain's hat that made Lulu think of Captain Birdseye.

'It is, yes.'

'So you're on *The Lark*?'

'That's right.'

'You're a long way from home.' He had obviously seen 'LITTLE VENICE' on the sign on the side of *The Lark*.

'Visiting friends,' said Lulu.

The other man was a few years younger and could have well been Captain Birdseye's son, though Lulu had long since stopped assuming relationships based on appearance. 'Are you travelling alone?' he asked.

'Just me and Conrad,' said Lulu. Conrad jumped down from her shoulders onto a green plastic chair.

'Well, fair play to you,' said Captain Birdseye. 'My days of dealing with locks single-handed are well behind me.' He gave her a salute. 'Enjoy the rest of your day.'

'You too,' said Lulu, sitting down. The two men walked down to the towpath and climbed onto a green and red narrowboat with solar panels covering its roof. Lulu had never been a fan of solar panels on canal boats. She understood the advantages of having free electricity on tap, but they always looked so unsightly.

'They spoil the appearance, don't they?' said Conrad.

'Yes, they do,' said Lulu. She frowned. 'Did you just read my mind?'

Conrad chuckled. 'I saw you looking at the roof of their boat, and your nose wrinkled just a little. So it was a straightforward deduction. Elementary, my dear Watson.'

'So I'm Dr Watson to your Sherlock Holmes? I'm the one who was a detective, remember?'

'A detective superintendent with the Metropolitan Police, no less.'

'Indeed,' said Lulu.

A young waitress appeared, wearing a Santa hat and carrying a tray. She began to clear the table where the two men had been sitting. 'I'll be with you in a moment,' she said to Lulu in a soft Wiltshire accent. Conrad dropped down from the chair and curled up beneath it as the waitress began collecting the used plates and mugs. The men had left a newspaper behind.

'Do you mind if I have a look at that?' Lulu asked, pointing at it.

'Not at all,' said the waitress, handing her the paper. 'And what can I get you to drink?'

'A glass of Pinot Grigio would be lovely. And water for Conrad.'

The waitress frowned. 'Conrad?'

'I'm sorry – my companion,' said Lulu, pointing at Conrad.

'Oh! I'm sorry, sir, I didn't see you there. Would tap water be okay?'

'Actually, he's quite partial to Evian. If you have it.'

'We most definitely do,' said the waitress. 'I shall be right back.'

The Cat and the Christmas Kidnapper

Lulu looked at the front page of the newspaper. It was the *Wiltshire Times* and the main headline was FEARS FOR MISSING SCHOOLGIRL. Beneath it was a photograph of a young girl, her hair in braids, holding a schoolbag to her chest. Lulu scanned the story. Ten-year-old Poppy Novak had vanished on her way home from school. She lived just under half a mile from the school and had left at four o'clock. When she hadn't arrived by six o'clock, her worried parents had phoned the police. A full search of the area had found nothing, and police feared she had been abducted.

Conrad emerged from the under the chair. He looked up at the newspaper, then jumped up onto the chair next to Lulu to get a better look. 'That's awful,' he said.

'Yes, it is,' said Lulu. 'I always hated missing children cases. I couldn't help fearing the worst, even though the vast majority turn up safe and sound in the end.'

'Do a lot of children go missing?'

'Oh, more than a hundred thousand children are reported missing every year in the UK,' said Lulu. 'But most are the result of confusion – basically, children not keeping their parents informed of their whereabouts. And sometimes younger children simply get lost and are found after a search. In cases of abduction, it's often relatives who are involved. Mum and dad split up, one parent gets custody and the other parent takes matters into their own hands. Abduction by strangers is quite rare, thankfully.'

'So do you think they'll find her?'

Lulu looked at the masthead. The paper was a weekly and had been published two days earlier. 'She's probably been found already,' she said.

'Can you check?'

'Can I check? Why?'

'I'm worried.'

'I suppose they probably have a website. Let me have a look.' Lulu picked up her phone just as the waitress returned with a glass of wine and a bowl of water. She put the bowl down on the floor and the glass in front of Lulu.

Lulu thanked her and then showed her the paper. 'Did this little girl ever turn up?' she asked.

The waitress peered at the paper and shook her head. 'That's little Poppy. No. There was another search for her yesterday – I was one of the people looking. She only lives ten minutes from the school and she walks along the main road, so no one can understand how anybody managed to abduct her. Her parents were on TV last night. They're in bits.'

'Novak, that's an unusual name, isn't it? Though there was a film star many years ago called Kim Novak.'

'I think her dad is from the Czech Republic. Her mum's a local girl whose father used to run the Queen's Head. That's the pub down the road. He died a few years ago and the pub was sold.'

'What do they think happened to the little girl?' asked Lulu.

'Nobody knows,' said the waitress. 'She seems to have vanished into thin air.'

'I do hope they find her safely.'

'We all do, but it's been five days now, so people are starting to fear the worst.' She handed a menu to Lulu. 'Can I get you anything to eat?'

Lulu studied the menu and smiled. 'Oh, fish and chips,' she said. 'I haven't had fish and chips for ages.'

'Garden or mushy peas?'

'It has to be mushy, doesn't it?'

'And for Conrad?'

'He can share my cod.'

'I'll bring a spare plate.'

'You're an angel, thank you.'

Conrad waited until the waitress had walked away before speaking. 'Children don't just disappear, do they?' he said.

'No, not really. Adults do. They just pack up and go if life gets too much for them. Teenagers sometimes run away, but they usually take their phones with them, so the police can track them down. But this little girl is only ten – and ten-year-olds don't disappear of their own accord.'

'So somebody has taken her?'

'If the police haven't been able to find her within twenty-four hours of her having gone missing, then that's the assumption.'

'That's terrible. Do you think you can help?'

'Me?'

'You were a superintendent. A detective superintendent.'

'That was a long time ago. And Wiltshire has a perfectly good police force. They'll be doing whatever needs to be done.'

Conrad sighed. 'I hope so.'

2

Lulu paid for their lunch and walked back to *The Lark* with Conrad at her heels. 'That was lovely,' he said. 'Absolutely delicious. Thank you.'

'You're quite welcome,' said Lulu.

'I always feel bad that I can't pay,' said Conrad. 'But you know, I have nowhere to keep a wallet.'

'And no opposable thumbs,' said Lulu. 'Anyway, I think the days of males being expected to pay are well gone.'

'I understand that,' said Conrad. 'But I feel we should at least go Dutch.'

'I've never understood where that expression comes from.'

'It goes back to the seventeenth century, when England and the Netherlands were fighting over trade routes. The English always accused the Dutch of being stingy, and "going Dutch" came to mean that each person would pay his or her own expenses during a date.'

'You are a very knowledgeable cat,' said Lulu.

'It has been said.'

They reached *The Lark* and Lulu climbed on board. Conrad followed her, and as always, she marvelled at how smoothly he moved. He seemed to glide through the air as if he were weightless, landing on the rear deck without making a sound. He sat on the metal seat at the back of the deck and she pressed the button to start the engine. It kicked into life, and a cloud of black smoke belched out over the water. Lulu jumped back onto the towpath, undid the three lines and then pushed the prow away from the bank before jumping onto the stern and grabbing the tiller. She eased *The Lark* into the middle of the canal, then increased the throttle.

Conrad jumped up onto the roof and sat facing forward, the wind ruffling his fur. 'Where will we moor?' he asked.

'Unfortunately we can't moor in the city centre. The council put a stop to it.'

'Why on earth would they do that?'

'I suppose not everyone appreciates narrowboats,' said Lulu. 'There's a note on their website that says we can moor on the Widcombe Lock flight and enter the city centre on foot.'

'Is it far?'

'Not really.'

Conrad turned his head to look at her. 'And what, pray tell, is the Widcome Lock flight?'

'It's a set of locks that takes the Kennet and Avon Canal down sixty feet to join the River Avon in Bath. It's about nine miles from here. So if we're lucky, we'll be there in three hours and we'll get to Amanda's house before six.'

'And Amanda is your goddaughter, you said?'

Lulu nodded. 'Her mother was a great friend.'

'Was?'

'She passed away about sixteen years ago, when Amanda was a teenager. Well, she was nineteen, at university, so almost out of her teens. Her father was always busy so Amanda used to come and stay with me and Simon during her breaks.'

'And was Amanda's mum a police officer, like you?'

Lulu shook her head. 'She was a lawyer. For a few years she was a member of the London Policing Board. That's how I met her, and we just clicked. Michelle, her name was. Michelle Taylor. We became good friends, and when Amanda was born Michelle asked me to be her godmother. That was almost thirty-five years ago.'

'What does a godmother do, actually?'

'That's a very good question. Basically, they're to act as stand-in parents if anything happens to the real parents. They're supposed to take an interest in the child's upbringing and personal development, and if the worst comes to the worst they can claim legal guardianship. That was never an issue with Amanda. Her father is still alive. But he and Amanda were never very close, and he remarried.' Lulu forced a smile. 'Several times, actually. I think maybe he was looking for someone to replace Michelle, but she really was one of a kind. Irreplaceable. Anyway, Amanda married over ten years ago and she moved to Bath. She has a daughter of her own now. Olivia. Lovely little girl. Her husband Donald is a professor at the university there.'

'And we're going to stay with them?'

'We are. They have a lovely house in the centre of Bath.'

Another narrowboat was coming towards them, so Lulu steered over to the right and slowed the engine. The oncoming boat did the same. The boater was a young woman in her thirties, wrapped up in a padded jacket with what looked like a colourful Peruvian chullo on her head. Made with llama wool and with long earflaps, it looked like the perfect headwear for a canal in winter, and Lulu made a mental note to keep an eye out for one. The woman waved and Lulu waved back.

'I love your hat!' Lulu shouted.

'Thank you!' the woman shouted back. 'I love your cat! Wanna trade?'

'Oh, my goodness me, no!' shouted Lulu.

The woman laughed and waved again. Her boat was called *Moorning Sunshine*, which was a nice pun. The dentist who had sold *The Lark* to Lulu had given it that name because he had bought the narrowboat as a lark. Lulu loved the name and had never even considered changing it.

Most of the journey to Bath was through open country-side, passing through the villages of Limpley Stoke, Claverton and Bathampton. If they had been touring, Lulu would probably have stopped off to walk around at least one of the villages, but she was on a deadline, and in three hours she passed over two aqueducts and two swing bridges and reached Bath Top Lock.

There was no wait to use the locks; being so close to Christmas, there were few travellers on the canal. The only narrowboats Lulu saw as she went through lock 13 and lock 12 were moored at the canalside. There was another boat heading east through lock 11, a trim 50-footer driven by a bearded young man wearing a parka with a fur-lined hood. His boat was called *Mary Jane*, and the strong smell of cannabis emanating from the vessel suggested the name was drug-related. The *Mary Jane* had reached the lock first and the man was dealing with it single-handed, so Lulu moored *The Lark* and went to help him.

'Thank you!' he called over from the other side of the canal as she went to work on her side of the lock, inserting her steel windlass and using all her weight to turn it.

'No problem, happy to help,' she replied.

'I'll return the favour,' he said.

The lock quickly filled up. They opened the gates and the young man drove through. He moored the *Mary Jane* as

Lulu drove into the lock, then hurried over to the gate on his side and pushed it closed. Lulu stepped off *The Lark*, keeping hold of the centre line, and pushed her gate closed.

'Oh, you have a cat,' said the man, spotting Conrad for the first time.

'He's Conrad,' said Lulu. 'And I'm Lulu.'

'Pleased to meet you,' said the man, raising his hand in greeting. 'I'm Tim.'

'Pleased to meet you, too,' said Lulu.

They walked to the other gates and opened the sluices to let the water out. Lulu kept hold of the line as the water level dropped, keeping *The Lark* in the middle of the chamber.

'Why don't you climb on board? I'll open the gates to let you out,' said Tim.

'Are you sure?' asked Lulu. It would mean more work for him, but it would be easier for her to control *The Lark* with the engine rather than the line.

'Go ahead, we've done the hard work.'

'Thank you so much,' said Lulu. *The Lark* had only dropped a few feet, so she was able to step down onto the roof. She hurried along to the stern and down to the rear deck. She pressed the button to start the engine and eased the throttle forward a fraction to keep the back of the boat clear of the gate, and in particular to keep it off the cill, a protruding concrete ledge below the uphill lock. The quickest way to sink a narrowboat was to catch the stern on the cill – it would definitely ruin your day.

The Lark continued to drop as water poured out of the sluices. Lulu used small changes of the throttle to keep the boat steady. Operating the throttle – or speed lever, as some boaters called it – was so simple that a child could do it. In fact, Lulu often saw children at the tiller, though usually under the watchful eye of an adult. All you had to do was push forward to go forward and pull back for reverse. Pulling the throttle lever to one side put the boat in neutral. Simple it might be, but it still required concentration and a deft touch to keep *The Lark* centred.

When all the water had poured out of the sluices, Tim pushed open one gate, hurried around and carefully crossed the lock on the closed gates, then pushed the second gate open.

'Thank you so much!' called Lulu. 'You're a gentleman!'

Tim laughed and gave her an exaggerated bow as she pushed the throttle forward and eased *The Lark* out of the lock.

'What a nice man,' said Conrad as they drove away from the lock.

'Canal people are generally good people,' said Lulu.

'Why is that, do you think?'

'That's a very good question,' said Lulu.

A middle-aged couple in matching Barbour waterproof jackets were heading towards them along the towpath, arm in arm, so Lulu didn't reply until they had passed by.

'I think it's because the pace of life is so much gentler on the canals,' she said. 'The top speed of a narrowboat is four miles an hour, but you spend most of your time at walking pace or even slower. There's no rushing. You simply can't hurry – it takes as long as it takes.'

'So you think that calms people down?'

'Partly. But I think it also means people who are in a rush – and that's probably most of the world these days – tend to avoid the canals.'

'Well, I prefer it that way,' said Conrad.

Lulu smiled. 'And so do I.'

There were boats moored on either side of the canal, but she spotted a gap on the left and eased back on the throttle. A narrowboat has no brakes, just forward and reverse, and it can be tricky to get the hang of manoeuvring in and out of tight places. Lulu had had more than enough practice and it took her only a few minutes to ease *The Lark* into the gap, even though there was only a yard or two of extra space fore and aft. She put the engine in neutral, then jumped off with the stern line. In less than a minute she had secured *The Lark* with three lines.

'Nicely done,' said Conrad as she climbed back onto *The Lark*.

'You should have seen me the first time I drove her out of Little Venice,' said Lulu. 'I was all over the canal, I really was.'

'Well, you're an expert now, that's for sure.'

'Why, thank you,' said Lulu. She went down into the cabin. It was just before six o'clock and the walk to Amanda's house would take them about half an hour. She could call for a taxi, but Bath was a lovely city and she was looking forward to a walk after several hours at the tiller. She took a quick shower, changed into a clean pullover and trousers and put on just enough make-up to add some colour to her face. Conrad sat on her bunk licking his front legs as she applied the last of the make-up. It was dark outside and Lulu had switched the lights on.

'You cats have it so easy,' Lulu said.

He looked up from his ablutions. 'How so?'

'Well, look at you. No showering, no having to choose

what to wear, no make-up needed. Just a few licks and you're good to go.'

'And I always look good.'

Lulu laughed. 'Yes, you do.'

'You look good, too.'

'Thank you.' She opened a cupboard and took out a Harrods carrier bag containing the Christmas presents she'd brought for Amanda, Donald and Olivia, then picked up the backpack in which she had packed enough clothes for her stay, including a pretty Karen Millen dress that she planned to wear on Christmas Day. She smiled at Conrad. 'You get to travel light, too. No clean underwear, no washbag, nothing to carry.'

'Just my good self.'

'Yes. Your good self.' Lulu nodded at her backpack. 'But I need pyjamas, underwear, and a couple of dresses.' She grinned. 'So, off we go.'

3

Lulu pulled on her sheepskin jacket and brown wool gloves with the fingers cut off. They went out onto the rear deck and she locked the door. After Conrad had jumped up onto her shoulders, she stepped carefully off *The Lark*.

A man and woman were standing on the rear deck of the adjacent boat, drinking from cans of lager and smoking small cigars. They had placed a small electric lantern on the roof of their boat. They were in their mid-fifties and wearing matching North Face fleeces. 'I love your cat,' said the woman, waving her can of lager. 'How long did it take to learn to do that?'

'I picked it up quite quickly,' said Lulu.

'No, I meant . . .' The woman giggled and didn't finish the sentence.

'Merry Christmas!' called her companion, waving his cigar in the air.

'Four more days to go,' said Lulu.

'We're leaving tomorrow, so you have a great Christmas.'

'I will do, thank you,' said Lulu. 'You too.'

She left the towpath and headed down a steep track towards the city. There was a metal handrail down the middle, and Lulu kept her right hand on it as she walked. A young couple were coming towards her, students maybe, in their late teens. The boy had his arm around the girl's shoulders and kept sniffing her long blonde hair. He saw Conrad first and his face broke into a cheerful grin. He whispered into the girl's ear and she looked up and smiled. 'Oh, that is so cool,' she said.

They stopped walking. Lulu thought it would be rude to just walk by, so she stopped too.

'Can I stroke him?' the girl asked. She had a Liverpool accent, so almost certainly a student, Lulu decided.

'Of course,' said Lulu. 'He always loves to be petted by a pretty girl.'

The girl reached up and stroked Conrad's neck, and he purred happily. 'I love his colours,' she said. 'What do they call that? Tortoiseshell?'

'I always say he's a calico cat,' said Lulu. 'People say that calico is an Americanism, but for me a calico has a three-colour coat with white, black and red-orange. Tortoiseshells lack the white and have a black and orange mottled coat. But there is a lot of discussion about that.'

'How did you teach him to sit on your shoulders?' asked the boy. He had a broad Yorkshire accent that immediately made Lulu think of a Hovis advert.

'Oh, he just decided to do that himself,' said Lulu.

'You didn't train him?'

'Oh no. Conrad isn't the sort of cat you can train.' She smiled. 'Actually, I don't think most cats can be trained. Or at least, they don't allow themselves to be trained.'

'Our family dog can do all sorts of tricks,' said the boy. 'He can stand up on his back legs and turn all the way around. And my dad taught him to do press-ups. How cool is that?'

'Very cool,' said Lulu, though actually she didn't think that a dog doing tricks was the least bit cool. She said goodbye and continued along the track.

'Good grief,' said Conrad, once they were out of earshot.

'I didn't think you'd be impressed by the idea of a dog doing press-ups.'

'Training is all about dominance, that's the thing,' said Conrad. 'A dog will do pretty much whatever you tell it to do, especially if there is food involved.'

'Because they're pack animals,' said Lulu.

'Because they have a need to be told what to do,' said Conrad. 'It's almost as if they have no free will.' He shuddered. 'I'm glad I'm not a dog.'

'Me too,' said Lulu. 'If nothing else, you'd be a lot heavier.'

Lulu loved the way people reacted to seeing that Conrad was riding on her shoulders. Usually it was surprise; eyes would widen and jaws would drop, often followed by a smile. People generally weren't shy about commenting, more often than not with a simple 'Lovely cat' or 'How wonderful'. She had never put Conrad on the scales, but she assumed he weighed between three and four kilograms, though when he was wrapped around her neck he felt almost weightless. Sometimes she would feel his warm breath on her ear, and occasionally he would shift position slightly, but most of the time he was as comfortable and reassuring as a warm scarf.

The only negative reactions tended to come from dogs – and their owners. Most dogs simply didn't notice that Conrad was on her shoulders, but the few that did would usually erupt into frantic barking and start pulling at their leads. Conrad took such outbursts in his stride and merely stared disdainfully down at them. The owners of the dogs rarely apologized for the barking, and more often than not they would glare at Lulu as if she was somehow the one at fault. Lulu always reacted the same way – with a smile. Rarely did she receive a smile in return, but when she did, it always gave her a good feeling. During her years as a police officer, she'd often found that smiling and showing respect would defuse a potentially volatile situation, although that didn't mean she ever let her guard down. 'Expect the best, but prepare for the worst' was the advice she'd been given by a grizzled sergeant by the name of Jimmy McLeod when she'd first started walking a beat, and she'd pretty much lived by it ever since.

They walked alongside a busy road and over a stone bridge that crossed the River Avon. The street lights were reflected in the water, giving it a fairy tale feel. To the right Lulu could see a weir in the distance, illuminated by floodlights. It was Pulteney Weir, built in the late Middle Ages to prevent the river from flooding Bath.

'This is a lovely city,' said Conrad.

'It is,' said Lulu. 'The Romans built baths and a temple here in AD 60, but the hot springs were known long before that. There's a beautiful abbey and most of the architecture is Georgian, using the local Bath stone. Wait until you see Amanda's house – it's quite something.'

'It reminds me of Oxford.'

'They're both very pretty cities,' said Lulu. 'We could visit the Roman baths while we're here.'

'I'm not a big fan of baths,' said Conrad.

'Why is it that cats don't like water? Dogs seem to love it.'

'Dogs are dogs,' said Conrad. 'They love chasing after sticks, too. I've never understood the point of that. I can tell you that the main reason we cats don't like water –

other than for drinking – is because of what it does to our fur. Wet fur is uncomfortable and it takes for ever to dry. And wet fur is heavy; it makes moving around really difficult. So we try to avoid it wherever possible. But dripping taps, they're fun. I could spend all day watching a dripping tap.'

Lulu chuckled. 'You're funny.'

They walked past terraces of townhouses, all built from the local beige Bath stone. Lulu doubted they had changed much over the past couple of centuries. Like Little Venice, her home in London, most of the buildings here were probably listed and changes weren't allowed. It didn't require much imagination to picture Beau Brummell and his Regency dandies swanning around in perfumed wigs, frock coats and silk stockings.

They reached the Circus, a ring of four-storey townhouses with rows of tall chimneys. The ring formed the intersection of three roads, and a lawn and towering plane trees occupied its centre. Several tourists were wandering around, taking selfies.

'Oh, well, now this is impressive,' said Conrad, looking around.

'Isn't it?' said Lulu. 'And can you believe – it was built in the late 1750s, early 1760s.'

'The houses look as good as new,' said Conrad.

Leaving the Circus via Brock Street, they walked along to the Royal Crescent, where Amanda lived. Like the Circus, the Crescent was an architectural spectacle: a 500-foot curved terrace of stone townhouses fifty feet tall, with striking columns and dormer windows in their slate roofs. The Crescent faced a large, well-manicured lawn, and beyond it was a sprawling park where dozens more tourists were taking photographs.

There were several dog walkers out, on the lawn and in the park, many of them following their charges with plastic bags in hand. Conrad chuckled. 'That always amuses me,' he said.

'What, exactly?'

'Well, suppose aliens arrived from another planet and saw human beings walking behind dogs, collecting their waste. Who would they assume was the dominant species?'

Lulu chuckled. 'You do have a point.'

'I do, don't I?'

Lulu looked out over the lawn. 'The really interesting thing about this is the ha-ha.'

'The what now?'

'The ha-ha. You can't really see it from here, which is of course the whole point.'

'You've lost me,' said Conrad.

Lulu pointed down the lawn. 'There's a vertical barrier there with a masonry wall, with quite a drop. But because the lawn slopes, you can't see it from here. It stops vehicles coming up across the lawn. And livestock. It's also referred to as a sunk fence or a deer wall.'

'And why is it called a ha-ha?'

'Apparently because that's what people usually say when they first see it.'

Conrad snorted. 'I'm not sure if I believe you or not.'

'Cross my heart,' said Lulu. She began peering at the numbers on the front doors they passed. 'Here we are,' she said eventually, stopping outside a house with a large Christmas wreath hanging on the front door. Fake snow had been sprayed on the inside of the windows. There were old-fashioned coach lights either side of the door, casting pools of light on the steps.

'Very festive,' said Conrad.

Lulu walked up to the front door and pressed the bell. After thirty seconds it was opened by Amanda, her dyed blonde hair held up with a white plastic clip. She was wearing a blue dress with large white flowers that looked as if it might be a Ted Baker, and there was a slim gold Cartier watch on her left wrist. She smiled when she saw Lulu, then her eyes widened as she noticed Conrad.

'There's a cat wrapped around your neck,' said Amanda. 'Is that the latest fashion in London?'

'This is Conrad, my plus one,' said Lulu.

'Well, he's very welcome,' said Amanda, pulling the door open wider. 'As are you.'

Lulu stepped across the threshold and air-kissed Amanda on both cheeks. Amanda closed the door and took the Harrods carrier bag from her. Conrad jumped down, making almost no sound as he landed on the carpet.

'Those are your Christmas presents,' said Lulu, nodding at the Harrods bag.

'Oh, you shouldn't have,' said Amanda. 'I'll put them under the tree.'

Amanda took the bag and led Lulu through to a large sitting room overlooking the park. There was a real, towering Christmas tree in one corner, festooned in tinsel and baubles, with wrapped presents stacked around the base. Eleven-year-old Olivia was sitting on a low leather sofa and she shrieked with excitement as they came in. 'Aunty Lulu!'

'Hello, Olivia. You look lovely.'

The Cat and the Christmas Kidnapper

Olivia was wearing a blue denim dress and had her long chestnut hair pulled back in a ponytail. She was tall and thin, gangly like a newborn foal as she jumped up and hurried over to hug Lulu. 'I'm so glad you're here for Christmas.'

'Me too,' said Lulu. She kissed Olivia on the top of her head. 'It's so lovely to see you again. No school today?'

'It's the last day, but Mummy and Daddy said I didn't have to go.' She stopped hugging Lulu when she spotted Conrad standing nearby. 'Oh, there's a cat!' she exclaimed.

'That's Conrad,' said Lulu.

Olivia stepped away from Lulu, staring at Conrad. 'Is he your cat?'

'I rather think that I'm his human,' said Lulu.

'Is he staying? Can he sleep on my bed?'

'Oh, you'd have to ask Conrad.'

Olivia knelt down in front of Conrad. 'Conrad, would you like to sleep on my bed tonight?' she asked solemnly.

Conrad looked at her with his shining green eyes and meowed.

'That's a yes, Olivia,' said Lulu.

Olivia clapped her hands together excitedly. 'He talks!'

Lulu smiled. 'Yes, he does. But only to people he likes.'

'He likes me?'

'Oh, I'm sure he does.'

'Meow,' said Conrad.

'And there you have it, from the cat's mouth,' said Lulu.

Amanda had taken the wrapped gifts from the Harrods bag and was placing them around the foot of the Christmas tree. Red, green and blue fairy lights flashed on and off, and at the top of the tree was an antique fairy that Lulu knew was an heirloom that had been in Amanda's family for generations.

She took off her backpack. 'Where shall I put this?'

'Just drop it by the sofa,' said Amanda. 'I'll show you your room later. Would you like a cup of tea?'

'Oh, I'd love one,' said Lulu. She glanced around. 'Is Donald here?'

'He's at the university,' said Amanda. 'There were some faculty meetings he couldn't get out of, but he should be here any moment.' She took Lulu down the hall and into a large kitchen with French windows that looked over a lawn with a swing set and slide. There was a kitchen island with four stools, and Amanda waved for Lulu to take a seat. As Lulu slid onto a stool, Amanda pulled open the door of a large stainless-steel fridge. 'I said tea, but it is wine o'clock,' she said. There was a lovely smell coming from the oven. Lulu didn't have Conrad's super-sensitive sense of smell, but she could definitely discern lamb and cauliflower cheese.

'It is indeed,' said Lulu.

'Are you still a fan of Pinot Grigio?'

'I am.'

Amanda pulled a bottle from the fridge, took out a corkscrew and two glasses and sat down opposite Lulu. She deftly extracted the cork and poured large measures into the glasses. Before either of them had a chance to drink, Donald appeared in the doorway, wearing a tweed jacket and brown corduroy trousers and carrying a battered leather briefcase.

'Well, look what the cat dragged in,' he said. 'Literally. I've just met Conrad entertaining Olivia.' He came over to the island, set his briefcase on the floor and gave Lulu a hug and a quick air kiss. 'So good to see you again. How long has it been?' He was five years older than Amanda and a couple of inches taller, with receding hair that he cut short. He had reading glasses hanging on a chain around his neck.

'Almost two years,' said Lulu.

'And you really did sail your boat here?'

Amanda raised the wine bottle and he nodded, so she hopped off her stool to fetch him a glass.

'Well, you drive a narrowboat rather than sail it, but yes. It's been quite a trip.'

'Doesn't it get cold at night?' asked Donald.

'Oh no, there's a multi-fuel stove and *The Lark* has its own central heating system. And I have a lovely quilt. It's quite snug.'

Amanda poured wine for Donald and all three of them clinked glasses.

'Dinner smells good,' said Donald. 'Are we going to eat here or in the dining room?'

'We have a guest,' said Amanda. 'So the dining room, of course.'

'Guests plural,' said Donald. 'Don't forget Conrad.' He sipped his wine. 'So, are you okay?' he asked Amanda.

Amanda nodded. 'Yes, fine.'

There was an uncertainty in her voice that Lulu found unsettling. Perhaps they had been arguing, or something had happened to upset Amanda? But Lulu was a guest and in no position to pry. 'I thought the universities had closed for the holidays?' she said.

'Oh, they have, but once the pesky students are out of the way it gives the vice-chancellor a chance to get busy with faculty business. Today's meeting was about increasing our quota of foreign students, because obviously they pay more. But I'm an academic, Lulu, not a salesman. If I'd wanted to be a salesman and live on commission, I'd be out selling solar panels or life assurance.' He took a sip of wine that rapidly turned into a gulp. Amanda was also gulping down her wine. Lulu kept a smile on her face, but she could tell that something was definitely wrong.

4

Dinner was delicious, that was the only word for it. The lamb was succulent and perfectly cooked, the roast potatoes had been basted in goose fat, the cauliflower cheese was the best that Lulu had ever eaten, and the carrots had been freshly picked from the vegetable patch before being boiled and bathed in butter. Amanda had made her own mint jelly using mint from the garden. There was chocolate mousse for dessert, and again it was delicious.

The dining room overlooked the rear garden, which was now illuminated with small Japanese pagoda lights. The table had eight seats, but there was only Lulu, Amanda, Donald and Olivia for dinner. Conrad was lying on a wooden trunk under the window, apparently sleeping.

They had finished off the bottle of Pinot Grigio, and Donald had opened another.

'Would you like a port to finish off?' asked Donald.

'Oh no, I'm fine with wine,' said Lulu. She grinned. 'Listen to me, I'm a poet.'

'And you didn't know it,' said Donald.

They both laughed. Amanda also laughed, but Lulu could tell that something was still troubling her.

'Amanda, that was fabulous,' said Lulu.

'Thank you. I must admit the potatoes were a rehearsal for Christmas Day.'

'They were perfect. And your mint jelly, that was amazing.'

'I have to confess, it's a Jamie Oliver recipe.'

'Well, hats off to Jamie,' said Lulu.

Olivia yawned, and Amanda smiled at her. 'Time for bed, young lady,' she said. 'Go upstairs and clean your teeth and I'll come up and say goodnight.'

'Can I take Conrad with me?'

Amanda looked over at Lulu. 'Is that okay?'

'Of course,' said Lulu.

Olivia reached out her arms and scooped up Conrad. He lay against her with his head resting on her shoulder as she carried him out of the room.

'I never had you down as a cat person,' said Donald.

'I don't think I was, until I met Conrad,' said Lulu.

'Have you had him since he was a kitten?'

'No, he walked into my life fully grown and introduced himself.'

'So he was a stray?' said Donald.

'I guess you could say that,' said Lulu. 'He just jumped onto my boat in Little Venice and never left.'

Amanda looked at her watch. 'Would you mind if we watch the news, Lulu?'

'Of course not,' said Lulu.

'Amanda, really?' said Donald.

Amanda's eyes hardened. 'I want to watch the news.'

Donald held up his hands in surrender. 'Fine. Right. The news it is.' He picked up his glass and the bottle, then waved Lulu to the door. 'We shall retire to the sitting room, m'lady.'

Lulu smiled, but she felt a little uneasy. Amanda was clearly tense, and Donald was also agitated. Something was wrong, but neither Amanda nor Donald seemed to want to address it. She picked up her glass and followed Amanda across the hall to the sitting room. There were two blood-red Chesterfield sofas at right angles to each other across a brass and glass coffee table. Amanda sat down on one of the sofas and picked up the remote. The television was above the fireplace. Amanda pointed the remote at the television and it clicked on.

Lulu sat down on the other sofa and sipped her wine. Amanda was staring at the screen as she clicked through the channels. Donald joined her on the sofa and put the wine bottle on the coffee table.

'Is everything okay?' Lulu asked.

Amanda didn't seem to hear her as she continued to flick through the channels.

Donald smiled awkwardly. 'Everything's fine,' he said, but without conviction. He took another sip of wine.

Amanda found what she was looking for and sat back, still holding the remote. There was a news programme on the screen, presented by a young woman with hair that didn't move and a rigid forehead that suggested Botox injections. The newsreader was talking about the local hospital unveiling an expanded maternity outpatient facility. A short film of a pregnant woman being examined by a nurse replaced the newsreader.

'How do you get on for electricity on your boat?' Donald asked.

He was clearly just trying to make conversation, Lulu realized, hoping to distract her from his wife's unusual behaviour. 'Oh, I have batteries, and the engine keeps them charged. And like I said, the stove heats the boat and provides hot water. So the electricity just powers the lights and the fridge,' she babbled. She was fairly sure that Donald wasn't really listening to her.

The newsreader was back on the screen. Amanda boosted the volume and Lulu realized that the woman was talking about Poppy Novak, the girl who had gone missing in Bradford-on-Avon.

Amanda was leaning forward, gripping the remote with both hands. Donald gritted his teeth as he stared at the screen; then he shuddered and drained his glass.

The broadcast cut to footage of a police press conference. A man and woman sat at a table, holding hands. Behind them was a photograph of a young girl, the same picture Lulu had seen on the front page of the *Wiltshire Times*. The woman was sweating profusely and kept dabbing at her forehead with a handkerchief. She was talking to a group of assembled journalists, tearfully describing what had happened to her daughter: Poppy had been walking home from school, as she did every day, but had never arrived. Mrs Novak went on to talk about Poppy's interests, her hobbies, how she was doing at school. She kept using Poppy's name. She would have been told to do that, Lulu knew, to make it as personal as possible. Whoever had taken Poppy needed to be reminded that she was a real person, a living, breathing human being, not just a victim.

At another table to the left of the Novaks was a man in his thirties with brown hair swept back from a broad forehead. He was wearing a grey suit with a cream shirt and a dark blue tie. There was a sign in front of him – 'DI SIMON KEMP'. The fact that he was a DI, a detective inspector, meant that he was probably the SIO, the senior investigating officer.

Mrs Novak finished speaking and looked tearfully into the camera.

The Cat and the Christmas Kidnapper

'Please,' said Mr Novak. 'Just give us back our daughter. Poppy doesn't deserve this. She's a child. She doesn't have a bad bone in her body.' Tears were welling up in his eyes and he looked down at the table as he blinked them away. He was in his late thirties, a big, strong man with bulging forearms that strained at his jacket. It was probably an old jacket, one he hadn't worn for a while, but he'd have been told that the public would have more sympathy for a man who looked presentable. He began to cry and his wife put her arm around him, tears running down her cheeks.

DI Kemp then announced that he would be taking questions and there was a flurry of them, all asking for more details of the investigation. It was clear from his replies that he had nothing to add and that the police were no nearer to finding the missing girl.

Then the segment was over and the newsreader began talking about the weather. Amanda muted the sound and put the remote down on the coffee table. She drained her wine glass and then refilled it with a shaking hand.

'Amanda, whatever's wrong?' asked Lulu.

Amanda forced a smile. 'I'm fine. Really.'

'Well, you're clearly not fine. You're close to tears and your hands keep shaking. If you're not feeling well then you really need to see a doctor.'

'I'm not ill, Lulu.'

'So what's wrong? Or is it something you don't want to share with me? If it is, just tell me and I'll mind my own business. I only have your best interests at heart.'

A tear trickled from Amanda's eye and she dabbed at it with the back of her hand. 'I'm okay. Really.'

'Maybe we should tell her,' said Donald quietly.

'No!' snapped Amanda, turning to glare at him.

'Lulu used to be a police officer. A detective. She might be able to help.'

'They said no police,' hissed Amanda. 'They specifically said no police.'

'Lulu is retired, so strictly speaking she isn't police,' said Donald.

He reached over to take Amanda's hand but she snatched it away. Tears were falling from both her eyes now. She leaned towards a box of tissues on the coffee table, pulled one out and dabbed her cheeks with it. 'We can't,' she sniffed. 'They said no police.'

'Has something happened?' asked Lulu.

'I'm going to tell her, Amanda. We need to know what to do.'

'They've told us what we need to do,' hissed Amanda. 'We send them the money, that's what we need to do.'

'Send who money?' asked Lulu.

'We've received a ransom demand,' said Donald. 'The kidnappers want fifty thousand pounds from us.'

Lulu frowned. 'Oh my goodness. Who's been kidnapped?'

'Well, that's where it starts to get a bit crazy,' said Donald. 'No one has actually been kidnapped. Yet.'

'Yes, they have,' said Amanda. She pointed at the television. 'That poor little girl.'

'Okay, she has been kidnapped. But she has nothing to do with us.'

Lulu's frown deepened. 'I'm sorry, I don't understand. The kidnappers want you to pay a ransom for Poppy Novak?'

Donald shook his head. 'No,' he said. 'Look, it's better if I show you the ransom note.'

'You mustn't!' said Amanda. 'All we need to do is pay the damned money and that will be the end of it.'

'And what if it isn't? What if we pay and they ask again? And again?'

'They won't. They said this was a one-time thing. Like an insurance policy.'

'Amanda, darling. You pay an insurance premium every year. That's how insurance works.' Donald flashed Lulu a tight smile. 'You'll understand more when I show you the letter.'

He got up from the sofa and left the room.

'Amanda, I'm so sorry if I've upset you,' said Lulu. 'That wasn't my intention.'

Amanda sighed. 'It's not your fault. I did suggest to Donald that we cancel your visit, but that seemed unfair after you'd come all this way.'

'It wouldn't have been a problem. We're not Mary and Joseph, desperate for a bed. We can always stay on *The Lark*. That's the beauty of a narrowboat. Home is wherever you moor your boat. In fact, we can go back tonight, it isn't a problem.'

'No, of course you're not doing that,' Amanda said. She dabbed at her tears again. 'We invited you here for Christmas and I've no intention of going back on that. We've so been looking forward to having you. I'm not going to let anyone or anything spoil that.'

'Only if you're sure, Amanda.'

Amanda nodded tearfully. 'I'm sure.'

Donald returned with a large white envelope. He tried to pass it to Lulu as he sat down, but she shook her head and held up her hands. 'Fingerprints,' she said. 'The fewer people who touch it, the better.'

'We've both touched it,' said Amanda.

'That's okay, but I should wear gloves.'

'Gloves?' repeated Donald.

'Latex would be best. But any gloves will do. Just so I don't handle it with my bare hands.'

'I have some Marigolds in the kitchen,' said Amanda.

'Perfect,' said Lulu.

'I'll get them,' said Amanda. She stood up and left the room, still dabbing at her eyes.

Donald placed the envelope on the coffee table and Lulu peered at it. The letter was addressed to Mr and Mrs Balfour, and the names and the address were typed – printed out, Lulu thought, rather than typed on a typewriter. There were two stamps, and the postmarks were dated four days previously.

'When did it arrive?' asked Lulu.

'This morning.'

'First-class stamps, but they were franked four days ago.'

'The post here is appalling,' said Donald. 'Has been for years. They're understaffed, I think. We used to have a regular postie, a lovely chap called Eric, but he retired and since then we've had a succession of people, none of whom appear to be local. Most of them seem more interested in playing on their phones than delivering letters.'

'Who's that you're talking about?' Amanda asked as she came back into the room.

'I was just saying that we haven't had a decent postie since Eric retired.'

'That's right. Years of carting those heavy bags around ruined his back,' said Amanda as she sat back down on the sofa. 'These days they push a trolley around. But we're lucky to get a delivery three times a week.' She held out a pack of bright yellow Marigold kitchen gloves. 'Will these do? They've never been used.'

'Perfect,' said Lulu. She tore the pack open and put the gloves on, wiggled her fingers and then picked up the envelope. She lifted the flap and slid out the contents. The top sheet was a letter in a large, easy-to-read typeface. Beneath it were two photographs. One was of Olivia, walking through the gates of her school wearing her uniform. The date was printed across the bottom of the picture: 17 December.

'How does Olivia get to school?' Lulu asked.

'Usually I take her,' said Amanda. 'Otherwise, Donald does. That says December the seventeenth, and I took her on that day.'

'I don't suppose you saw anyone taking photographs, did you?'

Amanda shook her head. 'No, I didn't.'

'He was probably sitting in a car some distance away,' said Lulu. 'Or she – it could have been a woman, of course. From the look of the photograph, it was taken with a long lens.'

Lulu put the picture down and picked up the second photograph. It was of Poppy Novak, the missing child. She was sitting on an armchair, holding a newspaper. She was smiling bravely, but she had been crying and her cheeks glistened with tears. Lulu squinted at the paper but couldn't make out the date.

'It was the day after she went missing,' said Donald. 'I used a magnifying glass.'

Lulu nodded. She could see the bottom of what looked like a camp bed to the left and a wardrobe to the right. 'The poor girl,' said Lulu. 'She looks scared out of her wits.'

She put down the photograph and picked up the letter. Like the envelope, it appeared to have been done on a printer. Lulu thought the font looked like Times New Roman, probably 14 or 15 point. It was all in capital letters.

YOU WILL KNOW BY NOW THAT WE HAVE KIDNAPPED POPPY NOVAK. HERE IS THE PROOF THAT WE HAVE HER. YOUR DAUGHTER OLIVIA WILL BE NEXT IF YOU DO NOT PAY US £50,000.

WE KNOW WHERE OLIVIA LIVES, WE KNOW WHERE SHE GOES TO SCHOOL, WE KNOW EVERYTHING ABOUT HER. WE COULD TAKE HER AS EASILY AS WE HAVE TAKEN POPPY NOVAK.

DO NOT CONTACT THE POLICE. IF YOU TALK TO THE POLICE, WE WILL TAKE OLIVIA AND YOU WILL NEVER SEE HER AGAIN. YOU HAVE ONE WEEK TO PAY THE MONEY INTO THE FOLLOWING BITCOIN ACCOUNT. IF THE MONEY IS NOT IN THE ACCOUNT BY THEN, WE WILL TAKE YOUR DAUGHTER. YOU HAVE BEEN WARNED.

At the end of the letter was a forty-digit code, a mix of upper-case and lower-case letters and numbers. Lulu knew enough about cryptocurrencies to recognize it as a Bitcoin receiving address. It would almost certainly be a one-off, generated for the transaction and virtually untraceable.

'Oh, my goodness me, this is terrible,' said Lulu.

'Yes,' said Amanda. 'It is. But all we have to do is pay them.' She looked at Donald. 'We are going to pay them, right?'

'Of course, yes,' said Donald. 'I spoke to the bank and they say they can do a transfer online from my account to what they call a Bitcoin wallet. Then we can move it to the address in the letter. But there isn't enough cash in our accounts. I'll have to sell some shares or unit trusts.'

'Then do it,' said Amanda.

Donald nodded. 'I will.'

Lulu peered closely at the letter. It had definitely been printed; there were none of the small imperfections that would have been produced by a typewriter.

'I suppose there's no way of tracing it, is there?' said Donald.

'Actually, there may be,' said Lulu. 'Most inkjet and laser printers add what's called a Machine Identification Code to every sheet that they print. The MIC is in the form of yellow dots, effectively a digital watermark that contains the serial number of the printer, and sometimes even the date and time that the document was printed.'

Donald reached for the sheet, but Lulu moved it away. 'Not without gloves,' she said.

He nodded. 'Okay, yes. I didn't see any yellow dots.'

'They're almost invisible to the naked eye,' said Lulu.

'So that means we can find out who sent it?' asked Amanda.

'Maybe,' said Lulu. 'But it is possible that the machine they used doesn't print MIC. I think some cheap imports don't use the technology. And even if we were to identify the serial number, that wouldn't necessarily mean you'd know who was using the printer. But it's definitely worth a try.'

'Can you do it?' asked Donald.

'I'm afraid not; it needs specialist equipment. You'd have to give it to a police forensics team.'

'No police,' said Amanda quickly. 'They said no police.' She looked at Donald. 'It's bad enough that we've told Lulu. We can't take the risk of telling the police.'

'I understand how you feel, Amanda,' said Lulu. 'But I don't think that whoever sent that letter will carry out the threat. Why would they? There's nothing to be gained.'

'They could hurt Olivia just to prove a point.'

'But would they do that? Hurt a child just to teach you a lesson? And if they knew that the police were involved, would they be likely to take the risk?'

'They've already kidnapped one child,' said Amanda. 'Poppy Novak. And they still have her. No one knows what's going to happen to that poor little girl. I don't want that to happen to Olivia. We kept her off school today, but we can't do that for ever, can we?'

'They took Poppy Novak when she was walking alone on the street,' said Donald. 'We always drive Olivia to and from school, and the school is a secure place.'

'So we have to watch Olivia all the time? We can't ever allow her out on her own? Is that the sort of life you want for her?'

'Oh Amanda, that ship has sailed,' said Donald. 'It's not like when we were kids and could spend the day out riding our bikes or playing in the woods. The world was a different place then. A safer place.'

Amanda sniffed and wiped her eyes again. 'I couldn't live with myself if anything happened to Olivia. We can afford their demands. Let's just pay it.' She looked tearfully at Donald.

'Well, as I said, I'll have to move some money from our share account and then I'll have to buy the Bitcoin. I've never owned Bitcoin before; it's always struck me as gambling. But it's a simple matter to buy some. It's all done online.'

'How long do you think it'll take?'

'I really don't know. Today's the twenty-first and the banks stay open until Christmas Eve, but then they'll be shut on Christmas Day and Boxing Day.'

'Can you do everything before Christmas Eve?'

'Possibly. Yes. I can certainly try.'

'I have to say that paying the ransom may not be the best idea,' said Lulu. 'Once you've transferred the Bitcoin it's gone for ever, and you've no guarantee that the kidnappers will keep their word. That's where they're being very clever, of course. Bitcoin is practically untraceable. Once it's in their wallet, they can move it halfway round the world in moments.'

'What do you mean?' asked Amanda.

'Basically, a crypto wallet is a place where you can securely keep your crypto,' said Lulu. 'That's short for cryptocurrencies. They promise anonymity. If you do pay the kidnappers with Bitcoin, once you've handed it over, it's gone for good.'

'But then we hopefully won't hear from them again,' said Amanda.

'The point I'm making is that if you pay by Bitcoin, there's almost no way the police can follow the money. If it's cash, they can use marked notes and maybe a tracking device – if the money moves through the banking system it can be followed, up to a point. But Bitcoin . . .' Lulu shrugged. 'The police will have nothing to work on.'

'I don't care about that,' said Amanda. 'All I care about is Olivia.'

'I understand that. Of course I do. But Amanda, think about Poppy Novak's parents. Think about how they must be feeling. Wouldn't you want to help them if you could?'

'What do you mean?'

'Well, it's obviously the same people, isn't it? They've sent you photographs of Poppy as a warning. So if you do help the police catch them, you'll be returning Poppy to her parents.'

'Lulu does have a point, darling,' said Donald.

'They can pay their own ransom,' said Amanda.

'From what I've seen and heard, they don't have two pennies to rub together,' said Donald.

'I don't think this is about making the Novaks pay a ransom,' Lulu said quietly.

'What do you mean?' asked Donald.

'Well, think about it,' said Lulu. 'The kidnappers have sent you Poppy's photograph as a warning. "We can do to Olivia what we've done to her. Pay us or else." What if you're not the only one they've written to? What if they've sent out ten letters like this one? Or a hundred? A hundred people each paying fifty thousand pounds – that's five million pounds. Even if only one in ten people pay up, that's half a million pounds for a few days' work.'

'Do you think that's what's happening?' said Amanda.

'I don't know. At this point, anything I say can only be guesswork. But I can't believe anyone would go to all this trouble for fifty thousand pounds.'

'I think we should just pay them what they want and hope that's the end of it,' said Amanda. 'If, as you say, lots of people have received the letter, better to be one of the payers than one of the non-payers.'

'But what about the Novak family?' said Lulu. 'There was no mention of ransom demands during their appeal. It sounded as if the police think that it's an abduction rather than a kidnapping.'

Donald nodded. 'That's true, darling,' he said to Amanda. He reached for her hand again but she pulled it away.

'They might just be keeping that information to themselves,' said Amanda. She looked hopefully at Lulu. 'They do that sometimes, don't they? Hold back things that only the criminal would know about.'

'Well, yes,' said Lulu. 'But there's a world of difference between an abduction, which might well have a sexual motive, and a kidnapping, where the motive is financial. I think if the police knew that there had been a ransom demand, they would have said as much. Really, Amanda, I think the police need to see this letter – if for no other reason than the Novaks will at least know that their daughter most likely isn't in the clutches of a sexual predator. Imagine how you and Donald would feel if you thought Olivia was in that situation.'

Amanda blew her nose into her tissue but didn't say anything.

'I think Lulu's right, darling,' said Donald. 'We owe it to the Novaks.'

'But they said no police.' She pointed at the letter. 'No police. As clear as day. What if they find out that we've disobeyed them?'

'I could speak to the police for you,' said Lulu. 'And I would make it clear that they aren't to go public with the information. If, as I suspect, other people have received similar letters, the kidnappers won't know who went to the police.'

'What if they see you?' said Amanda, dabbing at her eyes again. 'What if they're watching the house?'

'Do you think someone is watching the house?' Lulu asked. She looked over at Donald. 'Have you seen anyone?'

Donald shrugged. 'This is one of the most photographed streets in the country,' he said. 'There are always people outside staring and taking photographs, or walking their dogs at all times of day and night. It's quieter now, in the middle of winter, but really, there's always someone out there no matter the time of day.'

Lulu sat back. 'Okay. How about this, then? I know you invited me to stay, and you know how much I love staying with you, but why don't Conrad and I go back to *The Lark* tonight? On the off chance that your house is being watched, I'll just have been a dinner guest, so there's no reason why anyone would follow me. I'll take the letter and photographs with me, and first thing tomorrow I'll take them to the police. I'll make sure that they understand the situation and that they aren't to approach you. I'll just show them what you received and they can take it from there.'

'But if they see the letter, they'll know that it's us,' said Amanda. 'What if the information gets out?'

'I'll make sure it doesn't,' said Lulu.

Amanda shook her head fiercely. 'I don't think we can take that risk, Lulu,' she said. 'I'm sorry, I just don't.'

'Couldn't you just tell them that you've seen the letter and photographs, but not show them to the police or mention our name?' said Donald. 'Just keep our names out of it?'

Lulu reached for the photograph of Poppy Novak and turned it so that it was facing Donald. 'I don't see a window or curtains in this picture. So maybe she's being held in a basement, which means a house and not a flat.' She tapped the lower right corner. 'What do you see here?'

'A wardrobe, I suppose.'

'Yes, a wardrobe. But the police have access to databases that might well be able to identify the wardrobe, from the type of veneer, the base – lots of little clues that we're not aware of. Now, suppose they could show that this particular wardrobe was manufactured by, say, IKEA, between 2009 and 2015. And suppose only fifty of those wardrobes were sold in the West Country over that period. The retailers could well have the sales receipts on file and the police would be able to identify the buyers. It would be a relatively simple matter to visit their homes and check their bedrooms.'

'But they could have bought the wardrobe second-hand,' said Amanda. 'Or brought it with them from somewhere else.'

'Yes, that's possible. But we won't know unless we give the police a chance to investigate,' said Lulu. She tapped the photograph of Olivia. 'And look at this picture. Whoever took the photograph was almost certainly in a car, and you don't remember seeing them. But it could well be that the area is covered by a video doorbell camera, or by a council CCTV camera. We won't know unless the police get to see this photograph. If the car was caught on camera, the police might be able to get a registration number, and that could lead them straight to the kidnappers.'

'You make it sound so easy,' said Amanda.

'It's not easy, but it is possible. This letter and these photographs could be the best chance of catching the kidnappers and putting an end to this,' said Lulu. 'And getting the kidnappers behind bars means you will be able to relax.'

'Lulu is making a lot of sense, darling,' said Donald. He reached for Amanda's hand again, and this time she let him take it. 'I think we should let her at least try.'

Amanda bit down on her lower lip, then nodded slowly. 'Okay,' she said.

'I won't let you or Olivia down, Amanda,' said Lulu. 'I promise.'

5

The Uber dropped Conrad and Lulu close to the canal. Conrad, who had been sitting on Lulu's lap, jumped out onto the pavement. Lulu followed him with her backpack and closed the door. Donald and Amanda had made a big show of waving her off as she left their house. There were several dog walkers around and tourists taking night-time shots of the Crescent, so it was impossible to know for sure whether they were being watched.

Conrad waited until the taxi had driven away before looking up at Lulu. 'I don't understand,' he said. 'I thought we were staying the night with your friends.'

'We were, that was the plan,' said Lulu.

'But the plan has changed?'

'I'm afraid so.' They began walking up the narrow track towards the canal, Lulu keeping her left hand on the metal rail. The ground was icy and she didn't want to risk a fall. 'Someone has threatened to kidnap Olivia unless Amanda and Donald pay them fifty thousand pounds.'

'What?'

'I know, it sounds crazy. But they received a ransom demand which seems to have been written by the kidnappers of Poppy Novak, that missing girl we read about in the paper earlier. The letter says that if Amanda and Donald don't pay them fifty thousand pounds, they'll kidnap Olivia too.'

'That's terrible.'

'Yes, it is.'

'We have to do something, Lulu. We can't let anything happen to that sweet little girl.'

'I hear you,' said Lulu.

'Have they been to the police?'

'They're scared. The kidnappers – the would-be kidnappers, that is – told them not to talk to the police. So I've said I'll talk to the police on their behalf.' She patted her jacket. 'I have the letter they were sent. I'm going to show it to the police. Amanda was worried that if I left from their house to visit the police tomorrow, I'd be followed.'

'That's not likely, is it?'

'I'd say it's very unlikely. But Amanda is so upset, I thought it best that we just sleep in *The Lark* tonight and go to see the police tomorrow. Depending on what happens, we might well sleep in the house tomorrow night.'

'I could sense that something was wrong,' said Conrad.

'Yes, me too.'

'Perhaps you're developing catlike senses.'

'It was more my detective experience,' said Lulu. 'Amanda was clearly upset about something. We watched a police press conference about Poppy's case, and then it all came pouring out. We'll have to go to the police HQ, which is outside Bristol. We can get an Uber first thing.'

'There isn't a police station in Bath?'

'I did ask Amanda and Donald, but it seems that there's only a one-stop shop set up in the city centre that's open nine to five on weekdays. Probably just there to hand out crime numbers to victims of housebreaking or car thefts. Major crime would be handled from Bristol.'

'I obviously missed a lot when I was in Olivia's bedroom.'

'You can say that again.'

'I obviously missed a lot when I was in Olivia's bedroom,' said Conrad. He flashed her a sly smile. 'Did you see what I did there?'

'I did,' she said. 'Very clever.'

They reached *The Lark*. Conrad jumped smoothly onto the rear deck and Lulu followed him. 'I'm going to make myself a nice cup of camomile tea, and then you and I can talk this through,' she said as she unlocked the door.

'Do you think you'll be able to help?'

'I certainly hope so,' said Lulu.

6

Lulu woke before sunrise. Conrad was still asleep at the foot of the bunk, so she slipped off without waking him. She showered, and when she came back into the cabin he was sitting up. 'What time are we leaving?' he asked.

'I think about eight o'clock should work,' she said. 'So we have time for breakfast.'

Main police stations were usually open 24/7, but detectives were only human and even on major cases they had to sleep, so Lulu had decided there would be no point arriving at the station before nine o'clock. A quick check on Google Maps showed her that the Avon and Somerset HQ was actually at Portishead, close to the Bristol Channel, which was almost an hour's drive from Bath.

She pulled on a pair of blue jeans, a cotton T-shirt and a cashmere sweater, then made herself scrambled eggs and sausage. Conrad was a fan of scrambled eggs, but he preferred them without butter. In fact, the first time he had met Lulu he had pointed out that cats didn't react well to dairy. He had explained that most cats are lactose intolerant, and consuming dairy products can lead to diarrhoea and vomiting. So no butter for him, but Lulu loved her eggs creamy and buttery, so she cooked their portions separately. They ate their breakfasts at the table, Lulu accompanying it with a steaming mug of coffee while Conrad lapped at water in a blue and white Wedgwood saucer.

The Cat and the Christmas Kidnapper

After they had finished and Lulu had done the washing up, she used her phone to summon an Uber. When the car arrived it waited on the road at the bottom of the sloping track that led from the towpath. It was a grey Prius, driven by a lovely man called Ahmed who asked what sort of music Lulu wanted on the radio, whether the temperature was to her liking, and if she had a preferred route.

'It's my first time there, so you choose,' she said. 'And your car is toasty warm.' She was wearing her sheepskin jacket and was already starting to sweat.

'Music?'

'Again, you choose,' she said.

Conrad curled up on her lap and closed his eyes. Ahmed didn't speak again until they arrived at Portishead almost an hour later, which suited Lulu just fine. She had spent the hour deep in thought, worrying about Poppy Novak and trying to work out what the best option was for Amanda and Donald. She was sure that paying the fifty thousand pounds was a very bad idea, but she understood how Amanda felt.

'We're here, madam,' said Ahmed eventually. 'But it looks as if we can't drive in.'

The Prius had pulled up at a gatehouse with a red and white pole barrier blocking their way. A uniformed security guard walked over to talk to Ahmed. Lulu wound down her window. 'Hello. I'm here to speak to a member of CID,' she said.

The guard was in his fifties, overweight with steely grey hair and wire-framed glasses perched on the end of a nose flecked with broken blood vessels. He shook his head. 'Members of the public aren't allowed in,' he said.

'This is the headquarters of Avon and Somerset Police, isn't it?'

'It is, yes. But it's also the headquarters of the Fire Service, and we don't have any fire engines here.'

'Right, okay. But I need to report a crime.'

'You can go online and it will tell you where your nearest police station is.'

'Apparently that's a one-stop shop in Bath city centre, but the CID aren't there. And I really need to talk to a detective.'

'Then you'll have to call 101 and tell them.'

'I have something to show them,' said Lulu. 'Evidence.'

'They'll take the details over the phone and arrange to see any evidence you have,' said the guard.

'Could I talk to the SIO on the Poppy Novak case? DI Simon Kemp, I believe.'

The guard frowned. 'SIO?'

'Senior Investigating Officer,' said Lulu. 'I have information pertinent to his case.'

'That may well be, but as I said, members of the public can't just drop by. You have to visit your local police station or call 101.'

Lulu flashed him her most ingratiating smile. 'If it makes a difference, I was a detective myself, with the Met in London.'

'It doesn't,' said the guard. 'Now, if you could just reverse back and head on your way.'

'What's your name, please?' Lulu asked him.

The guard leaned forward so that she could see the name on his ID tag: Ronald Casey.

'Is it Ronald, or Ron?'

'It's Ron. But if you want to make an official complaint, use Ronald.'

'Oh no, I'm not the complaining type, Ron,' Lulu said. 'My name is Lulu, Lulu Lewis.' She nodded at Conrad. 'And this is Conrad, my cat. I absolutely understand that members of the public aren't to be admitted. That's such a sad reflection of the way that policing is going, isn't it? You can never find a police officer when you need one these days, and they seem to prefer to lock themselves away rather than walking around and interacting with the public. All in the name of efficiency, of course. And I absolutely understand that your job is to keep members of the public away from the building so that they can do whatever it is that they do in there in peace. But this is important, Ron, it really is. You've heard about the little girl who went missing? Poppy Novak?'

Ron nodded. 'Terrible business. My granddaughter is the same age.'

'Then I'm sure you realize how distraught her parents are right now. The thing is, Ron, I have evidence that I need to show the SIO, the senior investigating officer, and I think he needs to see that evidence that I have. So could you do me a huge favour, Ron? Could you make a phone call and explain that I'm here outside, that I am a former detective superintendent with the Met, and that I have some information that might well help find little Poppy Novak? Could you do that for me, Ron?'

'You're very persuasive,' he said.

'I try to be, when it's necessary. And in this case, it really is necessary.'

He stared at her for several moments. Then he nodded. 'Okay,' he said. 'Let me try.'

'You're an angel, Ron,' she said.

Ron went back into the guardhouse.

Ahmed twisted around in his seat. 'My mother always said that you catch more flies with honey than you do with vinegar,' he said.

'That is very true,' said Lulu.

After a couple of minutes, Ron reappeared. He smiled at Lulu and passed her a laminated form. 'If you drive straight ahead you'll see the admin building on your left. Someone will be waiting for you there. Your driver will need that to get out.'

'Ron, thank you so much.'

Ron nodded. 'I just hope they find that little girl,' he said.

He raised the pole and the Prius drove through. It was only then that Lulu realized just how big the compound was, with several large buildings and hundreds of vehicles lined up in multiple car parks.

She saw the admin building ahead of them and pointed at it. 'If you could stop here, Ahmed, that would be great.' He pulled up in front of the building. 'Can you wait here for me?' she asked.

'I'm sorry, madam, I cannot,' said Ahmed.

'No problem,' said Lulu. She climbed out and swung Conrad onto her shoulders.

'Five stars?' said Ahmed hopefully.

'Of course,' said Lulu. She closed the door and the Prius drove away.

Lulu looked up at the building. It was a very strange design, with two large white triangular pediments above two white columns that rested on top of a glass and steel entrance. The ground floor was made of yellow bricks, with orange bricks above them, and there were dormer windows set into the roof. It was as if a child had tried to copy the architecture of the Royal Crescent and had not done a very good job.

'I don't understand why you'd build a police station and then ban the public from entering it,' said Conrad.

'It's modern-day policing, unfortunately,' said Lulu.

'But it doesn't make any sense, does it?'

'Not to me, no. But then, I'm retired and no one cares what I think.'

A glass door opened and a woman in a dark blue suit came out. She was in her early thirties, a little over five feet tall but with heels that added a couple of inches. She had black wavy hair cut so that it brushed her shoulders as she walked. She smiled and waved. 'Hello,' she said. 'You must be Lulu Lewis?'

Lulu nodded. 'Thank you for seeing me.'

'Not a problem. I'm Juliet. Detective Inspector Juliet Donnelly – but please just call me Juliet. They said you used to be in the job?'

'I was a detective superintendent with the Met, now retired.'

'And you have information regarding the Poppy Novak abduction? Is that right?'

'I do, yes.'

'Come inside and let's have a chat.' Juliet took Lulu into the building. There were several chairs and sofas off to the right. 'Let's sit here,' said Juliet.

Lulu sat down on one of the grey plastic sofas and Juliet sat in a chair facing her. Conrad jumped down off Lulu's shoulders and sat next to her on the sofa. 'Does he go every-where with you?' Juliet asked.

'Pretty much, yes,' said Lulu. 'His name is Conrad.'

'Pleased to meet you, Conrad.' She smiled at Lulu. 'So, you understand that we don't run investigations here. This complex is mainly for admin and training. Forty-seven acres in total, with more than a thousand operational and police staff, with units like Road Policing and Purchasing and Supply. Major incident planning takes place here, and the Counter Terrorism Group and Armed Response Group are here. But we don't investigate crimes at Portishead, so there are very few operational officers on site.'

'So where would I find the SIO working the Poppy Novak case?'

'Well, that is a little complicated, I'm afraid. Poppy Novak was kidnapped in Bradford-on-Avon, which doesn't fall under Avon and Somerset. It's Wiltshire. There is a neighbourhood policing team in Bradford-on-Avon, but anything major like a kidnapping would be handled by Wiltshire Police's Trowbridge station.'

'But Bradford-on-Avon is just a few miles from Bath,' said Lulu.

'Yes, and the county border lies between them,' said Juliet. 'I can find out who the SIO is, but it won't be one of our officers.'

'I saw him on television last night – DI Simon Kemp.'

'Right, yes. But he would be with Wiltshire Police.'

'Oh my goodness. Then this is really going to get complicated, because the evidence I have originated in Bath. Which would be your patch.'

'What is this evidence, exactly?'

'It's a letter that was sent to friends of mine. A ransom demand of sorts.'

'You have it with you?'

'I do, yes. But before I show it to you, can we agree that you don't make it public without getting their permission?'

Juliet pulled a face. 'I'm not sure I can agree to that without knowing what the evidence is.'

'The thing is, whoever wrote the letter warned my friends not to contact the police. So they don't want anyone to know that the letter has been shown to anyone else.'

'Okay, I understand that. Have you worked kidnapping cases before?'

'I have, yes.'

'Then you know that we always proceed very carefully. I'm sure that everything will be done to protect your friends.'

'Okay. Good.' Lulu reached into her sheepskin jacket and pulled out the envelope, which she had placed in a Waitrose carrier bag. 'I didn't have an evidence bag,' she said. 'This was the best I could find. My friends have both handled the envelope and the material inside, but I wore gloves.' She smiled. 'Marigolds, as it happens.'

'Well, I can do better than that,' said Juliet. She reached into her jacket pocket and pulled out a pack of blue latex gloves. She opened the pack and put the gloves on before taking the carrier bag from Lulu, then carefully opened the envelope and took out the contents. She gasped when she saw the photograph of Poppy Novak. 'Oh my goodness,' she said. She peered at the newspaper in the photograph.

'It was taken the day after she was abducted,' said Lulu.

'How long have your friends been sitting on this?'

'It only arrived yesterday. It was held up in the post. The Christmas rush. Perhaps if you get the picture analysed, there might be clues in it as to its location. The furniture, the carpet. Something that might tell us where the room is.'

Juliet looked at the photograph of Olivia arriving at school. 'And who is this?'

'Olivia. My friends' daughter. If you read the letter, you'll understand everything.'

Juliet put down the photograph and picked up the letter. Her forehead creased into a frown as she read it. 'Olivia hasn't been kidnapped?' she said eventually.

'Olivia is fine, for the moment. But the threat is there.'

'So the kidnappers took Poppy Novak, but sent a ransom demand to . . .' She looked at the envelope. '. . . Mr and Mrs Balfour?'

'Donald and Amanda. Yes.'

'They live in the Royal Crescent,' Juliet said. 'So they have money?'

Lulu nodded. 'They're planning on paying.'

'With Bitcoin?'

'Yes.'

'Well, that's not a good idea.'

'I told them that.'

Juliet gathered the sheets of paper together, slid them back into the envelope and put the envelope into the carrier bag. 'I need to show this to my bosses,' she said.

'Please remember what I said about making it public.'

'I will, but I have to run this by my bosses before we go any further.' She stood up. 'Do you have any identification, Lulu?'

'I don't have a warrant card any more, if that's what you mean?'

'A driving licence will be fine.'

Lulu fished her driving licence out of her wallet and gave it to the inspector.

'Please wait here,' said Juliet. 'If you and Conrad want water or a coffee, just let them know at reception. Hopefully I won't be long.' She hurried off.

'She seems nice,' said Conrad.

'Good aura?'

'A very good aura,' he said. 'Trustworthy, open, honest.' One of Conrad's many talents was his ability to see people's auras. It was why he was such a good judge of character.

'Excellent,' said Lulu. 'Then we've come to the right person.'

7

It was more than half an hour before Juliet returned to reception. She didn't have the carrier bag or the blue latex gloves but she did have Lulu's driving licence, which she returned to her. 'The Assistant Chief Constable will see you, Lulu,' said Juliet. 'I'm to take you to his office.'

'Conrad, too?'

'Oh yes. I told the ACC about Conrad.'

Lulu stood up and bent down, letting Conrad jump onto her shoulders, before following Juliet to the lifts. They went up one floor and Juliet took them along a corridor to the ACC's office. A secretary sat at a desk in an outer office but she waved them right through.

The ACC was a man in his late forties with greying hair cut short and black-framed spectacles perched on the end of his nose. His face broke into a grin when he saw Lulu. 'Well, this is a turn-up for the books,' he said. 'I was sure it had to be you, boss, but I never had you down as a cat lady.'

'Oh, my goodness me,' said Lulu as she recognized him. 'Colin. Colin Morris. Long time no see. I had no idea . . .' She put her head on one side. 'Of course. You married a lady from Bristol, didn't you? When was that? Twenty years ago?'

'Nineteen. Three children since I arrived here, one away at university, the other two eating me out of house and home.' He stood up. He was wearing an immaculate uniform, with the rank badges of crossed tipstaffs within a wreath on his epaulettes. 'Great to see you, boss.' He walked round his desk and spotted Conrad as he approached Lulu to hug her. 'You really do have a cat.'

'Conrad, my constant companion,' said Lulu. 'He came up from London with me on my narrowboat.'

'That's a long journey.'

'The journey is half the fun,' said Lulu.

Conrad jumped down onto the grey carpet with a soft thud. The ACC hugged Lulu and patted her on the back before ushering her towards a sofa by the window. He grinned at Juliet. 'I was Lulu's bag carrier many years ago. I was still wet behind the ears, and truth be told I was struggling a bit, but she whipped me into shape and got me my sergeant's stripes.'

A bag carrier – also known as a scribe – was a detective who followed a senior investigating officer's every move, recording every decision the SIO made in the Book 194, also known as the key decision log. If at any point a senior officer wanted to check on the progress of an investigation, they could examine the Book 194 to check that all protocols were being followed and that nothing had been missed. Colin Morris had been Lulu's bag carrier for almost two years, and he'd been a good one.

'Oh, you were more than capable of getting your stripes yourself, Colin.'

'That's nice of you to say, boss, but I was finding being a detective hard going. It was a lot harder than I'd expected – I was thinking of asking for a transfer back to uniform before you took me under your wing. I learned so much from you. Not just about running a major investigation but about handling people, too.'

Lulu felt herself blush. 'That's so very kind of you to say, thank you.'

'It's the truth,' said ACC Morris. He waved at the sofa. 'Please sit, both of you.'

Lulu and Juliet sat down on the sofa and ACC Morris pulled up an armchair and sat opposite them across a low pine coffee table. The Waitrose carrier bag containing the envelope was on the table. The letter and photographs had been placed in official police evidence bags.

'Seriously, if it wasn't for the two years I spent with you, I doubt I'd be where I am today.'

'You're making me blush, Colin.'

'Then I'll stop.' He gestured at the carrier bag. 'And you come bearing gifts.'

'I gather it's an awkward situation, with the border being between Bath and Bradford-on-Avon.'

ACC Morris nodded. 'Yes, very much so. We did offer to help as soon as they went public that it was a possible kidnapping, but to be honest, it was already too late then. They should have called us the moment they knew she was missing, but they wanted to handle it themselves. Poppy Novak's home is only a few miles from our patch, so as soon as we were notified, we carried out a search on our side of the border. We've also made it clear that we'll offer any assistance they need, but frankly they have nothing to go on. No eyewitnesses, no CCTV, no nothing.'

'And no ransom note?'

'Certainly not as far as I know. I suppose it's possible that they have one and they're holding it back, but I won't know until I've had a chance to speak to my opposite number there.' He smiled and nodded at Juliet. 'I've asked Juliet to be SIO on our case. And no matter what the Wiltshire police say, this is very much our case. Yes, the Poppy Novak kidnapping is on their turf, but the extortion is our case to deal with. If there's one of these letters, there could well be more. So we need to get this envelope and its contents to our forensic people, and we need to give copies to the SIO of the kidnapping case. That'll be Detective Inspector Simon Kemp. Now, he'll obviously want the originals, but we have to make it clear that they stay with us, for the time being at least. Their forensics lab isn't a patch on ours, but even so, it might well be that we end up having to ask for assistance from the Met or the National Crime Agency. Perhaps even MI5 – their anti-terrorism people know all about tracking printers.' He gestured at the envelope. 'It was posted? Regular mail?'

'First class,' said Juliet. 'But it took four days. The sorting office is swamped, pre-Christmas.'

'So if we know where it was posted, we might get lucky with CCTV,' said ACC Morris. 'Any other thoughts?'

'We need to analyse the room contents in the photograph of Poppy,' said Juliet. 'It might help us locate it. Lulu's idea.'

The ACC wrinkled his nose. 'I'm not sure that we're geared up for that,' he said.

'The Met's online paedophile crime unit has experts in that field,' said Lulu.

'Do you know anyone?'

Lulu shook her head. 'I did, but they tend to move on

quite quickly,' she said. 'Their work is emotionally draining and most investigators can only take it for a few years.'

'I'll make a call,' said ACC Morris. He looked down at the carrier bag. 'I have to say, Lulu, this is going to get very complicated. There's quite a bit of politics involved, unfortunately. As I said, we've offered to help with the Poppy Novak case, but they've insisted on handling it themselves. And just between you and me – and Conrad, of course – I don't think that was a smart move on their part. In the summer of 2022, Her Majesty's Inspectorate of Constabulary found the Wiltshire force "inadequate" in three areas: responding to the public, protecting vulnerable people – especially victims of domestic abuse – and making use of its resources. From then on, the force was subject to external monitoring. Then in December 2022 a review reported a decline in the force's performance in investigating crime effectively.'

'Well, that's not good news, is it?' said Lulu.

'Unfortunately it means they have something to prove, which is possibly why they want to handle it themselves. But if we have an extortion case in Avon and Somerset linked to an abduction in Wiltshire, that makes things very complicated. Operationally, it puts us in a difficult position.'

Lulu frowned. 'I wonder if that's why Poppy Novak was kidnapped?'

'What do you mean?'

'Well, this has all been very well planned and executed, clearly. What if Poppy Novak was chosen because she lives in Wiltshire, and the threatening letters are being sent to families in your area? It makes it that much more difficult for the police to operate, doesn't it? I'm assuming they hoped that the families involved wouldn't go to the police – the ransom demand is very clear about that – but if they did, there's the extra wrinkle that the kidnapping would be investigated by a different police force. And from what you have said, it's a force that doesn't have a great reputation for investigating crime.'

The ACC nodded thoughtfully. 'That makes a lot of sense.'

'So what should I do?' asked Lulu. 'Shall I go to the Trowbridge station and ask to talk to DI Kemp?'

'You could, yes.' Juliet held up the letter. 'But they wouldn't be able to investigate the extortion. That would be down to us.'

'But DI Kemp needs to see that letter, because the MIC might help identify the printer. And there might be clues to Poppy's location in the photograph. It's all intel that he'll need.' Lulu looked from Juliet to Colin. 'It seems to me that some sort of joint investigation is called for. And if it's done through you, that would help insulate my friends from the inquiry.'

'I'm going to have to talk to your friends, come what may,' said Juliet.

'I'm sure that will be okay, but you mustn't go to their house. She's worried that the house is being watched.'

'That's very unlikely,' said Juliet. 'If they were asking for a million pounds, maybe; but for fifty thousand pounds? I think it's a try-on. They'll have sent out several of these letters, hoping that one or two will fall for it.'

'My friends don't want to take the risk,' said Lulu. 'And besides, they really don't have any information other than what was in the envelope.'

Juliet wrinkled her nose. 'I'll still need to talk to them. In person, ideally.'

'I'm sure we can arrange that.'

'Do you think they'll pay the ransom?' asked ACC Morris.

'I'm sure they will,' said Lulu. 'They seem to think it'll be the end of it.'

'To be fair, they might be right,' said Juliet. She sat back in her seat and sighed. 'This is a right can of worms. I think you're right, a joint investigation is probably the way to go.' She looked at the ACC. 'What do you think, sir?'

'I think you need to run the extortion case, Juliet. Get a team set up at Kenneth Steele House ASAP and start the ball rolling, then head over to Trowbridge today. I'll speak to my opposite number in Wiltshire and pave the way. The two cases are clearly connected. I suspect DI Kemp will try to take over your investigation, but you'll need to resist that.'

'Colin, do you think I could be involved in some way?' said Lulu. 'Not officially, perhaps, but I would like to be in the loop.'

'Juliet is a first-rate investigator, Lulu. Your friends are in good hands.'

'I'm happy for Lulu to be involved,' said Juliet. 'It's possible that her friends were chosen for a reason, so she may have some insight that could be helpful.'

'I don't really have a budget for consultancy fees,' said ACC Morris apologetically.

'Oh, I wasn't even thinking about money,' said Lulu. 'I'd just be happy to tag along.'

'If Juliet's okay with that, then full steam ahead,' said ACC Morris.

Conrad meowed from under the coffee table. 'And Conrad would like to tag along, too,' said Lulu.

ACC Morris smiled thinly. 'The more, the merrier, I suppose,' he said.

8

Juliet drove Lulu and Conrad into Bristol in a blue Tesla. The traffic was bad, presumably because the city was flooded with last-minute Christmas shoppers, and it took forty-five minutes to travel the eleven miles or so to Kenneth Steele House, a two-storey white-clad box on an industrial estate to the east of the city. There were plenty of marked police cars around and a car park for the people working in the building, but it was clearly not geared up for visits from members of the public.

'So, this isn't a police station, is it?' said Lulu as she climbed out of the car with Conrad on her shoulders. Next to the building was a radio tower that must have been a hundred feet tall.

'There are police stationed here, but it's more of an operational base than a neighbourhood police station.' Juliet was carrying a black North Face backpack.

'So you couldn't report a crime here?'

'Oh, no. You'd call 999 in an emergency or 101 if it wasn't an emergency.'

'But what if I wanted to talk to an officer, face to face?'

'Well, then you'd visit your local police station.'

'Yes, but the one in Bath is a one-stop shop thing which is closed in the evenings and at weekends.'

'But the phones are answered 24/7,' Juliet said. 'London is the same, isn't it? They're shutting stations to save money?'

'I suppose so. They've been closing down police stations all over the city, but there are still plenty around where you can walk in off the street and talk to someone in uniform.'

Juliet took them up a flight of concrete steps to the main entrance. 'And who exactly was Kenneth Steele?' asked Lulu, looking at a large sign above the door.

'He was chief constable in the late seventies. The first police chief of the amalgamated forces that became Avon and Somerset.'

'Nice to be remembered,' said Lulu.

Juliet led the way inside and along a corridor to an office on the ground floor at the back of the building, with two windows overlooking the car park. There were six tables, each with a computer monitor, a line of grey metal filing cabinets, and three large whiteboards on one wall. The whiteboards were covered in handwritten notes, computer printouts and photographs and maps, clearly connected to whatever case the previous occupants had been investigating. Two young men in almost matching blue suits were scrutinizing the whiteboards, but they turned around as Juliet entered the room. Juliet introduced them to Lulu as DC Sam McLean and DC Roger Warner. As they all solemnly shook hands, the door opened and two women appeared, carrying folders. They had police lanyards but Juliet introduced them as civilian support workers.

'Right, this is the team so far,' said Juliet. 'But I'm expecting more bodies later this afternoon, including DC Debra Hinton, who will be my scribe.' She opened her backpack and Blu-tacked copies of the envelope and its contents onto one of the whiteboards as she briefly brought the team up to speed on what had happened. 'Sam and Roger, I need you to go out to the school and see if you can work out where this photograph was taken. Find out where the photographer was positioned, and check for CCTV and doorbell footage. Whoever took that photograph might well have targeted other kids. The school has closed now for Christmas, but I want you both out there talking to local families. See if anyone saw anything. Get hold of the headteacher at home and see about a list of home phone numbers.' She took out evidence bags containing the envelope and sheets that Amanda and Donald had received and handed them to one of the civilian workers. 'We need everything processed for DNA and fingerprints. Our extortion case might not be treated as a priority, so you'll need to explain that it's linked to the Poppy Novak kidnapping. If you get any pushback at all, refer them to ACC Morris. Also, see what information we can get from the franking – I'm assuming part of the code will tell us where the envelope was posted. If that's the case, give the info to Sam or Roger. Any questions?'

Everyone shook their heads.

'Right. As I said, I'm expecting a few more bodies later today. Meanwhile, Lulu and I will head over to Trowbridge and touch base with DI Kemp, the SIO on the kidnapping case. Needless to say, we keep what has happened to ourselves. Refer any press enquiries to me, and only tell anyone you speak to that it's an ongoing investigation. Under no circumstances are details of the letter to be made public.' She nodded briskly. 'Onwards and upwards. We should be back in three or four hours.'

9

Trowbridge was an hour's drive south-east from Bristol, passing to the north of Bath. Trowbridge Police Station was a very strange building that looked like an avant-garde arts centre, with a large wavy black canopy over the main entrance. There were two circular holes in the canopy and four metal rods under each hole that had the look of the long-legged invaders from Mars in the *War of the Worlds* movie. A sign on the front door said that the station was open to the public from 8.30 a.m. until 5.30 p.m. Monday to Friday, 9 a.m. to 1 p.m. on Saturdays, and closed on Sundays.

They had to wait in reception for almost half an hour before DI Kemp came out to see them. Lulu didn't know if the inspector was busy or if it was a power play, but from his coolness as he greeted Juliet, she suspected the latter. He was wearing the same grey suit he'd had on during the press conference she'd seen on television, with a pale blue shirt and a red and black striped tie. There were dark patches under his eyes and flecks of dandruff in his hair, and his nails were bitten to the quick. He didn't look like a man who was getting a good night's sleep. Lulu knew that was par for the course for SIOs with difficult cases, especially where children were involved.

Juliet introduced Lulu, explaining that she was a retired Met detective superintendent. DI Kemp acknowledged her with a curt nod. He frowned at Conrad. 'There's an interview room we can use. Please follow me,' he said.

That was probably a power play, too, Lulu thought as she followed them down the corridor. Kemp could just as easily have taken them to his incident room.

The room he led them to was small, with a single window high up in the wall facing the door. It held a table and six chairs, and running around the wall was a plastic strip at waist height – a panic button. The room was clearly set up for interviewing witnesses and suspects. There was a double tape recording machine at one end of the table and two CCTV cameras were aimed at the table. A man was sitting in one of the chairs and scrambled to his feet when the door opened. He was in his late twenties, tall and gangly, in a brown suit that appeared to be a size too small.

'This is DC Arnold,' said Kemp.

'The bag carrier,' said Arnold with a grin. 'DC Max Arnold. Have pen, will travel.'

Kemp flashed Arnold a cold look, and the DC averted his eyes.

'Please, sit,' said Kemp. He took a seat by the wall and Arnold sat down next to him, taking a notebook and pen from his jacket pocket.

Juliet sat down facing DI Kemp, and Lulu took the chair opposite Arnold. Conrad jumped down off Lulu's shoulders and went to stand near the door, sniffing the air, his tail high.

'What's the story with the cat?' Kemp asked.

'No story,' said Lulu. 'He's my companion.'

'And he goes everywhere with you?'

'Pretty much, yes.'

Kemp frowned. 'It's as if he's listening to me.'

Lulu twisted round in her chair. Conrad was looking at Kemp, his ears up and his whiskers twitching. 'Oh, he is,' said Lulu. 'Every word.'

Kemp stared at Conrad, and Conrad stared back. Kemp was obviously trying to outstare him, and Lulu knew he was on a hiding to nothing. She smiled to herself when the DI eventually conceded defeat and blinked, turning back to the others. He smiled at Juliet without warmth.

'I'm told you have information pertinent to the Poppy Novak abduction,' he said.

'You're treating it as an abduction rather than a kidnapping?' asked Juliet.

'The girl has been abducted. There's been no ransom demand. We have no reason to think she went missing of her own accord, and two searches of the area have come up with nothing, so at the moment we are treating this as an abduction by person or persons unknown. We are focusing our investigation on the sex offenders who are known to live locally, and as there are so many of them, it's taking time.'

Juliet opened her backpack and took out the copy of the photograph of Poppy Novak. DI Kemp's jaw dropped when he saw the photograph. 'What the hell?' he spluttered. 'What is this?'

'It appears to be a photograph of Poppy Novak with a copy of the *Daily Mail* from four days ago. Proof of life.'

'Where did you get this from?'

'Have you not received a similar photograph?' asked Juliet.

'No, we bloody well haven't,' said Kemp. 'And I'm asking again, where did you get it from?'

'It was sent to a friend of mine,' said Lulu. 'Along with a ransom demand, of sorts.'

Kemp squinted at her. 'Remind me again who you are?' he said.

Lulu smiled brightly. There was nothing to be gained by antagonizing the detective, though he was clearly an unpleasant piece of work. 'Lulu Lewis. I used to be a detective superintendent with the Met.'

'Used to be?'

'Retired now, obviously. But as I said, this was sent to friends of mine who live in Bath. I'm here to represent their interests.'

Kemp looked at the photograph again. 'If the newspaper is from four days ago, why are you only bringing it to us now?'

'The kidnappers posted the ransom demand,' said Juliet. 'It arrived yesterday. We assume it was held up in the Christmas post.'

'A ransom demand – that doesn't make any sense. Why wasn't the ransom demand sent to Poppy's parents?'

'Presumably because they don't have any money,' said Lulu. 'And the thing is, the ransom demand isn't for the return of Poppy Novak. It's to make sure that the kidnappers don't take their daughter.'

'Which daughter?' said DI Kemp, clearly confused.

'The daughter of my friends. The people who received the ransom demand. It seems clear to me that the kidnappers only took Poppy Novak to prove what they're capable of.'

DI Kemp threw up his hands. 'That doesn't make any sense.' He looked over at Juliet. 'Can you explain this to me in a way that I'll understand? Because none of what she is saying is making sense.'

'It makes perfect sense,' said Juliet. 'It's just a little unusual.' She took the letter from her backpack and held it out.

'Don't we need gloves for this?' he said.

'It's a copy,' said Juliet.

DI Kemp took it from her. 'Where's the original?'

'Our forensics people are looking at it,' she said.

The detective's eyes narrowed as he read the letter. 'And this Olivia is where?'

'With her parents,' said Lulu. 'In Bath.'

'I'm going to need to talk to them, obviously,' said Kemp.

'They don't know the Novak family,' said Lulu. 'All they have is the letter and the photograph.'

'I'll still need to interview them,' said the detective. 'And I'll need the originals of the letter and the photograph. And the envelope they came in.'

'I'll be more than happy to send you the forensics reports when we have them,' said Juliet.

Kemp put the letter down. 'That's not what I said, DI Donnelly. The letter and the photograph are evidence in a kidnapping case, a case in which I am the senior investigating officer. I need to have that evidence.'

'I hear you, DI Kemp. But the documents are also evidence in an extortion case of which I am senior investigating officer. And until a minute ago, you didn't even know you had a kidnapping case.'

'So you're refusing to cooperate with my ongoing kidnapping case? You must realize that by doing so you're putting Poppy Novak's life at risk?'

'DI Kemp, that's why we've driven all the way over from Bristol to talk to you. We're very keen to cooperate. Your boss and my boss have made it clear that they want us to share what information we have. Now, we had the documents in Bristol, so it made sense to start the forensic examination there. As I said, once we have the results I will of course show them to you.'

Kemp put down the letter and picked up the photograph of Poppy Novak. He wrinkled his nose as he examined it. 'So this is a bedroom, from the look of it.'

'I would say so, yes.'

'And going by the newspaper, this was the morning after she was taken.'

Juliet nodded. 'Yes.'

'But there's been no further communication with your friends? No phone calls or follow-up letters?'

'Just the one letter. What about the Novaks? Has there been any contact with the family?'

DI Kemp shook his head. 'None. Which is why we were treating it as an abduction.' He scratched his chin. 'So the kidnappers take Poppy, tie her up in a bedroom somewhere, and demand a ransom of fifty thousand pounds from this Olivia's parents. Who are the parents, by the way?' He took a notebook and pen from his pocket.

'They'd rather that their names were kept confidential,' said Lulu.

'I'm not planning on making their names public,' said the detective. 'But I'll definitely need to interview them. What I don't need is a civilian telling me how I should be conducting my investigation.'

Lulu had to fight the urge to snap at him. She took a deep

breath, but before she could speak, Juliet chipped in. 'I'm sure Lulu isn't trying to tell you what to do, but we have agreed that the parents should be kept out of this as much as possible,' she said. 'The letter does make it very clear that they are not to speak to the police, and they were very worried about any repercussions if they did so. It was only after we assured them that their names would be kept confidential that they agreed to hand over the letter and photographs.'

'Photographs?' said Kemp. 'I see only one photograph.'

Lulu realized he was watching her carefully, alert for any sign of deceit. She instinctively knew that he would know if she was lying, so she steadily returned his gaze. 'There was a second photograph, but it was of Olivia being dropped off at school,' she said. 'The school is in Bath. Investigators will be trying to ascertain where the photograph was taken from.'

'And hopefully identify the photographer or their vehicle,' said Kemp. 'Okay, that makes sense.' He sat back in his chair. 'This information raises a number of issues,' he said. 'It seems we're no longer looking for a paedophile abductor. The motive is clearly financial, which means we've pretty much been wasting our time over the past five days.' He gritted his teeth, and Lulu noticed that he had clenched his hands.

'Well, the searches would have been necessary either way,' she pointed out. 'As would the checking of any CCTV and ANPR cameras.' Lulu was referring to the United Kingdom's network of fixed and mobile Automatic Number Plate Recognition cameras, which read registration plates and checked them against a database of vehicles the police were interested in. ANPR data from around the country was fed to the National ANPR Data Centre at Hendon in north London, the same site used for the Police National Computer. Police forces routinely used it as a technique for apprehending criminals, and she knew that these days the data centre received thousands of police requests each day.

'Whatever the motive, Poppy must have been taken against her will,' Lulu continued. 'As to the change of emphasis – in a perverse way, it's a good thing that we now know it's a kidnapping. As you say, the motive is financial, which means there is no reason for her abductors to harm her. If she had been abducted by a predator, after five days we would be assuming the worst. But now we know that she has been kidnapped for money, there's every chance she is being looked after. From the photograph, it appears she's being held in a house, which means, hopefully, access to a bathroom and a kitchen. Plus, we have an advantage: the kidnappers hopefully don't know that we're onto them. Which is why we need to tread carefully from here on in.' She paused. 'It's your investigation, obviously. I'm just an observer. But it does seem to me that there's an argument for keeping the fact that we know it's a kidnapping to ourselves.'

'To not tell the Novaks, you mean?'

'Oh, no, they need to be told, obviously. By now they must be at their wits' end. We can tell them that we no longer believe she has been abducted by a predator – but I don't think anyone else should be told. If the media gets hold of it and the kidnappers become aware that the police know what's going on, Poppy could be at risk.'

'Are you suggesting that my team can't be trusted?' snapped the detective. 'Because I resent that insinuation.'

Lulu realized that he was clenching his hands again, so

tightly that his knuckles were whitening. 'I only know that all journalists have their sources,' she said. 'Your team might well be as pure as the driven snow, but word gets around. People talk. Can you put your hand on your heart and vouch for every single person in this building?'

DI Kemp opened his mouth to reply. Then he sighed and sat back in his chair.

'I hear what you're saying, Lulu,' said Juliet. 'But if there is a shift in the investigation – and there will have to be – then the team are going to want to know why. They've been hunting for a paedophile for five days, and now they're not. They're going to need a reason for that.'

Lulu nodded slowly and took a deep breath. Of course, Juliet was right. Lulu had been thinking like Amanda's friend, not like a police officer. Lulu had promised to keep Amanda and Donald out of any investigation, but the priority so far as the police were concerned was to rescue Poppy and apprehend the kidnappers.

'I apologize, DI Kemp,' she said. 'I am a guest here, and it's completely wrong for me to be offering advice where it isn't wanted or needed. As you say, this is your investigation, and you must proceed as you see fit.'

'No offence taken, Mrs Lewis,' said Kemp. 'But DI Donnelly is right. I can't change the thrust of the investigation without explaining the reasons to my team. So far as the press is concerned, I'm not sure how best to proceed. We've been asking the public for any help they can give regarding a child abduction – could we say that we now believe Poppy has been kidnapped for financial reasons?'

'That seems reasonable,' Lulu acknowledged. 'The investigation is progressing. Things change.'

He looked at Juliet. 'Presumably you'll be looking for other victims who have received similar letters?'

'We are, but we don't want to cause a panic,' Juliet replied. 'Also, we're waiting to see what we get forensically. We're hoping that we can track down whoever took the photograph of Olivia. We need to get them on the back foot – to push them into a position where they decide just to cut their losses and let Poppy go.'

'Or they might decide to . . .' began Lulu, but she couldn't bring herself to finish the sentence.

'I don't see that happening,' said Juliet. 'There'd be no point. Nothing to be gained. And this is all about money, remember?'

'That's assuming that the kidnappers are professionals and acting logically,' said Lulu. 'They could just as well be amateurs who panic when they think they're going to get caught.'

'Nothing about that letter suggests amateurs, though,' said Kemp. 'Amateurs would ask for a bag of cash to be left in a supermarket car park. This whole Bitcoin thing suggests they know what they're doing. About that – I'm no expert, but are there ways of tracking Bitcoin?'

'I'm not an expert either. I think it's possible, but not easy,' said Juliet. 'And I'm sure our force doesn't have the technical expertise to do it. We'll need help from the Met, or maybe the National Crime Agency.'

'Actually, I have a friend in the cybercrime division at the NCA,' said Lulu. 'I could make a call.'

'That would be helpful,' said Juliet.

Kemp rubbed his chin thoughtfully. 'So how much can we make public? How do we explain the fact that the Novaks haven't received a ransom demand?'

'You could do another press conference,' said Juliet. 'Mr

and Mrs Novak appealing directly to the kidnappers. "Just tell us what you want", that sort of thing.'

'But we'd still get the same question, wouldn't we – about how we know it isn't an abduction?'

'We could just say the line of inquiry has changed. We don't need to give a reason,' said Juliet.

'Do you have to say anything?' said Lulu hesitantly. 'You can tell the Novaks, obviously, but swear them to secrecy. You can tell your team, but don't tell the media. For a few days, at least. So long as the kidnappers think that you're treating it as an abduction, their guard will be down. You can maybe take advantage of that.'

DI Kemp sighed. 'Okay.' He looked at Juliet. 'How long before you get feedback from your forensics people?'

'We should have DNA and fingerprint results later today,' said Juliet. 'I have a team checking out Olivia's school, looking for the place where the photograph there was taken. Then they'll be looking for CCTV and ANPR. That should hopefully be done by this evening. We'll get the Met checking this photograph.' She tapped the photograph of Poppy. 'They'll check out the furniture, the carpet, the wallpaper, looking for any clues as to where the room is. These guys are the experts. I've no idea how long it will take, but I'm not expecting instant results. I'm having the envelope examined to see if we can work out where it was posted. And we'll see what Lulu's Bitcoin expert has to say.'

'Sounds like you've got all the bases covered,' said Kemp.

'What about you?' asked Juliet.

'We've been treating it as an abduction, so we were going the sex offender route, mainly. Although we did carry out two extensive searches in case she had fallen ill or got locked in somewhere. Both scenarios were unlikely considering how close her home is to the school, but we wanted to rule them out, which I think we did. We were taking advice from the NCA's Child Rescue Alert unit. They suggested we keep any public appeals local to begin with.'

Lulu nodded. 'Once you start appealing nationally, you'll be inundated with sightings from Land's End to John O'Groats.'

'That's what they said, that we'd need dozens of bodies to be following up all the leads. They said we should keep our appeals to local papers, radio and TV in the first instance, and if she was still missing after five days to consider going national. Which is where we are today, of course.'

'Except a national appeal probably isn't going to help now that we know she's been kidnapped,' said Juliet.

'I think we need to go back to CCTV and ANPR footage,' said Kemp. 'They must have used a vehicle. And we know exactly when she left the school.'

'You have CCTV footage of her leaving?'

'The front of the school is well covered, so yes. You can see her leaving, then she talks to a group of friends before heading home.'

'And you spoke to the friends?'

DI Kemp's jaw tightened at the implied criticism, but he nodded. 'Of course,' he said. 'It was just chit-chat. Nothing untoward.'

'And did she have a mobile phone?' asked Lulu. 'So many children do these days.'

Kemp nodded. 'She did. We can see it pinging off a local tower as she leaves the school, and then she pings off a second tower. But nothing after that.'

'So the phone was switched off?' asked Lulu.

'It seems so, yes. We're trying to get data from the phone company but they have a backlog, apparently. I'll get onto them again today.'

'And the phone is off now, obviously,' said Lulu.

DI Kemp gave her a tight smile. 'Obviously. How hopeful are you of identifying the vehicle that was used to photograph this Olivia?'

'We'll know later today,' said Juliet. 'Then what we can do is cross-check any registration numbers we come up with against the numbers of the vehicles in the vicinity of Poppy's school when she went missing.'

'You think they would use the same vehicle?' asked Lulu.

'No way of knowing unless we check,' said Juliet.

'As this was obviously planned, they would have given a lot of thought to the type of vehicle they would use to take her away in,' said Lulu. 'A predator would be driving around in their regular vehicle, and the abduction would probably be opportunistic. But now we know that it's a kidnapping, that probably means Poppy Novak was targeted in a planned seizure, and that being the case wouldn't the kidnappers use a van, probably a van with no rear windows?'

'I think Lulu has a point,' said Juliet. 'A windowless van would have best suited their needs. Have you checked CCTV footage for vans?'

'We checked all vehicles, but that doesn't mean we were able to get registration numbers for them all,' said Kemp.

'No, but if you confined your searches to vans, you could widen your search area.' Lulu shrugged. 'It was just a thought.'

'It's a good thought,' said Juliet.

'Also, I wondered if we could go and have a look at Poppy's school, just to get a feel for the area.'

DI Kemp opened his mouth to protest, but before he could say anything, Juliet began nodding enthusiastically. 'I was going to suggest that,' she said. 'Are you willing to take us out to the school? And maybe introduce us to Mr and Mrs Novak at the same time?'

Kemp still looked as if he was about to argue, but then the fight seemed to go out of him and he sighed. 'Fine, yes, why not?'

10

'This is the school, coming up on the left,' said DI Kemp. He was in the front passenger seat of a grey Vauxhall Insignia being driven by DC Arnold. Juliet and Lulu were sitting in the back. Conrad was lying in Lulu's lap, snoring softly. The school was just four miles from the Trowbridge police station. 'During term time the children start leaving at three thirty and the last have gone by about ten past four, unless they have after-school activities,' Kemp went on. 'The school gates are locked at six. Everyone broke up for the holidays yesterday, but we've had detectives here during the past week speaking to parents arriving in the morning and leaving in the afternoon. We've found half a dozen people who are sure they saw Poppy leaving that day and their statements coincide with CCTV footage from the school's cameras. But no one saw her being taken, obviously.'

'They do remember which direction she was going?' asked Lulu.

'Oh yes, they all say she went the same way, heading for her home,' said the inspector.

DC Arnold turned down a side road and parked. They all climbed out. Lulu scooped up Conrad and put him on her shoulders. They walked back to the school. DI Kemp was wearing a black overcoat, and Juliet and DC Arnold were both wearing raincoats. It was a cold afternoon and the bullet-grey sky overhead was threatening rain.

DI Kemp led the way, walking along the pavement towards the school. DC Arnold followed him, his raincoat flapping against his legs. Juliet and Lulu walked together. The school was to their right, a two-storey sandstone building with a slate roof. There were playing fields at the rear of the building, a paved playground and a staff car park. The grounds were surrounded by railings.

DI Kemp turned right and Arnold hurried to keep up with him. There were houses all around, mainly detached stone cottages with pretty gardens, though there was the occasional line of terraced houses.

DI Kemp stopped outside the school entrance and waited for Juliet and Lulu to join him. 'All the pupils leave through this gate,' he said. 'Those parents who pick up their kids – and that's the majority – queue up outside, though not directly in front of the gates. There have been parking issues in the past but no complaints recently. The parents queue up in this road or wait along the road where we've just parked.' He pointed off to the right. 'And there are side streets there, either side of the main road, for any overflow.'

'But Poppy always walked home?' said Juliet.

Kemp pointed to the left. 'She lives that way. A ten-minute walk if she walked purposefully, fifteen to twenty if she dawdled.' He turned to face the school and pointed out the two CCTV cameras that covered the front entrance. 'She was seen on the cameras there. She stopped here and talked to several of her friends, then she started to walk home alone.'

He strode along the pavement, and DC Arnold hurried after him.

'It's quiet now,' said Juliet. 'But I expect it must be busy in term time, during the school run.'

Lulu nodded. 'And there'd be cars driving to and from the school. I can't see how she could have been taken without being seen.'

'What if it was someone she knew?'

'That would explain why she would get into a car, but even if it was voluntary, there's a good chance someone would have noticed.'

They started walking down the road. DI Kemp and DC Arnold had crossed over the street where they had parked and were waiting for them. They looked both ways and crossed. 'Do we know for sure that this is the way she went?' asked Lulu.

'This is the way home,' said Kemp. 'And we did find her on a doorbell cam about a hundred yards on. This way.' He strode off with Arnold at his heels.

There were cottages either side of the road, but most of them were shielded by tall hedges. Lulu looked around as she walked. There were no council CCTV cameras that she could see. 'Do you think he asked for dashcam footage from any vehicles in the area at the time?' she asked Juliet. 'I don't want to mention it to him, he seems a tad sensitive.'

'I'll bring it up,' said Juliet. 'As tactfully as I can.'

Kemp had stopped in front of a cottage that had had its hedge removed and the front garden replaced with paving stones. He pointed at a smart doorbell in the centre of the front door. 'We got footage from this house, and it showed Poppy walking by on her own two minutes after leaving the school.'

'And no vehicle obviously following her?'

'Traffic was moving at normal speed,' said the inspector. 'Because the camera is facing forward, it was useless for catching registration numbers.'

'And there are no other cameras between here and Poppy's home?'

'Unfortunately not,' said DI Kemp.

'Has there been an appeal for dashcam footage?' asked Juliet.

'Several,' said the inspector. 'And we received close to two hundred downloads. The problem is that it's a very narrow window of time, ten minutes or so, and there were several dozen children walking down this road. We've examined all the footage but most of it was irrelevant. Despite us being very specific about the time, we received footage from first thing in the morning until the early evening.'

'They probably just wanted to help,' said Lulu.

'I get that, but they took up a great deal of time,' said DI Kemp. 'Anyway, we did see Poppy on eight dashcams, but six of those were from cars parked outside the school. So we have six views of Poppy talking to her friends or walking away from the school. Then we have another crossing the road where we parked. And the final one is not far from here. About a hundred yards further down. I'll show you.'

A line of cars drove by, heading the way they had come. An old man in a flat cap was in the first car, a brand new Mini, gripping the steering wheel as if his life depended on it. There were half a dozen vehicles grouped up behind him, clearly wishing that he would get a move on.

They walked for another minute or so. DI Kemp was looking at the houses on their left. Eventually he stopped. They were about fifty feet from a crossroads. 'The last dashcam footage was here,' he said. 'She was walking, and on her phone.'

'Talking or texting?' asked Lulu.

'The footage shows her with her phone in front of her, so it isn't clear. We're still waiting for the phone company to get back to us. It's literally a second or two. The car was speeding. Fifty miles an hour, so it just flashed by. It's definitely her, but that's all it shows.'

'And nothing else between here and the house?' asked Juliet.

'Nothing.'

'Is it possible she turned left or right at the crossroads there?' asked Lulu.

'It's possible,' said DI Kemp. 'But why would she?'

'That I don't know,' said Lulu. 'But if the last footage was seen here, then either she was taken from this road, or she turned off it. If she was actually abducted on the road, then there's a good chance that it would have been caught on dashcam.'

DI Kemp shook his head. 'Not really. It would take just a few seconds for someone to grab her, especially if there was more than one kidnapper. And presumably they would time it so that there would be no other vehicles around. So I'm not surprised that we don't have footage of the actual kidnapping. But we do know that she was taken somewhere between here and her home.'

He started walking again. They reached the crossroads and went over. A white van went by, followed by a Range Rover. The road wasn't especially busy at this time of day, but it was rarely empty.

They passed a line of shops. Lulu looked over, but she

didn't see any CCTV cameras covering the pavement. The shopkeepers would obviously be more concerned about shoplifters than passing pedestrians.

'It's a strange road for a kidnapping, isn't it?' said Juliet quietly.

Lulu nodded. 'There are always vehicles around. Plus the kidnapper couldn't be sure if anyone was watching from one of the houses. It would all be down to luck, wouldn't it? They would have no way of knowing if anyone would pass by as they grabbed her.'

'And it would be a lot busier when the kids were leaving.'

'So why take a pupil from this road? Presumably there must be some pupils who walk down the side roads. They could have parked and waited for someone to walk by.'

'They could have parked on this road and grabbed,' said Juliet. 'That way they could have chosen a place that isn't covered by CCTV, which from the look of it is most of the road.'

Lulu nodded. 'I guess the question is, was Poppy Novak taken at random, or was she targeted?'

'Generally, kidnappers don't choose their victims at random,' said Juliet. 'Often predators just want a child, and probably any child will do. But kidnappers usually have a specific target. And this was obviously very well planned, with the picture of your friends' daughter already taken, plus the whole Bitcoin thing. I don't see that they'd go to all that trouble and then carry out a random kidnapping.'

'I agree,' said Lulu. 'If they just wanted a random pupil, then why not choose a side road to take her from? The fact that they didn't suggests that they targeted Poppy Novak. But why? What would make her so special?'

Juliet grimaced. 'You won't like the answer.'

'What do you mean?'

'From what I gather, the Novaks don't have much money. The wife has health problems and is on disability. Her husband is down as her carer. He worked as a delivery driver for a while but now he's a full-time carer. So the family lives on benefits.'

'Which means – what? The police wouldn't try to find their daughter because they're on benefits?'

'No, of course not. And you've seen how committed DI Kemp is to finding her. But think what would happen if it had been the daughter of your friends who had been taken? Nice middle-class family living in the Royal Crescent? Poor little rich girl? It plays differently in the media.'

'You're right, Juliet.'

'I am?'

'Yes. I don't like that answer at all. Not one bit.'

'But you understand that there's a perception about the Novaks? Family on benefits, forcing their daughter to walk home from school?'

'Presumably if they're on benefits, they don't have a car.'

'No one cares about that. All they care about is that Poppy had to walk home. And I guarantee that when people watched that television appeal, a high percentage of viewers would have been looking at the father and wondering if he was involved in some way.'

'Oh, that's awful.'

'But it's true. They'll have been wondering if he's been up to no good and she's run away, or if he's done something to her to keep her quiet. People always think the worst. Well, not all people, but a lot of them.' Juliet grimaced. 'She wasn't taken at random – this walk has proved that to me.'

DI Kemp and DC Arnold had stopped in front of a row of terraced stone cottages. There were four homes in the terrace, each with a single ground-floor window and a front door that opened from the street. 'This is the Novak house,' said DI Kemp, gesturing at a door with peeling black paint. He looked at his watch, a plastic Casio. 'It took us thirteen minutes to get here and we weren't rushing.'

'We were just saying, it's a strange road to choose for an abduction,' said Juliet.

'In what way?'

'It's just busy. A busy road.'

'Most roads are busy these days,' said the inspector.

A truck loaded with gravel went by, so close that the slipstream ruffled Conrad's fur and the front window rattled. DI Kemp pressed a doorbell and after a few seconds the front door was opened by a woman in her early thirties. It wasn't Mrs Novak, Lulu realized; this woman was taller and thinner and had blonde hair, cut short. She nodded at the inspector. 'Sir,' she said. She was wearing a dark blue suit over a white turtleneck sweater and had large black-framed spectacles perched on the end of her nose.

'Everything okay?' asked DI Kemp.

'All good,' said the woman.

DI Kemp introduced her as Constable Rachel Woodisse, a family liaison officer who had been assigned to support Mr and Mrs Novak. The main purpose of an FLO was to gather evidence and information from the family to contribute to any investigation, but they were also sent in to help families through periods of crisis, and to deal with any members of the media who wanted to make contact with the family. FLOs were usually assigned when there had been a murder, a road fatality or a major disaster, but a missing child was also often treated as a priority. Constable Woodisse wasn't a detective, but she was allowed to work in plain clothes to help put Mr and Mrs Novak at ease.

'Mrs Novak is in the kitchen,' she said, opening the door wide. 'The husband is in the garden.'

DI Kemp stepped into the narrow hallway. There was a small plastic Christmas tree on a side table with a fairy on top, slightly askew. He walked down towards the kitchen, followed by DC Arnold.

Constable Woodisse's eyes widened when she saw Conrad sitting on Lulu's shoulder. 'Oh, he's amazing,' she said.

'Yes, Conrad is an amazing cat,' said Lulu.

'You know, I have a certificate in feline behaviour from the International Society of Feline Medicine,' she said. 'I just love cats.'

'So you know how cats think?' said Lulu.

Constable Woodisse laughed. 'Oh, understanding the behaviour of a cat is one thing, trying to understand their thought processes is very different. But I can see that Conrad totally trusts you and is very much at ease in your company.'

'It's mutual,' said Lulu.

Constable Woodisse closed the door, and Lulu and Juliet joined the two detectives in the kitchen. Mrs Novak was sitting at a circular pine table in front of a window that overlooked a small garden. She had her hands cupped around a mug. Her eyes were red from crying and there was a box of tissues on the table next to her. An NHS walking stick was propped against the wall.

'This is Detective Inspector Donnelly and Lulu . . .' Kemp paused. 'I'm sorry, I've forgotten your surname.'

'Lulu Lewis,' said Lulu. She smiled at Mrs Novak. 'I'm so sorry about what's happened,' she said. 'It must be a nightmare for you.'

Mrs Novak nodded tearfully. 'So what's happened? Is there any update? Oh my God, is she – is she . . . ?' She couldn't bring herself to finish the question and began to sob.

'No, that's not why we're here, Mrs Novak,' said DI Kemp. 'We're just here to talk.'

'Swear to me that she's not . . . dead.'

'Mrs Novak, I swear, that's not why we're here,' said DI Kemp. 'As far as we know, Poppy is still okay.'

'As far as you know?' she sobbed. 'What does that mean?'

Mr Novak was in the back garden, standing with his back to the house and smoking a cigarette.

The kitchen was crowded, so DC Arnold slipped out between Lulu and Juliet and went to stand in the hallway with Constable Woodisse.

'DI Donnelly has some information that might be helpful for our inquiry,' said DI Kemp. 'That's why we are here.'

Mr Novak turned around and froze as he looked through the window, his cigarette a few inches from his mouth. He frowned, took a final drag and then threw away the remains of the cigarette before hurrying towards the kitchen door. He burst into the kitchen, his eyes wide. 'What's happened? Has something happened?' He put his hand on his chest and seemed to be having trouble catching his breath.

Kemp put his hands up. 'Josef, it's okay. Relax. Nothing has happened. Nothing bad, anyway.'

Mr Novak was still struggling to breathe, so Kemp pulled out a chair and guided him onto it. Lulu went over to the sink and poured a glass of water, which she handed to Mr Novak. He took the water from her and frowned when he saw Conrad on her shoulders. 'Who are you?' he asked.

'My name is Lulu,' she said. 'I used to be a detective superintendent in London.'

'Why are you in my house?' he gasped.

'Drink,' said DI Kemp, patting him on the shoulder.

Mr Novak sipped his water. His hand was shaking, and water slopped over the edge of the glass and down the front of his pullover.

'The first thing you both need to know is that we now believe that Poppy was kidnapped for money,' said DI Kemp. 'So we have every reason to believe that she is being looked after with the aim of returning her to you safe and sound at some point in the future.'

Mrs Novak began shaking her head in confusion. 'What's happening?' she said. 'Is Poppy okay? Is that what you're saying? She's okay?'

'We believe so, yes,' said DI Kemp.

'But you say they want money?' said Mr Novak. 'We don't have any money. There's no way we can pay a ransom.'

'They don't expect you to pay a ransom,' said DI Kemp.

Mr Novak frowned. 'I don't understand.'

'I'm going to show you a photograph that we have just received,' said DI Kemp. 'I must warn you that it is a little upsetting, but you need to focus on the fact that Poppy is alive and well.'

The Novaks frowned at the inspector, clearly bewildered. He reached into his coat and took out a copy of the photograph of Poppy. 'We have received this. The newspaper in the picture is from four days ago, after she was taken.'

He held out the sheet of paper and Mrs Novak snatched it from him with trembling fingers. Lulu noticed that her fingernails were bitten to the quick.

Mrs Novak stared at the photograph and wailed in pain. Woodisse hurried over to her and put her arms around her.

'I don't understand what's happening,' said Mr Novak.

'We believe that Poppy has been kidnapped, and that the kidnappers want money,' repeated Kemp.

'We don't have any money!' shouted Mrs Novak.

'Look around you,' said her husband. 'Does it look like we're flush with cash? We're struggling to pay our electricity bill.'

DI Kemp held up his hands. 'The ransom demand isn't for you, Mrs Novak. They want someone else to pay. And we assume that if they do pay, Poppy will be released.'

Mrs Novak looked at Lulu. 'Is it you? Do they want money from you? Is that it? Please pay them. Please give them what they want. I just want Poppy back.'

Lulu forced a smile. 'No, it isn't me, Mrs Novak. I'm sorry.'

Mrs Novak looked at Juliet. 'Is it you?'

'No, as DI Kemp said, I'm DI Donnelly. From Bristol. You can call me Juliet. The ransom demand was sent to a family in Bath. They are totally unconnected to you.'

'Are they going to pay?' asked Mr Novak.

'That's under discussion,' said DI Kemp.

'They have to pay!' snapped Mr Novak. 'You have to tell them to pay, straight away. We want our daughter back.'

Mrs Novak looked back at DI Kemp and waved the picture at him. 'Why is Poppy tied up like this? Where is she?'

'We don't know. I know this is difficult to understand, but in a way this is actually good news.'

'How is this good news?' sobbed Mrs Novak, tears running down her face. Constable Woodisse hugged her, but the sobbing continued.

'If the people who have taken Poppy want money, that means they will take care of her. This photo shows that she is still alive and being taken care of.'

'Does it look like she's being taken care of?' sobbed Mrs Novak. She waved the photograph. 'Look how scared she is! My baby must be terrified. You have to help her!'

'We will,' said DI Kemp. 'We will.'

'As DI Kemp says, this is good news,' said Juliet. 'We now have some physical evidence that might help identify the kidnappers. Before, Poppy seemed to have vanished without trace, but now we do have something to go on.'

'What evidence?' snapped Mr Novak.

'The letter that came with the photograph,' said Juliet. 'We're having it examined now.'

DI Kemp nodded. 'The thing is, we now have a definite line of inquiry to follow. Plus we now know that Poppy is alive.'

Mrs Novak waved the photograph. 'This is four days ago,' she said. 'Anything could have happened in the past four days.'

DI Kemp tried to take the photograph from her but she clasped it to her chest. 'No!' she said defiantly.

'Okay, okay,' said DI Kemp. He stepped back, his hands up. 'You can keep it. But please, don't show it to anybody.'

He looked at Mr Novak. 'We want to keep this to ourselves. We don't want the press to know about this.'

Mr Novak nodded. 'Okay,' he said.

DI Kemp looked at Constable Woodisse. 'In fact, no press contact at all from now on. Refer everything to me. Everything.'

'Yes, sir,' said the constable.

'Can I ask you a question, Mr Novak?' said Lulu quietly.

DI Kemp threw Lulu a withering look, but she ignored him and smiled at Mr Novak.

'I suppose so,' he said. 'I've been answering questions ever since Poppy was taken.'

'I know, I'm sorry about that. But did she walk home the same way every day?'

'Of course.'

'She never stopped off to visit a friend? Or pop into a shop?'

Mr Novak shook his head.

'And when she didn't arrive home, you phoned the police?'

'Yes.'

'You did, or Mrs Novak did? Who actually made the call?'

'I did.'

'And who did you call? 999?'

'Yes.'

'But before that, did you try to phone Poppy?'

He frowned. 'Of course. But she didn't answer.'

'And she wasn't in the habit of getting home late?'

'Never. She always came straight home. You never answered my question. Why are you here? You said you used to be a detective? Used to be. So what business is this of yours now?'

'Mrs Lewis used to be a detective superintendent in London, and she's working as a consultant with the Avon and Somerset Police,' said Juliet.

'More of an observer, actually,' said Kemp archly.

'Looks to me like there are too many cooks,' said Mr Novak. 'You'd be better off actually looking for Poppy than crowding into our kitchen.'

'We just wanted you to know that we're doing everything we can to bring Poppy back to you,' said Juliet.

'Mr Novak does have a point,' said DI Kemp. 'Too many cooks might well spoil the broth, so why don't we give him and Mrs Novak some space?'

'You want us to leave?' said Juliet.

'What happened in Bradford-on-Avon is the prerogative of Wiltshire Police, so any questions really should be coming through me, and they most definitely should not be coming through Mrs Lewis, who is a civilian, after all.'

'You said she was with Avon and Somerset Police,' Mr Novak snapped.

'I didn't actually say that,' said DI Kemp. 'Mrs Lewis was with the Metropolitan Police in London many years ago, and now she is a civilian. Anyway, I'll be running the investigation into Poppy's disappearance. Nothing has changed on that front.' He nodded at Juliet. 'We should leave Mr and Mrs Novak with Rachel. If you have any questions, we can run them through her.'

Juliet's jaw hardened as if she wanted to argue, but she nodded. 'Yes, of course,' she said.

It was a power struggle, Lulu realized. DI Kemp wanted to show the Novaks that he was still in control of the investigation. Juliet could have stood her ground – she was the same rank as Kemp and she was SIO of the extortion case, so she was well within her rights to insist on questioning the Novaks. But it was doubtful that they had any information they hadn't already given to the Wiltshire investigators, so at this point there was little to be gained by antagonizing Kemp.

'I'll drop by as soon as we have any news,' DI Kemp said to the Novaks. 'If you have any problems at all, discuss them with Rachel. But believe me, this is good news. I have every hope that we'll soon have Poppy back, safe and sound.'

Mrs Novak sniffed and blew her nose into a tissue. Mr Novak sat back in his chair and pulled a packet of Rothmans and a disposable lighter from the pocket of his jeans.

'Right, goodbye then,' said DI Kemp.

Mrs Novak blew her nose again and Mr Novak gave him a half-hearted wave before lighting a cigarette.

They left the house and walked back to the school. This time Lulu timed it. It took a little over twelve minutes.

'That went better than I expected,' said DI Kemp as they reached the school gates.

'They're under a lot of pressure,' said Juliet. 'But at least they can now see some light at the end of the tunnel.' She smiled at Lulu. 'I'll run you back to Trowbridge.'

'You know, I think I'll just call an Uber from here,' said Lulu. 'Bath is much closer than Trowbridge.'

'Are you sure?' asked Juliet. 'I'll happily drive you from Trowbridge before I head back to Kenneth Steele House.'

'An Uber makes more sense,' said Lulu. She held out her hand to DI Kemp. 'Thank you for allowing me to intrude on your investigation, DI Kemp. I apologize for any inconvenience I may have caused you.'

DI Kemp looked slightly taken back by the gesture, but then he relaxed and shook her hand. 'Not a problem, Mrs Lewis,' he said. 'I hope it was helpful.'

Lulu took back her hand and smiled at DC Arnold. 'And nice to meet you too, DC Arnold.' They shook hands and then Lulu took out her phone. She used it to book an Uber as the three detectives walked back to the car.

'You're always very polite to him, even though he clearly resents you being around,' said Conrad.

'You catch more flies with honey than with vinegar,' said Lulu.

'You see now, I've never understood why you'd want to catch flies in the first place. You humans have such strange expressions.'

'Like when we say that cats have nine lives?'

'Oh, that's not an expression,' said Conrad. 'That's a fact.'

11

The Uber driver's name was Kristof and he was still geared up for the pandemic, wearing a face mask and with hand sanitizer and wet wipes on offer. He asked Lulu if she had a preferred route, which she didn't, and if she had any objections to the classical music playing on the radio; again, she didn't. There were many things about the modern world that Lulu didn't like, but the technology that had produced Uber was a blessing that she never stopped being thankful for. It didn't matter where she was in the country – a few seconds on her phone would produce a car prepared to take her anywhere she wanted to go. And when she was on *The Lark*, she could moor pretty much anywhere and have provisions delivered as quickly as rubbing a lamp and summoning a genie. Uber truly was magic.

Kristof dropped them a hundred yards from the canal and Lulu waved him off with the promise of five stars. 'So what do you think about Juliet?' she asked Conrad as they headed for the towpath.

'I told you before,' said Conrad. 'Trustworthy, open, honest.'

'Because of her aura?'

'Her aura is a deep blue around her head and shoulders, with a white crown on top. That's a sign that she's open and honest. There was plenty of green, which again suggests she is kind, compassionate and open-hearted. Cats are always drawn to green auras.'

'You didn't mention seeing green in my aura when I first met you,' said Lulu. 'You said you saw lots of bright yellow and indigo.'

'Oh, there was definitely green. I would never have spoken to you if there hadn't been green in your aura. But it was the yellow that attracted me the most. A yellow aura suggests optimism and playfulness. It's a sign that you are open-minded and inquisitive and ready to take the next steps on your spiritual journey.'

Lulu chuckled. 'Remember how I was worried that I was about to die and that you were there to see me off?'

'You were quite worried about that, weren't you?'

'I was. You hear stories about cats being drawn to people who are dying.'

'No need,' said Conrad. 'You're fit, healthy and very strong. And I was drawn to the indigo in your aura. That was another reason I spoke to you. Old souls usually give off an indigo aura. It's a sign that they have wisdom accrued over many lifetimes. Sometimes it can mean you have psychic abilities.'

'Oh, I'm not psychic,' said Lulu.

'Well, you might say that, but how many times have you told me that despite the evidence to the contrary, you just knew in yourself that someone was guilty?'

'But that's different.'

'Is it, though?'

'It's copper's intuition based on experience.'

'It could be. Or it could be psychic ability. Anyway, there's definitely indigo in your aura.'

They reached the towpath and began walking towards *The Lark*. 'And what about DI Kemp?'

Conrad wrinkled his nose. 'His aura is cloudy and muddy. All of it. That's a sign that he is facing challenges or going through a difficult patch.'

'Well, that's an easy guess, considering that he's SIO of a kidnapping case that's going nowhere fast.'

'And there's green there, but not the bright green that you and Juliet have. His is a muddy, dirty yellow-green that suggests he's being deceitful.'

'I didn't think he was telling us lies when we met him.'

'Auras aren't lie detectors, Lulu. That's not how it works. But DI Kemp is definitely under a lot of stress at the moment.'

'Hopefully the information we've given him today will help him find little Poppy.'

'I do hope so,' said Conrad.

A teenager with a shaved head, a spider's-web tattoo on his neck, multiple ear and lip piercings and a large bull mastiff on a lead was walking towards them. The dog looked up at Conrad, sniffed and wagged its tail. The teenager nodded at Lulu. 'Afternoon,' he said. 'I love your cat.'

'Why, thank you,' said Lulu. 'You dog is something special, too.'

She turned her head as the teenager walked by. The dog was walking at his side, so close that the lead was hanging loosely.

'You can't judge a book by its cover, can you?' said Conrad.

Lulu chuckled. 'You're reading my mind again.'

'It was an easy read,' said Conrad. 'From a distance, you'd expect the worst, wouldn't you? A skinhead with tattoos and piercings and a musclebound dog on steroids. But then they were as nice as pie.'

'You're right, of course,' said Lulu. 'But then you usually are. So what about Mr Novak? The father?'

'Ah,' said Conrad. 'I was wondering when you would ask about him.'

'Was there something wrong?'

'Can I ask you a question?'

'Of course,' said Lulu.

'When you were in their kitchen, you were asking Mr Novak some questions. Very simple questions. Questions of fact. Who called the police? On what number? Did Poppy usually come straight home? All questions that he must have answered before.'

'I was trying to get a baseline read,' said Lulu. 'That's interrogation 101. You ask the subject some basic, non-threatening questions to which you already know the correct answers. This establishes a baseline for how they respond when telling the truth. But I never got beyond that stage, because DI Kemp cut me off.'

'But you learned something, right?'

'What makes you say that?'

'I was watching you. You and Mr Novak. Both of you. I felt that you had learned something about him, even though you only asked a few questions.'

'You are a very perceptive cat.'

Conrad smiled. 'It has been said. So what did you learn?'

'It was the way he was reacting. It was easy to read Mrs Novak. She was out of her mind with worry. You saw the way she grabbed that photograph of Poppy and wouldn't let go of it. The way she was shaking, the genuine tears that she cried.'

'She was distraught,' said Conrad.

'Yes, that's the word. Distraught. But Mr Novak – well, he was tense, upset even, but he wasn't distraught, was he?'

They reached *The Lark* and Lulu climbed onto the rear deck.

'No, he wasn't,' said Conrad. 'When we first saw him, he was in the garden, smoking. He turned around and saw us all but there was no panic, no trepidation, no dread. His child has been abducted and a pack of police officers appear in his house. He has to assume the worst. But he took another pull on his cigarette before he started moving towards the house. He put his cigarette to his mouth, smoked it, and then flicked away the butt. Only then did he start walking. I thought that was . . . strange. And he didn't seem as upset as his wife, right?'

'Exactly,' said Lulu.

Conrad jumped down onto the rear seat and Lulu unlocked the door.

'I wondered if it was because he's a man, so he was hiding his concern. Stiff upper lip and all that.'

'His daughter is missing,' said Lulu. 'And at that stage, so far as he was concerned, Poppy could have been taken by a sexual predator. No father could possibly maintain a stiff upper lip under those conditions.' She walked carefully down the steps into the cabin and switched on the lights.

'So you were testing him with regular questions?'

'That was the idea. And you could see that he was answering them quite calmly. He clearly wasn't happy about being questioned, but he was nowhere near as volatile as his wife. She was almost in hysterics. Her tears were very real, as was her distress.'

'He wasn't crying.'

'Well, as you said, he's a man, so perhaps he was holding back the tears.' Lulu used a match to light one of the stove burners and put the kettle on the flames. 'Remember how Mrs Novak clasped the photograph to her chest and wouldn't give it back?'

'I think it made her feel closer to Poppy,' said Conrad.

'Yes, that's how it looked to me. But Mr Novak barely looked at it, did he?'

Conrad nodded. 'You're right. He didn't. He seemed more concerned about who you were and what you were doing there.' He wrinkled his nose. 'What do you think that means?'

Lulu shook her head. 'I wish I knew.'

'Could he be involved?'

'He could, yes. But he doesn't have a car, and not much money by the look of it. He'd have needed a vehicle and somewhere to keep Poppy. Plus he didn't look the sort to be knowledgeable about cryptocurrency.'

'True. But there's obviously more than one person involved. He could be part of a gang, couldn't he?'

'Most definitely, he could be. Yes.' Lulu's phone rang and she looked at the screen. 'Well, that's a coincidence,' she said. 'That's Kirsty Grant calling, my NCA crypto expert.'

Kirsty Grant had been an enthusiastic detective constable when Lulu had been a detective chief inspector. Lulu had always been impressed with Kirsty's quick mind and grasp of figures and hadn't been at all surprised when she had transferred to the Serious Organised Crime Agency to deal with complicated fraud cases, later moving to the National Crime Agency, where she had specialized in cryptocurrency scams.

Lulu took the call. 'Kirsty, thank you so much for calling back.'

'I was bowled over to get your message,' said Kirsty. 'I thought you'd retired.'

'Oh, I have,' said Lulu, sitting down on the sofa. 'But I'm helping on an inquiry down in the West Country. A friend of mine has received a ransom demand and the kidnappers want payment in Bitcoin. The case is being handled by Avon and Somerset and Wiltshire forces, but neither is really geared up for cryptocurrency investigations.'

'Happy to help in any way I can, Lulu. At some point I'll need a case number so that we can do it officially.'

'Not a problem, Kirsty, thank you. Okay, I guess the first thing I need to know is, how easy is it to identify the owner of a Bitcoin wallet? The kidnappers have given us a wallet address and said that's where they want the money to be sent. I've always thought that everything about Bitcoin is anonymous.'

'You'll hear a lot of people say that Bitcoin is anonymous, but it isn't,' said Kirsty. 'It's pseudonymous. Basically, every Bitcoin transaction is public, traceable and permanently stored in the Bitcoin network. You can enter the sender's address into a blockchain explorer and instantly access all information related to the wallet, including full transaction history, date of origin and account balance. That will lead you to the wallet address – a string of alphanumeric characters.'

'Which is what we have,' said Lulu.

'Well, the problem is that the wallet is effectively a pseudonym. An alias. It is possible to link the wallet to a real-life identity, but that would be beyond the scope of the average user. For that you'd need a blockchain analytics firm. And they're not cheap.'

'But they can identify who owns a particular wallet containing particular Bitcoins?'

'You need to stop thinking of Bitcoins as real coins, virtual or otherwise. Bitcoin is more like a list of transactions that have ever taken place between all addresses. It's a chain of events, and anybody can examine that chain. It will lead you to a wallet, but the Bitcoin itself isn't actually in the wallet. I'm sorry, it's difficult to explain. To be honest, it sometimes makes me dizzy.'

'Would you be able to get one of these analytics firms to take a look at the wallet our kidnappers are using?'

'Absolutely. And kidnapping falls within our jurisdiction, so I can get right on it. But there's every chance that once the money has been paid, it will be moved straight into another wallet. And another. Wallets are easy to set up and virtually free. A lot will depend on who they use to set up the wallet. Traditional financial institutions and centralized crypto exchanges are legally bound to perform the Know Your Customer checks that governments have put in place to combat money laundering. Now, if the kidnappers were stupid enough to go that route, they'd have given up their address, date of birth and government ID.'

'They've been very professional in every other respect, so I am fairly sure they'll be covering their tracks.'

'Even so, there's still a chance that they did something that will help identify them. Send me a text with the wallet address and I'll start the ball rolling.'

'And what about getting the money out of Bitcoin and into cash? Can you go to any bank and get cash?'

'No, absolutely not,' said Kirsty. 'Digital currencies are outside the traditional banking system, so the banks can't handle them. The easiest way would be to open up an account with a cryptocurrency exchange, but all the legitimate ones would be making the money laundering checks before they would pay out to a bank account.'

'I'm guessing that our kidnappers wouldn't be transferring the ransom to an identifiable bank account,' said Lulu.

'Almost certainly not,' said Kirsty. 'Plus, they'll probably be using a proxy server or a VPN and do everything through Tor.'

'Tor?'

'The Onion Router. Basically, the dark web. A real pro would use a VPN to access Tor. Double anonymity.'

'But still traceable?'

'Well, the fact that all transactions are public means that the blockchain can always be examined. You can't hide that. But a VPN and Tor makes it that much harder to identify the ultimate owner of the wallet.'

'And what about when the kidnappers withdraw their money? Presumably they won't keep it in Bitcoin.'

'Yes, that's when they're most vulnerable,' said Kirsty. 'But the bad guys have a lot of options. There are peer-to-peer exchanges which allow people to basically swap crypto assets and cash for a fee, usually a percentage. But if they know someone in the criminal fraternity who has cash and who wants Bitcoin, you could arrange an in-person sale. Basically put the Bitcoin in a portable hard drive and sell that for cash. That would be totally untraceable. And you could do it anywhere. You could make the transfer at a coffee shop, on a beach, in a pub car park. And even if you were seen, there's nothing to see. Even if the cops were there and seized the money and the hard drive, the drive would be encrypted.'

'The perfect crime.'

'Well, selling a hard drive, even one loaded with Bitcoin, isn't a crime,' said Kirsty. 'It might be that the Bitcoin was the proceeds of crime and could therefore be seized, but that's a whole different ball game.'

'What about getting Bitcoin out of an ATM?' said Lulu. 'Could that work?'

'Again, there's no such thing as a physical Bitcoin, so an ATM can't pay out Bitcoin.'

'I mean withdraw the equivalent in real money from an ATM. Is that possible?'

'Yes and no. There are more than thirty thousand Bitcoin ATMs across the United States. A lot are solely for purchasing, though some do allow withdrawals. They're not like common or garden ATMs, though. They're a bit more complicated. The ATM will show you a QR code and you use your mobile to transfer them the Bitcoin, and then the ATM will pay out the cash in dollars. Withdrawal fees are hefty, though. They can be as high as ten per cent.'

'What about the UK? How many Bitcoin ATMs are there here?'

'Last time I checked, there was one. In Birmingham. But I doubt it will be there for long.'

'How so?'

'There used to be more than a hundred in the UK, more than half of them in London. Drug dealers and assorted bad guys were making full use of them, so the Financial Conduct Authority shut them down. Some countries follow the same hard line and don't allow them, others are less stringent. So the last time I checked there were just under two hundred in Germany and over a hundred in Austria, but only one in India and one in Belgium. But I think it's unlikely your kidnappers would be using an ATM to withdraw their money. They'll have limits on how much they can pay out, and there's a limit on how much they carry. I think in the UK, an ATM is at capacity at between sixty and seventy thousand pounds. And I can't see any ATM being allowed to pay it all in one go. I think it's much more likely there'll be a peer-to-peer exchange.'

'Which could be totally anonymous?'

'Again, yes and no. Remember, the blockchain is always visible. So once the buyer starts to use the wallet on the hard drive, the transactions can be seen. If the buyer isn't as security conscious as the seller, they might slip up and be identified.'

'And once you have the buyer, you can get him to lead you to the seller?'

'Hopefully. It's not an exact science, unfortunately. But I'll be on the case, Lulu. Are you expecting the ransom to be paid soon?'

'It's complicated, Kirsty. I said ransom, but it's more extortion linked to a kidnapping. A little girl has been kidnapped, and we believe ransom demands have been sent to other parents saying that if they don't pay, their children will be kidnapped too.'

'Oh, that is clever,' said Kirsty.

'Isn't it? And they're demanding fifty thousand pounds, which is affordable for a lot of people. Not for everyone, obviously, but there are plenty of people in Bath who have access to that sort of money. It means they can kidnap one child but demand money from – well, it's open-ended, isn't it?'

'Absolutely. They could send out dozens of demands. Hundreds. It's like email scams. If you send out enough emails, there'll always be a percentage that will pay.'

'Well, the friends of mine who received the letter are set on paying,' said Lulu. 'They think it will give them peace of mind.'

'Their call, I suppose,' said Kirsty. 'I would advise against paying, but then, my child isn't at risk.'

'Exactly,' said Lulu. 'My instinct would be to not pay and to help with the police investigation, but then I see their daughter and imagine how I would feel if she was taken.'

'If they do pay, or if you know anyone else has paid, let me know. You realize, of course, that if they are sending out multiple demands, there is every chance that they will be using multiple wallets? If it was me, I'd be using a different wallet for each demand. Then, as and when payments came through, I'd funnel them through a central wallet.'

'That's good thinking.'

'Thank you. My husband always says I'd make a great criminal.'

Lulu chuckled. 'I think he's right.' They ended the call, and she put her phone down on the table.

'Good news?' asked Conrad.

'I think so,' said Lulu cautiously. 'If Amanda and Donald do pay the ransom, there's a chance the police may be able to follow the money.'

'And catch the kidnappers?'

'Possibly – although it's probably easier said than done.'

'Well, you know what they say: the best-laid plans of mice and men . . .'

'Do they tend to make plans, mice?' asked Lulu.

'They're not known for it,' said Conrad. 'That's why mousetraps are so effective. A much better saying is the one about the second mouse always getting the cheese.'

'That always seemed a bit harsh to me,' said Lulu.

'Life is harsh,' said Conrad. 'For mice, anyway.'

12

Lulu woke at dawn. She showered and changed into clean clothes without waking Conrad, but by the time she was making herself a cup of coffee he was sitting on the small sofa, diligently licking his fur. She poured water into his favourite Wedgwood saucer, then bent down to open the fridge door. She was just reaching for a packet of bacon when her phone rang. It was Amanda.

'How did it go yesterday?' asked Amanda.

'Yes, good, under the circumstances,' said Lulu. 'DI Kemp, the detective who was at the press conference, is doing everything by the book, and Juliet, the detective who is handling your case, is very on the ball. The letter has already been sent to forensics and she has a team working to see if they can find out who took the photograph of Olivia.'

'What are you doing now?'

'I was actually just about to start cooking breakfast.'

'Why don't you come here for breakfast? Donald is going to do one of his trademark fry-ups.'

'With potato bread?'

'And black pudding. Though I've never seen the attraction of pig's blood.'

'You're not worried about me being seen there?'

'I was discussing this with Donald last night,' said Amanda. 'Nobody knows who you are, and if they do follow you they'll see the boat and that'll be the end of it. You're just a friend, staying over for Christmas. I was being silly expecting you to leave.'

'No, I understand. Really.'

'Please come back and stay with us, like we planned. And Conrad, too, obviously.'

'Well, Conrad does love black pudding.'

'He's welcome to have mine,' said Amanda.

Lulu ended the call and put the phone on the table.

'Black pudding?' said Conrad.

'And potato bread. Donald's mother is a Belfast girl, so she taught him to appreciate the Ulster fry.'

'The Ulster what now?'

'The Ulster fry. It's like a full English breakfast with bacon, eggs, sausages, fried tomato and black pudding. Sometimes with beans and/or fried mushrooms, though there are differing views on that. What makes it different is the addition of fried soda bread, and potato bread.'

'That sounds like a lot to eat.'

'Oh, and that's before you add the toast and butter. You have to remember that back in the day most jobs used to involve manual labour, and the average worker needed to stock up on calories first thing to get them through the day.'

'So they're offering you breakfast? I thought they were scared of you being seen around their house.'

'They've had a change of heart.'

'Well, that's nice. Shall we walk or call an Uber?'

'I'm happy to walk,' said Lulu.

'Then a walk it is,' said Conrad. 'Though in my case, it'll be a ride, of course.'

Lulu grabbed her sheepskin jacket and pulled it on, then locked up *The Lark*. Her breath feathered in the air as she walked along the towpath with Conrad on her shoulders. Most of the narrowboats moored had their diesel engines running to charge their batteries, and smoke was curling from their chimneys. Winter always sorted out the serious boaters from the dabblers.

The sky overhead was white, and Lulu realized there was a chance they might actually have a white Christmas. The streets were full of families wrapped up against the cold walking to the city centre, and there were smiles and laughter all around. Lulu couldn't help but smile as she headed to the Royal Crescent. Christmas always brought out the best in people.

Well, not everyone, obviously. Whoever had carried out the Poppy Novak kidnapping had definitely soured the Christmas spirit. She frowned as she walked. Everything about the kidnapping and the extortion letter had clearly been well thought out, which meant it couldn't be a coincidence that it was happening over the holiday period. It had all been too well planned; the timing couldn't be random. The kidnappers were probably hoping that there would be fewer police and forensic experts on call, and that it would be harder to get CCTV or phone data to help with an investigation.

Before she knew it, they had reached the Royal Crescent. Lulu was almost surprised to turn the corner and see the sweeping curved terrace. Dog walkers and tourists were out in force, and there seemed to be children everywhere. As she approached Amanda and Donald's house, her eyes scanned left and right, looking for any signs of surveillance. There were plenty of cameras around, but they were in the hands of tourists photographing the houses.

She walked up to the front door and rang the bell. After a few moments, Amanda opened the door and beamed at her. 'Welcome, welcome,' she said. 'And welcome to you, Conrad. Does he always ride on your shoulders like that?'

'A lot of the time,' said Lulu. 'It's just easier, and people don't keep tripping over him.'

Amanda ushered them inside and closed the door. Conrad jumped down onto a chair and Amanda helped Lulu off with her sheepskin jacket. 'Donald's in the kitchen, go on through,' she said, hanging the jacket on a coat hook. Lulu headed down the hallway with Conrad at her heels.

Donald was standing at the cooker. He turned around, grinning, and waved a spatula in the air. 'Perfect timing,' he said. He was wearing a pink apron with 'IF YOU'RE READING THIS, BRING ME A BEER' in capital letters. 'How do you like your eggs?'

'As the Americans say, over easy.'

'There's no real English equivalent, is there?' said Donald. 'But for an over easy they flip the egg over for a few seconds, which I never like doing. I prefer to baste the egg with the hot fat.'

'Me too,' said Lulu.

Olivia was sitting at the island, staring at her smartphone, but she put it down when she spotted Conrad. 'Can I pick Conrad up?' she asked.

'If he likes you,' said Lulu. 'Bend down and hold your arms out. If he wants to be picked up he'll walk towards you. If he doesn't, he'll walk away, and you shouldn't chase him.'

Olivia slid off her stool and crouched down with her arms outstretched. 'Like this?'

'Just like that,' said Lulu.

Conrad looked at Olivia, his tail straight up like an antenna, his whiskers twitching.

'I promise I'll be gentle with you, Conrad,' Olivia whispered to him.

Conrad walked towards her, watching her with his piercing green eyes. He edged between her arms and she scooped him up. He rested his front paws on her shoulders and purred.

'That means he's happy,' said Lulu.

'He's so soft,' said Olivia, nuzzling her cheek against his neck.

'Let's eat at the island,' said Amanda as she walked into the kitchen. 'It's cosier.'

She set out knives and forks while Donald put the finishing touches to the breakfasts. Lulu had eaten his Ulster fry before and he never disappointed. He made his own potato pancakes and soda bread, and he always served the freshest eggs, usually with bright orange yolks. Lulu slid onto a stool. The breakfast Donald placed in front of her was cooked to perfection.

'He does do a wonderful breakfast,' said Amanda, getting onto her stool.

'It's the most important meal of the day,' said Donald. 'Come on, Olivia, put Conrad down and eat.'

Olivia kissed Conrad on the back of his neck and carefully placed him on the floor before climbing onto her stool.

Donald poured coffee for the adults and gave Olivia a glass of orange juice. They chatted as they ate their breakfast, about Christmas, about Olivia's homework, about whether or not it was going to snow, about what Olivia wanted to study at university, even though that was years away. From time to time, Amanda would glance anxiously at Lulu and her voice would take on a hard edge, as if something was troubling her. Which, clearly, it was.

Eventually they were finished, and Amanda gathered up their plates. Lulu looked at Conrad. 'Would you like to go to Olivia's room, Conrad?'

Conrad meowed.

'He said yes!' said Olivia.

'He did, didn't he?' said Lulu.

'Come on, Conrad,' said Olivia, heading down the hallway. Conrad trotted after her, his tail in the air.

'That is one amazing cat,' said Donald.

'He's very special,' said Lulu. She looked over at Amanda, who was standing by the sink. She seemed to be close to tears. 'Amanda, are you okay?'

Amanda shook her head. 'Not really,' she said. She turned back to the island. 'Do you think they're any closer to catching the kidnappers?' she asked.

'I think the fact that they've seen your letter has made it more likely,' said Lulu. 'Their previous efforts were aimed at identifying sex offenders in the area, and obviously that has changed. Now they'll be treating it as a kidnapping, which means a different offender profile. I spoke to the NCA about the Bitcoin wallet, so that's being looked at. And the DI from Bristol has had detectives out looking around Olivia's school to see if they can work out where the photograph was taken.'

'Are you still working on the theory that the kidnappers have sent out lots of letters?' asked Donald. 'That we're not the only ones being threatened?'

'We are, yes. We haven't found anyone yet, but I think it's only a matter of time.'

'How many letters, do you think?'

Lulu looked pained. 'I'm sorry, but there's no way of knowing.'

'It might only be a few letters. A handful.' Donald shook his head. 'I don't like those odds, Lulu. There's safety in numbers, but if there are only a small number who have been threatened then I'd rather be one of the ones that have paid. If they do carry out their threat, they won't be going after the people who have paid them. That wouldn't make any sense at all, would it?'

Lulu sighed. 'Oh, Donald, you can't apply logic to people like this. The fifty thousand pounds might be a test. If you pay that, maybe then they actually do kidnap Olivia, because you've already shown that you have money and that you're prepared to hand it over.'

'Please don't say that, Lulu,' said Amanda. 'We have to believe that they'll keep their word.'

'They're criminals, Amanda. They break the law. It's what they do.'

'What part of "don't say that" do you not get?' said Amanda sourly.

'You need to face facts, Amanda, and if that means my telling you something that you don't want to hear, then so be it. But believe me, I have your best interests at heart, I really do.'

'I know you do,' said Amanda. She reached for Lulu's hand and gave it a gentle squeeze. 'I'm a bit on edge. Sorry.'

'We're all on edge,' said Donald.

'I really think it might help if you spoke with the detective who's looking at the letter you received.' Lulu saw Amanda open her mouth to protest and raised a hand to stop her. 'I know what you're going to say, and I didn't mean that she should come here. Or that you should go to the police station. But I did think of a way that you could meet that wouldn't arouse any suspicion. Okay?'

'Only if you're absolutely sure,' said Amanda.

'I am,' said Lulu.

'Okay then. But don't let me down, Lulu. I'd never forgive you if something went wrong.'

Lulu's stomach lurched. She was trying to do her best to help, but Amanda was right: if anything did go wrong, it would be her responsibility. She gave Amanda what she hoped was a confident smile and took out her phone. As Donald cleared away their plates, she phoned Juliet. Juliet answered almost immediately.

'Hey,' Lulu said. 'I'm with the Balfours, and I've just had an idea about how you could meet them in person, under the radar.'

'I'm all ears,' said Juliet. 'I do think it best that we meet, and the sooner the better.'

'Do you have a dog?'

'A dog?' Juliet repeated. 'No.'

'Can you borrow one?'

'Borrow one? I suppose I could, yes. But why would I . . . ?' She laughed. 'Ah, right. I get it.'

13

Donald locked the door behind them. Amanda was standing on the pavement with Olivia, both wrapped up in puffa jackets and thick scarves. Lulu was behind them, the collar of her sheepskin jacket up and Conrad lying across her shoulders.

'Right, off we go,' said Donald, slipping his keys into the pocket of his black cashmere overcoat. There was a cold wind blowing up from the park but there were still plenty of people around, many of them walking dogs.

'I still don't see why this is necessary,' said Amanda, looking around nervously.

'She really wants to meet you,' said Lulu. 'And you were so against the police coming to the house. This way, we're just out for a walk. Nothing unusual about that. We all need some fresh air from time to time.'

'What if they're watching?'

'Amanda, she won't be wearing a uniform or be arriving in a police car. Just smile and relax and enjoy the walk.'

Amanda put her arm around Olivia. 'Stay close, darling,' she said.

'Can we go shopping?' Olivia asked.

'Oh, I don't know,' Amanda said anxiously. 'It's going to be so busy . . .'

'Please, Mum? I've still got presents to buy!'

Amanda looked over at Donald for support. He just

smiled. 'We could do with something to cheer ourselves up,' he said. 'We could walk to the Christmas market after this.'

'Yes, yes, yes!' said Olivia excitedly, taking her father's hand.

'Looks as if I'm outvoted,' said Amanda.

They walked across the road and onto the grass. Amanda was still looking around anxiously, so Lulu slipped her arm through hers. 'It's going to be fine,' she said. 'Please try to relax.'

Amanda took a deep breath. 'I can't believe this is happening. It's as if I'm in a nightmare and I can't wake up.'

A Jack Russell began barking excitedly at Conrad. Lulu looked at the yapping dog, then realized it was on the end of a long lead being held by Juliet. She was wearing a purple wool coat, knee-length boots and black leather gloves. She flashed Lulu an apologetic smile. 'This is Jake, my neighbour's dog. I told her I needed Jake for an undercover mission and she was fine about it. Sorry about the barking.'

'It's ideal,' said Lulu. 'Jake gives us the perfect cover for a chat.'

'Camouflage,' said Juliet, smiling at Amanda. 'My name is Juliet,' she said, keeping her voice low so that Olivia couldn't hear. 'Detective Inspector Juliet Donnelly. Lulu showed me the letter you received, and I wanted to let you know that we're taking the case very seriously.'

Jake fell quiet under Conrad's baleful stare. Then he spotted Olivia and began wagging his tail furiously. Lulu was fairly sure she heard a contemptuous snort from Conrad.

Juliet smiled at Olivia. 'Do you like dogs, Olivia?'

'I love them,' she said.

'This is Jake, and he really does need some exercise. Would you like to take him for a run?'

'Yes!' said Olivia excitedly. 'I'd love that.'

Juliet handed her the lead. 'Just don't let him loose because I'm not a hundred per cent sure that he'll come back.'

Olivia took the lead and began walking away. Jake continued to bark excitedly.

'Don't go too far!' called Amanda. 'And stay where we can see you.' But Olivia was already off and running with the Jack Russell at her side, barking excitedly.

'How much does she know?' asked Juliet.

'Nothing,' said Donald. 'We didn't want her to worry.'

'To be honest, I really don't think you have anything to worry about. I'm sure it's an idle threat.'

'How sure?' said Amanda.

Juliet frowned. 'What do you mean?'

'I mean, how sure are you that they won't carry out their threat?'

'Well, that's impossible to say, isn't it?'

'Are you ninety per cent sure? Ninety-five? Eighty?'

'Amanda, I can't put a number on it, obviously.'

'The kidnappers can, and they have. If we pay them fifty thousand pounds, they'll leave Olivia alone.'

'There's no guarantee that they'll keep their word.'

'That's what Lulu said.'

Juliet nodded. 'In fact, if you do pay the fifty thousand, they might well think there is more to be had.'

Amanda sighed. 'Lulu said that, too.' She looked over at Donald. 'This is a nightmare,' she said. She shaded her eyes with the flat of her hand and peered at Olivia, who was still running with the dog. 'I'll die if anything happens to her.'

Donald put his arm around her. 'Nothing is going to happen,' he said.

'You can't say that, Donald. You don't know for sure. Nobody knows.' She glared at Juliet. 'You shouldn't have come here. I really am not happy about you being seen with us like this.'

'I drove here in my own car, and as you can see, I'm very much in plain clothes,' said Juliet. 'I'm just a dog walker, taking her charge out for some exercise.'

'You look like a policewoman,' said Amanda.

'Really?'

Amanda nodded. 'There's a confidence about you, the way you hold yourself, the way you walk. Lulu is the same.'

'I shall try to stand less confidently,' said Juliet.

She allowed her shoulders to slump theatrically, and Amanda laughed in spite of herself. 'Much better.'

'I didn't realize that I still looked like a police officer,' said Lulu.

'All right, a police officer with a calico cat around her neck. Am I being oversensitive?'

'You're being protective of your family, and there's absolutely nothing wrong with that,' said Juliet. 'But I don't see any signs of surveillance. And if there was surveillance, all they can see is a woman with a dog talking to a woman with a cat. And I won't be here for long.'

Amanda sighed. 'Why us? Why the hell did they choose us?'

'Olivia's school is in a wealthy catchment area,' said Lulu. 'It's a state school, but a lot of the parents have money, so there could well have been other parents targeted. We wouldn't know, would we? The letter says you mustn't talk to the police, and the only reason you told me was because I was staying with you. You didn't talk to any other parents about this, did you?'

'Of course not,' said Amanda.

'Exactly,' said Lulu. 'Why would you? So there could be dozens of families at the school who are going through exactly what you and Donald are going through, and none of them are talking to each other.'

'So we should be talking to other parents at Olivia's school,' said Juliet. 'How many children attend?'

'About four hundred,' said Donald.

Juliet sighed. 'That's a job and a half.'

'I think there might be a shortcut,' said Lulu. 'The first thing Amanda and Donald did when they got the letter was to keep Olivia away from school. I think that would be the reaction of most parents, to protect their child and keep them safe. So whatever school staff you can get hold of during the holidays, ask them for a list of children who were absent over the past few days. You could do that with schools across the county. Then all you'd need to do is approach the parents of those children.'

Juliet smiled. 'That's clever,' she said. 'That's very clever.'

'Thank you.'

'I'll get the team working on it, starting local and moving across the county.'

'I think it'll pay off,' said Lulu. 'What about DI Kemp? Is he making any progress?'

'He's started looking at offenders in the area who've been involved in kidnapping and extortion. And he's doing another house-to-house along the route they think Poppy took, this time asking specifically about any vans that might have been seen.'

'I really think he should be checking the side roads, too. If there was a van, it might well have parked up earlier.'

'I suggested that.'

'And what did he say?'

'Some comment about teaching my grandmother to suck eggs, but he was hanging up on me so I didn't get the full gist. I think he's taking the idea under consideration.'

'His idea of looking at previous offenders is a good one.'

'Yes. I'm doing the same, looking at anyone in Bath and the surrounding area who might have done time for extortion or kidnapping.' She smiled at Amanda. 'We're doing everything we can, and obviously you can keep a close eye on your daughter.'

'I'm not letting her out of my sight,' said Amanda.

'That being the case, I'd really think twice about handing over fifty thousand pounds.'

Amanda grimaced. 'I'm not sure.'

'If you do pay, you need to realize that there's every chance you'll never see your money again,' said Juliet. 'Even if we eventually catch the kidnappers, the money could have been spirited off to who knows where.'

'We'll think about it,' said Amanda. She waved to Olivia. 'Olivia! Come on back!'

'What I would say is that it might be better to see if other parents at the school have also received letters,' said Lulu. 'Hopefully that'll be clearer by tomorrow, right?' She looked at Juliet, who nodded enthusiastically. 'Why not wait until after lunch?' said Lulu. 'I might have heard back from the NCA about the Bitcoin wallet by then.'

Amanda was still waving at Olivia. 'Okay, yes, all right,' she said. She called over to Olivia again, and waved with both arms. 'Come here now, Olivia!' she shouted.

Olivia waved back.

'Olivia, I'm serious!' Amanda yelled at the top of her voice. 'Come back now!' Heads were turning in their direction.

Donald put an arm around her. 'It's okay, Amanda. She's fine.'

'She has to stay close. I don't want her wandering off.'

'We can see her from here.'

'I don't want anything to happen to her,' said Amanda, her voice trembling.

'And nothing will,' said Donald.

Olivia knelt down and hugged Jake.

'She's happy,' said Donald. 'Let her have some fun.'

'Well, I'll leave you to your shopping,' said Juliet. 'It's been a pleasure meeting you, and rest assured we'll be doing everything we can to resolve this. If you have any questions or concerns, Lulu has my number.' Jake barked excitedly and began tugging at the lead. 'Have fun at the Christmas market,' Juliet called back, as she let him drag her away.

14

Their walk to the Christmas market took them around the Circus and down Gay Street, one of the city's main thoroughfares, lined with impressive stone townhouses. At the end of Gay Street they turned left and walked by the Roman baths. Lulu knew that the baths had first been used more than two thousand years ago, when the city had been a small town known as Aquae Sulis. A century after the Romans left, the baths were in ruins, but now they were one of the most visited attractions in the UK. It was a short walk from the baths to Bath Abbey, also known as the Abbey Church of Saint Peter and Saint Paul. It was built in Perpendicular Gothic style, in the shape of a cross, and the west front had a sculpture of Jacob's Ladder, with angels climbing stone ladders to heaven. It was a working abbey, with up to twelve hundred worshippers attending services.

Each Christmas, some two hundred stalls and decorated chalets were set up in the historic abbey courtyard along with a towering Christmas tree. Cheery stallholders sold hand-crafted gifts and Christmas decorations, and there was the delicious smell of freshly cooked street food in the air. Coloured lights illuminated the magnificent abbey, alternating between red, blue and yellow.

'This is lovely,' said Lulu, soaking in the festive atmosphere.

'It's my favourite time of the year,' said Amanda. 'You

can't move for tourists during the summer months, but over Christmas it's mainly locals.'

A violinist was busking in the shadow of the abbey, and they stopped to listen. He was playing a classical piece that Lulu knew – the Winter concerto from Vivaldi's *Four Seasons* – plucking the strings to represent rain and doing an excellent job of it.

'Do you play an instrument, Olivia?' Lulu whispered.

'I'm learning the flute at school,' she said.

'Oh, I love the flute,' said Lulu. 'So does Conrad.' Conrad was curled around her shoulders, his head tilted on one side as he looked at the violinist, a bearded man in his thirties wearing a patchwork waistcoat and brown corduroy knickerbockers. 'He hears frequencies that we don't, so it sounds different to him.'

Olivia looked up at her, frowning. 'How do you know that?'

Lulu smiled. She knew it because Conrad had told her, but obviously that had to remain a secret. 'Cats have very sensitive hearing, better even than dogs,' she said. 'Between 45 and 64,000 Hz. Humans hear sounds between 20 to 20,000 Hz. So when Conrad hears music, he hears something very different to what we're hearing.'

'How is he with K-pop?' asked Donald.

'K-what now?' said Lulu.

'K-pop,' said Donald. 'Teams of good-looking Korean boys in tight trousers singing love songs.'

'Dad!' said Olivia.

'I'm only joking,' said Donald, ruffling her hair.

'Who did you listen to when you were ten, Donald?' asked Lulu.

'David Bowie. Roxy Music. Queen.'

'We had much better music back then, didn't we?' said Amanda. 'Olivia hasn't even heard of Fleetwood Mac.'

'Times change,' said Lulu. She looked up at the abbey as the lights changed from red to blue. 'It's such a beautiful building,' she said.

'Isn't it?' said Donald. 'And it's been like this for about four hundred years. In fact, there's been a church here in one form or another for a thousand years, and in the thirteenth century it was a cathedral. Then Henry VIII shut it down in 1539 and kicked out all the monks. It was Elizabeth I who decided it should be restored and organized a public whip-round to pay for it. The restoration took nigh on fifty years, and this is how it turned out.'

'I love it,' said Lulu.

'It's run sustainably, too,' said Amanda. 'The abbey uses hot water from the Roman baths to run its central heating. Olivia did a science project on it last year, didn't you, Olivia?' Amanda looked around. 'Where is she?'

Lulu turned through a complete 360, but didn't see the little girl. 'She was here a moment ago.'

'Well, she's not here now,' said Amanda. 'Olivia!' she called at the top of her voice. 'Olivia, where are you?'

'She can't have wandered far,' said Donald, but Lulu could hear the uncertainty in his voice.

'Why don't we split up and look for her?' said Lulu, but Amanda was already walking away, calling Olivia's name.

'You go that way,' Lulu said to Donald, pointing at the abbey. 'Phone if you find her.'

'Do you think something's happened to her?' asked Donald.

'There's no point in speculating, let's just find her,' said

Lulu. She patted him on the shoulder. They could hear Amanda calling for Olivia off in the distance.

Lulu walked towards a line of food outlets, decorated chalets each offering a different cuisine. She passed a toffee apple stall, a kebab stall and a fish-and-chips outlet. People were queueing to hand over their money or swipe their cards, but there was no sign of Olivia. Conrad was looking, too, his head swivelling from side to side. A child screamed off to their right and they both looked towards the sound, but it was a small boy, shouting excitedly.

They reached the end of the food chalets. Lulu looked left and right. There were more food stalls to the left, and to the right were stalls selling handmade Christmas decorations, ornaments and crackers. Olivia had not long ago eaten breakfast so if she was browsing, it probably wasn't for food. Lulu turned right.

Donald was calling Olivia's name now. Heads were turning. 'Olivia!' Lulu shouted. 'Olivia!'

'Aunty Lulu!' Olivia shouted, further down the line of stalls.

A surge of relief washed over Lulu. 'Olivia!' she shouted again.

Olivia stepped away from the stall and waved. Lulu hurried over to her. She was standing in front of a display of Christmas ornaments, and she pointed at one excitedly as Lulu approached. 'Look!' she said. 'It's Conrad!'

Lulu looked at the ornament she was pointing at: a glass sphere with a calico cat sitting under a Christmas tree with a red and green bow around its neck. Lulu had to admit, the cat did look exactly like Conrad. 'Oh my goodness, you're right.'

'The markings are exactly the same. And look at the green eyes.'

Lulu moved closer to get a better look. Yes, the eyes were definitely the same colour as Conrad's.

'I'm buying it to put on our Christmas tree. Then every year I'll remember when I first met him.'

'That is a lovely thought,' said Lulu.

The stallholder, a woman in her fifties wearing a fake fur coat and a Santa hat, was rummaging through a large cardboard box full of ornaments swathed in bubble wrap. 'You know, dear, I think that's the only one I have,' she said.

'Oh, that's okay,' said Olivia. 'I'll take the one on display.'

Lulu took out her phone and called Amanda, who answered almost immediately. 'I've found her,' said Lulu. 'She's doing some last-minute Christmas shopping.'

'Oh thank you, thank you, thank you.'

'I'll bring her back, just give us a couple of minutes. Can you call Donald and let him know she's okay?'

'Of course, yes,' gasped Amanda. 'Oh, thank you, Lulu. Thank you so much.'

Amanda ended the call and Lulu put her phone back in her pocket. The stallholder carefully removed the calico cat decoration from the display, covered it in bubble wrap and put it into a small box. 'That'll be five pounds, please.'

Lulu thought that was expensive for a bauble, but she didn't say anything. Olivia handed over the money and took the box. She was so excited that Lulu couldn't help but smile. 'Come on,' she said. 'Let's show your mummy what you've bought.'

Donald and Amanda were waiting close to the violinist, who was now playing a tune that Lulu recognized but couldn't name. Olivia ran over to them and held up her purchase but Amanda ignored it. Instead she knelt down and grabbed her daughter, clutching Olivia to her chest. 'Don't you ever run away like that again,' she said.

'I didn't run away,' Olivia protested. 'I was shopping.'

Amanda hugged her tighter. 'You need to stay where we can see you,' she said.

'Mummy, I was shopping, I wasn't running away. I got the cutest ornament, it has a picture of Conrad on it.'

Amanda frowned. 'Conrad?'

'Do you want to see it?'

'Sure,' said Amanda. 'But first, promise me you'll stay close to us.'

Olivia sighed theatrically. 'I promise.'

'Good girl.' Amanda straightened up and Olivia opened the box and unwrapped the ornament. Amanda took it. 'Oh, that is strange,' she said. 'That is Conrad to a T.' She held the ornament close to Conrad's face. He meowed and wrinkled his nose. 'The markings are the same and so are the eyes. Lulu, did Conrad ever model for Christmas ornaments?'

'Not that I know of,' said Lulu.

'It's wonderful,' said Donald. 'It definitely needs to go in pride of place on the tree.'

'Oh my goodness – *Schindler's List*,' said Lulu, looking over at the violinist.

'I'm sorry, what?' said Donald.

Lulu gestured at the violinist. 'He's playing the theme from *Schindler's List*.'

'So he is,' said Amanda. 'I thought I recognized it.'

'It's a strange choice for the Christmas market,' said Lulu.

'It's a beautiful tune,' said Donald. 'But yes, the context is a bit jarring.' He smiled. 'Right, let's get some shopping done. And is everyone okay for my shepherd's pie tonight?'

'So you're cooking again?' asked Amanda. 'Be still, my beating heart.'

'Well, I know how hard you work at getting Christmas dinner ready. And shepherd's pie just seems appropriate, that's all. You know – *while shepherds washed their socks at night . . .*'

'So many dad jokes,' said Olivia, shaking her head.

'I use real shepherds, too,' said Donald. Olivia groaned.

15

When Lulu woke up the next morning, it took a few seconds for her to realize that she wasn't in her bunk on *The Lark*. She blinked as she looked up at the ceiling of Amanda's guest bedroom, then sat up, rubbing her eyes. Conrad was already awake, sitting at the foot of the bed.

'You slept well,' he said.

'It's a really comfortable bed,' said Lulu. 'The sheets are Egyptian cotton and the pillows are the ones that mould themselves to your head.' She looked at her watch. It was just before nine o'clock – well after the time she normally woke up. She had gone to bed just before midnight. It had been a lovely dinner, served in the dining room overlooking the park. Donald's shepherd's pie had been a delight, as had his crème brûlée. He had admitted that the secret to his shepherd's pie wasn't real shepherds, but half a glass of red wine and a couple of bay leaves. He had made a big show of using a small propane torch to achieve the crackly sugar top on the crème brûlée, and it had tasted heavenly. They had drunk a very good bottle of Nuits-Saint-Georges with the shepherd's pie and a bottle of Sancerre Sauvignon Blanc after Olivia had gone to bed. It had been a wonderful evening, and by the end of it they had almost forgotten about the threatening letter and Poppy Novak's kidnapping. Almost – but there were still moments when Lulu noticed tension in Amanda's face and a flicker of fear in her eyes.

Lulu slid off the bed and padded over to the en-suite. There was a large bath and a walk-in shower, but it was no contest – it had been more than a month since she had enjoyed a proper bath. She turned on both taps, added a good measure of Laura Mercier Almond Coconut Honey Bath, and cleaned her teeth as the bath filled up.

Conrad came into the bathroom. He sniffed the air. 'Oh, that smells good,' he said. 'There's honey, and coconut, and nuts. Almonds, I think. And I'm getting notes of cocoa, figs, cinnamon and nutmeg. It literally does smell good enough to eat.'

'Probably best not to,' said Lulu. She turned off the taps and slid into the water with a sigh. 'Oh, that feels good,' she said.

'Well, you know my views on water,' said Conrad. 'I shall wait for you in the bedroom.' He walked out, his tail in the air.

Lulu spent half an hour luxuriating in the hot bath, then dressed and went downstairs. Amanda and Donald were in the kitchen. 'I just had the most wonderful bath,' she said, sliding onto a stool at the island. Conrad settled himself next to the island.

'What do you do on your boat?' asked Amanda. 'I picture you washing with a wet flannel.'

Lulu chuckled. 'I have a very nice shower,' she said. 'But I do miss a bubble bath. Where is Olivia?'

'She's upstairs talking to her friends online. She's allowed two hours online a day and she's taking them this morning.'

'Fancy another Ulster fry?' asked Donald.

'Oh, no, thank you. I think I put on a kilo with the last

one,' said Lulu. 'Just scrambled eggs would be fine. Conrad will probably eat the same, but no butter or milk in his.'

'Lactose intolerant?'

'Exactly.'

'Two scrambled eggs coming up, one without dairy,' said Donald, and he began cracking eggs into a bowl.

'So what are your plans for today?' Lulu asked Amanda.

'We were planning to go down to the abbey at eleven – there'll be carol singers. But now I'm not sure I want to go out.'

'No, we should definitely go,' said Donald. 'Olivia was looking forward to it. Darling, we can't let these people ruin our lives. It's still Christmas, after all.'

Amanda sighed. 'I suppose so.'

'And what about Christmas dinner?' said Lulu. 'Will you do the preparation today? I'm a mean potato peeler, if you need any help.'

'I was planning to get started this afternoon, and I'd love you to help, thank you.'

'Does that mean I get a pass on kitchen duties?' asked Donald.

'That depends on the quality of this morning's eggs,' said Amanda.

The scrambled eggs were delicious. Conrad clearly enjoyed his, as he left the dish spotless.

Just after half past ten they all pulled on their coats and walked down to the abbey, where more than fifty carol singers had assembled in the courtyard. It was a lovely concert with the singers clearly enjoying themselves. Hundreds of people gathered to listen, their breath feathering in the cold morning air.

They had only been there for thirty minutes when Lulu's phone rang. She took it out. It was Juliet. 'Sorry,' she said apologetically. 'I have to take this. It's Inspector Donnelly.' She put the phone to her ear and walked away. 'Hi, Juliet, is everything okay?'

'Everything's fine,' said the inspector. 'We've had a stroke of luck, actually. I had the team following up your idea about checking on other pupils who were kept off school during the final week of term. It's been tricky because of the holidays, but we've been reaching out to emergency contacts and safeguarding leads, and they've been extremely helpful. We struck gold with a private school in the north of the city. A lovely woman there was able to give us a full list of pupils who hadn't been at school over the past few days. I'd like to go and have a chat this afternoon. Debra has been delayed and won't be on the team until tomorrow morning, but I also think you'd be an asset because of your experience with the Balfours.'

'Not a problem. I'm more than happy to help,' said Lulu.

'Where are you? I'm just getting in my car.'

'Near the abbey. Just soaking up the Christmas atmosphere.'

'Why don't you walk down to the police station? It's only a couple of minutes away and it's easy for me to stop outside. I'll be there in ten minutes.'

'Perfect,' said Lulu. She put the phone away and went back to Amanda and Donald. 'I'm afraid I'm going to have to love you and leave you,' she said.

'Has something happened?'

'Juliet needs my help with something,' said Lulu. She

didn't want to raise their hopes unnecessarily in case the visits came to nothing. 'I shouldn't be more than a couple of hours. I'll see you back at the house.'

She waved goodbye to Olivia and blew her a kiss. She walked down Manvers Street until she reached Bath Police Station on her right. It was closed and there was a sign detailing its opening times: 9.30 a.m. until 5 p.m. Monday to Thursday, 9.30 a.m. until 3.45 p.m. on Friday, and closed Saturday and Sunday.

'So criminals in Bath don't work in the evenings or at the weekend?' asked Conrad.

'It looks that way,' said Lulu.

'That's crazy, right?'

Lulu chuckled. 'I think so, but then I'm old school. I think the best form of policing is a constable in a uniform walking around his patch.'

'You walked a beat, didn't you?'

'I did. And I was a better police officer because of it. But there's no doubt that having a control centre with mobile officers responding as and when needed is cost-effective. And that's the way the world is these days – everything comes down to money. Unfortunately.'

They waited outside the police station for a few minutes before Juliet arrived in her blue Tesla. Lulu held Conrad to her chest as she climbed in. 'Oh, this is toasty warm,' she said. Conrad settled down in her lap.

'The Tesla has great climate control, but you have to be careful on long journeys because it can really drain the battery,' said Juliet. 'But we're good today because we're fully charged.' She pulled away from the station. There was a large screen on the dashboard showing a map of the city and their destination to the north.

'How far can you drive on one charge?' asked Lulu.

'They say about three hundred miles, but so much depends on how fast you're driving and what other things you have switched on. The lights, the heating, the windscreen wipers, they all take power. But day-to-day running around in the cold weather like we have now – probably about two hundred and fifty miles between charges. What about your narrow-boat? What sort of range does it have?'

'Well, my tank holds two hundred litres of diesel. And if I'm pottering along at three miles an hour, *The Lark* probably burns a litre an hour, so we're good for about two hundred hours.'

'So six hundred miles on one tank?'

'Yes, about that. But you would never drain the tank like that. You keep topping it up.'

'And what about water?'

'The water tank holds five hundred litres, which can last me a couple of weeks. But again, I top off the tank whenever I can.'

'It really is self-contained, isn't it?'

'Absolutely. For thousands of people, their boat is their only home.'

They drew up at a set of traffic lights. Juliet gestured at the map. 'So, as I told you, this private school came up with a list of parents who have kept their children at home in recent days. Six had applied officially, as they were taking their children skiing.' She smiled. 'It's that sort of school. Five were kept off for medical reasons, but of those five, only three provided a doctor's note. We'll be visiting the other two.'

'And how much do we tell them about what's going on?' asked Lulu.

'I plan to play that by ear, depending how cooperative they are. The fact they've withdrawn their children from school shows how worried they are. And assuming they were told not to contact the police, they'll be none too pleased to see us on their doorstep. If they clam up, then we might have to explain that they're not the only ones to have been threatened.' Juliet smiled thinly. 'Assuming they have received a letter, of course. They may well just have a child with the sniffles.'

They drove for another ten minutes before Juliet pulled up in front of a detached stone house on the side of a hill overlooking the city. There were two cars in the driveway but plenty of space to park in the street. 'Right, so this is Mr and Mrs Elliott, and their son is Liam, aged eight,' said Juliet as she switched off the engine. 'Mr Elliott is a solicitor and his wife is what they call a homemaker, I suppose. I have to say, I much prefer *homemaker* to *housewife*. Housewife always seems to imply that the woman is in some way married to the house, doesn't it?'

'Homemaker does sound much more creative,' agreed Lulu.

They climbed out of the car. 'Now, that is an impressive view,' said Lulu, as she surveyed the view with Conrad in her arms. From where they were standing they could see all the city's landmarks – the abbey, the Roman baths, Pulteney Bridge, Royal Victoria Park and the Royal Crescent – and the hills beyond.

'I'm guessing the view is reflected in the asking price,'

said Juliet. 'It's certainly well beyond the means of a detective inspector.'

'They clearly have money,' said Lulu. She nodded at the two cars parked in front of the house: a Mercedes SUV and a BMW 5 Series. 'You only have to walk past the house to see that. And Donald and Amanda – well, their home in the Royal Crescent shows that they have money.'

'There'd be no point in trying to extort families on benefits,' said Juliet.

'Like the Novaks,' said Lulu.

'Yes, like the Novaks.'

They walked up the driveway towards the front door. Conrad was on Lulu's shoulders, looking around.

'Did you have Conrad with you when you worked for the Met?' asked Juliet.

'No, he came into my life long after I'd retired.'

'I was just thinking how useful he would be during interrogations,' said Juliet. 'He has a knack for putting people at ease, doesn't he?'

'Very much so,' said Lulu.

There was a wreath of holly leaves and berries hanging on the front door. Juliet pressed the bell and they heard a buzzing sound off in the distance. After a few seconds a man in a blue cardigan and baggy jeans opened the door and peered at them over the top of round-lensed spectacles.

'Mr Elliott?' said Juliet.

The man frowned at them. 'Yes?'

Juliet smiled. 'I'm a detective, Mr Elliott. Inspector Juliet Donnelly. I'd rather not show you my warrant card on the doorstep, but I'd be more than happy to produce it inside. This is my colleague, Lulu Lewis.'

Mr Elliott noticed Conrad for the first time and his frown deepened. 'There's a cat around your neck.'

'Think of him as camouflage,' said Lulu. 'No one watching would think that a cat lady like me would be a police officer. But as Juliet said, maybe we would be more comfortable inside.'

'What's this about?' asked Mr Elliott.

'I think you know,' said Juliet.

The man's eyes narrowed. 'Go away,' he said, attempting to push the door closed.

Juliet put a hand up to keep the door open. 'We've had a good look around, Mr Elliott, and we're sure that nobody is watching the house. And if anybody was watching, all they would see is a couple of friends visiting. We came here in my personal car.'

'A Tesla,' said Lulu. 'A wonderful vehicle, and definitely not a police car.'

Mr Elliott maintained his pressure on the door for a couple of seconds, and then he relaxed and opened it. 'Inside,' he said.

Juliet and Lulu stepped inside and Mr Elliott closed the door behind them.

'Is Mrs Elliott here?' asked Juliet.

'She is, yes. She's watching TV.'

'And what about Liam?'

'He's upstairs in his room. He's allowed an hour a day on social media and he has half an hour to go.'

'Oh, I do admire your firmness,' said Juliet. 'My ten-year-old is on Instagram most of the time and I haven't had the nerve to give her a curfew. My eight-year-old is more into TikTok, but she still loves to read, thankfully.'

'It's all about setting limits,' said Mr Elliott. 'The internet is not a safe place. Especially for children.'

He took them through to a sitting room where his wife was sitting on an overstuffed sofa. She had frizzy permed hair and was wearing a purple velour tracksuit. There was a box of tissues on the coffee table in front of her. She was watching a game show, and she looked up quizzically as Juliet and Lulu walked into the room.

'Darling, these two ladies are with the police,' said Mr Elliott.

'No!' said his wife. 'Are you stupid? They specifically said no police.'

'They just appeared at the door, darling,' said Mr Elliott. 'I didn't call them.'

Mrs Elliott glared at Juliet. 'You have to leave now,' she said. She stood up. Her cheeks had reddened and her hands were trembling. 'Please. Just go.'

'Mrs Elliott, just hear me out. The letter you've received – you're not the only ones. The parents of another local child, about the same age as your son, have received a similar letter, demanding fifty thousand pounds. We don't believe your son is in imminent danger. The kidnappers of Poppy Novak have, we believe, sent out many identical letters on the assumption that a number of parents will panic and pay.'

Mrs Elliott looked across at Lulu. 'Is this true?'

Lulu nodded. 'It is, yes.'

Mrs Elliott frowned. 'Is that a cat?'

'His name is Conrad,' said Lulu. 'He goes everywhere with me.'

'But he's a calico, right? Aren't calico cats always female?'

'Most are, yes,' said Lulu. 'But Conrad is a very unusual cat.'

Juliet reached into her handbag and took out a photocopy of the letter the Balfours had received. She gave it to Mrs Elliott, who read it quickly and then thrust it at her husband. 'It's the same,' she said. She had a ring with a massive ruby on her right hand and a gold Rolex on her left wrist. There was another large ruby on a thin gold chain around her neck.

'That letter came with a photograph of Poppy Novak, and also a photograph of their daughter arriving at her school.'

Mrs Elliott began gasping for breath and sat back down heavily.

'Are you all right, Mrs Elliott?' asked Juliet.

'Asthma,' said Mr Elliott. He hurried over to a sideboard, grabbed an inhaler, and rushed back to his wife. She took it and sucked on it greedily. 'She'll be okay,' said Mr Elliott. 'It's the stress.'

'I'm so sorry,' said Juliet. 'I had no idea.'

Mr Elliott held up the sheet of paper. 'Are they paying?' he asked.

'We're not sure,' said Juliet. 'It's still being discussed.'

Mr Elliott scrutinized the letter again.

'Mr Elliott, would you please show me the letter that you were sent?'

'No!' exclaimed Mrs Elliott. She glared at her husband. 'No police!' she hissed. 'They said no police.'

'I think we've already crossed that bridge,' said Mr Elliott. 'They're here already. Even if they leave now, they'll still have been seen if there is anyone watching.'

'As I said, Mr Elliott, I'm sure your house isn't being watched,' said Juliet.

'What about drones?' said Mrs Elliott. 'They could be using a drone.'

'That's very unlikely,' said Juliet. 'The point is, Mrs Elliott, the more people who have received letters like this, the less likely it is that they'll be acted upon.'

'You don't know that for sure,' said Mrs Elliott. 'You can't know that. You're not a mind-reader.'

Juliet opened her mouth to reply, but Mrs Elliott cut her off with a shake of her head. 'It doesn't matter,' she said. 'It's immaterial. We've already paid.'

Juliet's jaw dropped. 'Really?'

Mrs Elliott nodded emphatically. 'The day we got the letter. How could we not pay? There's no way that we would put our son at risk.'

Juliet looked at Mr Elliott. 'You paid, just like that?'

He nodded. 'I've owned Bitcoin and other cryptos for years. I was advising my clients to get into it over a decade ago, when it first passed a thousand dollars. I won't tell you how much I invested, but I can tell you that fifty thousand doesn't even make a dent in my Bitcoin holdings.'

'You're a very lucky man, Mr Elliott,' said Lulu.

'It isn't luck, Mrs Lewis,' he said. 'I could see the way it was headed, and it seemed to me to be a no-brainer. Several of my clients followed my advice and got very rich because of it. I wouldn't necessarily recommend investing in Bitcoin today; the market is far too volatile, and if you get the timing wrong you could lose your shirt. But anyone who bought when I did – well, they'll be sitting pretty now.'

'And you had no hesitation in paying?'

'I didn't want anything to happen to Liam. He's our only son and there is nothing I wouldn't do to protect him.' He grimaced. 'If we'd had to sell the house, we'd have done that. But we didn't have to. A few taps on my computer keyboard, and the problem was solved.'

'But you've put everything in jeopardy by coming here,' said Mrs Elliott. 'No police, they said.'

'Mrs Elliott, they've got what they wanted. They won't be interested in you now,' said Juliet. 'As I said, we already know of one other family who have been threatened, and we believe there are more.'

Mr Elliott gave the letter back to Juliet. 'We don't want any involvement with this,' he said. 'We want to put it behind us and move on.'

Juliet put the letter into her handbag. 'I do understand that, Mr Elliott. I'm a mother myself. We do whatever we have to do to protect our children. That's human nature. But I need you both to consider the parents of Poppy Novak. Their daughter has been kidnapped, and they have no idea if they will ever see her again. Unlike you, they don't have money. They're on benefits and they live in a council house. They have no assets, they weren't able to buy Bitcoin when it was cheap – they barely have enough to cover their bills. They can't pay a ransom, they simply can't. And there's no guarantee that Poppy will be released. Can you imagine what they're going through?'

'Of course I can,' said Mr Elliott. 'I saw them on TV. I could see how shattered they were.'

'That's a good word,' said Juliet. 'They are shattered. Absolutely shattered. And there's no end in sight for their torment. The police are doing everything they can, but really, there's not much to go on. No one saw Poppy being abducted and no one seems to know where she is. But the letter you received might provide a much-needed clue. DNA, perhaps. Or fingerprints. Or perhaps we can identify where the letter was posted. We don't know what evidence there might be, which is why we really need our forensics people to examine it.' She smiled and nodded. 'You've paid the kidnappers what they wanted. They're not going to know that you gave the letter to us.'

'And the police already have the letter that was sent to my friends,' said Lulu. 'There's no reason to believe that the kidnappers will even know that we contacted you.'

Mr Elliott went over to his wife. 'I think we should help,' he said. 'Imagine if the roles were reversed, if it was Liam who had been taken and the Novak family had information that could help find him? You'd want them to do whatever they could, wouldn't you?'

Mrs Elliott nodded glumly. 'I suppose so.'

'It's the right thing to do, Lisa.'

She nodded again. 'All right. Go on.'

Mr Elliott patted her on the shoulder, then went over to the sideboard and took out three sheets of paper. He brought them over to Juliet. Juliet produced three plastic evidence bags and held them out one by one so that he could slide each sheet in. One was a typewritten letter; one was a photograph of a young boy in a dark blazer with an Arsenal backpack over one shoulder; and the third was the photograph of Poppy Novak.

'What about the envelope?' asked Juliet.

'I threw that away,' said Mr Elliott. 'I don't know why I kept those, to be honest.'

'I'm glad that you did,' said Juliet. 'The day that photo-graph of Liam was taken, did one of you drive him to school?'

'I always do the school run,' said Mrs Elliott.

'Did you see anyone taking photographs?' asked Juliet.

'I didn't, no. But I wouldn't have been looking. I drop Liam off, I wait to see that he goes through the school gates, then I drive home.'

Juliet held up the photograph in its clear bag. 'Do you have any idea where the photographer might have been positioned?'

Mrs Elliott peered at the photograph. 'There's a small car park opposite the school that's used by the teachers. Parents are allowed to drive through to drop off their children but they're not supposed to park there.'

'Do you know if there's CCTV in the car park?'

'I think there might be,' said Mrs Elliott. 'I know there's definitely a camera down the road, because there's a bus lane there and I got fined for driving in it last year. They sent me a photograph of my car as proof.'

'Thank you for that,' said Juliet. 'I'll leave you to get on with your day. We're grateful for your time and for your help. And I hope you have a merry Christmas, despite everything.'

'I hope you get the girl back safely,' said Mr Elliott.

'We'll certainly do our best,' said Juliet. 'And if we do catch the kidnappers, we will make every effort to recover the money you've paid.'

Mr Elliott shook his head. 'We don't care about that. All we care about is Liam. The money doesn't matter.'

16

The second family lived about half a mile from the Elliotts'
house. As Juliet drove, Lulu studied the letter Mr Elliott had
given them. It was almost identical to the letter Amanda and
Donald had received and appeared to have come from the
same printer, although that would need confirming by the
forensic experts. The letter referred to Liam and not Olivia,
and the Bitcoin wallet was different.

'This is very well organized, isn't it?' said Lulu.

'They're not amateurs, that's for sure.'

Conrad was sitting in Lulu's lap, and she stroked him. He
purred contentedly. 'They're clearly not choosing people at
random. Both the Elliotts and the Balfours are in a position
to pay. They must have known that.'

'It's not difficult to find out who has money these days,'
said Juliet. 'Everyone is on Facebook, Instagram and TikTok,
even the kids. They can find out where they live, what cars
they drive, where the kids go to school, who their friends
are. It's scary just how much information is out there. A few
hours on a phone and the bad guys can get all the intel they
need. They know what the kids look like, they know what
school they go to – all they have to do is park up and wait
for a photo opportunity.'

'It's a very clever crime,' said Lulu. 'It was clearly easy to
abduct Poppy Novak, whereas taking Liam Elliott or Olivia
would be a much more challenging operation. But once they

have Poppy, it makes the threat real. And by choosing parents who could easily pay, they made it less likely that they would go to the police. So who are we going to see now?'

'Mr and Mrs Khan. Salim Khan is a businessman who owns a chain of shoe shops across the West Country. His wife is Noor Khan, a homemaker. They have three children who go to the same school, and they kept all three off school for the last two days of term. They told the school that the girls had Covid, but there have been no other reports of Covid infections.' She nodded at a large stone detached house ahead of them. It was surrounded by a thick privet hedge and there was a Porsche SUV parked on a tarmac driveway. There was enough space in the drive for several more vehicles, so Juliet had plenty of room to park the Tesla.

As they climbed out of the car, a man appeared at the front door. 'Can I help you?' he asked, in a voice that suggested that was the last thing he wanted to do.

'Mr Khan? I'm Detective Inspector Juliet Donnelly. I'm here to . . .'

'You need to leave now,' the man hissed. 'Get back in your car, now.'

'All we need is a few words . . .' Juliet began, but Mr Khan silenced her with a wave of his hand.

'No. You need to go. Now.'

Juliet began walking towards him, but he stepped back into the house and slammed the door shut.

Lulu joined Juliet, and they both stared at the door. 'Well, that didn't go well, did it?' said Lulu. She was holding Conrad in her arms and she raised him up so that he could climb onto her shoulders.

'His attitude really says everything, doesn't it?' Juliet

stepped forward and pressed the doorbell. There was no answer. She pressed it again.

Lulu bent down and pushed the letterbox open. 'Mr Khan, we have something to show you. Please open the door.'

Juliet pressed the doorbell again. This time the door opened a few inches. 'You need to go away,' Mr Khan said.

Juliet reached into her handbag and took out the letter she had taken from the Elliotts. She held out the evidence bag. 'If you received a letter like this, you need to talk to us about it.'

Mr Khan shook his head. 'I haven't received a letter.'

'You haven't looked at it, Mr Khan.'

'I don't need to look at it. Now please, go away or I'll call . . .' He broke off as he realized what he was about to say. 'Just go.'

Before he could close the door again, Juliet shoved her foot into the gap. 'Mr Khan, you can either speak to us now, or I can arrange for a vanload of uniformed constables in high-vis jackets to call round. I'm sure you don't want that.'

'You've no idea what you're doing,' said Mr Khan, his gaze darting over her shoulder. He was only in his forties, but looked older; his hair was greying, his face was creased with worry and there were dark patches under his eyes. 'Please, just go away.'

'We can't, Mr Khan. It's important we talk to you. Poppy Novak's life may depend on it.'

'She's nothing to do with me. This is my house, and it's my family that's being threatened here. You need to leave.' He glared at her. 'I won't call the police, obviously, but I will call my lawyer, and he'll sue you for harassment and anything else he can think of. I'll make sure you lose your job and that your force is sued for millions. Now go. Or I'll phone my lawyer. I swear.'

'You're making a mistake, Mr Khan. We only want to help,' said Juliet. She slowly withdrew her foot. 'But I can see you're under a lot of pressure, so we can leave this until another time.'

The door slammed in their faces. Lulu and Juliet walked back to the Tesla.

'We can try again when he's a bit more receptive,' said Juliet. 'I don't think there's anything to be gained by putting him under more pressure. I mean, we could charge him with obstruction, but what would we gain? And if he simply refuses to talk to us . . .' She shrugged. 'Well, that's his right, isn't it?'

They got back into the car. 'Where shall I drop you?' Juliet asked as she started the engine and drove back onto the road.

'Close to the Royal Crescent,' said Lulu. 'I'll be staying with Amanda and Donald tonight and I don't think they'd want you pulling up outside.'

'Not a problem,' said Juliet.

'So that's three,' said Lulu, stroking Conrad, who was back on her lap. 'And if there are three, there are certain to be more.'

Juliet nodded. 'That appears to be the case. Their plan was to abduct Poppy Novak and then use the threat of further abductions to make as many other parents as possible pay up.'

'And presumably, once they have enough money, they'll release Poppy. There's no point hurting her, is there?'

'If there's no way she can identify them, then yes, they

can just let her go,' said Juliet. 'If they're smart, they'll be hiding their faces whenever they interact with her.'

'So why not just go public with what we know?' said Lulu. 'If we make it public that the kidnappers are using her abduction to extort money from other families, then no one else will pay. And if the money dries up, they'll release Poppy.'

'That would be a gamble, Lulu. We don't know who the kidnappers are or how they'll react. For all we know, they might kill her just to prove a point.'

'That would be truly evil.'

Juliet nodded. 'There are evil people in this world, that's for sure. But these people do appear to be professionals, and if that's the case, then it's all about the money. We need to talk to DI Kemp. We can't really do anything further without talking to him first.'

'So you'll talk to him?'

'I'll call him as soon as I've dropped you off.'

Lulu took out her phone and called Kirsty Grant. 'Sorry to bother you, Kirsty – I have another Bitcoin wallet for you to check,' said Lulu.

'Not a problem. I'm in the office anyway. No rest for the wicked.'

'So, are you working over Christmas?' asked Lulu.

'I'm supposed to be off until the twenty-seventh,' said Kirsty. 'But I'll be monitoring things from home, and obviously if you need anything, just call. A kidnapped child trumps everything.'

'I'll send you a screenshot of the Bitcoin wallet,' said Lulu. 'The kidnappers sent it to another set of parents in Bath and they've already paid up, transferring fifty thousand pounds.'

'I'll get right on it, Lulu.'

Lulu ended the call, then sent Kirsty a screenshot of the Bitcoin wallet used in the letter that had been sent to the Elliotts. Once the message had gone through, she put her phone back in her pocket. 'My Bitcoin expert is on the case,' she said.

'Is she hopeful she can track the money?'

'Hopeful, yes – optimistic, no. If the kidnappers have gone to all this trouble to set this up, they'll have worked out a way to convert the Bitcoin into cash without being caught. But at the moment, it's our best hope of finding them.'

17

Juliet dropped Lulu and Conrad a short walk away from the Royal Crescent. 'Let me know what your NCA Bitcoin contact has to say,' said Juliet.

'I will. Are you okay if I tell the Balfours that you're investigating the other letters? It might make them feel better.'

'I don't see why not, but that information isn't to be made public. Not until I've cleared it with DI Kemp. Let's talk again tomorrow. If nothing else, I'll be able to wish you a merry Christmas.'

'Will you be phoning him?'

'I think I'll drive over and have a face-to-face with him. Try to build a relationship. I want us to be cooperating rather than competing.'

'It's always the best way,' said Lulu. She waved as Juliet drove away.

'Do police officers compete with each other?' asked Conrad as Lulu began walking towards the Royal Crescent.

'Some competition can be healthy,' said Lulu. 'If competition makes everyone work harder, that's a good thing. But sometimes a detective might be so focused on solving a case that he doesn't share as much information as he should.'

'He?' said Conrad.

Lulu chuckled. 'It does tend to be testosterone related.'

'Did that happen to you a lot when you were a police officer?'

'It did, I'm afraid.'

'How did you react?'

'Oh, I fought my corner. I always did. The worst times were when a more senior officer would take credit for my work, but you can't do much about that. I have to say, once I moved up the ladder I always tried to make sure that my team took all the credit that was due to them.'

'I didn't get the impression that DI Kemp is a team player.'

Lulu smiled. 'You are such a good judge of character, Conrad.'

'Well, I chose you, didn't I?'

'Yes, you did. And I'll always be grateful for that.'

As they approached Amanda and Donald's house, Lulu looked around. As usual, there were plenty of dog walkers in the park and tourists taking selfies, but she couldn't see anyone obviously watching the house. She rang the doorbell and after a few seconds Donald opened it. He was wearing his apron again and holding a potato peeler. He smiled when he saw Lulu and Conrad. 'I was about to give up on you,' he said. 'Come in, come in.' He bundled them inside and closed the door. 'Amanda is upstairs with Olivia.'

'Is something wrong?' asked Lulu.

'No, Olivia wanted her hair blow-dried and she loves it when her mum does it. They'll be down in a few minutes. Come through to the kitchen. I've started work on tomorrow's veg.'

Conrad jumped down off Lulu's shoulders and landed on the floor with barely a sound. He and Lulu followed Donald into the kitchen. There was a pile of potato peelings on the counter and a pan of peeled potatoes on the cooker. Donald put the peeler down next to a bag of carrots.

'Wine?' asked Donald.

'Wine not?' Lulu said, but realized from the confused look on his face that he hadn't understood her. 'Wine would be good,' she said. 'And some water for Conrad, if it's not too much trouble.'

'Nothing is too much trouble for Conrad the cat,' said Donald. 'Is tap water okay?'

'He prefers bottled, if you have any.'

'Still or sparkling?' asked Donald. He chuckled. 'Still, of course. Whoever heard of a cat drinking sparkling water?'

He took a bottle of water from the fridge and poured some into a saucer, which he put down in front of Conrad.

'And what about you, Lulu? I have a bottle of Pinot Grigio that's already open if you're happy with that.'

'Very happy,' said Lulu.

She slid onto one of the stools at the island as Donald poured her a glass of wine.

Amanda appeared in the doorway. 'I thought I heard the doorbell,' she said, and smiled over at Donald as he lifted the wine bottle enquiringly. 'Oh yes, just a small one for me.' She took the stool opposite Lulu. 'So, what was so important that they dragged you away from the Christmas carols?'

'It's good news, I suppose,' said Lulu. 'It's exactly as we thought. We've spoken to two other sets of parents who have received letters similar to the one you received. Well – one set of parents admitted it and gave us what they'd been sent, but the other father wouldn't really speak to us. But from his attitude, it was clear that he was hiding something.'

'So you're saying they received an identical letter to ours?' asked Donald as he poured the wine.

'A letter just like yours, and a photograph of their son.

The boy goes to a different school from Olivia, a private one in the north of the city. And that's significant, because if they have targeted two schools, they could well have targeted more.'

'So you're suggesting there's safety in numbers?' said Amanda. 'I don't think that's a gamble we're prepared to take. I'm sorry.'

'No need to apologize,' said Lulu. 'I understand. But really, this is good news. It confirms that these people aren't interested in kidnapping other children – they're just using the threat of kidnapping to extort money.'

Donald set their glasses down in front of them. 'But you don't know that for sure, do you?'

'Not for sure, no,' said Lulu. 'But the balance of probabilities is that this is about extorting money and not about carrying out further kidnappings.'

'These other parents, did they pay?' asked Amanda.

'The ones we spoke to, yes, they did.'

'Fifty thousand pounds?' asked Amanda.

Lulu nodded. 'In Bitcoin. But they were told to send it to a different Bitcoin wallet from the one they gave you.'

Amanda looked over at Donald. 'You see? They paid, so we should pay too. If we pay, they'll leave us alone and we can stop worrying. I don't want to keep panicking every time Olivia is out of our sight.'

'I'm not sure that's the way to go,' said Lulu. 'If they've sent out three letters, they could well have sent more. A lot more.'

'You keep pushing the safety in numbers line,' said Amanda. 'But who are they going to go after, Lulu? The ones who pay, or the ones who don't pay?'

'I understand that logic, I really do. But what if they're using this as a test to see who will and who won't pay? And what if they decide to extort money again, on the assumption that if someone pays once, they'll pay twice?'

'That's just speculation,' said Amanda.

'It is, yes. We simply don't know what they'll do next. But my gut feeling is that they're not targeting individuals – they're targeting a group, the same way scammers do with emails. They send out millions of emails, and even if only a tiny percentage fall for the scam, they can still make a lot of money. I think the kidnappers have sent out quite a few threatening letters, and they're hoping that some will bite.'

'So you don't think Olivia is in any danger?' said Donald.

'I really don't,' said Lulu. 'I was obviously concerned when you showed me the letter and the photographs, but now we know that it's part of an ongoing extortion plot, it's clear that you weren't singled out.'

'But we *were* singled out,' said Amanda. 'They singled out Olivia – they singled out our family. They chose us.'

'I'm sorry, I meant that the kidnappers didn't target you as individuals. They targeted wealthy families with young children, and you're in that category.'

'Are they any closer to catching them?' Amanda asked.

'I think things are moving in the right direction,' said Lulu. 'My Bitcoin expert at the NCA is looking at the payment this other couple has made, so that's a definite line of inquiry. Plus, we can analyse the photograph the kidnappers took of the little boy. Juliet will be checking CCTV in that area and cross-referencing any vehicles with the ones that were seen outside Olivia's school.'

'They might have used different vehicles,' said Donald.

'Yes, they might,' said Lulu. 'But it's a good start.'

'So your advice is that we shouldn't pay?' said Donald.

'I think this will be over quite soon,' said Lulu. 'And if you do pay, there's no guarantee that it will be possible to get your money back.'

Donald nodded at Amanda. 'Maybe we should wait, just for a day or two. Nothing's going to happen over Christmas, is it?'

'Criminals don't work over the holidays, is that what you're saying?' said Amanda.

'Do they?' Donald asked Lulu.

Lulu chuckled. 'Well, criminals have families, and like everyone else, they want to spend time with their families.'

'Yes, well, little Poppy Novak isn't going to be spending time with her family, is she?' said Amanda. 'Can you imagine what her parents are going through?'

Lulu nodded. 'I can, yes. It must be a nightmare for them. That's why I think you shouldn't pay. Because if parents like you do pay, there's no incentive for them to let Poppy go, is there?'

Amanda frowned. 'I don't understand. What do you mean?'

'Well, if people keep paying, then they're likely to keep her. The threat will still be there. If they release her, there's no threat. I've suggested to Juliet that the police go public with what they know, that this is all about extortion and not about abducting Poppy. Once people realize that, they simply won't pay, and there'll be no point in the kidnappers holding Poppy any longer.'

'But what if they . . .' Donald left the sentence unfinished.

'There would be absolutely no point in them hurting her,'

said Lulu. 'This is all about money, about financial gain. Once it's clear there's no money to be had, the sensible thing will be just to let Poppy go.'

'Sensible?' repeated Amanda. 'You think the kidnappers might be sensible?'

'Everything they've done so far has been well planned, well thought out,' said Lulu. 'From the initial abduction to the threatening letters, and especially the demands for Bitcoin. These people are professionals.'

'Lulu may be right,' said Donald quietly. 'Perhaps going public really is the best way.'

'We're not talking to the press,' snapped Amanda. 'Absolutely not.'

'Not us,' said Donald. 'That's not what I meant. Lulu said the police would go public; they wouldn't have to mention us. They could explain about the threatening letters, and if everyone who got one just refused to pay, then it would be game over.'

Lulu nodded. 'Exactly.'

Amanda sighed. 'I just don't know what to do for the best,' she said.

'Why don't we at least wait until Juliet has had the chance to talk to Inspector Kemp?' said Lulu. 'Once we know what they've decided, you'll be in a better position to decide what to do.'

Amanda sighed. 'I suppose so,' she said. She sipped her wine, looking at Donald over the top of her glass.

He gave her a reassuring smile. 'It's going to be okay, darling,' he said.

'I hope so,' Amanda said. She looked over at the vegetables that Donald had been working on. 'Thank you for that. Why don't I cook tonight? I've some lovely sea bass in the fridge. Why don't I do sea bass with pea, mint and asparagus mash?'

'Oh, that sounds delicious,' said Lulu.

'It's another Jamie Oliver recipe,' said Amanda. 'I'm a fan.'

'And Conrad loves sea bass,' said Lulu.

'Sea bass it is, then,' said Amanda. 'I'll do the stuffing at the same time. Pork and cider. It's delicious. We thought we'd eat at half past three tomorrow, after the King's Speech. Is that okay with you, Lulu?'

'Perfect.'

18

Lulu opened her eyes to find Conrad standing beside her, butting her shoulder softly with his head. 'Wake up,' he said.

'I am awake,' Lulu said, blinking in the gloom. 'What time is it?'

'It's about four o'clock, but as I'm not wearing a wrist-watch, I can't be sure.'

'There's no need for sarcasm,' said Lulu. 'You're the one who woke me up. Now what's wrong?'

'I heard a noise.'

'It's an old house. They're always creaking. Same as *The Lark*. You hear noises all the time.'

'This sounded like footsteps.'

'Maybe it was Donald or Amanda?'

'The footsteps were downstairs. And I didn't hear anyone go down.' He tilted his head to one side and his ears pricked up. 'Now I hear footsteps on the stairs.'

Lulu sat up and turned her head from side to side, listening intently. 'I don't hear anything,' she whispered.

'You're not a cat. And it can't have escaped your attention that I am.'

'I have to say, Conrad, this early-morning attitude is a bit much. What shall I do? Shall I call the police? How certain are you?'

'That I can hear footsteps? A hundred per cent sure. But I'm not certain whose footsteps they are.'

'I'm not sure the police will come out just because we've heard footsteps.'

'Now who's being sarcastic?' said Conrad primly.

'I wasn't being in the least bit sarcastic,' said Lulu. 'I was stating a fact. The police will need a reason for sending someone out.' She swung her feet off the bed and stood up slowly. She was wearing grey jogging bottoms and a Depeche Mode T-shirt. 'Are you sure it's not Donald or Amanda?'

'I can't tell,' said Conrad. 'But whoever it is, they're outside Olivia's room.'

'Maybe it's Amanda checking up on Olivia? She's really worried about her.'

'Maybe,' said Conrad, but Lulu could tell from his tone that he wasn't convinced.

She tiptoed over to the door and placed her ear against it, but couldn't hear anything. She reached for the door handle and slowly twisted it. Conrad jumped down off the bed and joined her as she eased the door open. Keeping a tight grip on the handle, she peered into the hallway. It was in darkness. She listened intently and heard a soft creaking noise, but it could just have been the house settling. She looked down at Conrad. 'Can you hear anything?' she murmured.

'Footsteps,' he said in a low voice.

'I'm going to switch the light on,' Lulu replied.

'I can see in the dark,' said Conrad.

'Yes, well, I can't,' said Lulu. 'I don't want to go tripping over something and breaking a hip.'

'Said no cat, ever.'

'Conrad!'

'I was joking,' he said. 'Switch the light on if you think it will help.'

Lulu flicked the light switch by the door. A wedge of light sliced through into the hall. She stepped out of the bedroom, still listening intently. Conrad followed her, tail straight up, nose in the air. Ahead of them were the stairs. To the left was Olivia's bedroom, to the right was the master suite where Amanda and Donald slept.

Lulu's mind was whirling. She couldn't hear anything amiss, but she had absolute faith in Conrad's abilities. She realized she had left her phone on the bedside table. What was she going to do if there was an intruder in the house?

She took another couple of steps down the hall. Conrad was by her side, nose twitching. 'I can smell something,' he said. 'Minty.'

'Minty? Like toothpaste?'

'No. Minty and chemically.'

'Can you hear anything?'

'Footsteps.'

'Where?'

Conrad turned his head from side to side. 'Olivia's room.'

'Could it be Olivia? Children sometimes sleepwalk.'

'Too heavy. And there's two of them.' He looked up at her. 'You should phone the police.'

Lulu nodded. But as she turned, the door to Olivia's room opened and a figure appeared in the doorway. Lulu flinched as if she had been struck. It was a man, wearing dark over-alls, training shoes and a ski mask. The man froze as he saw Lulu.

Lulu backed away but Conrad stood his ground.

The man stepped slowly into the hall. There was another man behind him, also wearing a ski mask and overalls. Lulu gasped when she saw that the second man was holding Olivia in his arms. Olivia's head was back, her eyes were closed and her mouth was open.

'No!' Lulu shouted. She rushed towards the two men, her arms outstretched, fingers forming claws. 'Leave her alone!'

The first man stepped forward and shoved Lulu in the chest with gloved hands. The impact made her gasp and she staggered backwards.

There was a blur to her left as Conrad sprang forward, front paws out. His claws raked the man's ski mask and the man fell back, cursing. Conrad continued his attack by raking the man's chest with his back claws.

Lulu's back smacked into the wall and then her head pivoted and the back of her head made a sickening crunching sound, which was followed by a wave of excruciating pain. She moaned. As her legs gave way and she slid down the wall, the last thing she saw was Conrad twisting in mid-air so that he landed on the carpet on all fours. Then everything went black.

19

'Lulu? Can you hear me?'

Lulu opened her eyes and winced. The light was on and it made her eyes water, so she closed them again.

'Conrad?' she mumbled.

Someone squeezed her hand. 'No, my name is Archie. Can you open your eyes?'

Lulu did as he asked. She was back in the guest bedroom. Her head was throbbing. 'They've taken Olivia. They . . .'

The man squeezed her hand again. 'The police are here already. They're downstairs, talking to Amanda and Donald. My name's Archie. I'm a paramedic.'

Lulu blinked her eyes to focus. Archie was in his thirties, with receding hair and a kindly smile. He was wearing a green uniform and had a nametag on his pocket. He gestured at a young red-haired woman standing behind him. 'This is my colleague, Tracey. We're going to check you out and then whisk you off to hospital.'

'What about Olivia?'

'You'll have to talk to the police about that.'

Lulu tried to sit up, but pain lanced through her head and she gasped and fell back.

'Try not to move, Lulu. Now, how old are you?'

'Old enough,' she said. 'I'm perfectly okay. I can tell you who the prime minister is and what the capital of Luxembourg is, so my brain is just fine.'

Archie frowned. 'What is the capital of Luxembourg?'

'It's also Luxembourg.'

'Well, that's good to know.' Archie smiled and nodded. 'Okay, so can you turn your head to the side? Let me have a look at the damage.'

Lulu did as she was told.

'You've obviously had a bang there,' said Archie. 'I'm going to let Tracey run a few checks on you, Lulu. Then I think we'll need to take you to A&E for a scan.'

'Really, I'm fine,' said Lulu. 'Where is Conrad?'

'Conrad?'

'My cat.'

'He's sitting at the foot of the bed. He's fine. But clearly he's worried about you.'

'Listen to me, Archie. There were two men, and I think Conrad scratched one of them. You need to get a cotton bud and take samples from Conrad's front claws, right and left. There could be DNA evidence, and the longer we leave it, the more chance there is that we'll lose it.'

'Don't the police have experts for that?'

'They do. Yes. But it's Christmas, and there's no telling how long it will take to get someone here. You need to preserve the evidence as quickly as possible.' She saw the confusion on the paramedic's face. 'I used to be a police officer. Please, can you do that for me?'

'Of course,' said Archie.

Archie stood up and moved to make way for Tracey. There was a nervousness in Tracey's movements that suggested she hadn't been a paramedic for long. She pressed a digital thermometer into Lulu's ear for a few seconds, then slipped a blood pressure cuff onto her left arm. 'Temperature and blood pressure are normal,' she said after taking a reading.

'Thank you,' said Lulu.

She saw Archie use a cotton bud to scrape against Conrad's claws and breathed a sigh of relief.

Tracey clipped an oxygen monitor onto Lulu's left index finger and took her pulse while she waited for a reading. 'Pulse and oxygen levels are good,' she said.

'Thank you,' said Lulu again, but then realized that Tracey wasn't talking to her, she was talking to Archie, who was working on Conrad's claws with a second cotton bud.

Tracey patted Lulu on the shoulder. 'How much pain are you in, Lulu? On a scale of one to ten, where one is a slight discomfort and ten is a really bad toothache.'

'When I don't move it's a three, just a headache. But when I tried to sit up it was a five or six.'

'That's good,' said Tracey. She took a small torch and shone it into each of Lulu's eyes.

'So what do you think, Tracey?' asked Archie. He put the two cotton buds into a small plastic bag.

'I think we definitely need to take the patient in for a scan, but there's nothing life-threatening.'

'I think we should call Lulu by her name rather than calling her "the patient", don't you?'

Tracey's cheeks flushed. 'Sorry. Yes. I definitely think Lulu needs a scan.'

'Is that really necessary?' asked Lulu.

'It is,' said Archie. 'A nasty bang like that could easily cause internal bleeding, and you might well feel fine now but it could be a different story in a few hours. And if you did take a turn for the worse, Tracey and I would be in big trouble – and we don't want that, do we?'

Lulu couldn't help but smile. 'You're quite right,' she said. 'I really wouldn't want that.'

'The scan will be done as a matter of urgency, and assuming you get the all clear, you should be in and out within an hour or so.'

'One hears stories about people waiting in A&E for hours and hours,' said Lulu.

'That does happen, but cases like yours are a priority.'

'Please don't say it's because I'm an old lady,' said Lulu.

Archie laughed. 'That's not what I meant and you're clearly not old. I meant a bang on the head. That's the priority.' He looked at Tracey. 'And how do you propose that we get Lulu to the ambulance?'

'I can walk,' said Lulu.

'We'll never get a loaded gurney down the stairs, so it has to be a stretcher.'

'Really, I can walk,' said Lulu.

'I'm sure that you think you can,' said Archie. 'But if there's internal damage, walking could exacerbate it. So, yes, it's a stretcher for you.'

Lulu sighed. 'Health and safety.'

'You say that as if it's a bad thing,' said Archie.

A uniformed police officer in a high-vis vest appeared at the door. He was in his fifties with steel-grey hair and a darker moustache. 'Is she well enough to talk?' he asked.

'I'm fine,' said Lulu.

'Lulu keeps saying she's fine, but the damage to the back of her head suggests otherwise,' said Archie. 'We're about to take her to hospital.'

'I just need to know if you can describe the men who hurt you?' the policeman asked Lulu.

'They were wearing ski masks, and it was dark,' said Lulu. 'They came out of Olivia's room and one of them shoved me against the wall.'

'You saw them take Olivia?'

'She was either sleeping or unconscious. I couldn't tell. One of the men was carrying her.' She pointed at Archie. 'Conrad, my cat, scratched one of the men. Archie has taken swabs from his claws.'

Archie held up the Ziploc bag and the policeman took it.

'For the SOCO team,' said Lulu. 'It might take them some time to get here, so we needed to preserve the evidence. Conrad launched himself at one of the men, the one who pushed me, and I'm pretty sure he scratched him. So there could be blood and DNA evidence.'

'That's good thinking – Mrs . . . ?'

'Lewis. Lulu Lewis. I used to be a police officer. A detective superintendent with the Met. The Balfours have already been talking to DI Juliet Donnelly about another case, so if you could give her a call and let her know what's happening, that would be great.'

The officer frowned. 'Another case?'

'It's complicated,' said Lulu. 'But I know DI Donnelly would appreciate the call.'

'I know her. Our paths have crossed a few times, and yes, I'll do that,' said the policeman. 'And just to confirm, you didn't see the two men's faces?'

'No. The ski masks and overalls meant I won't be able to identify them. And neither of them spoke.'

'So no sense of their ethnicity? Or any distinguishing features?'

'I'm sorry, no. One was about six feet tall and had big feet. Size thirteen or fourteen, maybe. The other was five ten, five eleven maybe.'

'You noticed the man's big feet?'

'My father had big feet. He was a thirteen. It's something I always notice. The one with the larger feet was the one who pushed me.'

The policeman nodded. 'Okay. Well, I'm sure that a detective will want to speak to you later.'

'So CID are on their way?'

'For a kidnapped child? It's all hands to the pumps, even on Christmas Day.'

'I'd forgotten it was Christmas Day,' said Lulu. 'Please do make sure that DI Donnelly is informed. She might well want to be SIO on this case.'

Tracey appeared at the door holding a lightweight aluminium stretcher. 'This is just to get you to the ambulance, Lulu,' she said. She placed the stretcher on the floor, parallel to the bed. 'If you can carefully sit up, we'll help you onto it.'

Lulu wanted to protest that she was sure she could walk down the stairs, but she knew that they had made up their minds she had to be carried. They were right, of course. If they didn't follow the correct protocols and something bad happened, they would be held responsible. 'Okay,' she said. Tracey helped her sit up, then eased her off the bed and onto the stretcher. 'I don't suppose Conrad can come with me,' Lulu said.

Archie laughed. 'No. I'm afraid it's humans only.'

20

Lulu's fears about A&E were unfounded – the ambulance arrived at the Royal United Hospital within five minutes, thankfully without the use of flashing lights or sirens, and three minutes after arriving at the hospital she was being examined by a young doctor who looked as if she was barely out of her teens. The doctor carried out the same tests that Tracey had done, then cleaned the wound on the back of Lulu's head. An orderly then wheeled her to a room with an MRI scanner, where an equally young technician had Lulu lie with her head in a huge white machine that whirred and rattled as it did whatever it was supposed to do. Half an hour later, the young A&E doctor was studying the results of the scan and reassuring Lulu that there was no sign of any damage. 'Just the normal sort of atrophying that we would expect in the brain of a woman of your age,' said the young doctor.

'I suppose that's good news,' said Lulu, though she did wish that the doctor had phrased it more diplomatically. No one liked to be reminded of their own mortality.

'I don't think you need stitches – the flesh is more bruised and crushed than cut. And a plaster won't be much use unless we shave that part of the head.'

'Oh, I wouldn't like that,' said Lulu.

'That's what I thought,' said the doctor. 'Just keep it clean. I'll give you some antiseptic ointment to put on it. Now, there's no need for us to admit you, but if over the next day or two you experience any headaches or dizziness, or extreme tiredness, come straight back. If you feel you need painkillers, try paracetamol. Two tablets every six hours, no more than eight over a twenty-four-hour period.'

'So I can go?'

The doctor smiled and nodded. 'You can. I would suggest you call a taxi, but if you want to wait until an ambulance is free . . .' Her expression suggested that an ambulance probably wasn't going to be an option.

'I'm more than happy to call an Uber,' Lulu said. 'Thank you so much for all your help. It can't be much fun having to work on Christmas Day.'

'Actually, it's quieter than usual, and I don't have family so I'm happy enough with a Christmas Day shift. It's New Year's Eve where it gets stressful.'

Lulu's phone rang and she looked at the screen. It was Juliet. 'I'm sorry, I need to take this,' she said.

The doctor waved and walked away.

'Lulu, I'm at the Balfours' house now. Where are you?' asked Juliet.

'I've just been released from hospital,' Lulu said.

'Is everything okay?'

'My brain is atrophying, but that's to be expected at my advanced age, according to the child doctor who examined me.'

'They said you were knocked out.'

'One of the kidnappers pushed me against the wall. I did pass out, I suppose, because I woke up in bed. I'm assuming Donald carried me there. Is there any news about Olivia?'

'Nothing so far, but we're checking CCTV to see if we

can find their vehicle. It's Christmas morning, so there isn't much traffic around.'

'Will you be SIO on the case?'

'Yes. I've already spoken to ACC Morris and he's said that I should head up the investigation. And obviously he's going to increase the size of my team, although there won't be too many bodies available on Christmas Day.'

'I'll get an Uber and see you at the house,' said Lulu.

'Why don't I come and get you?' said Juliet. 'You're not far away, and Ubers might be few and far between. It'll give us a chance to chat.'

'Thank you. Do you think you could possibly bring a sweater, some jeans and maybe my boots? I'm sitting here in my pyjamas.'

Juliet laughed. 'Of course. I'm on my way.'

It took Juliet just ten minutes to arrive at the hospital. She walked into reception with two Waitrose carrier bags, one containing Lulu's clothes and the other her boots. Lulu took them into the toilets and reappeared a few minutes later. 'Much appreciated,' she said to Juliet. 'I came in on a stretcher.'

'It sounded quite serious.' Juliet peered at the back of Lulu's head. 'Oh, that looks nasty.'

'It's bruised, that's all,' said Lulu. 'I'm good to go.'

They walked out to Juliet's Tesla. 'How did the family react to you having to work on Christmas Day?' said Lulu.

'The kids thought I was Santa when I got up. Hubby sleeps through anything.'

'I'm so sorry. This is going to ruin your Christmas.'

'It's not the first time,' said Juliet. 'They're used to it, unfortunately.'

They climbed into the car.

'How are Amanda and Donald taking things?' Lulu asked.

'Better than I had expected,' said Juliet, as she started the engine. 'Donald is putting on a brave face, as men do, but he's clearly worried. Amanda has retreated into herself. She was hysterical at first, I'm told, but now she's just quiet. You know her better than me – what's she like in a crisis?'

'She used to work for a hedge fund before she married Donald and had Olivia. Pretty unflappable, I'd have said, but everything changes when a child is in danger.'

Juliet nodded. 'It certainly does. Initially she kept demanding to know what we were doing to find Olivia, but now she's just sitting in Olivia's bedroom with Conrad.'

'Conrad's good in a crisis,' said Lulu. 'He can be a calming influence.'

'Yes. Last I saw, he was sitting on her lap and she was stroking him.' Juliet pulled out of the car park and drove away from the hospital. 'So, to bring you up to speed, the kidnappers entered through the kitchen door. Looks as if they picked the lock. We're assuming they came in through the garden.'

'They would have seen the bedroom lights go off from there,' said Lulu.

'We found traces of chloroform in Olivia's bedroom, so they must have drugged her. But after you disturbed them they went out of the front door and got into a waiting car.'

'So the car was seen?'

'Sorry, no. Waiting vehicle, I should have said. No one has reported seeing anything yet. The only person who saw the kidnappers was you, and I'm told you didn't see much?'

'They wore ski masks and overalls. Did you get the DNA sample from the paramedic?'

'I did, thank you. That was good thinking on your part. It's on its way to our forensics lab in Bristol as we speak, marked urgent. Along with the note that the kidnappers left.'

'Note?'

Juliet nodded. 'The first detectives on the scene found it, on Olivia's bed. It looks as if it was printed on the same machine that did the letter the Balfours received.' She pulled up at a red light and took the opportunity to take out her phone. She scrolled through to a picture and handed the phone to Lulu just as the light turned green.

Lulu peered at the screen. The words on the letter were all in capital letters.

WE HAVE OLIVIA. NOTHING WILL HAPPEN TO HER PROVIDING YOU TRANSFER £250,000 TO THE BITCOIN WALLET WE GAVE YOU BEFORE. YOU HAVE 48 HOURS TO COMPLY.

She wrinkled her nose. 'So they're upping the ante,' she said. 'Now they want a quarter of a million pounds.'

'You have to wonder what changed,' said Juliet. 'Their initial plan was presumably to get a number of parents to hand over fifty thousand pounds so that their kids would be left alone. That made sense. But now they've taken Olivia and want a quarter of a million for her return.'

'Perhaps that was their plan from the start,' said Lulu. 'Get them primed to pay and then ask for more.' She read the note again. 'Forty-eight hours isn't long, is it?'

'Especially when you realize it's Christmas Day and Boxing Day, so the banks are shut.'

'It's not very threatening, is it? It doesn't spell out what will happen. In fact it's the opposite, basically saying that nothing will happen to her providing they get what they want. I mean, the sentiment is there, sure, but it's not an aggressive letter.' She looked at the phone. 'No mention of the police, did you notice that?'

'I did. The first letter was very specific about not talking to the police.'

'I suppose they might have assumed that after an abduction, the police would obviously be called in,' said Lulu.

'Even so, you might have expected them to make the same threat again.'

'Have Amanda and Donald seen the note?'

'They've seen it, yes, but they didn't find it. They heard you being attacked in the hall, and when they left their room they heard the kidnappers heading down the stairs. The kidnappers got into whatever vehicle they were using and fled the scene before Donald and Amanda reached the pavement. Donald called 999 and then carried you into the bedroom. Two uniformed officers attended and secured the scene, but it wasn't until CID got there that the note was found.'

'It's all very strange, isn't it?' said Lulu. 'I don't understand the escalation. Why take the risk of carrying out another kidnapping? And one that involved breaking into a house, too. Abducting a child on the street is difficult enough, but creeping through an occupied house at night is much more high risk.'

'I wonder if it was always part of the plan? First kidnap Poppy Novak. Then send out letters to however many parents demanding money to keep their children safe. Then kidnap Olivia to show that they're serious. It's bad enough for the Balfours, but when it gets out that Olivia has also been taken, then presumably every other parent who received a letter is going to think about paying. I wonder if the kidnappers will be sending out photographs of Olivia saying that their kids will be next?'

'That's so . . . clinical,' said Lulu.

'Clinical?'

'Maybe that's not the right word. It just seems so well planned, as if they're moving people around like chess pieces. As if they've had a plan right from the start, and we're only seeing it bit by bit as it happens.'

'But it has all been planned, hasn't it?' said Juliet. 'Right from the start. Whoever they are, they're professionals. I can't believe they haven't done this before.'

'Maybe they have,' said Lulu. 'There have been abductions in the past where the victim has been found or returned with no ransom having been paid. Or the assumption has been that no ransom was paid. It could have been that the ransom itself was just a threat to force other people to part with their money. The National Crime Agency would probably have a national database of kidnappings. The thing is, these people, whoever they are, seem to be experts at staying below the radar. I don't see how we'd be able to identify cases of extortion linked to kidnappings where the victim was returned. But I have good contacts within the NCA, so let me put out some feelers.'

21

It was just after ten o'clock when Lulu and Juliet arrived at the Royal Crescent. 'So what do you plan to do today?' asked Lulu as they walked towards the Balfour house.

'I'm hoping to have at least eight detectives on the team before lunch, so I'll need to brief them,' said Juliet. 'We've had uniforms knocking on doors along the Royal Crescent, but I want some detectives to repeat the process. Later today, I'm hoping to get that list from Olivia's school administrator of children who were absent over the last few days of term; and I need detectives to chase up out-of-hours contacts at other schools in the area. Christmas or not, we'll get them to dig out the information. Then I'm going to visit the homes of any likely families we find out about, because I think it's going to need a gentle touch.'

'Oh, that was such a good show,' said Lulu.

Juliet frowned. 'What was?'

'*The Gentle Touch*. It was on in the early eighties.' Lulu laughed. 'Oh, before you were born, of course. It was a police procedural, well ahead of its time. Long before *Prime Suspect* and the like. Jill Gascoine played a detective inspector based at Seven Dials police station. She was actually one of the reasons I joined the police. I wanted to be her. Or at least I wanted to be the character she played.'

'I wanted to be Helen Mirren,' said Juliet. 'Or rather, Jane Tennison.'

'Not Juliet Bravo?' Lulu laughed again. 'No, of course, that was in the early eighties too.'

'Juliet Bravo?'

'Another TV cop show with a female lead. This one starred Stephanie Turner, and she ran a police station in Lancashire. Before your time. Yes, I was a big *Prime Suspect* fan back in the day. And Jane Tennison made detective superintendent long before me.'

They reached the house. There was a uniformed constable in a high-vis jacket standing outside the front door, and he stepped aside so that Juliet could ring the doorbell. The door was opened by Donald. He was wearing a black polo-neck sweater and jeans, and he hadn't shaved. He looked exhausted, but he managed a smile when he saw Lulu. 'I'm so glad you're okay,' he said.

'How's Amanda?'

Donald grimaced. 'Not good. She's sitting in Olivia's bedroom.' He looked at Juliet. 'Is there any news?'

'Nothing yet,' said Juliet. 'As soon as I hear anything, you'll be the first to know.'

Donald opened the door wide and Juliet followed Lulu into the hall. 'I'll go up and see Amanda,' said Lulu.

'I'll take you,' said Donald. He smiled at Juliet. 'Make yourself at home in the kitchen.'

Donald and Lulu headed up the stairs as Juliet went down the hall to the kitchen.

The door to Olivia's bedroom was shut. Donald knocked quietly before easing it open. 'Darling, Lulu is back,' he said.

Amanda was sitting on Olivia's bed, gazing out of the window that overlooked the garden. She was wearing red and blue striped pyjamas.

'Amanda?' said Lulu quietly. There was no reaction, so Lulu walked over to the bed and sat down next to Amanda. Conrad was curled up on Amanda's lap.

'Are you okay?' asked Lulu, even though she knew the answer. Amanda's daughter had been snatched in the middle of the night; how could she possibly be okay?

Amanda forced a smile but her eyes were blank, devoid of any emotion. 'Obviously not,' she said. 'How about you? Donald says they hit you.' She spoke mechanically, without emotion, and continued to stare out of the window. Donald walked over and put a hand on her shoulder but she showed no reaction.

'One of them pushed me and I banged my head against the wall. Nothing serious.'

Amanda continued to stroke Conrad. 'I can't bear this, Lulu. I really can't.'

'We'll get through it,' said Lulu. 'This is a kidnapping, Amanda. It's all about money. They won't hurt Olivia, it's all about keeping her safe.'

'We're paying the ransom. Today.' Amanda looked up at Donald. 'Right? We're paying?'

'If that's what you want, yes,' Donald said.

'Are you sure that's wise?' asked Lulu.

'If we'd paid the fifty thousand pounds when they first asked for it, they wouldn't have taken Olivia.'

'We don't know that for sure, Amanda.'

'I'm not making the same mistake again. We're paying and that's the end of it.'

'Have you got the money? I thought there was an issue with the banks?'

'I've spoken to Ivan, the guy I worked for at the hedge

fund. He's richer than God and he's already promised me that he'll lend me whatever I need. He spends more than a quarter of a million on wine in a year – and that's just the wine he drinks, not the bottles he puts in his cellars.'

'Did you tell him that Olivia had been kidnapped?'

'I just said that I had a family emergency and that we needed a short-term loan. He didn't ask for details. It means nothing to him in the grand scheme of things, and he's a friend, not just a former boss. And it's not as if we don't have the money, it's just that it's not liquid. Anyway, long story short, the cash will be in our account later today and Donald says he's sure he can do the Bitcoin transaction.'

'Have you spoken to Juliet about this?'

'It's nothing to do with her.'

'Well, she is SIO on the case. Senior Investigating Officer. She's organizing the team that's looking for Olivia.'

Amanda snorted contemptuously. 'Do you think she'll have any more luck than they've had looking for Poppy Novak? She's been gone over a week already and they don't seem to be any closer to finding her. I'm not putting Olivia through that. I want her back, and I want her back today.' For the first time, she turned to look at Lulu. The blankness had gone and now her eyes were burning with a fierce intensity.

'I know you do, Amanda. But it's not as simple as that. You need to be sure that the money you send gets to the right people. And you need proof of life.'

Amanda gasped. 'Oh, why would you say that? Why would you even think that she's . . .' She couldn't bring herself to finish the sentence.

'Darling, don't upset yourself,' said Donald.

Lulu held up her hands. 'That's not what I meant, Amanda. It's a technical term. It means that the kidnappers need to prove that they have her, and that she is okay. What if you transfer the Bitcoin and she isn't released?'

'They left a note, didn't they? And the note says that if we pay them two hundred and fifty thousand, they'll give Olivia back to us. So that's what we're going to do.'

Conrad jumped down off Amanda's lap and padded over to Lulu. He rubbed himself against her legs and she stroked the back of his neck.

'Do you need anything, Amanda?' Lulu asked.

Amanda shook her head. 'I just want my daughter back.'

Lulu scooped Conrad up and put him on her shoulders. 'I'll be in the kitchen with Juliet,' she said. 'Do you want something to eat? Or a cup of tea? Coffee?'

Amanda shook her head but didn't say anything.

'You should try to get some sleep,' said Donald. 'Or at least lie down. Did you take one of your sleeping pills?'

'I don't want to sleep, Donald. I want to be awake for when they call.'

'Okay, whatever you think is best. I'll take Lulu downstairs but I'll be back shortly.'

Amanda stared at the wall, motionless.

Lulu and Donald went downstairs and into the kitchen.

'How is she?' asked Juliet, who was sitting at the island.

'She's shattered, in shock, obviously,' said Lulu. 'She's determined to pay the kidnappers.'

'We think it's best,' said Donald.

The doorbell rang. 'Are you expecting anyone?' Juliet asked.

Donald shook his head.

'It's probably one of my team,' said Juliet. She slid off her stool and headed down the hall.

'Do you want a coffee?' Donald asked Lulu.

'I'd love a cup of tea.'

'Tea it is,' said Donald. He went over to the kettle and switched it on.

'You're sure about paying the kidnappers?' Lulu asked.

'I don't see that we have any choice,' said Donald. 'What happens if we don't pay?'

'Then they'll have to communicate with you again. And every time they make contact, they give us a chance of tracing them.'

'But if we give them what they want, we get her back straight away.'

'That's not guaranteed, Donald. You have to be aware of that.'

They heard footsteps in the hall. It was Juliet with DI Kemp behind her. He was wearing a black raincoat with the collar up. 'I came over as soon as I heard what happened, Mr Balfour,' he said. 'I'm so sorry. Rest assured we'll do whatever we can to get your daughter back.' He held out his hand. 'I'm DI Simon Kemp, I'm in charge of the Poppy Novak kidnapping investigation.'

Donald shook his hand. 'Any progress on that front?'

'It's still very much an active investigation,' said Kemp, which Lulu knew was his way of saying 'no, none at all'.

DI Kemp looked over at Lulu, and for a crazy second or two she thought he had read her mind. 'I'm told the men who took Olivia assaulted you, Mrs Lewis?' he said.

'Just a bang on the head,' said Lulu.

'And you didn't get a look at their faces?'

'No. They were wearing overalls and ski masks.'

'But they left a note, I understand.'

'It's with our forensics people at the moment,' Juliet said. 'It seems identical to the one they received about Poppy.'

'Do you want tea?' asked Donald.

'Tea would be good, thank you,' said DI Kemp. 'Milk and two sugars.' He and Juliet climbed onto stools.

'No tea for me,' said Juliet. 'I was going to call you, DI Kemp, but I thought you might appreciate a couple of hours in bed.'

'My bag carrier wasn't as considerate,' said DI Kemp. 'He got a call from someone on your team and rang me straight away.'

'Is DC Arnold on the way?' asked Juliet.

'I said I'd come over solo, as this is going to be your case. Though I wanted to ask you about running a combined investigation, seeing as it's clearly the same kidnappers.'

'I think it's a better fit with our extortion case,' said Juliet.

DI Kemp flashed her a tight smile. 'I was pretty sure you'd see it that way,' he said. 'But obviously we need to work closely together on this. Presumably they used a vehicle?'

'We're pulling in CCTV and canvassing for witnesses.'

'At that time of the morning, there won't be many people looking out of their windows,' said DI Kemp. 'Was there anything helpful in the note?'

'Pay up or else,' said Juliet. 'Except now they want two hundred and fifty thousand pounds paid into the Bitcoin wallet.'

'Any sort of deadline?'

'Forty-eight hours,' said Juliet.

'And what's your game plan?'

His question was addressed to Juliet, but it was Donald who answered. 'We're going to pay it. End of.'

He brought over two mugs of tea, gave one to DI Kemp and handed the other to Lulu.

'I'm not sure that's the best course of action,' said DI Kemp.

'Best for whom?' asked Donald.

'For a start, you have no guarantee that paying the ransom will result in your daughter being released.'

'Well, that really is the definition of kidnapping, isn't it?' said Donald. 'They get their money, we get our daughter back.'

'That's the theory, yes. But we don't get many kidnappings by strangers here in the UK. Usually it's when business partners fall out, or a parent takes a child during a custody battle. What we've seen with Poppy Novak and your daughter is a very rare occurrence, so it's hard to make predictions. But I can tell you that in the US, the FBI reckons fewer than half of all kidnappings end up with the hostage safely back home.'

Lulu saw Donald's jaw tighten and his hand begin to tremble. 'But America isn't England,' she said quickly. 'They're chalk and cheese when it comes to crime. They have more than forty thousand shooting deaths a year, and we have a couple of dozen. You can't compare what happens here with what happens in the United States.'

'Of course, you're right, but I'm just pointing out that payment of a ransom doesn't always guarantee the safe return of the hostage,' said DI Kemp. He sipped his tea.

'So what would you suggest?' asked Juliet.

'I think you need to set up a line of communication,' said DI Kemp. 'The notes are all well and good, but they only go one way. We need some sort of phone or email communication, some way that we can ask them questions. If nothing else, they need to provide proof of life.'

Lulu nodded. 'I explained that to Amanda, but she just wants to pay them.'

'As do I,' said Donald.

DI Kemp held up a hand. 'I'm not against paying a ransom, but it has to be handled carefully. And we need to establish ground rules. For instance, how will Olivia be handed back? Will they drop her off somewhere? How will she get home? And above all, how will they prove she's all right before any money is handed over?'

'How do we do that?' asked Donald. 'They've never called us, and we don't have their number.'

'A press conference, perhaps,' said DI Kemp. 'You and Mrs Balfour appeal for the kidnappers to get in touch. You could say there's a problem with the money transfer and you need to talk to them. And that you need proof that they have Olivia and that she is okay.'

'How does any of that help?' asked Donald.

'It allows us to build a relationship with them,' said Kemp.

'If they do make contact, we might be able to trace them,' said Juliet. 'And if we can persuade them to accept cash instead of Bitcoin, that gives us a better chance at following the money.'

'There is that,' said Kemp. 'But it's equally important that the kidnappers see Olivia as a person, not just a bargaining chip. That's what a press conference will do – it will personalize Olivia. And once they see her as a person, they're less likely to allow her to come to harm. My advice would be to do that as quickly as possible.'

'Did it help when the Novaks appeared on TV?' asked Donald. 'Did the kidnappers get in touch?'

'When the Novaks did their press conference, we were under the impression that a sexual predator had taken Poppy, so it was only about personalizing her. We were focused on appealing for whoever it was to let her go. We would probably have played it differently if we had known it was part of a kidnapping for money scheme.'

'These people are professionals, aren't they?' said Donald. 'Professional criminals?'

'I assume so,' said Kemp.

'Because only professionals could have taken Olivia the way they did last night?'

'Again, yes. That would be the obvious inference.'

'So if they are professionals, they're not likely to start phoning us or doing anything else that might lead to them being caught. They'll know exactly why we're asking them to make contact.' He looked at Lulu. 'Right? What do you think, Lulu?'

'I don't think they're stupid, that's for sure. They clearly have a plan that they've put a lot of thought into.'

'Exactly,' Donald said. 'And there's no reason that plan would involve hurting Olivia or Poppy. This is all about the money. And once they have their money, there's no reason at all not to release both of the girls.' He looked back at Kemp. 'We'll just pay the ransom. No tricks, no shenanigans. We behave like professionals and we'll assume that the kidnappers will reciprocate.'

'Okay, I hear you,' said DI Kemp. 'But you have to

understand that what's happened is going to be made public sooner rather than later.' He glanced at Juliet. 'Looks like you've started a house-to-house?'

'The uniforms were knocking on doors first thing and we have detectives doing it now.'

Kemp looked back at Donald. 'It's going to be obvious what's happened from the questions those detectives ask. Within hours, the street outside is going to be filled with photographers and TV crews and the kidnapping is going to be headline news.'

'Is he right?' Donald asked Juliet.

She nodded. 'I'm afraid so.'

'So what I'm saying is that if you give a press conference, at least you'll have control of the narrative,' said Kemp. 'You'll be able to present the facts as you see them, rather than have a scenario plucked from the air by a head-line-hungry journalist.'

Donald frowned and rubbed his chin. 'I'll have to talk to Amanda.'

'Maybe I should talk to her,' said Kemp.

'I'd rather you didn't,' said Juliet. 'This is my case, and dealing with two DIs might cause confusion.' She smiled. 'Remember how keen you were to remind me that you are SIO on the Poppy Novak case?'

DI Kemp held up his hands. 'I wasn't trying to muscle in on your case; it was just a suggestion. It's just that we are almost certainly after the same perpetrators. And most of the leads at the moment do seem to be on this side of the border.'

'We'll be sharing any intel, obviously,' said Juliet.

'What's your best hope?' asked Kemp.

'Ideally an eyewitness who saw them driving off with Olivia. If not, then CCTV footage that gives us a registration number. And we're still hoping we can ID the printer that produced the notes.'

'What about the experts you were getting to check the photograph of Poppy?'

'It's in hand,' said Juliet. 'What about your investigation?'

'We're waiting for a list of people who have served time for kidnapping and extortion who might be in the area. As soon as we have that we'll start knocking on doors. Other than that, it's going cold. I'm hoping that what happened here could give us something concrete to go on. That's one of the reasons I was hoping for a press conference; we could link the two cases and get some momentum going. We have two victims now, so the more people looking, the better. Someone must have seen something.'

'The problem with public appeals is that you get inundated with false leads, every one of which has to be checked,' said Juliet. 'It works best when you have a concrete description of a person or a vehicle, but we don't have that.'

'I disagree,' said DI Kemp. 'We know that there were two men, plus a driver, in a vehicle with a drugged child. We could ask anyone who was on the road at the time to check their dashcams.'

'I think a public appeal would be counterproductive,' said Juliet. Her tone suggested that she had made up her mind and wouldn't be dissuaded.

'Okay, well, what about an interview with a national newspaper? A one-on-one. A sympathetic journalist who could get the story out there.'

'The end result would be the same,' said Juliet. 'The story

will get picked up and we'll be overwhelmed with false leads that will only add to our workload.'

'The genie's out of the bottle,' said Kemp. 'The press is going to be all over it, sooner rather than later.'

'And when they do start asking questions, the press office will reply that we are investigating two missing children but that we cannot confirm that the two investigations are linked.'

Kemp looked pained. 'It's never a good idea to lie to the press. We know that the two cases are linked. The Balfours were sent a photograph of Poppy Novak, and not long afterwards their daughter was kidnapped.'

'We wouldn't be denying there is a link. We just wouldn't be confirming it.'

'That's playing with words, and you know it,' said Kemp. 'The two cases are definitely linked – the fact that the Balfours received a photograph of Poppy Novak confirms that.'

'But that information hasn't been made public. And I want it to stay that way.'

DI Kemp took a sip of tea, and Lulu had the distinct impression he was playing for time while he got his thoughts in order. Eventually he put down his mug and nodded. 'Okay, I hear what you're saying. And I understand your reservations. No one likes chasing up dead ends, and as always, we have a manpower problem.

'But look at it this way. Two children have been taken, one of them plucked from her bedroom in the middle of the night. We have already gone public with Poppy Novak, and word is going to get out soon about Olivia. The public, no matter what we do, are going to link the two cases, and if we're not careful they'll put two and two together and get five – five being that we have a serial child abductor out there.

Can you imagine the fear that would generate, if people believed a predator was taking young children from their homes? Every family with kids would go into lockdown. The media would be all over it and our bosses would find themselves under a lot of pressure. In my experience – pardon my French – shit rolls downhill, so we'd be the ones suffering.'

Juliet nodded slowly.

He did have a point, Lulu realized. Parents would be fearful, and the obvious reaction would be to keep their children at home where they could keep an eye on them. But Olivia's kidnapping meant that nobody's home was safe. Fear was a terrible thing; it could split communities and provoke overreactions. Fingers would be pointed, names would be whispered, and before long the streets would be full of vigilantes waving pitchforks and flaming torches. Well, not literally pitchforks and flaming torches, but the social media equivalent.

'This is not how I wanted to spend my Christmas Day,' said Juliet.

'You and me both,' said DI Kemp.

Juliet looked over at Lulu. 'Did you ever have a case like this when you were in the Met?'

'Kidnappings? A couple, yes. But both were gang related, and we had zero cooperation from the families of the victims. The case we had that has more in common with this was a serial rapist who was attacking women in parks across north London. He always attacked from behind and strangled his victims until they passed out, so we never had a description. He tended to pick on women who had been drinking, and several of his first victims were homeless, so we didn't realize we had a serial until about six months into his spree. We had a similar discussion to the one you're having now. To go public would have created a climate of fear. Women would feel that it wasn't safe to go out alone, vigilantes would take the law into their own hands, and innocent people could get hurt. And of course, if he knew we were onto him, he might have simply stopped or moved away and we'd never have caught him.'

'So what did you do?' asked Juliet.

'We decided to withhold the fact that we were hunting a serial rapist,' said Lulu. 'We knew we couldn't hold that information back for long, so we upped our resources and went all out to catch him. He had six different hunting grounds, all parks in north London, so we increased uniform foot and mobile patrols in five of the parks and put two undercover officers in the remaining one, with full surveillance in place. The two female officers took it in turns to walk through the park, dressed and acting the part. They were wired and we had half a dozen big beefy officers in place. On the third day, he attacked one of the women and we caught him.' She grinned. 'Job done.'

'And you couldn't have done it if you'd gone public with the fact that you were after a serial rapist,' said Juliet. She looked over at DI Kemp. 'I think we should be doing the same – going all out to capture the kidnappers without creating a climate of fear.'

'But if these kidnappers have taken two kids, they could take three. Or four. I think we have to assume that they won't stop at two, and we have to act accordingly.'

'And by act accordingly, you mean hold a press conference with the Balfours warning that other children are at risk?' said Juliet.

'We don't have to say that, obviously. But we need to put out an appeal for the kidnappers to make contact, and to let everybody know that they need to be looking out for Poppy and Olivia. Not going public made sense when you were hunting a serial rapist, but these guys know we're already after them. We've already had two press conferences with the Novaks, and they'll probably have seen all the police activity here in Royal Crescent. We wouldn't be revealing any of our cards by going public, so I don't see there's any downside. The upside is that we might force the kidnappers to open a line of communication, and we might reach someone who saw Olivia being taken.'

Juliet wrinkled her nose and tilted her head to one side. Her eyes narrowed as she considered what he had said. DI Kemp drank his tea, watching her over the top of his mug. It was an interrogator's trick, Lulu realized: leave a silence and wait for the other person to fill it.

Eventually it was Donald who spoke. 'I don't think either I nor Amanda want to be interviewed about this,' he said. There was an apologetic tone to his voice and he avoided eye contact with the two detectives. 'We've decided that we're going to pay the ransom today, so I don't see that there's anything to be gained by media exposure.'

'That's obviously your decision, Mr Balfour,' said DI Kemp, putting down his mug. 'But as I've said, you have to understand that paying the ransom does not guarantee that your daughter will be released.'

'Perhaps not, but I think we do know for sure that if we don't pay, Olivia won't be released.'

'Unless we find the kidnappers,' said Kemp.

Donald raised his head and looked the detective in the

eye. 'You haven't found Poppy Novak's kidnappers, have you? And from what I've heard, you're no closer to finding them than when she was first taken.'

'To be fair, Donald, I'm SIO on Olivia's case,' said Juliet. 'And it's only been a few hours since . . .'

Donald held up his hand to silence her. 'I'm sure you're an excellent detective and that you're more than capable of running an investigation, and you might well have what it takes to find the kidnappers. But I'm enough of a realist to know that it's going to take time. Days at best, more likely weeks. And I don't want Olivia to be in that situation for one minute longer than is necessary. I keep thinking about how absolutely terrified she must be. I can't bear it.' Tears were welling up in his eyes.

Lulu slid off her stool and put an arm around Donald. 'It's going to be okay,' she said. 'We'll get Olivia back. I know we will.'

Donald sniffed and wiped his nose with the back of his hand. 'Women's intuition?' he said.

'Based on years of experience,' Lulu said. She hugged him. 'You need to stay strong, for Amanda and for Olivia. Okay?'

Donald nodded tearfully. 'Okay,' he said.

22

Lulu's phone rang and she looked at the screen. It was Kirsty. 'I'm sorry – I need to take this,' she said.

Amanda and Donald were sitting on the sofa. Amanda was still wearing her striped pyjamas. Conrad was on her lap and she was stroking him absent-mindedly. Juliet had gone upstairs to check on the SOCO investigation. DI Kemp had left, clearly unhappy at their refusal to take part in a press conference.

Lulu went into the hall. 'Hi Kirsty, thanks for calling. Any news?'

'Lots,' said Kirsty. 'There were five transfers from the wallet, all within two minutes of the Bitcoin being paid in by the Elliotts. The five transfers went to five different wallets, and then within another two minutes, the Bitcoin from each of those five was split up and transferred to another five. By that I mean we went from one wallet to twenty-five wallets in the space of four minutes. I'm assuming that they're using some sort of automated process – either that, or they have a whole team of operators. It's a cascade effect, and there's no way of knowing how many wallets it's going to end up in. We're probably at hundreds already.'

'So these are professionals?' asked Lulu.

'Oh, there's no doubt about that,' said Kirsty. 'This has all been very well planned. They're using wallets in Russia,

Ukraine, the Czech Republic, all countries that are crypto fraud hotspots.'

'The Czech Republic?' repeated Lulu.

'Prague, Brno and Ostrava so far,' said Kirsty. 'Are you interested in Czechia, which I think is what we're meant to call it these days?'

'The father of the little girl who was abducted in Wiltshire is from there,' said Lulu. 'So it might be significant.'

'I'd say we're looking at half a dozen countries already, with more to come. They were obviously splitting the Bitcoin up into smaller and smaller amounts, and then after about ten hours they began combining the amounts. That took place mainly in Russia, and then the Bitcoin came back to the UK, and at about three o'clock in the morning it went quiet. There has been nothing since.'

'Which means what?'

'The Bitcoin was probably transferred to a hard drive wallet, which would then have been moved physically. I say hard drive, but it could just as well be a thumb drive or an SD card. Anything that can be used to store data.'

'So you can't follow the blockchain? That's what you called it, right?'

'That's right. In a way, it's a dead end. The wallet is on a hard drive or whatever and when it's unplugged, the data stays where it is until it's reconnected down the line. The thing is, the hard drive could then be taken anywhere in the world and exchanged for cash, or drugs, gold, anything of value. The buyer would just plug the hard drive into a computer or a tablet or even a phone and check that the Bitcoin is there, then hand over whatever they are exchanging the Bitcoin for.'

'But when they do eventually move the Bitcoin again, you'll be able to track it?'

'Absolutely. But we've no way of knowing when that will be.'

'Can you keep an eye out for it?'

'Of course,' said Kirsty. 'I mean, I'm at home now and won't be back in the office until the twenty-seventh, but I can monitor everything on my laptop. What about you? What are your Christmas Day plans?'

'I'm staying with the Balfours, and there's something I have to tell you. Their daughter was kidnapped last night and they've received another ransom note. The first one, the one that was just threatening to kidnap Olivia, was for fifty thousand pounds. But now they have actually taken her, and they're demanding two hundred and fifty thousand pounds.'

'Oh Lulu, that's terrible. The police are involved, obviously?'

'Yes, they're at the house now. They're carrying out full forensics, checking CCTV, everything. But as we already know, these people are professionals. I'm sure they'll have covered their tracks.'

Kirsty sighed. 'Why did the kidnappers change tack, do you think? I thought the whole point was they were only making threats?'

'That's what I thought,' said Lulu. 'But maybe that was always their plan – to threaten several parents, and then kidnap another child to prove they were serious.'

'Well, if they do pay, let me know. My phone will be on round the clock.'

'Thank you, Kirsty. I'll hope you at least get some time with your family.'

'The two missing children come first, Lulu. They're my priority right now.'

Kirsty ended the call. Lulu bit down on her lower lip as she stared at the screen. Kirsty would do whatever she could to help, Lulu knew that, but tracking the Bitcoin ransom was always going to be a long shot.

Juliet came down the stairs and looked at Lulu expectantly. 'Kirsty is looking at the Bitcoin handed over by the Elliotts,' Lulu told her. 'She thinks it might be on a thumb drive now, which makes it untraceable, for the moment at least. She did say something interesting, mind. She said that some of the money went through the Czech Republic.'

Juliet's eyebrows shot up. 'The Czech Republic?' she repeated. 'That's where Mr Novak is from.'

'Do you think DI Kemp looked into Mr Novak at any point?'

'Family members are always put under the microscope when a child is abducted,' said Juliet. 'If there had been anything untoward, I'm sure he would have found it. But I'll raise it with him, obviously.'

'How's it going with SOCO?' asked Lulu.

'Plenty of prints, but as the two men you saw were wearing gloves, it's reasonable to assume they belong to family members. There's traces of chloroform on the carpet; they must have spilled some when they were knocking her out. But chloroform is easy enough to get. They're having more luck in the garden. There are several footprints in the soil around the door where they gained entrance.'

'What about CCTV?'

'There are no cameras in the Royal Crescent, and not a single video doorbell. So no CCTV footage. But there are council cameras in the area, and we'll be checking footage from the time the kidnapping occurred.'

'Juliet, do you think that they should pay the ransom?'

'That has to be their decision, of course.'

'But what do *you* think they should do?'

'That's a difficult question, Lulu. Do you have children?'

Lulu shook her head. 'No.'

'As a parent, you'd do anything to keep them safe. If one of my kids was kidnapped . . .' She shuddered. 'I'd do anything. Literally anything. The safety of my kids trumps everything.'

'What's your experience of paying ransoms? Are the victims usually released?'

'Oh, Lulu, this is Avon and Somerset. Kidnappings hardly ever happen here, and when they do it's usually a parent in a messy divorce who runs away with their own child. Kidnappings for money, well, they never happen, not here. But I'm assuming if you pay, the victim is returned safe and sound. I can't see them killing a child, can you? I mean, abducting a child is bad enough, but to kill a child in cold blood . . .' She shuddered again. 'Who could possibly do that?'

'There are a lot of sick people in the world, Juliet. But hurting children is as bad as it gets. These people do seem to be professionals, and they'll know that if they do hurt Poppy or Olivia and they get caught, they'll be behind bars for the rest of their lives.'

'I hope you're right,' said Juliet. She looked at her watch. 'I'm going to have to go,' she said. 'I need to talk to the team, and then I'll call DI Kemp and bring him up to speed on what SOCO have found.'

'Will you get to spend time with your family?'

'I'll miss the present-opening. Well, I've missed that already. I'm hoping to get back to do the cooking at some point today. But I'm on this 24/7 now, as are all the team. What about you?'

'I'll stay here until it's resolved, one way or another.'

'I wonder if you could do me a favour, Lulu. Usually in a case like this I'd be sending in a family liaison officer, but considering that it's Christmas – would you mind taking on that role?'

'Of course, I'd be happy to. I'm sure Donald and Amanda would prefer not to have a stranger in the house.'

'Thank you.' Juliet looked at her watch again. 'I have to rush, sorry. If anything happens, if anyone calls, you have my mobile number. Call me any time, day or night.'

'I will do,' said Lulu. She walked Juliet to the front door.

'The SOCO team will be here a while longer and will probably let themselves out,' said Juliet. 'I'll come back later this afternoon to check in.'

Lulu opened the door. A large constable in a high-vis jacket was standing on the step, his arms folded.

'We'll have someone out front for the rest of the day,' said Juliet. 'The house is still a crime scene, obviously, and we don't want any journalists pestering the Balfours.'

'That's the last thing they need,' said Lulu.

'I wish there was more I could do,' said Juliet. 'It's just the worst time of the year to get things done. I'll press the DNA people for results of the swab from Conrad's claws – that has to be our best hope of identifying the kidnappers.' She forced a smile. 'We were lucky that Conrad was there.'

Lulu nodded. 'Yes, we were.'

23

Amanda refused to eat all morning. Donald asked her what they should do about cooking the turkey, and she burst into tears and said she wouldn't be cooking Christmas dinner until Olivia was home. Lulu understood what she meant. There was no way that they would be able to enjoy their food while they were worrying about Olivia.

At about eleven o'clock, Amanda went upstairs to sit in Olivia's bedroom, but the SOCO team were still there. She returned to the sitting room with tears in her eyes and sat down on the sofa again, and Conrad stepped carefully onto her lap. She stroked his fur.

Lulu was sitting in an armchair by the window. She didn't know what to say. There were simply no words. If there had been a bereavement, then there would be ways of expressing empathy and sympathy, of sharing memories of the loved one who had departed. But Olivia wasn't dead – she had been taken, and they had no way of knowing where she was or what she was going through. There was nothing Lulu could say, other than that the police would be doing everything they could. That was probably true, but it was no comfort. They had no control over the situation and there was nothing to do but sit, wait and worry.

They all jerked as the phone rang in the hallway.

'Is that them?' asked Amanda, looking at Donald.

Donald didn't say anything. He got to his feet and hurried out of the room.

'Is that them?' Amanda repeated to Lulu. There was a faraway look in her eyes, as if she wasn't aware of her surroundings. Lulu smiled but didn't reply.

Amanda looked over at the door. They heard Donald pick up the phone and the murmur of his voice. Then he shouted 'And don't call here again!' and slammed the receiver down.

His cheeks were flushed when he walked back into the room. 'Damn journalists!' he said. 'Have they got nothing better to do with their time?'

'How did they get our number?' asked Amanda. 'We're ex-directory.'

'Probably hacked it,' said Donald. 'That's what they do, isn't it?' He began to pace up and down.

'Don't let them upset you, Donald,' said Lulu. 'They're just doing their job.'

'They're bloody parasites, that's what they are,' he said. 'Intruding on grief. It's not right.'

He dropped down onto the sofa next to Amanda and patted her on the leg. 'I'm sorry,' he said.

'It's not your fault,' she said. She smiled, but her lower lip was trembling.

Time ticked by. Several times, Donald asked if he should cook something to eat, but Amanda just shook her head. Lulu didn't feel like eating either.

A phone rang in the kitchen, and Amanda jerked as if she had been stung. 'That's my mobile,' she said.

'I'll get it,' said Donald, hurrying out of the room. He

returned a few seconds later, holding her still-ringing phone. 'Number withheld,' he said.

She reached for it, frowned at the screen, and then took the call. She listened, then moaned and hurled the phone across the room before bursting into tears.

Lulu rushed over and sat down next to Amanda. 'Whatever's wrong?' she asked, putting an arm around her.

Donald picked up the phone and put it to his ear. 'Hello?' he said. He sneered as he listened, then ended the call with a stab of his finger. 'Another bloody journalist,' he said. He put the phone on the coffee table. 'Can't we block them or something?' he asked Lulu.

'They can use pay-as-you-go mobiles,' said Lulu. 'And it's not an offence to phone somebody for information.'

'It's stalking,' said Donald. 'It's intrusion. It's just . . .' He flailed his arms in the air, lost for words.

'You should turn the ringer off,' said Lulu. 'They'll keep trying.'

'No!' said Amanda quickly. 'We need to know if the kidnappers call. We have to keep the phones on.'

'They haven't phoned before,' said Lulu. 'They've only communicated through letters. There's no reason to believe that they'll suddenly start using the phone.'

'But they might,' said Amanda. 'We don't know. And we need to have the phones on in case the police call.'

'If there's any news, Juliet will probably call my number,' said Lulu. 'If one journalist managed to get your number, others probably will too. You don't have to switch it off – just mute it so that the ringing doesn't annoy you.'

Amanda nodded. She picked up the phone and muted it

before putting it back on the coffee table. 'What do they hope to gain by speaking to us?' she said.

'They want a story for their paper or their website,' said Lulu. 'Clickbait. The more people who click on their websites or buy their papers, the more money they make from advertisers.'

'But what do they expect us to say? We don't know anything.'

'They just want a reaction from you. To know how you're feeling.'

'But that doesn't help anyone, does it?' said Amanda.

'It's not about helping, though, is it?' said Donald. 'They don't want to help.'

Lulu's phone rang and she took it out. Donald pointed at it. 'See? They won't give up!'

Lulu looked at the screen and shook her head. 'It's Juliet.' She put the phone to her ear. 'Hello?'

'Lulu, we've struck lucky with the DNA sample from Conrad's claws. Can I pick you up outside in about fifteen minutes?'

'Of course.'

'My bag carrier still hasn't turned up and I'd appreciate an extra pair of eyes on the case.'

'Two pairs,' said Lulu. 'I'll bring Conrad.'

As she was putting her phone away, Lulu heard footsteps on the stairs. It was the SOCO team, still wearing their white coveralls and blue shoe protectors. Lulu went into the hallway. Three of the officers went out of the front door, but the fourth, a woman in her thirties carrying a large black case, smiled and nodded at Lulu. 'I'm Emma,' she said. 'Emma Burke. Are you by any chance Lulu?'

'I am, yes.'

'Excellent,' she said. 'Juliet said I should liaise with you. We're done with Olivia's room now. Lots of prints and DNA, obviously, so we need to start eliminating family. We have Olivia's hairbrush and toothbrush, so we have her DNA and fingerprints, but we'll be needing samples from anyone else in the house.'

'That would be Donald and Amanda, Olivia's parents. And I was here, of course.'

Lulu took Emma into the sitting room and explained to Donald and Amanda what she needed to do.

Emma nodded and smiled at Amanda. 'So, I'll take your fingerprints electronically with a handheld scanner, and I'll need to take a swab from your cheek. It's all quite painless.'

'Did you find anything in Olivia's room?' asked Donald.

'Plenty of prints, but then we'd expect that in a child's bedroom. We were told the kidnappers were wearing gloves, so they'll probably all be from family. We found some hairs and traces of soil. The soil was probably brought upstairs on the shoes. We'll check the hair, but they were wearing ski masks, right?'

Lulu nodded. 'They were. Juliet said you found footprints in the garden?'

'We did, yes. Several very good prints.' Emma looked over at Donald. 'What shoe size are you, Mr Balfour?'

'Me? Eight.'

'These were ten, and they're training shoes. Nike, I think, but I'll have to wait until I'm back in the lab until I'm sure.'

'I never wear Nikes,' said Donald.

'You do have a pair of Nike golf shoes,' said Amanda. 'But they have those little spikes in, don't they?' She turned to Emma anxiously. 'Was there any blood? Did they hurt her?'

'We found no blood at all,' said Emma. 'Not a spot. We did find traces of chloroform, so we think that they soaked a cloth in chloroform and used that to knock Olivia out.'

'Oh no!' said Amanda, clasping her hands to her face. 'My poor baby.' She looked across at Donald, tears welling up in her eyes. 'She must have been terrified.'

Emma gave Amanda a consoling smile. 'At least if she was asleep, she wouldn't have known what was happening. That's something.' She bent down and opened her case. 'Right, let me get your prints and DNA and I'll be on my way.'

24

Lulu and Conrad only had to wait a couple of minutes outside the house before Juliet arrived in her Tesla. Lulu climbed in and fastened her seatbelt. Conrad sat in her lap.

'How are the Balfours?' asked Juliet as she put the car in gear and drove away from the kerb.

'As well as can be expected,' said Lulu.

'They're still going to pay?'

'I think so, yes. Paying the ransom at least gives them some control over the situation. They just want to do something. The alternative is to sit and wait for you to find the kidnappers.' She managed a pained smile at Juliet. 'I wasn't being critical,' she said. 'I know you're doing your best.'

'I know how frustrating it can be. But identifying the DNA is a big step forward. ACC Morris called the lab and asked that they prioritize the sample from Conrad's claws, and they got a hit.'

'That's amazing.'

'Shows you what friends in high places can do,' said Juliet. 'Anyway, the DNA from Conrad's claws was a match to one Steven Chorley, who works as a courier in Chippenham and the surrounding area. He owns and drives a white Renault van and we're running the registration number through ANPR as we speak.'

'Why did you have his DNA on file?'

'He was arrested four years ago on charges of assault and

affray after an argument in a pub. The charges were later dropped but his DNA stayed in the system, luckily for us.'

'But no other criminal record?'

'No. Just the assault and affray arrest and the odd speeding ticket. Lives with his wife and two children on a council estate outside Chippenham.'

'And he's definitely the guy that Conrad scratched?'

'The odds are twenty billion to one that he's not. Pretty good odds, considering there are only eight billion people on the planet.'

Juliet headed out of Bath on the A4 and drove towards Chippenham. In less than twenty minutes they were driving through an estate of drab, featureless council houses on the outskirts of the city. The Tesla's satnav led them to a row of brown-brick terraced houses facing a square grass area.

'There's his van,' said Juliet, pointing at a line of parked vehicles. She looked around and spotted a police patrol car. 'And there's our guys,' she said, and drove over, reversed and parked next to it.

The passenger-side window of the patrol car wound down. There was a grey-haired sergeant in the passenger seat and he nodded at Juliet. 'There's people in there, but we haven't seen him, so we can't say for sure that he's inside.' He gestured at the Renault van. 'That's his. How do you want to play it?'

'There were no weapons used in the kidnapping, so I think Lulu and I should just knock on the door.'

'Are you going to arrest him?'

'That's the idea, yes. We found his DNA at a kidnapping scene, so we need to take him in for questioning.'

'What if he does a runner?'

'You can block his van in, then he's on foot.'

'I'm not a great one for running,' said the sergeant. He nodded his chin at the driver, a young Asian woman. 'But Jasmine here is swift on her feet.'

'Good to know,' said Juliet. 'To be honest, once we tell him we have his DNA at the scene, he'll probably realize there's no point in running. Is there a back way out?'

'There's a small walled garden behind the house. He could get out that way.'

'Maybe you could cover that, just in case he does run. Jasmine can use the car to block the van if necessary.'

'Is that a cat?' asked the sergeant, noticing Conrad for the first time.

'This is Lulu Lewis, a former Metropolitan Police super-intendent, who's assisting me on the case. Conrad is with her.'

Conrad stood up and stretched.

'Lovely cat,' said the sergeant. 'I have two tuxedos at home.'

'Tuxedos?' repeated Lulu.

'Black-and-white toms. They look for all the world as if they're wearing evening dress,' said the sergeant. 'They've never come on duty with me, though.'

'Conrad is a special cat,' said Juliet. 'In fact, he's the reason we're here. He scratched Mr Chorley, which is how we got his DNA.'

'That's one smart cat,' said the sergeant.

'Meow,' said Conrad.

'He says thank you,' said Lulu, and the sergeant laughed. 'So he talks?'

'Incessantly,' said Lulu. She and Juliet climbed out of the car. Lulu picked Conrad up and placed him on her shoulders.

The sergeant got out of the patrol car, put on his peaked hat and walked over to an alley that led behind the row of terraced houses.

'Are you planning on playing good cop, bad cop?' asked Lulu with a sly smile.

'I always find that chatty cop, smiley cop works best,' said Juliet.

'So I'll be smiley cop?'

'Let's see how it goes,' said Juliet. 'We can keep our options open.'

They walked slowly towards the house. There were three windows – two upstairs that were probably bedrooms and a larger one to the left of the front door, which featured a large holly wreath. As they got closer, Lulu realized that the wreath was plastic. 'Merry Xmas' was written across it in curvy red writing.

Juliet pressed the doorbell and after a couple of seconds the door was opened by a woman in her thirties with long permed hair and black-framed spectacles that gave her the look of a frazzled librarian. She was wearing a baggy polo-neck sweater, a short denim skirt and a pair of grubby Pokémon slippers.

Juliet held out her warrant card. 'Good afternoon, Mrs Chorley. I'm Detective Inspector Donnelly and this is my colleague, Lulu Lewis. We'd like a word with your husband.'

'He's not here,' said Mrs Chorley. 'What's this about?'

There were sudden shouts from behind her – two children arguing, from the sound of it. Mrs Chorley twisted round. 'Jordan, Noah, keep the noise down. We've got visitors.'

'We need to speak to your husband, Mrs Chorley.'

Mrs Chorley turned back to look at them. 'I just told you, he's not here.'

'That's his van outside, isn't it?'

'Someone picked him up at about half past ten this morning. He said he had to do an extra shift.'

'But he's a courier, right?' said Juliet. 'He'd need his van, surely?'

'Sometimes he works in the warehouse. They usually pay him overtime for that. It's because of the Christmas rush, obviously. He only got back in at five o'clock this morning after working a night shift. But they're short-handed, so he had to go in when they phoned him. The boys were in tears, but Steven said he was needed by Santa Claus so that all the children in the world would get their presents on Christmas Day.'

'Did he say when he'd be back?'

'He didn't,' said Mrs Chorley. 'I phoned him to see when we could expect him and that's when I found out that he'd left his phone in the bedroom. I suppose he was in such a hurry that he forgot it.'

'Would you mind letting us borrow the phone, Mrs Chorley?' asked Juliet.

The woman frowned. 'Is something wrong?'

'We need to know your husband's whereabouts,' said Juliet. 'His phone might help to answer our questions.'

Mrs Chorley's frown deepened. 'Don't you need a warrant for that?'

'Only if you have a problem with giving us the phone,' said Juliet. 'If you do have a problem, we could get a judge to issue a warrant. But it's Christmas Day, and I don't think any judge would want to be disturbed on Christmas Day, do you?'

'I suppose not. Look, you said you want to know about Steven's whereabouts, but I've already told you, he's at work. You can see him there.'

'We will do, Mrs Chorley, but we really would like a look at his phone. Could you get it for us?'

Mrs Chorley smiled, but there was a worried look in her eyes. 'Has Steven done something wrong?' she asked.

'That's what we're looking into,' said Juliet. 'At the moment we're just making enquiries. Can we come inside? Better we don't have the neighbours wondering what's going on.'

Mrs Chorley's jaw tightened and for a moment Lulu thought that she was going to close the door in their faces. Then she relaxed and opened it wide. 'Go through to the kitchen,' she said. 'The boys are in the living room on their PlayStation.'

Lulu and Conrad followed Juliet down a narrow hallway to a small kitchen which overlooked a tiny paved area with rubbish bins against one wall and two children's bicycles against another. The kitchen was shabby and the appliances were old, but it was clean and the fridge was covered with family photographs held in place by magnets. Mrs Chorley appeared at the door. 'Please sit down. I'll get Steven's phone,' she said, gesturing at a small circular pine table with four chairs.

Lulu and Juliet sat down. Conrad jumped off Lulu's shoulders and landed on the linoleum with a dull plop. He sniffed the air, his tail pointing straight up like a radio antenna. Then he padded across the floor towards the door.

'Now where's he going?' asked Juliet.

'Probably just having a look around,' said Lulu. 'He is a very curious cat.'

'Didn't curiosity kill the cat?' asked Juliet.

'I'm told that's apocryphal,' said Lulu.

'By whom?'

Before Lulu could answer, Mrs Chorley returned with a Samsung smartphone, which she handed to Juliet. 'I don't suppose you know the PIN, do you?' Juliet asked.

'Actually, I do. Steven doesn't know that I do, but I do.' She gave Juliet the PIN and sat down at the table. 'Is Steven in trouble?' she asked after a moment.

'We're still gathering information,' said Juliet. 'How has he seemed over the last day or two?'

'He wasn't happy, but then he's been working so hard. Fifteen hours a day and more. So he's been snapping at me and the kids, but I do understand – he's not getting enough sleep. It's the busiest time of the year, obviously.'

Juliet tapped at the screen and wrinkled her nose. 'Who was it who called him this morning?' she asked. 'There's a phone number but no name.'

'Steven didn't say, but it must have been someone from work. Whoever it was picked him up half an hour later.'

'Did you see who it was? Or what car they were driving?'

Mrs Chorley shook her head. 'No. Sorry. Look, what do you think he's done?'

'At this stage we're just making enquiries,' said Juliet. She held up the phone. 'Would you mind if we keep this for a while? It will help us to determine where Steven has been over the past few days.'

'I suppose so,' said Mrs Chorley.

'I can't help but notice all the photographs on the fridge,' said Lulu. 'Some of them are really good.'

'Oh, that's Steven. He's always been mad keen on photography. It was his dream to be a professional photographer and have his own studio, but our dreams don't always come true, do they?' She smiled a little sadly. 'I certainly didn't get my dream.'

'What was that?' asked Lulu. 'Your dream?'

'I always wanted to work with animals. To be a vet, maybe. Or to own my own riding school.'

'You like horses?'

'I love all animals. But yes, horses especially.'

'Do you ride?' Lulu asked.

Mrs Chorley snorted dismissively. 'Does it look as if I can afford to ride horses? We never had any money when I was a kid and I have even less now. Even with all the hours that Steven works, we barely have enough to get by.'

'Have you thought about doing volunteer work for the RSPCA?'

Mrs Chorley frowned. 'Really? You can do that?'

'I have friends who do it in London. They always need helpers, in all sorts of roles.'

Juliet nodded. 'They have a shop in Chippenham. You could reach out to them. And there's the Bath Cats and Dogs Home charity, which isn't far from here,' she added. 'I know for a fact that they are always looking for volunteers.'

'It's not easy when you have two young kids.'

'You could do a few hours a week, while the boys are at school,' said Lulu. 'I get that life isn't easy, but you should never give up on your dreams.' She smiled encouragingly. 'So does Steven have his own equipment?'

Mrs Chorley nodded. 'He has a Canon camera and some long lenses. All of it second-hand.'

'Is it digital or film?' asked Lulu.

'Digital,' said Mrs Chorley. 'Film costs an arm and a leg. But digital is free once you have the equipment.'

'Do you think we could possibly borrow the camera, Mrs Chorley?' Lulu asked.

'Why? Why would you want his camera?'

'For our enquiries,' said Lulu. 'It would be helpful to know what he has been photographing.'

'I don't think that Steven would be happy if I handed over his camera.'

'I understand. But he's not here, and it would help us with our enquiries,' said Lulu.

'And it wouldn't be difficult for us to get a warrant,' said Juliet. 'But as I said, it's never a good idea to disturb a judge on Christmas Day.'

Mrs Chorley grimaced, then sighed theatrically and stood up. 'Right, fine,' she said, and headed out of the kitchen. They heard her going heavy-footed up the stairs.

'Well spotted about the camera,' said Juliet.

'Lucky guess,' said Lulu.

'No, astute observation,' said Juliet. 'I saw the photographs on the fridge too, but I didn't make the connection.'

They heard Mrs Chorley coming down the stairs, and then she appeared in the doorway holding a Canon SLR with a long lens attached. Lulu and Juliet stood up. Juliet took the camera from Mrs Chorley.

'How long will you need it for?' Mrs Chorley asked.

'Just a day or two,' said Juliet, although Lulu realized that probably wasn't true. If Steven Chorley had used the camera to take photographs of Olivia and Poppy, it would be evidence – evidence that could well see him behind bars for a long time. 'We'll take good care of it. If your husband should call you, would you tell him I need to speak with him?' Juliet took a business card from her bag and gave it to Mrs Chorley. 'My mobile number is on the card.' She smiled. 'We'll see ourselves out.'

As they headed for the front door, Conrad came down the stairs, his tail still a stiff antenna. 'Now where have you been, you naughty boy?' said Lulu, scooping him up and putting him on her shoulders.

Juliet opened the front door. The two boys started shouting excitedly in the living room as Lulu and Juliet stepped outside. Juliet pulled the door closed and they walked over to the car. The sergeant hurried over from the rear of the house, flicking away a cigarette butt that bounced along the tarmac in a shower of sparks. 'Not there?' he said.

'He left at ten thirty this morning. Somebody picked him up,' said Juliet.

'That's a pity,' said the sergeant. 'So, we can stand down?'

'You can, and thank you for your help. Have a great Christmas.'

'I'll be working right through,' said the sergeant.

'Sorry to hear that,' said Juliet. 'The family can't be happy.'

'My wife passed away two years ago, and both of my kids emigrated. One in New Zealand, one in the States. So I'd rather be working than sitting at home with an M&S chicken dinner for one.' He grinned. 'That makes me sound like a right sad bugger, but trust me, I'm happier working the holidays.' He winked and headed over to the patrol car.

Juliet and Lulu climbed into the Tesla. Conrad slipped down from Lulu's shoulders to settle in her lap.

'So what do you think happened?' Juliet asked as she pulled away from the kerb.

Lulu sighed and stroked Conrad's fur. 'I think someone tipped Chorley off that we were onto him.' She smiled. 'Or rather, that *you* were onto him. He obviously hadn't realized that the DNA on Conrad's claws could identify him. He took Olivia, delivered her somewhere and then went home to play at happy families. But someone else realized that the DNA would identify him and made the call. Chorley left the house in a hurry, and he left his phone behind because he knew that it could identify his location.'

Juliet nodded. 'Exactly.'

'So I took two things from the conversation with Mrs Chorley. The first is that Olivia is probably somewhere between the Balfours' house and Chorley's house – not quite on a straight line, but not far off. Olivia was taken at a quarter past four in the morning. Chorley arrived home at five o'clock, according to the wife – so, about forty-five minutes after the kidnapping. It took us less than thirty minutes to get here from the Royal Crescent. That means dropping off Olivia only added fifteen minutes to his journey. So there can't be much of a deviation from the route we took, a few miles at most.'

'Fifteen minutes at forty miles an hour is still ten miles.'

'It would take some time to get her out of the car, and there would probably be some discussion with whoever is holding her,' said Lulu.

'Agreed, but at that time of the morning he could well have been speeding. There wouldn't be much traffic around.

So I think there's still a wide area to cover, but you're right, it does cut down the options. And it means we know where to concentrate the CCTV and ANPR search.' Juliet smiled. 'What was the other thing?'

'Well, someone obviously tipped Steven Chorley off and told him to run – but how did *they* know the police were after him?'

'That's a very good question,' said Juliet. 'What's the answer?'

'I'm afraid I don't have an answer. Just the question,' said Lulu. 'I shall give it some thought.'

25

Juliet brought the Tesla to a halt a short distance from Donald and Amanda's house. There was a small group of photographers gathered on the pavement, wearing winter gear and carrying long-lensed cameras. A uniformed constable in a high-vis jacket stood in front of the door, his arms folded, his face a blank mask.

'Parasites,' muttered Juliet. 'Are you okay to walk by them?'

'I don't see that I have any choice,' said Lulu.

'You wonder what they think they'll achieve, standing in front of the house like that,' said Juliet. 'A picture of a worried parent standing in the window? How is that newsworthy?'

'I suppose they hope someone will come out and talk to them,' said Lulu. 'Or that they'll get a photograph of Olivia being returned.'

'Now that I would like to see,' said Juliet. She sighed. 'Okay, I need to get Chorley's phone and camera to our tech people. I'm sure Chorley will have deleted a lot of stuff but it's amazing what they can recover these days.'

'Will they be working on Christmas Day?' asked Lulu.

'Skeleton staff, but ACC Morris will make sure we get priority. I'll have to brief the team and I'll need to bring DI Kemp up to speed. Busy, busy, busy.'

'And what about your plans?'

'I'm going to try to get home this afternoon to drum up Christmas dinner. My husband isn't the best cook.'

'Turkey and all the trimmings?'

Juliet laughed. 'Some of the trimmings. I can't be bothered with Brussels sprouts, and the stuffing will be Paxo and the gravy will be Bisto; but yes, home cooked. But my phone will be on, and if we find Chorley or there's any break in the case at all, I'll be on it. Olivia and Poppy are my priority. No question.'

'I did have a thought,' said Lulu.

'I'm listening.'

'This is clearly not a one-man operation. There were two men in the house, including Mr Chorley. I suspect they had a driver waiting outside. And I very much doubt that they would have left Poppy Novak on her own. So that's a minimum of four people. And for a job like this, they probably wouldn't be strangers. They'd have to know and trust each other.'

'That makes sense.'

'So I thought it might be worth checking on the circumstances of Mr Chorley's assault and affray charge to see if any of his friends were involved.'

Juliet nodded approvingly. 'Birds of a feather.'

'Exactly.'

'I'll get right on it,' said Juliet.

Lulu opened the door, held Conrad to her chest, and climbed out. Juliet waved and drove away.

'So, did you find anything upstairs in the Chorley house?' Lulu asked Conrad as the Tesla disappeared into the distance.

'Neither sight nor sound of him,' said Conrad. 'The chicken had most definitely flown the coop. I didn't see the overalls that he was wearing when he carried out the kidnap – he must have changed somewhere else. And no sign of size ten Nikes. But I did see some other shoes that were definitely size ten.'

'So he's probably still wearing the Nikes,' said Lulu. 'That's good. If he's caught wearing them then it's open and shut, footprints and DNA.'

'Do you think they'll find him?'

'Oh, I think so. These days it's hard to disappear. And he has a wife and children; it's very hard to walk away from family. I'm guessing his plan, if he has one, is to get the ransom money and start a new life with them, overseas maybe, but that's easier said than done. So yes, the short answer is I do think they'll find him, and sooner rather than later.'

'I saw something else upstairs. A printer. I think Mr Chorley used it to print photographs, but he might have used it to print the threatening letters.'

'Oh, that is interesting. I'll tell Juliet when I see her again.'

'Do you think Mr Chorley is the mastermind behind this?' Conrad asked.

Lulu smiled. 'Mastermind?'

'You know what I mean. Do you think that he planned it all, or is someone telling him what to do?'

'That's a very good question, Conrad. And I'm afraid the answer is that at this stage I just don't know. We need to bring him in for questioning. Once we start talking to him, I think it'll all become clear.' She turned towards the house and stared at the photographers. 'Juliet is right. They're parasites. Feeding off other people's misery.'

'Do you know why they're called paparazzi?' asked Conrad.

'It's Italian for mosquito, isn't it? Because they're so annoying.'

'It's more complicated than that,' said Conrad. 'It actually goes back to Federico Fellini's film *La Dolce Vita*. Fellini had a hyperactive news photographer in the film, and he named him Paparazzo. The name stuck.'

'Well, they're certainly as annoying as mosquitoes.'

'I didn't see any of them buzzing around Poppy Novak's house.'

'That's true.'

'Why is that?'

Lulu sighed. 'Maybe Juliet is right; maybe the girls are being treated differently. Maybe the journalists see a "nice" middle-class girl like Olivia as more newsworthy than working-class Poppy Novak.'

'That's awful if it's true.'

'Yes, it is. Truly awful.'

As they approached the house, the photographers began to call out to Lulu.

'Are you with the police?'

'Can you get Mr Balfour to come out and talk to us?'

'Is there any news?'

'Oy, lady, look this way!'

Lulu kept her face turned away as she headed for the front door. The police constable pressed the bell for her. Donald opened the door and ushered her inside.

'How did it go?' he asked.

'We think we've identified one of the kidnappers,' said Lulu. 'One of the men who took Olivia.'

'Oh, wow, that's good news. Has he been arrested?' He closed the door.

'We know it's him, but he isn't at home. They're searching for him now.'

'Who is he?'

'A courier. He drives a white van. And he owns a camera with a telephoto lens. It's definitely him.'

'That's amazing, Lulu. How did you identify him?'

'He was the one Conrad scratched, and his DNA was on file.' She set Conrad down on the floor and shrugged off her sheepskin jacket. Donald hung it up for her. 'Where's Amanda?' Lulu asked him.

'In Olivia's bedroom. She's been there since you left. See if you can get her to eat something, would you? She hasn't eaten all day.'

'I will,' said Lulu. She went slowly up the stairs with Conrad close at her heels.

Amanda was sitting on Olivia's bed, still in her pyjamas, her hands clasped together in her lap, a faraway look in her eyes. Lulu sat down next to her and patted her hands. 'How are you feeling?' she asked.

Amanda didn't react. She was staring at a framed photograph on Olivia's dressing table: Amanda, Donald and Olivia standing in front of Sleeping Beauty Castle at Disneyland Paris.

Lulu patted Amanda's hands again. 'We will get her back, Amanda.'

'Can you promise?' whispered Amanda.

Lulu's jaw tightened. It was a cardinal rule of policing to never make promises, because no one could see into the future. No one knew for sure what was going to happen.

'We have definitely identified one of the kidnappers, so now it's just a matter of time,' she said.

'I just want her back,' said Amanda. 'I'll do anything, Lulu. Anything.'

'Everything is being done that can be done,' said Lulu. 'We have his phone, and there's every chance that will lead us to him and his accomplices. It's just a matter of time.'

Tears were running down Amanda's face. There was a box of tissues on the dressing table next to the Disney photograph. Lulu leaned over, pulled out a handful and gave them to Amanda. 'Why don't I make you a nice cup of tea?' she said. 'And you need to get out of those pyjamas and have a shower. Or maybe a bath. When Olivia comes back we don't want you looking as if you've just dragged yourself out of bed, do we?'

Amanda dabbed at her tears and sniffed. 'I can't bear this, Lulu. I really can't.'

'You have to,' said Lulu. 'You have to be ready for when Olivia comes home. She'll need her mum. And her dad. She'll need you both to help her get through this. So dry your eyes, and I'll run you a nice hot bath.'

26

Juliet returned to the Balfours' house at half past four, after phoning to confirm that she was on her way. Donald answered the door when she rang and showed her into the sitting room. Amanda and Lulu were on the sofa, with Conrad sitting on the floor between them. Amanda was wearing a flower-print dress and had fastened her hair back with a red plastic clip. Lulu had even persuaded her to apply a little lipstick and mascara, though Amanda had drawn the line at blusher.

'Well, things are starting to move,' said Juliet.

'Please, sit down,' said Donald, waving her to an armchair next to the Christmas tree.

Juliet sat. 'So our digital forensics team pulled out all the stops and they have already found photographs of fifty other children on the camera taken at three schools,' she said. 'Chorley had deleted them but kept the memory card so the team were able to recover the photographs.' She looked over at Amanda. 'Steven Chorley is the man that Conrad scratched. We identified his DNA and went around to his house earlier today. He wasn't there, but we got his phone and his camera.'

'I'm surprised that he didn't get rid of the memory card,' said Lulu.

'He'd been using it for a long time and there were hundreds of photographs of his sons; I assume he didn't want to lose them. Either way, it's clear that a large number of children have been targeted. I have detectives contacting the head teachers at home and we'll try to get access to the school records as soon as possible.'

'Fifty is a heck of a lot of children,' said Donald.

'I suspect they took photographs of lots of children and then later they would do their research to see which came from families with money,' said Juliet. 'Most children are on social media these days so it wouldn't be difficult to find out where they lived, what possessions they had and so on.'

'The cars that the children arrived in would also be a clue,' said Lulu.

'What about Olivia?' asked Donald. 'Was her photograph on the camera?'

Juliet nodded. 'It was. And so was Liam Elliott. Once we've identified the rest of the children in the photographs we can talk to their parents. But it's becoming clear that this is a huge operation.'

'I had a thought,' said Lulu. 'Chorley must have some way of printing his photographs, so I was wondering if he might have a printer somewhere in the house. Upstairs, maybe.'

'Oh, I should have thought of that. I'll see about getting a warrant.'

'Mrs Chorley would probably let you look around without one. She seemed quite amenable.'

'She did, but it's starting to look as if we're going to be charging her husband, so at this stage I'd rather do it all by the book.'

'Understood,' said Lulu. 'What about his phone? Was that helpful?'

'He'd deleted all messages and several contacts, most of which we've retrieved. The numbers he deleted were pay-as-you-go, probably burners. The messages are innocuous enough, but they could have been using code.'

'But this was his regular phone, right?' asked Lulu.

'It was.'

'So there's a good chance that he also had a burner phone?'

'I'm sorry,' said Amanda. 'What is a burner phone?'

'It's a cheap pay-as-you-go phone that someone buys, uses and then throws away,' said Lulu. 'If the user pays in cash there's generally no way of tracing them. Drug dealers will often have dozens of burner phones on the go at any one time. The point I was making is that we have his regular phone, which he probably didn't use for the kidnapping.'

'True, but the ten a.m. call was made to his regular phone, and it was that call that sent him packing,' said Juliet.

'Maybe his burner phone was switched off,' said Lulu.

'That's what I thought,' said Juliet. 'We're running a trace on the number that called his phone. The GPS will almost certainly have been switched off, but we should be able to ascertain which towers it pinged off.'

'I'm sorry, you've lost me again,' said Amanda. 'Pinged off? What does that mean?'

'There are thousands and thousands of mobile phone towers in the UK,' explained Juliet. 'Whenever you use your mobile phone, the signal travels back and forth to the nearest tower. The mobile phone company can calculate the general area where the phone is by measuring the time it takes for a signal to travel back and forth. And they can track the movement of the phone by seeing how the signal switches between towers. So even if the user of the phone has turned off the GPS, we can still get a rough idea of where the phone was.'

'So you can use that information to find where they're keeping Olivia?' said Amanda.

'We won't be able to pinpoint her position exactly, but it will narrow down our search area. Unfortunately, we don't have the details of Mr Chorley's burner phone yet. But we have the number that called Mr Chorley's regular phone so we can start looking at that. The problem is, we need to talk to the phone company and it's Christmas Day.'

'Are they not working?' asked Donald.

'They have a skeleton staff, but they are aware that we are a priority so I expect to hear from them sooner rather than later.'

Amanda flinched as her phone rang out. 'Why won't they leave us alone?' she said. She looked over at Juliet. 'Can't you arrest them for breach of the peace or something?'

'I'm afraid we have a free press,' said Juliet. 'If they hack your phone, that's an offence, but we can't arrest them for calling you.'

Donald picked up the ringing phone and looked at the screen. 'It's Ivan,' he said. He gave Amanda the phone.

Juliet frowned at Lulu. 'Ivan?'

'The hedge-fund entrepreneur that Amanda used to work for,' Lulu whispered. 'The money man.'

Amanda took the call and listened intently. 'Oh, thank you,' she said eventually. 'Yes, of course. I will. Absolutely, of course. Yes. God bless you, Ivan.' She ended the call and smiled at her husband. 'The money will be in your account within the hour,' she said.

27

'I need you to be absolutely sure that you think this is the right thing to do, Donald,' said Juliet. They were sitting at the dining table, with the curtains drawn and the lights on.

'We've talked it through, and it's what we both want,' said Donald. He was sitting next to Amanda and she reached over and took his hand.

'We have to do something, and this is the only thing we can do,' said Amanda. 'Otherwise we're just waiting, powerless.'

Lulu was sitting at the end of the table and Conrad was curled up on the chair to her left. Donald was holding his phone and staring at the app he was using to transfer the Bitcoin that he had purchased once the money from Amanda's former boss had arrived in his account. He was breathing slowly and deeply, as if trying to stay calm.

Lulu was holding her phone in front of her. She was on a FaceTime call with Kirsty Grant of the NCA. Kirsty was in her home office, facing a wall of monitors. 'Is everything okay?' Kirsty asked.

'Donald is just about to start the transfer,' said Lulu.

'Okay, let me concentrate on my screens,' said Kirsty. 'I'll call you back when I have something.' She ended the call and Lulu put the phone down on the table. 'Kirsty is monitoring the wallet, so whenever you're ready,' she said.

Donald nodded. He took a deep breath and slowly exhaled. 'Okay,' he said.

He looked over at Amanda and she nodded enthusiastically. 'It's the right thing to do,' she said. There was a box of tissues on the table and she took one and dabbed at her eyes.

Donald glanced at Juliet. 'You don't agree, do you?' he said.

'It's not my call, Donald,' Juliet said. 'You and Amanda have to do what you think is best. And at least with Kirsty on the case there is a chance of following the money. I've told you what I think, but Olivia is your daughter, not mine.'

Donald smiled thinly. 'I'm going to do it,' he said. 'It's for the best.' He swallowed, then tapped the phone's screen. 'It's done.' He sat back, staring at the screen. 'Wow, a quarter of a million pounds, gone, just like that.'

'Were you expecting more?' asked Lulu.

'I suppose not. But it's the lack of checks that surprises me. When I was talking to the bank about moving money into my current account, they had all sorts of questions. If you transfer money online there are PINs and phone confirmation, and at every step you're asked if you're sure you want to continue and are you sure that you're not being scammed. But for this, one press of a button and poof, it's gone. Off to God knows where.'

Amanda reached over and patted his hand. 'We'll have her back soon,' she said. She looked over at Juliet. 'How long do you think it will take the kidnappers to let Olivia go?'

'There's no way of knowing,' Juliet said.

'But today, right? I want Olivia to open her presents.'

'I wish I could sound more optimistic, but it's out of our hands. All we can do is wait, I'm afraid.'

'Why don't I make us all some tea?' said Lulu.

'I'll do it,' said Donald.

'No, you stay with Amanda,' said Lulu. She stood up.

'I'll come with you,' said Juliet. 'I could do with a cuppa before I head back to the office.'

They headed along the hall to the kitchen. Conrad stayed where he was, under the chair.

Lulu switched on the kettle as Juliet slid onto a stool. 'So you're not going home?' asked Lulu.

'I'll get back in a couple of hours and hubby is taking care of the kids,' said Juliet. 'Your idea of checking out Chorley's affray arrest was a good one, by the way. Basically it was a pub argument that got out of hand, Chorley and two of his friends against four locals in a pub in Chippenham. They ended up brawling in the street, the cops were called and they all spent a night in the cells. Nobody was badly hurt, so the charges were dropped. The DNA and fingerprints stayed on the system despite the three-year limit expiring.'

'Was approval sought from the Biometrics Commissioner?' asked Lulu. The Biometrics Commissioner's role was to keep under review the retention and use by the police of DNA samples, DNA profiles and fingerprints. The commissioner could approve data of unconvicted people being held for up to three years, but after that the police needed the permission of a judge to extend the time.

'Yes. But nothing happened after the three years. Strictly speaking the data should have been deleted, but it wasn't.'

'Might that be a problem?' asked Lulu.

'I'll need to check with the Crown Prosecution Service after the holidays. But I think we should be okay. And there's other evidence – you were bang on about the printer. We got a warrant and a couple of our guys went in and searched the house. The printer was in the box room and our forensics people are examining it as we speak.'

Lulu dropped teabags into four mugs. 'Do you think they'll have the result today?'

'I don't see why not. All they have to do is print a page and check it against the two letters we already have. Anyway, we checked out Chorley's two friends, the ones that were charged with affray. Their names are Jordan Mitchell and Ricky Palmer. Palmer hasn't been in trouble since, but Mitchell is a nasty piece of work. He had several run-ins with the police as a teenager and was in and out of young offenders' institutions. He wasn't charged with the pub affray, but a few weeks later he shoved a glass in a man's face in another pub and did eighteen months in HMP Erlestoke.'

'Is he still in contact with Mr Chorley?'

'Mrs Chorley was asked about Mitchell and she said that her husband did see him from time to time.' Juliet wrinkled her nose. 'Seems she isn't a fan, but he and her husband met at primary school and Mr Chorley refused to give up the friendship.'

'Have you spoken to Mitchell?'

'We knocked on his door, but there was no one at home. He lives alone in a village called Colerne. Wife moved out after he came out of prison and he'd started taking his frustrations out on her and their boy.'

The kettle finished boiling and Lulu poured hot water into the mugs.

'Mitchell is the registered owner of a blue Ford Fiesta, which wasn't at the house, so we're looking for it and running the registration number through ANPR.'

'Phone?'

'We don't have a number for him.'

'No number on Chorley's phone?'

'Unfortunately, no. Not under Jordan or Mitchell or anything similar.'

'And what about the other friend?'

'Ricky Palmer? We've visited him. He lives with his girl-friend and has either been at work or with her over the past few days, so we can rule him out.'

Lulu fetched a bottle of milk from the fridge. 'It could have been Mitchell who picked up Chorley yesterday morning.'

'Hopefully ANPR will bear that out. I have a good feeling about this, Lulu. If Mitchell and Chorley are involved, there's every chance that we'll find them, and sooner rather than later.'

'I had a thought about where they might be keeping Olivia and Poppy.'

'I'm all ears.'

'We know that they're not using their own houses. At least, not the homes of Chorley and Mitchell.'

'Well, they'd have to be pretty stupid to use their own homes, and we know they're not stupid. This has all been very well planned.'

'Exactly. So they'll have put a lot of thought into where to keep the girls. Somewhere secluded, somewhere no one will see them coming and going or hear any shouts for help.'

'A deserted farmhouse, or something like that?'

'Yes, if this was a film then it would be a deserted farm-house, or a disused factory, or an abandoned ship in the docks. But in the real world, opportunities like that are few and far between. And there's always the risk of the real owner turning up, no matter how long a place has been abandoned. Or somebody notices that there are people now using a previously abandoned place. But what if they signed up for an Airbnb? They'd be able to choose exactly what they wanted online, and neighbours, if there are any, would be used to strangers coming and going. I'm sure it's not too difficult to open an Airbnb account under a false name.'

'Don't the owners check people in and out?'

'I'm not sure. But even if they do, one of them can do the checking in and then once they have the keys they can come and go as they please. As I said, no one would be paying strangers any attention as there'd be strangers coming and going all the time.'

Juliet nodded. 'I like it,' she said. 'I'll get the team on it.'

'I'm assuming the website will say which properties are being rented out and which are still available.'

They both jumped as the doorbell rang. Juliet hurried to the sitting room and Lulu followed her. Juliet popped her head around the door. 'Are you expecting anyone?' asked Juliet.

Amanda shook her head. 'No,' she said. 'Do you think . . . ?' She looked at Donald. 'Oh my God,' she said. She stood up and grabbed a handful of tissues and dabbed at her eyes as she hurried to the hall. Donald rushed after her. Juliet stood back to give them room.

Lulu looked over at Juliet. Clearly Donald and Amanda were hoping that Olivia was at the door, but Juliet shook her head. Lulu knew what she meant. There was no way that the kidnappers would take the risk of delivering Olivia to the house; they'd drop her somewhere where there was no risk of them being seen.

Lulu stood up and followed Donald and Amanda into the hall. Amanda reached the front door and pulled it open. There was a young girl standing there, wearing a long red coat and with a white scarf wrapped around her neck. Lulu's hand went up to her mouth and she gasped.

The little girl opened her mouth and began to sing. '*Away in a manger . . .*' She had a strong, confident voice and she smiled as she sang. As Amanda opened the door further, Lulu could see that there were more children standing behind the little girl. There were two boys, in their early teens, on either side of a younger girl. All of them were wearing similar white scarves. '*. . . No crib for a bed . . .*'

Amanda had the door wide open now. There were half a dozen adults in the group. Two middle-aged women were holding collecting tins with 'HELP THE AGED' labels. They were carol singers. Amanda wailed and the strength faded from her legs. She grabbed at the front door with both hands but she still slid to the floor. Donald knelt down beside her.

The carol singers stopped mid-song and the girl in the red coat began to cry.

Juliet hurried along the hallway. The carol singers appeared flustered, with the children looking up at the adults, clearly wondering what was going on. 'I'm sorry, now's not a good time,' said Juliet, and she closed the door.

'I thought there was a police guard outside,' said Lulu. Conrad was at her feet, rubbing himself against her legs.

'You and me both,' scowled Juliet. She took out her radio and headed for the kitchen.

Donald had helped Amanda to her feet. Lulu stepped forward and took Amanda's left arm while Donald held her right. 'Sitting room,' said Donald. 'She can lie on the sofa.'

'I'm fine,' said Amanda. 'Please don't fuss.'

'You fainted, Amanda,' said Lulu.

'I just need a cup of tea.'

'And you can have one,' said Donald firmly. 'When you're on the sofa.'

They walked her to the sitting room and lowered her onto one of the sofas, facing the fireplace. 'Really, you don't have to fuss like this,' said Amanda. 'I just got overexcited. I thought it was Olivia at the door and when it wasn't . . .' She sat up. 'I'm fine, really.'

'Donald, there's tea made in the kitchen,' said Lulu.

'I'll get it,' he said.

As he left the room, Juliet returned, putting her radio away. 'The constable's shift was up and he decided to head off before his replacement showed up,' she said. 'I'm so sorry about that, Amanda, that should never have happened. They should never have rung the doorbell like that.'

'I feel so stupid,' said Amanda, clasping her hands together. Conrad jumped up onto the sofa and put a paw on her lap. She smiled and scooped him up and kissed him on the top of his head. 'I don't know what came over me,' she said. 'Obviously the kidnappers aren't going to deliver her to our front door, are they?'

Juliet nodded. 'It's much more likely they would drop her off somewhere isolated, where they wouldn't be seen.'

'When do you think they'll let her go?' asked Amanda.

Juliet gave her an uncomfortable smile. 'There's really no way of knowing.'

Lulu's phone rang in the dining room. 'I'd better get that,' she said, and hurried out. It was Kirsty calling, on FaceTime. Lulu took the call.

'Good news and bad news,' said Kirsty. 'Which is my life in a nutshell, I suppose.'

'You saw the payment?'

'Oh yes. And the kidnappers were onto it straight away. Similar to what happened with the Bitcoin handed over by the Elliotts. The Bitcoin was split up and moved around through multiple wallets.'

'Overseas?'

'All over. They left us behind within minutes and even with three of my colleagues on the case we're still lagging.'

'But you'll be able to follow the money, right?'

'Eventually, yes. The blockchains are there for ever. But it'll take time, and they could well get into thousands of wallets, which means it'll take days, possibly weeks to follow it. And by the time we've followed every blockchain they could well have most of the money on a thumb drive somewhere. Same as they did with the Elliotts' Bitcoin payment.'

'That's not good,' said Lulu.

'To be fair, it was never going to be easy,' said Kirsty. 'Anyway, we'll stick at it and I might be able to bring in a few extra hands to the pump. I'll keep you posted.'

Lulu thanked her and ended the call. She stared at her phone, mulling over what Kirsty had told her. The money had been paid and the kidnappers had whisked it away. Now they had their money, would they release Olivia?

She went back into the sitting room. Amanda looked up expectantly as she stroked Conrad. 'Any news?'

'They're following the Bitcoin, but it'll take time,' said Lulu. 'I'm sorry.'

Amanda looked over at Juliet. 'If anyone finds Olivia,

they'll call you straight away, won't they?' She was close to tears again.

Juliet nodded. 'Every patrol, every station, every constable on the beat, they have all been given Olivia's photograph and her details. The moment she appears, I'll be notified.'

Amanda pulled a tissue from the box on the table in front of her. She dabbed at her eyes. 'That's good,' she said.

Juliet caught Lulu's eye and flashed her a tight smile. Lulu knew what she was thinking. The ransom had been paid, but that was no guarantee that the kidnappers would release Olivia. That was in the lap of the gods.

28

They filled the next hour or two by watching *The Great Escape* on television, although nobody's mind was on the film. After it had finished, Donald went into the kitchen to make tea. Lulu went over to sit beside Amanda and patted her on the leg. 'I know the waiting feels impossible,' Lulu said. 'All you can do is try to take it one minute at a time.'

Amanda sighed and closed her eyes. 'It's as if time has stopped,' she said. 'Everything has frozen. I keep looking at my watch and the time just stays the same.'

'You need to try to think about something else. I know that's easier said than done, but dwelling on it won't help. You and Donald have done everything you can – it's out of your hands now. You've paid the ransom, now it's up to them to release Olivia. You worrying about it won't make it happen any sooner.'

'It's all I can think about, Lulu.'

'I understand that. Of course I do.'

Conrad jumped up onto the sofa. He stood staring at Amanda with his bright green eyes, then made a soft mewing noise. He pawed gently at her arm and she smiled and patted her lap. 'Come on then,' she said. Conrad stepped slowly onto her lap before curling up. Amanda stroked him and he purred softly. 'Cats are the best therapy, aren't they?' said Amanda.

'They are,' said Lulu. 'And Conrad is especially good at it.'

'Do you think they're looking after Olivia?'

'I'm sure they'll be taking good care of her,' said Lulu. 'This is all about money; there's absolutely nothing to be gained by frightening her. And one of the men we think is involved is a father himself. He has two young sons.'

'How could a parent do something like this?' said Amanda. 'How would he be able to live with himself? How would he like it if one of his children was kidnapped?'

'I suppose he's only thinking about the money,' said Lulu. 'But as a father, I'm sure he won't want her hurt in any way.'

'You don't think this will be hurting her?' Amanda snapped. 'They took her from her bed in the middle of the night. On Christmas bloody Eve.'

'I'm sorry,' said Lulu. 'I was just trying to make you feel better and I've ended up making it worse. I should just keep my mouth shut, shouldn't I?'

Amanda grimaced. 'No, I'm the one who's sorry,' she said. 'I had no right to snap at you. You've been so supportive. I'm an idiot, I'm sorry.'

'You've nothing to be sorry about, Amanda. Just know that I'm here for you. Anything you need or want, all you have to do is ask.'

Tears were welling up in Amanda's eyes and she blinked them away. 'You're a good friend, Lulu.'

'I'm more than that, I'm your godmother, remember?'

Amanda forced a smile. 'How could I forget?' She reached over and patted Lulu on the leg.

Donald returned with a tray on which there were three mugs of tea, a plate of sandwiches and a packet of Jaffa

Cakes. He placed it on the table and sat down in the armchair. 'You need to eat, darling,' he said.

Amanda sighed. 'I'm really not hungry.'

'There's salmon and cucumber, and pâté and cornichons. You can't say they're not your favourites.'

She shook her head. 'They are; you know they are. I just don't feel like eating.'

'A Jaffa Cake, then. Go on.' He smiled. 'Go on, go on, go on.'

Amanda's face broke into a genuine smile for a few seconds, then the blank mask fell back into place. 'If it'll shut you up,' she said.

Donald opened the packet, took out three Jaffa Cakes and put them on a plate. He offered the plate to her and she took one and bit into it. Donald offered the plate to Lulu and she also took one. She bit into it, more to encourage Amanda than because she was hungry, but after she had eaten the Jaffa Cake she started on the sandwiches.

Donald picked up the remote and found another film to watch; this time it was *Home Alone*. After a while they were all chuckling at Macaulay Culkin's antics and by the time the film had finished they'd eaten all the sandwiches and Jaffa Cakes.

Lulu went to bed just after ten o'clock. Amanda and Donald seemed determined to stay up all night, but Lulu knew that she needed to sleep. She also knew that as soon as there was any news, Juliet would phone.

As soon as they were in the bedroom, Conrad jumped up onto the bed and sat staring at Lulu with his emerald-green eyes. Lulu took off her pullover and placed it on a chair by the dressing table. 'This is all very strange, isn't it?' said Conrad.

'Unusual, yes,' said Lulu. 'Very unusual.'

'The way the kidnappers are behaving, there's no real logic to it, is there?'

'I don't know about that. They take a child and they ask for money for her return. There's a terrible logic to that.'

'But that isn't how they started out, is it? The first child they took, Poppy Novak, they didn't ask for a ransom for her, did they?'

'Well, the idea was to use her abduction as a way of threatening the other parents, so no ransom was necessary. It was never about getting money from Poppy Novak's parents.'

'It was about getting the nice middle-class parents to pay up.'

'Exactly.'

'So what changed? Why did they change their plan?'

'You mean why did they decide to kidnap Olivia?'

'If it was about extorting money with the threat of abduction, why did they go ahead and take her? They took a risk getting into the house, a risk which led to you identifying one of them.'

Lulu sat down on the bed next to him. 'I see what you mean. It was a complete change of plan, wasn't it?'

'Very much so. Everything had been planned to perfection. Someone had put a lot of thought into this, every step had been carefully planned and executed. The photographs, Poppy Novak's abduction, the letters, the Bitcoin wallets. And then, just as things were proceeding exactly as the kidnappers had planned, they changed their strategy and broke in here to take Olivia.'

'And you're saying that something happened to make them change their plan?'

'They wouldn't have altered what was clearly a winning strategy on a whim, would they? Cause and effect, obviously.'

Lulu smiled and stroked the back of his neck. 'And clearly you know what happened.'

'I do, yes.'

Lulu paused for a few seconds and then chuckled. 'You're going to make me ask, aren't you?'

'You know me so well.'

'I do, yes. Okay, Conrad, tell me. What happened to make them change their plans?'

'We did,' said Conrad. 'You and I happened. We turned up and discovered what was going on and the kidnappers had to change their strategy.'

Lulu frowned. 'You're saying that we're to blame for Olivia's abduction?'

'I'm saying that if we hadn't turned up, the kidnappers would have stuck to their original plan. But you did turn up, and that's why they took Olivia and not one of the other children they had targeted.'

Lulu frowned. 'But why react by taking her? What does that achieve?'

'It keeps you busy. A former detective superintendent with the Metropolitan Police, with decades of experience. The last thing they would want is for you to be looking at the Poppy Novak case. They had the measure of the local police, but you were a wild card. And you had direct access to Amanda and Donald. You weren't a detective asking questions, you were a family friend, privy to all sorts of inside information.'

Lulu sighed as she considered what Conrad had said. He was a very wise cat, and perceptive, and while she didn't like what he'd told her, she knew that he was probably right. The kidnappers had worked out exactly what they wanted profits-wise from their criminal endeavours. They would have calculated the risk/reward ratio and decided that the risk of abducting a working-class schoolgirl as she walked home was worth the hundreds of thousands of pounds they stood to make from the middle-class parents who didn't want the same to happen to their children. The Elliotts had already paid. A dozen more families might well also decide that handing over fifty thousand pounds was money well spent if it meant that their children would be spared. The kidnappers had taken Poppy Novak without incident, and all they had to do now was to wait for the money to flow in. The risk had been taken and now they were reaping the rewards. How much could they earn? Half a million pounds? Six hundred thousand? A million? Taking Olivia would earn them an extra quarter of a million pounds, but the audacious kidnapping more than doubled their risk.

'You're wondering why they would put themselves at risk by kidnapping another girl,' said Conrad.

'Are you reading my mind?'

'I can't read minds, Lulu. But I do understand how people think, so I can follow your train of thought. And you're right. It does make it riskier for them, and they've already paid the price because it allowed us to identify Steven Chorley. But Olivia's kidnapping has probably added to the reward part of the equation.'

'Because it puts pressure on the other parents? The fact that Olivia has been abducted from her bed means that their children are also vulnerable?'

'Exactly. I would expect more parents to pay up once they hear what's happened to Olivia. But again, I would ask why they took Olivia and not one of the other children they targeted? This house is not easy to break into, I'm sure there are much easier premises to enter. And if they did any surveillance at all, they would surely have seen you coming and going, so they would have known that there was at least one extra person in the house. That should have deterred them and made them look elsewhere. I think they know who you are, Lulu. I think that's why they broke in and took Olivia, because they wanted to throw you off your stride.'

'But how would the kidnappers know who I am?' Her jaw dropped. 'Oh, my goodness me.'

'You see it now, don't you?'

Lulu nodded. 'I do, yes. Of course. How did I miss it?'

'Remember we talked about Steven Chorley being tipped off in that morning phone call?'

'I do, of course.'

'Whoever tipped him off must know a lot about police procedure,' said Conrad. 'And the phone call was at ten o'clock in the morning. Whoever it was didn't speak to Chorley before that, so obviously wasn't aware that he had been scratched. If he had been aware, he'd have told Chorley to run straight away. So whoever it was learned of the scratching quite some time after the event. Or perhaps it wasn't the actual scratching they heard about, but the fact that the police had Chorley's DNA from Conrad's claws.'

Lulu shook her head in disbelief. 'So it was either a police officer or someone involved with SOCO who tipped him off.'

'Which means the kidnappers have an inside man,' said Conrad.

'Or woman,' said Lulu.

'Indeed,' said Conrad. 'Someone who knows you, and who you've probably met. That's a problem, isn't it?'

'A big one,' said Lulu.

29

Lulu's phone rang and she opened her eyes. She sat up. Conrad had been dozing at her feet, but he was also awake and stretching. Lulu groped for the phone and blinked at the screen. It was half past eight in the morning and it was Juliet calling. Her heart began to race. Had the kidnappers released Olivia? Was she on her way home?

'Bad news, I'm afraid,' said Juliet as soon as Lulu took the call. 'I'm being sidelined.'

'Sidelined how?' asked Lulu, as she sat up. 'Why?'

'DI Kemp has requested a tri-force major crime investigation team to look at both kidnappings. With himself as SIO. Which means I now have to answer to him.'

'Can he do that?'

'Unfortunately, yes. There are a number of existing operational collaborations between Gloucestershire, Wiltshire and Avon and Somerset. Major crimes is one. It's a way of maintaining quality across the forces, they say, but really it's about cost savings. Anyway, with one kidnapping in Wiltshire and another in Bath, and with clear connections between the two, and with our main suspect resident in Wiltshire, DI Kemp has requested and been granted a tri-force team with him in charge.'

'Well, that's annoying,' said Lulu. 'He wasn't making any progress on the Poppy Novak kidnapping until we gave him the letter and photographs. And it was your forensics people who identified Steven Chorley.'

'Yes, I think us going to see Mrs Chorley was the straw that broke the camel's back.'

'In what way?'

'He clearly wasn't happy yesterday when I told him that we'd been to Chippenham. He said that I should have told him we were crossing the border and given him the opportunity to be there when we questioned Mrs Chorley.'

'But it was your case. Your forensics people identified Chorley's DNA from the kidnapping of Olivia Balfour. The fact that the suspect lived in Wiltshire is neither here nor there.'

'My opinion exactly. But he was also annoyed that I hadn't kept him in the loop about the DNA. He said that I should have told him straight away that we had the DNA of one of the kidnappers.'

'Again, it was your case. And it's not as if telling him would have speeded things up, is it? The important thing was to identify who the DNA belonged to, not the fact that we had it. And once your forensics people had identified Chorley, the important thing was to get to his house as soon as possible. It wasn't about hogging the glory, it was about acting promptly.'

'He didn't see it that way. He was quite frosty with me when I spoke to him, and clearly afterwards he must have spoken to Wiltshire's chief constable about making it a joint operation. And she backed his request.'

'What about ACC Morris? Can't he help?'

'He's the one who just told me about the tri-force team,' said Juliet. 'He's in a difficult position because he's often pressing for tri-force investigation teams, so he can't really argue against this one. And as the first abduction and the only suspect are on their patch, there is a logic to making DI Kemp the SIO.'

'Even though you're the one who's been making progress on the case?'

'The important thing is that we get Poppy and Olivia back, not who gets the glory.'

'I hear what you're saying, Juliet, but it seems to me that you and your team are the ones most likely to crack this case. DI Kemp is no further on from the day that Poppy went missing.'

'I can't argue with that,' said Juliet. 'But what's done is done, and we have to deal with the world the way it is, not the way we want it to be.'

'Which means what, investigation-wise?'

'Basically, everything my team does now has to be run by DI Kemp. And he's in charge of allocating resources.'

'What about the digital forensics?'

'So far as I know, I'm still their point of contact. We'll have to see if that changes.'

'So if you do get a fix on Chorley, you'll have to tell DI Kemp and he'll make the arrest?'

'Theoretically, yes,' said Juliet. 'But we'll take it one step at a time.'

'Any joy with ANPR for Chorley's van after the kidnapping?'

'I'm still waiting to hear from Hendon,' said Juliet. 'I'm guessing they'll be on a skeleton staff over the next few days, but I'll be pressing them today. Assuming that Chorley was heading to Chippenham, he'd have been across the border within a few minutes.'

'So it's almost certain that Olivia is being held on the Wiltshire side?'

'That's my gut feeling, but it is possible that he dropped her closer to Bath and then headed home. I don't want to guess and be wrong.'

'Let me know if there's any progress,' said Lulu.

'How were the Balfours last night?'

'Tense. Worried. Jumping every time the phone rang. I think they assumed that Olivia would be released straight away. To be honest, I assumed the same. The fact that they still have her is a worry.'

'And what about your crypto expert?'

'Kirsty says the money was divided and sent around the world, then brought back together in the UK, and then the blockchain stopped – so presumably the Bitcoin has been parked on a hard drive.'

'Is there any way of knowing geographically where the hard drive is?'

'I'm afraid not.'

'But the kidnappers definitely have their money? The ransom has been paid?'

'Yes. All quarter of a million pounds of it. There's really no reason for them to keep her prisoner now.'

'Unless they decide to ask for more money,' said Juliet. 'We'll have to keep our fingers crossed on that score. Oh, I started the ball rolling on Airbnbs in the area. Turns out there are thousands across Wiltshire and Avon.'

'I know it's become very popular, though I've never stayed in one. With *The Lark*, I can take my home with me when I travel.'

'The sheer number is daunting, I'm afraid. Plus, when we

do a search on the website, it doesn't show the properties that have been rented out, it only shows the ones that are available, which doesn't help us. We've tried phoning the company but no one is answering. The only way we can see of doing it is to look at vacancies next year, and then look at what's available now and then by a process of elimination we can work out which are rented at the moment. But it takes several minutes to do a single property and there are thousands to check, though we're concentrating on the ones in the area we identified. It's a long shot, but at the moment I'll take any shot I can get.' She sighed and ended the call and Lulu put the phone back on the bedside table. She climbed out of bed. 'I'm going to shower,' she said to Conrad.

'And I shall have a cat wash,' he said. He began licking his left paw.

'You cats have it so easy,' said Lulu. She padded along to the bathroom, cleaned her teeth and showered, then wrapped herself in one of the fluffy white towels Amanda had provided. Conrad was at work on his rear left paw when she returned to the bedroom. It was Boxing Day but she decided that under the circumstances it probably wasn't appropriate to dress up, so she pulled on a jumper and blue jeans. She kept her make-up to the minimum, brushed her hair and then checked herself in the wardrobe mirror. 'That'll do,' she said.

'You look lovely,' said Conrad.

'Why thank you, kind sir.' She bent down so that he could jump onto her shoulders and walked out into the hall. She went barefoot down the stairs. She popped her head around the sitting-room door, but it was empty. The curtains were drawn, presumably to shield everyone from the prying eyes of the paparazzi. She went over and gently made a gap to look through. There were half a dozen photographers standing on the pavement. One of them saw the curtains move and began snapping away. Lulu let the curtain fall back into place.

'Don't they ever sleep?' asked Conrad.

'Most of them are freelancers, they're paid by results,' said Lulu.

She walked down the hall to the kitchen. Amanda was sitting at the island with her hands around a mug of coffee, wearing the same clothes she'd had on the previous day. Donald was standing by the toaster and he also hadn't changed.

'Please don't tell me you stayed up all night,' said Lulu. Conrad jumped down from her shoulders and landed on one of the stools.

'How could we possibly sleep?' said Amanda. There were dark patches under her eyes and her hair was lank and lifeless.

'You need to get some rest,' said Lulu.

'We'll rest when Olivia's back,' said Donald. 'Coffee and toast? Or I could do you a full English if you'd prefer?'

'Toast will be fine, thank you,' said Lulu. She slid onto the stool opposite Amanda. 'You really need to get some sleep,' she said. 'Staying awake for days isn't good for you.'

'I can't sleep,' said Amanda. 'I can't rest, I can't relax. It's torture.'

'I understand,' said Lulu. She reached over and patted Amanda's arm. 'But you need to stay strong. For Olivia.'

Donald put a mug of coffee on the island in front of Lulu. 'We've been talking, and we've decided that we need to do some sort of press conference,' he said.

'Okay,' said Lulu cautiously. 'I'm not sure that's the best idea.'

'Well, we assumed that the kidnappers would let Olivia go straight away, but it's been more than twelve hours and she's still not back.'

'That was always the risk, Donald. You knew that. It was always going to be a problem when paying with Bitcoin; there was no official handover where you gave them the money and they returned Olivia.'

'Do you think they'll give her back to us?' asked Amanda.

'Oh, Amanda, I don't know what to say. I don't know who these people are. They talk about honour among thieves, but in my experience there is no such thing.'

'So what are they doing? Are they going to ask for more money?'

'I really don't know,' said Lulu. 'I'm not sure what I can tell you. Some kidnappings do end badly, there's no getting away from that. But many cases end with the hostages being released. It might be that the kidnappers are having difficulties in releasing her.'

'What do you mean?' asked Donald.

'Well, there is every chance that Olivia and Poppy Novak are being held together, so they might be worried that Olivia could tell the police something that would lead them to find Poppy. Or she might have heard them say something, a name perhaps, or some personal information. Something the police might find useful.'

'So they might not release her, is that what you're saying?' said Donald.

'I wish I could tell you what you want to hear,' Lulu said. 'But I'm trying to be realistic. Hand on heart, I really don't believe the kidnappers will hurt Olivia, but I fear you might have to wait a while before she is released.'

'We can't wait,' said Amanda. 'We want her back, now.'

'And that's why you want to hold a press conference? To appeal to the kidnappers to let Olivia go?'

Donald shook his head. 'No, our plan is to tell the world that we paid, how much the ransom was, and how we handed the money over in Bitcoin. Then we say that despite paying, the kidnappers haven't let her go. We can say that the kidnappers haven't kept their word and that they're not to be trusted. And that anyone else who is considering paying a ransom should know that they don't keep their word.'

Amanda nodded enthusiastically. 'You see, if everyone knows that they haven't released Olivia, then no one will pay. Their whole scheme will fall apart. Who would pay if they thought the kidnappers won't keep their word?'

Lulu nodded thoughtfully. What they were saying did make sense. If no one paid, then the kidnappings would become a pointless exercise. And if there was no money to be made, the kidnappers would have no choice other than to release the two girls. They had the fifty thousand pounds that the Elliotts had paid, and the quarter of a million pounds that Donald and Olivia had handed over, but that would be it. No one else would pay. The only way that the kidnappers could keep their scheme going would be to release Olivia as they had promised. Lulu could appreciate the logic of what Donald and Amanda wanted to do, but she knew that the police wouldn't approve. They wanted to control the flow of information to the media and would almost certainly veto a press conference in which the Balfours would explain that they had paid a ransom. She took a deep breath. She had to stop thinking like a police officer; she was Donald and Amanda's friend, and she had to put them first. And there was a logic to what they were proposing that Lulu couldn't really argue with. 'I think you might be right,' she said eventually.

'Will you help us?' asked Donald.

'Help you how?'

'You know people in the media, don't you? Could you set it up for us?'

Lulu hesitated before replying, 'Okay. If you're sure that's what you want.'

Amanda nodded emphatically. 'It is.'

30

Lulu pulled back the curtains and peered through the gap. There were now more than a dozen photographers and reporters standing on the pavement, and two TV news crews. Two large vans with satellite dishes were parked down the road, one belonging to the BBC and the other had ITN's logo on the side. A metal podium had been set up in front of the house with a row of microphones on top.

Lulu let the curtain fall back into place. 'I think we're good to go,' she said.

Amanda and Donald were sitting on the sofa, holding hands. Donald was wearing a grey suit, white shirt and a dark blue tie. Lulu had insisted that Amanda wore a dress, and helped choose it: a dark blue sleeveless Ted Baker model that she paired with a white cardigan. Lulu had brushed her hair but Amanda had insisted on not applying any make-up and Lulu hadn't pressed her. Conrad was sitting at Amanda's feet, offering moral support.

Lulu had decided not to tell Juliet about the press conference. She would almost certainly object, and as DI Kemp was now effectively in charge of the case, she would have to run it by him. Donald and Amanda had made up their minds, and it was Lulu's duty as a friend to support them.

Donald and Amanda stood up and hugged. Donald kissed his wife on the top of the head. 'You don't have to come with me, darling,' he said.

'No, I need to be there,' she said.

'After you've said what you want to say, I'd suggest that you answer a few questions,' said Lulu. 'If it feels as if it's getting too intrusive, just stop.'

Donald nodded. 'Will you say something?'

'I think best not. If I speak then they'll want to know who I am and what my involvement is. Better I just stay in the background.' She gave him an encouraging smile. 'It'll be fine.'

'What about coats? Shall we wear coats?'

Amanda shook her head. 'We won't be out long.'

Lulu took them into the hall and put a hand on the door lock. 'Remember to breathe,' she said. 'The cameras will start clicking like crazy as soon as I open the door, and some of them will be using flash, but it should calm down once you start to speak.'

'Do I smile or not?' asked Donald. 'I don't feel like smiling.'

'Just do whatever comes naturally,' said Lulu. 'You're not an actor and this isn't a performance.'

'Okay,' said Donald.

'Ready?'

Amanda and Donald both nodded. Amanda reached for her husband's hand and held it tightly.

'Here we go,' said Lulu. She opened the door and immediately the cameras started clicking like angry insects, accompanied by flashes of white light. She kept her eyes averted as she opened the door wide. The uniformed constable on the doorstep moved aside to let them pass. Donald and Amanda walked hesitatingly to the podium while Lulu stayed by the door, holding it ajar.

The Cat and the Christmas Kidnapper

The cameras continued to click away. Lulu had no idea what they hoped to achieve by taking so many photographs; surely one or two would be enough.

Lulu had suggested that he read from a prepared statement, but Donald had insisted on speaking off the cuff, albeit with a few keywords written on a card. He had spent more than fifteen years lecturing and knew from experience that reading a prepared script was received with less enthusiasm than speaking directly to his audience. He figured that applied to journalists as much as students.

He took a deep breath and slowly looked around the pack, making eye contact with as many journalists as possible, another technique he had picked up from lecturing. Gradually the cameras stopped clicking. 'My name is Donald Balfour,' he said eventually. 'This is my wife, Amanda. Our daughter Olivia was kidnapped early on Christmas morning. She was taken from our house by the same people who have kidnapped Poppy Novak. We know that because prior to Olivia being abducted, we received a letter from Poppy's kidnappers saying that if we didn't pay them fifty thousand pounds, they would also abduct our daughter.'

The click-click-click of the cameras began again, increasing in volume and intensity.

'Before we had a chance to pay the money, the kidnappers broke into our house and abducted Olivia. There were two men involved, plus a driver, we think, and it appears that they used chloroform to drug her. They left a note demanding that we pay a ransom of two hundred and fifty thousand pounds. We paid the ransom yesterday afternoon, but they have not yet released our daughter or made any attempt to communicate with us.'

Amanda sniffed and dabbed her eyes with a tissue.

'We have been made aware that other parents have received letters threatening that their children will be abducted unless they pay a ransom of fifty thousand pounds, and that at least one of those families has paid. But from our experience of dealing with the kidnappers, they are not to be trusted. We handed over a quarter of a million pounds and Olivia is still being held. Let that be a warning to everybody.'

'What are the police doing to get your daughter back?' called out a female journalist.

'They're doing their best, but they haven't managed to find Poppy Novak and we were not prepared to see if they had any more luck finding Olivia. That's why we paid.'

'Did you get proof of life before you handed over the cash?' asked a reporter standing next to a television crew.

'No. We didn't. And it wasn't cash; the kidnappers demanded Bitcoin and that's what we gave them.'

'Mr Balfour, are you saying that you were told to pay fifty thousand pounds *before* Olivia was kidnapped?' shouted another reporter.

'They sent us a letter and a photograph of Poppy Novak and said that if we didn't give them fifty thousand pounds, they would kidnap Olivia.'

'Can we see them, the letter and the photograph?' asked the reporter.

'The police have them,' said Donald.

'And other parents have received similar letters?' said the reporter with the TV crew.

'That's what the police say,' said Donald. 'The idea was that the kidnappers would be paid *not* to kidnap children.

It was a sort of insurance policy. But I'm here to tell you that the kidnappers are not to be trusted. Yesterday we paid the kidnappers a quarter of a million pounds and they still haven't returned our daughter.'

'How do you feel about this, Mrs Balfour?' shouted a female reporter who was holding a large clipboard.

Amanda frowned. 'What do you mean, how do I feel? I'm distraught. I haven't slept since she was taken.' She dabbed at her eyes. 'No mother should have to go through this. No parent should.' She began to sob.

'Mr Balfour, can you tell me how much your house is worth?' asked a young male reporter in a dark blue puffa jacket.

Donald frowned. 'What?'

'Your house? How much is it worth? Our readers always like to know.'

'*Daily Mail*,' muttered a tall woman in a Burberry coat who was recording with an iPhone.

Donald opened his mouth to snap at the reporter, but Lulu stepped forward, put an arm around his shoulder and guided him towards the front door. 'That's all the questions we will be answering for the moment,' she said. 'The family would be grateful if you would respect their privacy at this challenging time.' She pushed the front door open. The cameras were clicking frantically and the photographers were shouting, trying to attract their attention. Lulu ignored them and ushered Donald and Amanda inside. The shouting and clicking intensified but she kept her face turned away from the cameras as she followed Donald and Amanda into the hall and closed the door behind them.

'Was that idiot seriously asking me how much our house

is worth?' muttered Donald. He had his arm around Amanda, who was still dabbing at her eyes.

'It's the *Daily Mail*,' said Lulu. 'It's their thing. That, and sexism and casual racism, is what people buy it for. Don't let him upset you.'

'My daughter has been kidnapped, and that's what he asks.'

'They'll run the story, Donald. That's what matters.'

31

Lulu and Amanda sat at the kitchen island while Donald made them mugs of tea. Conrad was sitting on the stool next to Lulu. Two hours had passed since the press conference. There was a small television on the wall by the door and they had it tuned to the BBC with the sound muted.

Lulu was holding her phone, flicking through the websites of the national newspapers. The days of readers having to wait for the first edition of a newspaper to hit the streets were long gone. All the papers had websites that were updated in real time. The *Daily Mail* was the first to release the story, complete with a dozen photographs of the press conference that were virtually identical, along with photographs of Olivia and Poppy Novak. The third paragraph had the value of the house, presumably obtained from the Land Registry or a local estate agent.

The Sun was the second paper to run the story, followed by the *Mirror*. *The Times* had the story up and running an hour after the press conference had finished, though Lulu couldn't read the article as it was hidden behind a paywall. The theme of the articles she could read was the same – that the Balfours had paid a £250,000 ransom but the kidnappers had not released their daughter. Poppy Novak was mentioned in all the articles, but almost as an afterthought. The main focus was always on Olivia and her parents.

'It's coming on now,' said Donald, gesturing at the television.

Lulu reached for the remote and boosted the volume. A newsreader was explaining about the press conference while the screen showed Donald and Amanda walking towards the podium. The newsreader went quiet as Donald began to speak. They showed the press conference in full, though ended it just as the *Daily Mail* reporter began to ask about the house price. The picture then changed back to the newsreader explaining about the two kidnappings. Photographs of Olivia and Poppy flashed up on the screen, followed by a short clip of the press conference held by Mr and Mrs Novak. At least the BBC didn't seem to have forgotten about Poppy.

The news bulletin came to an end and Lulu muted the sound.

Donald sighed. 'I hope it works,' he said.

'You gave it your best shot,' said Lulu.

Donald carried over two mugs of tea and placed them on the island. 'You think it was a bad call, don't you?'

'I think it was your call, and that's what matters. My problem is that I still think like a police officer.'

'And as a former police officer, you think it was a mistake?' asked Donald.

'I would never say that, Donald. Olivia is your daughter; only you and Amanda can decide what's the right thing to do. The rest of us are spectators.'

'You're more than that,' said Amanda.

Lulu smiled sadly at her. 'I'm sorry; that's not what I meant. Of course I love Olivia and would do anything to get her back safe and sound, but I can only imagine how you and Donald feel. So I don't think anyone has the right to tell you what to do.' She sighed. 'And I do understand the logic of going public, I really do.'

'I suppose we'll know soon enough,' said Donald, going back to get his mug of tea.

Lulu's phone burst into life, startling them all. Lulu picked it up and looked at the screen. 'It's Juliet,' she said. She took the call.

'Well, that was a surprise,' said the inspector.

'I'm sorry about that,' said Lulu.

'You didn't think to give me a heads-up?'

'It was Donald and Amanda's decision. They felt that it was time to put pressure on the kidnappers.'

'Oh, I understand exactly why they did what they did, but you need to prepare yourself for the wrath of DI Kemp. I'm just off the phone to him. He seemed to be under the impression that I had known about the press conference, so obviously I had to put him right.'

'Sorry if I've made your life difficult,' said Lulu. 'That wasn't the intention.'

'You haven't,' said Juliet. 'DI Kemp is SIO, I'm just a cog in the machine now. But he's spitting feathers.'

'What in particular has upset him?'

Juliet chuckled. 'Pretty much everything,' she said. 'He says you've jeopardized the investigation and put the children at risk. He says it was irresponsible and said some horrible things about the constable on your door. Seems to think that he should have put a stop to it.'

'That's not his job,' said Lulu.

'Of course it's not. And he works for Avon and Somerset, not Wiltshire Police, so DI Kemp has zero authority over him. To be honest, his outburst seemed to be out of all proportion to what happened and I told him as much.'

'How did he react to that?'

'He hung up on me.'

'I'm sorry you got caught in the middle of this, Juliet. That really wasn't my intention.'

'It's fine. DI Kemp might be SIO, but we're the same rank and on different forces, so there's nothing he can do to me. I hope it works out, Lulu. I really do.'

'What will happen if Olivia is released today?'

'All officers on duty have been given her photograph, and Poppy Novak's picture. When she turns up she'll be taken to the nearest police station for forensic examination and then she'll be taken home. I'll be told immediately she's found and of course I'll ring you straight away. My phone is with me all the time. I'm on top of this, Lulu. I promise.'

'I know, thank you. But do try to enjoy some family time.'

'I will,' said Juliet. She ended the call.

Lulu put the phone down and realized that Amanda and Donald were looking at her. 'No news yet,' she said. 'As soon as anything happens, Juliet will call us.'

32

The doorbell rang and Amanda flinched. It was coming up to six o'clock and they were all in the sitting room. Donald had made cups of tea and sandwiches and opened another packet of Jaffa Cakes, but no one had wanted to eat.

Amanda looked over at Lulu, who shook her head. 'It won't be Olivia; Juliet said she'd ring,' said Lulu. 'Let me get it.'

'Okay,' said Amanda, settling back on the sofa. Conrad was sitting in her lap and seemed to be asleep. Donald was sitting next to Amanda. He had been scrolling through newspaper websites on his phone. There was an old episode of *Midsomer Murders* on the television, a reassuring world that had never existed where a mature detective with an enthusiastic sidekick solved murders by knocking on doors and asking questions.

Lulu went out into the hall. As she opened the front door she heard the clicking of cameras. There were still half a dozen photographers outside, but they had been moved from the pavement to the grass. She opened the door wider, and the clicking intensified. Two men were standing on the doorstep – DI Kemp and DC Arnold. Kemp was wearing a black raincoat with the collar turned up, and Arnold had on a blue parka. They both had their hands in their pockets against the cold.

'We'd like to come in,' said DI Kemp.

'Of course,' said Lulu, opening the door fully. She stayed behind it; she really didn't want to be photographed. The two detectives stepped into the hall and Lulu closed the door.

'Where are Mr and Mrs Balfour?' asked DI Kemp.

'In the sitting room,' said Lulu.

'Was the press conference your idea?'

'No, absolutely not,' said Lulu. 'In fact, I advised against it.'

'And what about DI Donnelly?'

Lulu frowned. 'What about DI Donnelly?'

'Was she here? Did she know?'

'No, and no,' said Lulu.

'You didn't think to tell her?'

'Donald and Amanda wanted to do it. It was their decision.'

'It was irresponsible and could well have damaged our investigation. You had no right to hold a press conference without informing me first.'

'You were the one who first suggested a press conference, remember?' Lulu said. 'You said Donald and Amanda should do a joint press conference with the Novak family. Control the narrative, you said.'

'Yes, I did say that. But I meant that we, the police, would control what was said and we would get the information out there that we wanted getting out. We'd get the public involved, appeal for information that would help us find Olivia and Poppy. Instead, Mr Balfour went rogue. He seemed to go out of his way to attack the kidnappers, accusing them of not keeping their word. And it was totally out of order that they paid the ransom without checking with me first.'

'It's their daughter who was kidnapped. Decisions like that are for them to make, not the police.'

'I didn't say that I'd make the decision, but I should have been consulted. You all clearly felt comfortable telling DI Donnelly that they were paying the ransom – and I gather she was with you when the money was paid.'

'DI Donnelly is SIO of the Olivia Balfour kidnapping. You are SIO of the Poppy Novak case.'

'As of today I'm in charge of both investigations.'

'So I gather. But at the point they paid the ransom, Juliet was SIO.'

'At the time of the press conference, did you or did you not know that I was Senior Investigating Officer?'

Lulu's jaw tightened. She didn't appreciate the way that the inspector was speaking to her, but she didn't want to lie to him. 'DI Donnelly informed me this morning that you had requested a tri-force major crime investigation team be set up with you in charge, to investigate both kidnappings.'

'So why didn't you contact me when the idea of a press conference was first mooted?'

'I'm not a police officer. I'm a friend of the family who is here to offer moral support. Actually, more than that, I'm Amanda's godmother, and that takes precedence over everything else. As I've told you, I initially advised them against it, but at the end of the day it was their decision and I respect that. I suggest that you do the same.'

'What exactly did you think he would achieve with a rant like that?'

'Donald took the view that if he didn't put some pressure on the kidnappers, the situation was going to drag on and on. And I could see his point. You're no nearer finding out where Poppy Novak is, are you? How many days has it been?'

'It's a difficult case.'

'I'm not saying it isn't. But the Balfours look at the lack of progress on the Novak case, and that worries them. Olivia is their only child. She's their life, and I don't know what they would do without her. They will literally do anything to get her back – which is presumably one of the reasons why the kidnappers chose them. They paid without arguing, even though I pointed out the risks involved. Then, when she wasn't released immediately, they decided to hold a press conference. Again, I was hesitant about this, but it was their decision. You may well think that both of those decisions were bad ones, but it's not your child that has been taken.'

'My view would be the same even if it was one of my kids.'

'Until it has actually happened, I don't think you can say that with any certainty,' said Lulu. 'Now perhaps you can answer a question for me. You're SIO in charge of the joint investigation, but how close are you to making an arrest?'

'The investigation is ongoing.'

'But no progress with ANPR or CCTV? You're no closer to arresting the men behind the kidnapping or finding out where they are holding the girls than the day that Poppy Novak first went missing.'

'There's a process to go through. You know how it works,' said the inspector. 'What about your cryptocurrency contact? Any luck in following the money?'

'We can follow the trail through various wallets, but that doesn't mean we know who owns the wallets,' said Lulu. 'The money that both the Elliotts and Balfours paid appears to have ended up on portable hard drives, but we don't know where those drives are. Will you be pursuing the idea we had about Airbnbs? Now we know that Olivia was dropped off somewhere between here and Chippenham, it should be possible to narrow down the number of possibilities.'

'We're looking into it,' said DI Kemp.

'And why are you here? To give the Balfours a hard time?'

'To explain to them that there are other people involved in this case, and that in future they need to clear statements with me before announcing them to the media.'

'Can I offer you some advice, DI Kemp? Not as a former police officer, but as a friend of the family.'

DI Kemp nodded. 'Go ahead.'

'I'd suggest you go easy on Amanda and Donald. They are both under an incredible amount of pressure at the moment and the cracks are starting to appear. With the greatest of respect, the last thing they need right now is more pressure from you. They really do need to be treated with kid gloves.'

'I'm aware of the situation they're in, and the Novaks are in the same situation. The difference is that the Novaks haven't gone rogue.'

'No, the difference is that the Novaks have no choice in the matter. They couldn't pay a ransom even if they wanted to. They have no choice but to wait for you to get their daughter back. They're powerless. Amanda and Donald do have choices, and they've acted in the way they thought best for their situation. You can't criticize them for that.'

'I hear what you're saying, Mrs Lewis. I'll put my best kid gloves on. But I'll need something in return.'

'What, exactly?'

'You've effectively been acting as a family liaison officer for the Balfours. I'd like that to continue, but perhaps with a bit more emphasis on the liaison. If there are issues with the Balfours that require resolving, I would prefer to at least know about them. I was only told about the ransom payment after the event, and today's press conference came out of the blue. When things like that happen, it makes it look as if I don't have a grip on the investigation.'

'Maybe you should give me your number.'

DI Kemp nodded. 'I'll do that. And DC Arnold will give you his number, too, just in case I'm tied up.'

DC Arnold held out his hand. 'If you give me your phone, I'll put both numbers in,' he said.

Lulu unlocked her phone and gave it to him. 'Would you two gentlemen like tea or coffee?' she asked.

'We won't be staying long,' said DI Kemp.

'Are you working all day?'

'I was with the kids this morning, and I plan to be back before their bedtime. Long hours go with the job, as you know.'

Lulu nodded. 'It helps to have an understanding spouse.'

'She understands, but that doesn't mean she's happy about it. I just hope she doesn't kick me into touch like her predecessors.'

'You've been married before?'

'Sandra is my third,' said the inspector. 'I was hoping third time lucky, but . . .' He pulled a face. 'I won't bore you with my problems.'

DC Arnold gave Lulu her phone back. 'All sorted,' he said.

'So, we'll have a quick word with Mr and Mrs Balfour, then we'll be off,' said DI Kemp.

Lulu took them along the hall to the sitting room. Donald and Amanda were still on the sofa.

DI Kemp nodded at Donald. 'Nice to see you again, Mr Balfour,' he said. He held out his hand to Amanda. 'And you, Mrs Balfour. As of today, I'm in charge of the investigation into your daughter's kidnapping.'

Amanda frowned as she shook the detective's hand. 'What about Juliet?'

'Juliet will still be working on the investigation, but she now reports to me.' He gestured at DC Arnold. 'And this is Detective Constable Max Arnold.' He opened his wallet and took out a business card, which he gave to Amanda. 'Here's my card. It has my mobile number on it, so any time you want to talk to me, just call.'

Amanda took the card and looked at it. 'I don't understand why Juliet isn't still working on the case.'

'She is – it's just that now she answers to me.'

Amanda's frown deepened. 'But why?'

Lulu saw DI Kemp's smile harden a little. He clearly didn't enjoy having his authority questioned. 'Basically, it makes better use of resources to have your daughter's abduction and the abduction of Poppy Novak investigated from the same office. Poppy was abducted in Wiltshire, the same kidnappers have obviously taken your daughter, and the two suspects we have are both residents of Wiltshire. Believe me, Mrs Balfour, there will be no reduction in resources and DI Donnelly will still be working on the case.' He nodded reassuringly, but Amanda continued to stare at the card. DI Kemp switched his attention to Donald. 'So, you went ahead and paid the ransom?'

Donald nodded. 'We did. We thought it best.'

'And then earlier today you held a press conference basically saying that the kidnappers are not to be trusted. I have to say that I don't think that was the wisest course of action. You really have no idea how they'll react to that.'

'We took the view that it has all been about the money, and them getting their money depends on people believing what they say. If the families who received the threatening letters know that the kidnappers aren't to be trusted, why should they pay?'

'I do wish you had spoken to me first,' said DI Kemp.

'Why? The last time you were here, you wanted us to do a joint press conference with Mr and Mrs Novak.'

'Yes, as a way of appealing to the public for information – not because I wanted to goad the kidnappers. And I certainly didn't want you to tell the world about the letters the kidnappers have been sending out. That we wanted to keep to ourselves.'

Donald shrugged. 'I don't know what to say to you, DI Kemp. Our priority is to get our daughter back.'

'But as we both know, that hasn't worked out the way you'd hoped.'

'We'll see,' said Donald.

'Yes, we will. I just hope the kidnappers don't decide that as you paid the quarter of a million pounds so easily, it would be worth their while asking for more.'

Donald's face fell. 'Do you think they might do that?'

'Who knows? You've already called them out for not being true to their word. What would they have to lose?'

Amanda looked at Donald. 'Is that possible? Might they do that?'

'I don't see how they could,' said Donald. 'If they did

that to us, surely nobody else would pay. The only reason you'd pay a ransom is if you believed that you'd get your child back.'

DI Kemp held up a hand. 'Let's not get ahead of ourselves,' he said. 'You've paid the ransom and you've rattled their cage; let's see how that pans out. In the meantime, we're doing everything we can to track them down. As I said, we have identified two of them, so it's only a matter of time. You have my card, so call me any time. I'll make sure that we keep you in the loop.' He looked over at Lulu. 'I know that Mrs Lewis is doing a great job of taking care of you, but if at any point you feel you would benefit from having a family liaison officer, just let me know.'

'Oh, I think we're doing just fine with Lulu,' said Donald.

'And Conrad,' said Amanda, stroking his fur.

'Conrad seems to have made himself at home,' said DI Kemp.

'He is a very sociable cat,' said Lulu. She smiled brightly. 'Shall I show you to the door?'

33

Time slowed to a crawl after DI Kemp and DC Arnold left. Lulu had to fight the urge to keep looking at her watch. She and Donald took it in turns to make mugs of tea. They watched television most of the time. They watched a cartoon film, but Lulu had no idea what the film was about, though there was a princess in it who reminded her of Olivia and a dragon who spoke very like Conrad, with a deep, authoritative voice and a tendency to use sarcasm.

The film was coming to an end when Lulu's phone rang. Her heart leapt when she saw that it was Juliet calling. She took the call and opened her mouth to speak, but the inspector beat her to it. 'We've got her. We've got Olivia.'

'Oh, that's amazing,' said Lulu. 'That's brilliant.' Amanda and Donald were both looking at her, and she gave them a thumbs up and nodded enthusiastically.

'The kidnappers dropped her in a village called Batheaston, about three miles east of Bath. They told her to walk to a church and the vicar called the police. The officers who turned up called me and took her straight to the Royal United Hospital to be checked out. I'm there now.'

Amanda and Donald were standing up now, and hugging each other.

'She's fine, she's at the Royal United Hospital but everything is okay,' said Lulu.

'We'll go there now,' said Donald. 'It's only a mile away.'

'Amanda and Donald are coming now,' said Lulu.

'No, no need,' said Juliet. 'There's a car outside waiting and we'll be done in a few minutes. She's absolutely fine, they're just taking forensics samples from her clothes and then she's good to go. Tell the Balfours we'll be there in about ten minutes.'

'That's brilliant, Juliet. Thank you so much.'

'See you soon.'

Lulu ended the call. 'It's true?' asked Amanda. 'They've really found her?'

Lulu nodded. 'They let her go in a place called Batheaston. She's fine, they're just forensically examining her clothes and then Juliet will bring her straight here. They'll be about ten minutes. She's on her way home, Amanda. It's over.'

'Oh my God,' said Amanda, sagging against Donald. 'I can't believe it.'

Donald hugged her and kissed her forehead. 'We'll never let her out of our sight again,' he said.

Amanda smiled over at Lulu. 'Thank you, Lulu,' she said. 'Thank you so much.'

'I didn't do anything,' said Lulu. 'I think it was your press conference that did it.'

'For being here,' said Amanda. 'We couldn't have got through this without you.' She beamed, blinking away tears. 'I can't believe it. I'm not dreaming, am I?'

Lulu shook her head. 'No, it's happening. She's coming home.'

Amanda buried her face in Donald's chest and sobbed.

The next ten minutes crawled by, but this time Lulu had a reason to keep checking her watch. Amanda kept going over to the window and peering through the gap in the curtains, and each time she did the photographers would start shouting and the cameras would click away. Lulu wanted to tell her that a watched pot never boiled, but she knew there was no point. Donald offered to make tea and Lulu said she'd love a cup, but really she just thought he needed something to keep himself occupied. He offered her a sandwich, but she said no. Her stomach was churning so much that she knew she wouldn't be able to eat.

Lulu was halfway through her cup of tea when her phone rang again. It was Juliet. 'We're just about to pull up in front of the house,' she said. 'We're in a Mercedes Sprinter van. I don't want to wait outside with all the photographers there, so can you have the door ready?'

'Of course,' said Lulu.

'Ten seconds and we'll be there. We're on Royal Crescent now.'

Lulu ended the call and turned to Amanda and Donald, saying, 'She's just—' but before she could finish, Amanda had jumped to her feet. She dashed across the carpet and down the hall. Donald and Lulu hurried after her.

The doorbell rang as Amanda pulled the door open. Immediately they could hear the click-click-click of cameras and photographers shouting Olivia's name. Olivia was standing next to Juliet, wearing a hospital robe over blue scrubs. The scrubs were clearly too big for her, and someone had rolled up the sleeves and legs.

'Oh my darling!' Amanda shouted. She picked Olivia up and clasped her to her chest. The clicking of the cameras went into overdrive. Juliet eased Amanda and Juliet inside and closed the door as Donald hugged his wife and daughter.

Juliet beamed at Lulu. Lulu grinned back, and then Juliet

stepped forward and gave her a hug. 'I can't tell you how relieved I am,' said Juliet.

'I know, it's amazing. How is she?'

'The doctors say she's absolutely fine. They treated her well enough, and there was nothing physical. No bruises, no nothing.'

Lulu sighed with relief. 'That's something, at least.'

Amanda was carrying Olivia down the hall to the sitting room. Donald followed with tears in his eyes. He stopped and hugged Juliet. 'Thank you,' he said. 'Thank you for bringing our daughter home.'

He released her and disappeared into the sitting room.

'To be fair, I didn't really do anything,' Juliet said to Lulu. 'I just collected her from the hospital. It's the Balfours who deserve the credit – it was clearly the press conference that got things moving.'

'Have you talked to Olivia?' asked Lulu.

'A little,' said Juliet. 'I thought it best to wait until she was with her parents. After all she's been through, I didn't think she needed a barrage of questions from strangers.'

'Has she said anything about what happened?'

'She said that Poppy was being held with her. And that the men holding them wouldn't let them shower or clean their teeth. And the men wore ski masks and overalls.'

'Same gear they had on when they broke into the house,' said Lulu.

'They took her pyjamas and swabs from her skin at the hospital, but it looks as if the kidnappers were careful forensically.'

Donald came out of the sitting room. 'She wants spaghetti Bolognese and a Snapple,' he said and hurried to the kitchen.

Lulu and Juliet went into the sitting room. Olivia was sitting on the sofa with Conrad on her lap; Amanda sat beside her with her arm around her. 'Donald is going to cook some food for her,' said Amanda. 'And we'll run her a bath and into some clean clothes. Is that okay?'

'Of course. We took all the swabs we need at the hospital.'

Amanda bit down on her lower lip. 'She wasn't . . . ?'

'Oh no, nothing like that,' said Juliet. 'We just needed to check if there was any DNA or hairs that didn't belong to her or Poppy. It's standard procedure. That's why they kept her pyjamas.'

Olivia had her head down as she stroked Conrad. She was whispering softly to him.

Juliet sat down in one of the armchairs. 'Olivia, could you tell us a bit about what happened?'

Olivia shrugged but didn't say anything.

'Where were you kept? Could you see anything?'

'We were in a basement.'

'And you said that Poppy Novak was with you?'

Olivia nodded.

'How was she?'

'She was scared. But she was happier when I was there. She said it was good to have a friend.'

'When they took you to the basement, did you see the house?' asked Lulu. 'Did you see anything at all?'

'I was asleep. I woke up in the basement so I don't know how I got there.'

'And when you left? What did you see?' asked Lulu.

Olivia wrinkled her nose. 'I didn't see anything. They put this hood thing over my head and made me lie in the back of a car.'

'What about the men who were keeping you in the basement?' asked Juliet. 'What did they look like?'

'I never saw their faces,' said Olivia. 'I told you, they always wore ski masks. And overalls. It was hard to tell them apart.'

'How many do you think there were?'

'There were two that came down into the basement, and sometimes we heard another man upstairs. Maybe two.'

'Was there anything noticeable about their voices?' asked Lulu.

'Not really. They all sounded the same. But they didn't really say much.'

'Did you hear any sounds coming from outside the house?'

'Sirens sometimes. Like an ambulance. Or a fire station.'

'During the day? Or the night?'

'I don't know,' said Olivia. 'We never knew what time it was. There was a light but they left it on all the time, so we didn't know if it was day or night.'

Conrad jumped off Olivia's lap, walked over to the door and began scratching at it. Juliet looked over at him. 'Looks like he wants to go out,' said Juliet.

'Yes, it does,' said Lulu. She went over to the door and opened it. Conrad slipped out into the hall and padded along to the kitchen. Lulu followed him.

Donald was frying mince and onions. 'Is everything okay?' he asked.

'Call of nature,' said Lulu, gesturing at Conrad. 'We'll just go out into the garden.' She opened the kitchen door and Conrad ran out. Lulu followed him and closed the door. They walked in silence to the middle of the lawn.

'So you want a private word, is that it?' Lulu asked in a low voice.

'I could hardly talk to you in there, could I?' said Conrad. 'And it is important.'

'I'm listening,' said Lulu.

'I can smell curry on her.'

'Curry?'

'Indian food. Turmeric, coriander, cumin, black cardamom. It's on her clothes and her hair. You can't smell it?'

'No. But then we both know that your sense of smell is so much better than mine. Fourteen times better.'

'You remembered.'

'Of course. I remember everything you tell me. So she's been around Indian cooking, or at least Indian food?'

'Apparently. Yes.'

'That could be very helpful.'

'That's what I thought.'

Lulu leaned towards Conrad so that he could jump onto her shoulders. They went back inside and through the kitchen, where Donald was dropping spaghetti into a pan of boiling water. 'Won't be long now,' he said.

Amanda was still sitting next to Olivia. 'Olivia wants a bath,' she said.

'That's understandable,' said Lulu. Conrad walked over to the sofa and jumped up onto Olivia's lap.

'A bubble bath,' said Olivia, stroking Conrad's back.

'That sounds perfect,' said Lulu.

'With a bath bomb. From Lush.'

'Even better. Olivia, can I ask you what you had to eat while you were with them?'

'Not much, their food was rubbish.'

Lulu smiled. 'Rubbish? Why?'

'They ate curry most of the time and I hate curry.'

'You don't hate curry,' said Amanda. 'You love Thai green curry.'

'That's Thai curry, that's different. This was Indian curry.' She shuddered. 'It was horrible. But I could eat the rice, and they had some triangular pastry things stuffed with vegetables that were okay.'

'Samosas, they're called,' said Lulu. 'So you had curry both days?'

'They gave us sandwiches the first morning I was there. And Coke.'

'Did they make sandwiches for you?' asked Lulu.

'No, they were supermarket ones.'

'You don't remember the label, do you?' asked Lulu.

'They were Waitrose. They were quite nice, but after that it was just curry.'

'And did they cook the curry for you or was it a takeaway?'

Olivia frowned. 'Why do you care so much about the food, Aunty Lulu?'

'I want to know if they took good care of you,' said Lulu.

'Well, they didn't. I had to ask to use the toilet and they wouldn't let me take a shower. They gave me a bucket but I said I wouldn't use it.' She shuddered. 'It was horrible.'

'So was it a takeaway they gave you? Or did they microwave ready meals?'

'It was takeaway. Poppy loved it. She said her family eats curry a lot.'

'Do you remember anything about it? Did you see the carrier bag it came in?'

Olivia frowned. 'I did, yes. Bombay Palace. I thought it

was a stupid name because the food was so bad. Not like something people would eat in a palace.'

'And the food was always hot?'

Olivia nodded. 'He'd have two plastic bags, one for him and one for us. He gave us our bag with plastic forks and we ate it in the basement while they ate theirs upstairs.'

Lulu smiled. 'You say "he". Was it always the same man who gave you food?'

'Yes. But we heard other people moving around.' She sighed and looked over at Amanda. 'Mum, we have to get Poppy out of there.'

'The police are looking for her. I'm sure it won't be long before they find her.'

'No, you need to pay a ransom. That's why they let me go. Can we pay for her, too? Her parents don't have any money.'

'We'll see,' said Amanda.

'Mummy, if we don't pay, nobody will.'

'Let me talk to your father,' said Amanda.

As she spoke, Donald appeared in the doorway holding a tray on which there was a plate of steaming spaghetti and a bottle of Snapple. 'Dinner is served,' he said, placing the tray on the coffee table in front of Olivia.

Conrad jumped down and walked over to stand by Lulu.

'We'll leave you to your dinner and your bath,' said Juliet. 'Perhaps we could talk to you again tomorrow morning.'

'Okay,' said Olivia, picking up a fork and plunging it into the pasta.

Juliet took out her phone as they walked into the hall and closed the sitting-room door. 'That was very useful,' she said. 'They're within walking distance of a curry house called

Bombay Palace.' She tapped on the screen of her phone and then smiled. 'There's a Bombay Palace in Corsham, about five miles to the west of Chippenham.' She looked up. 'And if I remember right, there's a fire station in Corsham. It's an on-call station, so the firefighters all have other jobs and respond to emergency calls when paged. And emergency calls mean sirens.' She grinned. 'You did it, Lulu. Well done you.'

Conrad was looking up at Lulu with a smug smile on his face. He had been right, but then again, he usually was.

'Let's not count our chickens just yet, Juliet. Are you going to talk to DI Kemp?'

Juliet's smile faded. 'I have to, unfortunately. He's my boss now.'

'Which means he'll take the credit.'

'Oh, I'll make sure we're in at the kill,' Juliet said. She grimaced. 'Bad choice of words.'

'It's okay,' said Lulu. 'I know what you mean.'

34

'That's them ahead of us,' said Juliet. She slowed the Tesla. Lulu was in the passenger seat with Conrad on her lap. They were on the A4, Bath Road, on the outskirts of Corsham. It had taken DI Kemp and his team less than three hours to find the house where they thought Poppy Novak was being held: a three-bedroom stone cottage that was ten minutes' walk from the Bombay Palace curry house.

DI Kemp's grey Vauxhall Insignia was parked in a lay-by. Ahead of his car were two armed response vehicles – white BMW SUVs. In front of the ARVs was an ambulance. Two paramedics stood at the rear of the ambulance, vaping.

DI Kemp climbed out of the passenger side of the Vauxhall and walked over to the Tesla. Juliet wound down the window. 'Thank you for waiting,' she said.

'No problem. Seems only fair, as you nailed it.'

'It was Lulu who identified the Bombay Palace,' said Juliet.

DI Kemp smiled coldly at Lulu. 'Nice work,' he said. 'So, we have eyes on the house. One of my team visited the restaurant with photographs of Steven Chorley and Jordan Mitchell, and a member of staff recalled Mitchell picking up several takeaways over the past few days. The cottage is listed on Airbnb and has a basement, where we assume Poppy is being held. Mitchell's car is outside the cottage but we haven't seen any movement. The lights are on. I've booked a firearms team just to be safe. We'll let them go in first. The house is half a mile from here, and there's a bend in the road to the west of it. We can stop there and the firearms team can approach on foot. Once they're in, we can drive up.'

'Sounds like a plan,' said Juliet.

DI Kemp frowned when he saw Conrad sitting on Lulu's lap. 'Does that cat go everywhere with you?'

'Pretty much, yes. Don't forget, it was Conrad who got the DNA that helped us identify Chorley.'

'I'll be sure to mention that in my report,' said the inspector, his voice loaded with sarcasm. 'Right, we're ready to go now, so stick close to me. We'll be monitoring the firearms team on channel six.' He nodded to them, then walked back to the Vauxhall.

Juliet tuned her radio to channel six and gave it to Lulu to hold. The ARV pulled out of the lay-by. The Vauxhall followed.

'Here we go,' said Juliet, edging the Tesla into the road.

They drove in convoy for a minute or so and then Kemp's Vauxhall indicated and pulled in at the side of the road. Juliet stopped behind him and put her flashers on. The two ARVs disappeared around the bend.

The radio burst into life with transmissions between the members of the firearms team. It was easy for Lulu to picture the six officers leaving their vehicle and fanning out as they approached the cottage. Two went around to the rear of the building. One of the four at the front was holding an Enforcer – a sixteen-kilogram battering ram of hardened steel that was often nicknamed The Big Red Key. It could open pretty much any locked door, even one that had been reinforced, with a couple of well-timed swings.

The two officers at the rear radioed that they were in position.

Lulu heard one officer bang on the door of the house and announce that there were armed officers outside and that the door was to be opened immediately. There was no reaction, and after five seconds or so the officer banged again. 'Armed police!' he shouted. 'Open the door or we will break it down!'

Seconds later, there was a loud crash as the Enforcer did its job, followed by shouts of 'Armed police!' as the officers piled in.

Lulu had been at dozens of such forced entries during her years with the Met. She knew exactly how the officers would be moving through the cottage, guns at the ready, clearing each room. There were shouts of 'Clear!' and 'Armed police!' but nothing that suggested they were meeting any resistance. When there was a final shout of 'All clear!' Lulu realized that the cottage must have been empty.

She looked over at Juliet. From the look of disappointment on the inspector's face, it was clear that she had come to the same conclusion.

The Vauxhall pulled out and drove down the road. The Tesla followed. They went around the bend and for the first time they saw the cottage: stone built with a steeply sloping tiled roof, surrounded by a high privet hedge. There was a blue Ford Fiesta parked on a gravelled driveway. The two ARVs were in the road outside the cottage. The Vauxhall parked behind the SUVs, and DI Kemp and DC Arnold climbed out.

Juliet parked the Tesla on the other side of the road. A sergeant wearing a Kevlar vest, helmet and body armour was briefing DI Kemp as Lulu and Juliet walked over.

'All the rooms are clear but there are signs that a child

was being held in the basement,' said the sergeant as he cradled his carbine. 'The stairs lead down from the kitchen.'

'Thank you,' said DI Kemp.

'If it's okay with you, we'll leave you to it,' said the sergeant.

'Absolutely,' said DI Kemp. 'Sorry it was a false alarm.'

'Better safe than sorry,' said the sergeant. 'Happy Boxing Day.' As he turned away, he spotted Conrad sitting on Lulu's shoulders. He frowned. 'There's a . . .' he began, but then shook his head. 'Never mind,' he said. He walked over to the SUVs, where the firearms officers were stowing their weapons and removing their protective gear.

Lulu and Juliet followed DI Kemp and DC Arnold into the cottage. To the left was a sitting room, with two small sofas angled towards a television and a coffee table littered with newspapers. The curtains were drawn. To the right was a dining room, with a scratched oak table surrounded by four high-backed wooden chairs. The curtains were also drawn.

The hall led on to a large kitchen with a window overlooking a rear garden. There was a Belfast sink piled high with dirty plates and mugs. By the door was a rubbish bin. Lulu pressed the foot pedal and the lid popped open. Inside were several empty cans of lager and fast-food containers full of pungent-smelling Indian food.

In one corner, an open wooden door led to the basement. Kemp went down the stairs first, Arnold following.

Lulu went over to a kettle on the counter and touched it gingerly. 'Still warm,' she said to Juliet. 'They're not long gone.'

Juliet gestured at the door. 'Do you want to have a look?'

'I'll leave that to the professionals,' Lulu said. She pointed at the overflowing sink. 'Plenty of DNA and fingerprints there. They were clearly in too much of a rush to clean up.'

Juliet headed down the stairs after the two Wiltshire detectives.

'Are you thinking what I'm thinking?' asked Conrad quietly.

'I rather think I am,' whispered Lulu.

'Are you going to talk to Juliet?'

'I think I have to, don't I?'

'I rather think you do,' said Conrad.

They heard footsteps, and Juliet reappeared in the kitchen. 'This is definitely the place,' she said. 'There are two camp beds down there and some leftover food containers.'

'Have you checked out the garden?' asked Lulu.

'The garden? Why?'

'Oh, it's always worth getting the lie of the land,' said Lulu. She opened the kitchen door and stepped out onto a small flagstone terrace. Juliet joined her, and Lulu pulled the door closed. 'Don't you think this is all a bit convenient?' she said.

'Convenient? For whom?'

'For the kidnappers. They were here only a few hours ago. The kettle is still warm, and from the look of it they didn't finish their takeaway. It looks to me as if they were tipped off, grabbed Poppy and left. And they left behind Jordan Mitchell's car. Why would they do that?'

Juliet sighed. 'Because they knew we were looking for the car.'

'Exactly.'

'Which means that they know we know about Mitchell.'

'The same way that they knew we were after Chorley.

Chorley got a phone call telling him to ditch his phone and his van not long before we arrived at his house. And the kidnappers get a call to abandon this cottage just hours before we arrived.'

A cold wind blew from the hedge and Juliet shivered. 'You know what this means, don't you?'

'I'm afraid so. Very few people knew about today's operation in advance. The ambulance and the ARVs would have been told at the last moment, and I'm sure it wasn't you or me who tipped them off.'

'So it has to be Kemp or Arnold.'

'Or someone else on Kemp's team. It's possible he told them what was happening and one of them tipped off the kidnappers.'

'That's a good point. You're right. He's obviously going to be briefing his team every day.'

'I might have a way of finding out for sure,' Lulu said thoughtfully. 'When you get the chance, and DI Kemp and DC Arnold are within earshot, ask me how Kirsty is getting on chasing up the Bitcoin.'

'Will do,' Juliet said.

They heard a noise in the kitchen. Through the window, they saw DI Kemp appear from the basement stairs. Lulu opened the door. 'Nothing in the garden,' she said.

'There's plenty of evidence that the girls were down in the basement,' said Kemp. 'I'm calling in a forensics team, but it's Boxing Day so I don't know how quickly they'll be here. There are usually a few domestic stabbings during the festive season but hopefully they'll be out some time today. I've called for a uniform to preserve the crime scene and there's a car on the way.'

Lulu and Juliet followed him to the front door. DC Arnold followed, talking into his mobile phone.

'On the plus side, at least we know that Jordan Mitchell is definitely involved,' said Juliet. 'What about releasing his photograph and Steven Chorley's to the press?'

'I'm going to keep a lid on it for a day or two,' said Kemp. 'We know we're looking for Mitchell and Chorley now, and I'd rather it was our people doing the looking. Once we start asking the public for information we'll be inundated, and we'll have to follow up every single tip-off. And with Boxing Day manpower, that'll leave us seriously understaffed. I'm assuming they'll stay local. Everything they've done has been in the area, hasn't it? The homes of the two victims, the homes of Mitchell and Chorley, this cottage and the place where they released Olivia. The problem is that now we don't know what vehicle they're using, and there isn't much in the way of CCTV or ANPR around here.'

'Maybe that's why they chose this cottage,' said Lulu.

'Possibly,' said Kemp. He reached the front door and opened it. The two ARVs had gone.

They walked down the path towards the pavement. 'Any news from your NCA lady?' Juliet asked Lulu.

'She called this morning. The blockchain hasn't reappeared, so it looks as if the Bitcoin wallet is still on the hard drive. Which is good news for Donald and Amanda.'

'Why's that?' asked DI Kemp.

'Oh, it's a security measure that Kirsty invoked when Donald did the Bitcoin transfer. It's a new option available for Bitcoin transactions. If the wallet stays offline for more than forty-eight hours, the transaction is effectively cancelled and Donald will get his money back. I don't fully understand it – the whole cryptocurrency thing is a mystery to me. But Kirsty is an expert, and she says the NCA have used this technique to bring down a couple of criminal enterprises. Anyway, we'll know one way or another forty-eight hours after the Bitcoin goes offline.' She frowned. 'Or was it thirty-six?' She shook her head. 'It doesn't matter, she'll call me when she knows.' She flashed a smile at Juliet. 'Are you okay to drop me back at the Balfours', or shall I grab an Uber?'

'Oh, I'll drop you, of course.' Juliet nodded at DI Kemp. 'I'll have another chat with Olivia. If she gives up anything new, I'll call you.'

'Please do,' he said.

Lulu and Juliet walked back to the Tesla in silence. Juliet waited until they were sitting inside the car before speaking. 'So what was that about?' she asked.

Lulu took out her phone. 'As we were saying, someone is tipping off the kidnappers,' she said. 'I don't think there's any doubt about that. If it's either of those two, they'll check that the Bitcoin wallets are okay, and Kirsty will be able to see the blockchain online again.' She pulled a face. 'That's what I'm hoping, anyway. I wasn't joking when I said this whole cryptocurrency business is a mystery to me.' She tapped the phone to call Kirsty. 'Happy Boxing Day,' said Lulu when the NCA officer answered. 'I hope I haven't interrupted anything?'

'I'm just wondering if I should have a third glass of Pinot Grigio.'

'Oh, I'd say that's a definite yes,' said Lulu. 'I'm a big fan of Pinot Grigio. But I wonder if you could do me a big favour?'

'Ask and you shall receive,' said Kirsty.

'Would you mind keeping an eye on the two blockchains – the one from the Elliotts' wallet, and the one from Donald Balfour? They were both downloaded to hard drives and we lost touch with them. I just want to know if anything changes.'

'That'll happen automatically,' said Kirsty. 'I've set up a notification so that I get a text when either of the wallets reappears. I'll call you as soon as I have anything.'

'You're an angel,' said Lulu, and she ended the call.

'So you've set a trap,' said Juliet, pulling away from the kerb.

'I have, yes. Let's just hope that it works.'

35

Lulu watched DI Kemp in the side mirror as Juliet drove away from the cottage. He was staring after their car. Then DC Arnold walked up to him and said something, and the two detectives walked back towards the cottage.

'You know, it would explain why they've made such little progress on the Poppy Novak case,' said Juliet. 'The only breakthroughs they've made have been down to the information we've given them.' She smiled at Conrad. 'And of course the DNA that Conrad got for us.'

'So it's down to us to find the kidnappers,' said Lulu.

Juliet nodded. 'I think so.'

'Where do we start?'

Juliet sighed. 'That's a good question.'

'Well, we know that this has all been very well planned, right from the beginning,' said Lulu. 'But as of today, that plan has fallen apart. They rushed out of the cottage, taking Poppy with them, with only hours to spare. I can't see that they could have planned for this, so at the moment they must be making it up as they go along. We know that they're not using Chorley's van or Mitchell's Fiesta, so whatever vehicle they are using must belong to another member of the gang. And there aren't too many places they can go, not on Boxing Day. They know we're onto them, so they can't go home. They can hardly check into a hotel with Poppy, not after her face has been plastered over the country's newspapers, and I doubt they'll be sleeping in their vehicle.'

'So they'll have no choice but to let her go, is that what you mean?'

'I think,' Lulu said, 'that if they were going to let her go, they'd have just left her in the basement. The fact that they took her with them means they're probably hoping to get more money.'

'From the rich families? Families who don't want their children to be abducted?'

'Well, the Novaks don't have money, do they? Or maybe they think that the Balfours will pay for Poppy's release. Olivia and Poppy have a connection now – maybe the kidnappers think they can exploit that. Whatever they're thinking, it's clearly not over yet, so we have to find them.'

Juliet pulled over at the side of the road. 'I don't think CCTV or ANPR is going to help. Cameras are few and far between out here,' she said. 'And we don't know what vehicle we're looking for. Forensics might come up with DNA or fingerprints that will help us identify the rest of the gang, but that's going to take time.'

'They have to stay local, don't they?' said Lulu. 'Everything has taken place within a few square miles. The kidnappers we know about are local; the cottage where they kept Poppy and Olivia is local; Poppy is from Bradford-on-Avon, Olivia is from Bath. I don't see that they'd now run to London or Birmingham. They're sure to stay where they feel comfortable, aren't they? And they run a risk of being spotted if they drive around with a kidnapped girl. They need to lie low, and quickly.'

'Do you have an idea?'

'They booked the cottage through Airbnb, we know that. And they probably chose it because of the basement. I wonder if they considered other options, and if those options might still be available.'

Juliet frowned. 'So you think they've booked another Airbnb?'

'I think that's unlikely on Boxing Day. But there'd be nothing to stop them breaking in, would there? Especially if they'd already visited.'

'So we could drive around and look at the local Airbnbs that are showing as available?'

Lulu nodded. 'Not all, just the ones that could be suitable for hiding a child. Cottages, detached houses, buildings with no overlooking neighbours. There probably won't be too many that fall into that category. What do you think?'

Juliet took out her phone. 'I think it's an inspired idea. Let's both check out the website and see how many possibilities there are.'

'Probably within a ten-mile radius of Corsham,' said Lulu. 'I can't see them being comfortable driving further than that with a kidnapped child. Bath is within a ten-mile drive but it seems logical to assume they wouldn't choose a place in the city. I think they would also steer clear of the centres of villages in the area, as there would always be the risk of a neighbour noticing the arrival of a car with two or more men and a young child. They'll probably avoid Chippenham because that's where Chorley lives; ditto they'll avoid Colerne, because that's where Mitchell lives. Too much chance of being recognized.'

'That makes a lot of sense,' said Juliet.

'And we don't run this by DI Kemp?'

Juliet snorted. 'No, we don't.'

Lulu and Juliet spent the next half hour on their phones looking for possibilities. Of the limited number of Airbnbs available in the area, many were obviously unsuitable. Even assuming they had driven as far as ten miles from Corsham, once they applied the criteria they had set, there were only thirty-seven homes that would fit the bill. Juliet wrote down the addresses in her notebook and handed it to Lulu.

'You can be navigator,' she said. 'I suggest we start around the Corsham area and move outwards.' She nodded at the large screen on the dashboard to the left of the steering wheel. 'The Tesla's satnav is spot on,' she said. 'Just input the addresses and Tessa will show us the way.'

'Tessa? Your car has a name?'

'Says the lady who calls her cat Conrad.'

'That's his name, Juliet.'

Juliet laughed. 'Oh, he named himself, did he?'

Lulu smiled but didn't answer, because if she did she'd only have to deal with a lot more questions. She tapped in the location of the nearest Airbnb and sat back. 'Okay, Tessa, do your thing.'

Juliet started driving. They reached the address in less than two minutes: a barn conversion surrounded by apple trees. The lights were off and there were no vehicles parked in front of it. 'Looks deserted. What do you think?' asked Juliet.

'Best we do a quick check to see if there are any signs of a break-in,' said Juliet. 'They could have broken in and then moved their vehicle somewhere else.'

Lulu nodded. 'You're right,' she said. She opened the door and stepped out, scooping Conrad onto her shoulders. She walked down the driveway, checked that the door and windows were okay, and then did a quick walk around the back of the building. 'Looks fine,' said Conrad.

'Yes, all good,' said Lulu.

'Do people really name their cars?'

'Some people do, yes.'

'That's ridiculous, isn't it?'

Lulu chuckled. 'I think it's tongue-in-cheek. I don't think Juliet expects her car to come to her when she calls its name. Though with a Tesla, who knows?'

She walked back to the car and climbed in, slipping Conrad onto her lap. 'No problems,' she said. She tapped in the next address as Juliet pulled away from the kerb.

Over the next two hours, they checked another fourteen properties. All were unoccupied with no signs of forced entry. Lulu was just tapping in the sixteenth address when her phone rang. It was Kirsty.

'Whatever acorn you planted grew into an oak tree,' she said. 'Both hard drives were activated and both blockchains were back online. There were a few wallet-to-wallet transactions and then the blockchains went offline again, presumably back onto the hard drives.'

'So whoever it was, they wanted to check that the money was still there?'

'Exactly. Does that help you?'

'Oh, it does, Kirsty. Thank you so much. Best Christmas present you could have given me.'

Lulu ended the call and smiled at Juliet. 'Somebody just activated the hard drives,' she said.

'That's good news and bad news, isn't it?' said Juliet. 'We know where the kidnappers are getting their inside information from – but it means catching them is going to be that much harder.'

They drove to the next house, a large detached cottage shrouded with ivy. It had a two-car garage, the roof of which was topped by a large metal weathervane featuring a crowing cock. Most of the lights were on and there were three cars parked outside – two BMWs and a Mercedes.

Juliet brought the Tesla to a stop in the road. 'That's hardly low-profile, is it?' she said. She took out her radio and contacted the incident room in Kenneth Steele House, asking a DC to run the registration numbers of the three cars through the DVLA computer and then cross-check the names of the registered owners with the Police National Computer.

It took the DC just five minutes to confirm that two of the vehicles belonged to residents of Bath and the third to the owner of the cottage. Juliet thanked him and put the transceiver away. She smiled at Lulu. 'Good thing we didn't call in a firearms team. It would have ruined their Christmas party.'

Lulu tapped in the next address, a three-bedroom modern house. It turned out to be just two hundred yards away on the outskirts of the village of Marshfield. There were no lights on and no cars parked outside. This time, Juliet did the walk round to check for any signs of a break-in.

'I suppose a lot of police work is like this,' said Conrad, as he and Lulu watched Juliet disappear behind the house. 'Checking lots of possibilities until you find the right one. Knocking on doors, talking to people, gathering information. Taking things step by step.'

'That's right,' said Lulu. 'It's actually quite boring most of the time, even though the stakes are high. It isn't like it is on the TV, where a seasoned lone wolf detective with a drink problem and anger management issues goes off on a personal crusade to catch a bad guy. But then, if they showed what a real police investigation is like, no one would watch.'

Juliet returned and climbed back into the Tesla. 'All secure,' she said, starting the car.

Lulu tapped the next address into the satnav. It was on the other side of Marshfield – a barn conversion with a full-size billiards table and a sauna, according to the Airbnb listing. Pets were not welcome.

The nearest neighbour was a couple of hundred yards away, and the barn conversion was shielded from the road by a line of fir trees. There was a white Nissan Qashqai parked in the driveway.

Juliet slowed down. 'Can you get the registration number?' she asked. Lulu pulled out her phone and took a quick shot of the car as they drove by.

Once they were clear of the house, Juliet pulled over and radioed the incident room again, reading out the registration number from the photograph Lulu had taken. The DC came back on the radio after two minutes.

'The registered keeper is one Rob Ballantine. Lives in the Broadmead area of Bristol,' said the DC. 'Car doesn't appear to be insured. Mr Ballantine did three years in HMP Erlestoke for domestic burglary and carrying an offensive weapon.'

'Oh, that's interesting,' said Juliet. 'Can you check if there was any overlap between his stay in HMP Erlestoke and Jordan Mitchell? Mitchell was there for eighteen months.'

'Will do, boss,' said the DC. 'Bear with me.'

'Broadmead is a rough area of Bristol,' Juliet explained to Lulu. 'There's a lot of homelessness, drug issues and petty crime.'

The DC came back on the radio. 'Ballantine and Mitchell were at HMP Erlestoke together for seven months,' he said. 'Mitchell was released first and Ballantine some time after. They're not shown as contacts on the PNC.'

'I think we can assume that they know each other,' said Juliet. 'And I'm looking at his car parked outside a house in Marshfield which is supposed to be empty. Right, in view of the previous offence for an offensive weapon, I'm going to need an ARV, two if there are two available, a patrol van with at least six uniforms, and an ambulance. No sirens. Make it clear I want no blues and twos. Here's the address.' She read out the address of the house. 'And just to confirm once more – no sirens. I'll be parked down the road from the house in my blue Tesla. They can reach me on the radio when they're en route.'

'Just one thing, boss – you realize that the house is in Wiltshire?'

'I thought Marshfield was in Somerset.'

'It's literally on the border. But the village is about twelve miles from Trowbridge and thirty miles from Bristol, so if speed is important you'd be better off doing it through Wiltshire Police.'

'I appreciate what you're saying, but I'd prefer that we use Avon and Somerset resources for this, so let's assume the house is on our side of the border.'

'Not a problem, boss. I'll get that sorted.'

Juliet put down the radio and gave Lulu a wry smile. 'The last thing we want is to do this through Kemp,' she said.

She turned in her seat to look at the house. 'My heart is pounding like it's going to burst out of my chest.'

'Me too,' said Lulu.

'I really hope Poppy is in there,' said Juliet.

'I'm sure she is.'

'Really?'

Lulu nodded. 'I can feel it in my bones. Copper's intuition.'

'You know, if we do find her in there, it's all down to good, honest police work. You and me checking on possibilities one after the other until we strike gold. It's a change from DNA, CCTV and ANPR. That's how we solve most cases these days.'

The ARV made good time, thanks to the lack of traffic on the Boxing Day roads. They called in on the radio to say they were three minutes away and running silent.

When the AVR, a white BMW SUV, appeared, Juliet climbed out of her Tesla and waved them down. They pulled in and Juliet jogged over. A sergeant in the front passenger seat wound the window down. She was in her thirties with blonde hair tucked into a police baseball cap. Juliet recognized her as Sandy Deville, one of the force's longest-serving firearms officers.

'I thought it was you, Juliet,' she said. 'Is this about the kidnapped girl?'

'Poppy Novak, yes,' said Juliet. 'They released Olivia Balfour this morning and we have every reason to believe Poppy is being held in this house.'

'Any likelihood of firearms?'

'Not that we know, but one of the kidnappers has form for using an offensive weapon.'

'No problem,' said Sandy. 'There's a second ARV four

minutes away so we'll wait until they get here.' She opened the door and climbed out. Her front passenger got out of his side and opened the rear door of the SUV. The firearms officer in the back handed out Kevlar vests and pulled their carbines from the gun safe. They were adjusting their vests when the second ARV arrived, and within a few minutes there were six firearms officers ready to go in.

As they gathered on the pavement to be briefed by Sandy, a grey Mercedes Sprinter van arrived with seven uniformed officers on board. Juliet went over to speak to the unit's sergeant.

Lulu stayed where she was, in the front seat of the Tesla with Conrad on her lap. Conrad was sitting up, watching the six armed officers form a line and head to the driveway. One of them was holding an Enforcer.

'It's all very military, isn't it?' said Conrad. 'They look more like soldiers than police officers.'

'That's deliberate,' said Lulu. 'The idea is to overpower the criminals with a show of force so that nobody has to actually pull the trigger. It's supposed to be safer that way.'

'It's scary.'

'Yes, it is. But it's very unusual for a firearms officer to actually fire their weapon other than when they're training. Most go through their whole career without pulling the trigger in action.'

The last of the firearms officers disappeared down the driveway. The officers from the Mercedes van were lining up along the pavement to the left of the drive. Juliet was with them.

An ambulance appeared and pulled in behind the police van.

'I hope Poppy is okay,' said Conrad.

'So do I.'

They heard shouts in the distance, then the splintering of wood, and more shouts. Then silence. The silence dragged on and on, which Lulu took as a good sign. Two paramedics in green overalls carrying red and white kitbags walked along the pavement towards the driveway. Two officers appeared from the direction of the house. They moved to either side of the driveway to make way for Juliet, who was holding Poppy Novak, who was wearing her school uniform.

'We've got her!' said Lulu excitedly. 'Oh, that is wonderful. Just wonderful.' She opened the car door and climbed out, scooping Conrad onto her shoulders.

'She's fine,' said Juliet.

'What about the kidnappers?'

'They have Chorley and Mitchell in custody, and there's a third guy who is presumably Rob Ballantine. Ballantine put up a bit of a fight but they subdued him without firing a shot.' She grinned. 'He's going to have a few bruises.'

'That's great, Juliet,' said Lulu. 'Not the bruises, obviously – I mean, great that Poppy is safe and sound.'

'There are four mugs in the kitchen sink, so it could be there's another member of the gang we don't know about. I'll get a forensics team out and we'll see what we get in the way of DNA and fingerprints.'

One of the paramedics tried to examine Poppy, but she refused to release her grip around Juliet's neck.

'I think we should take Poppy straight home, don't you?' said Juliet. 'I don't think we need to bother with forensics. There are more than a dozen witnesses to her rescue.'

'I think you're right,' said Lulu. 'The important thing is

to get her back to her mum and dad. What do you think, Poppy? Do you want to go home?'

Poppy nodded and sniffed, hugging Juliet tightly.

'Home it is,' said Juliet.

36

The three kidnappers were placed in cells at Kenneth Steele House overnight. Juliet and Lulu took Poppy home and delivered her to her delighted parents. There were no photographers outside the house, and it was only when the Avon and Somerset Police press office released a statement that the media learned Poppy had been found and the kidnappers arrested.

Juliet asked Lulu if she wanted to be present while the suspects were interrogated, and Lulu readily agreed. Juliet picked her up at nine o'clock in the morning, and half an hour later they were walking through reception at Kenneth Steele House.

DI Kemp was waiting to meet them, clearly not happy. 'Why the hell wasn't I informed that you had found Poppy Novak?' he said. DC Arnold stood beside him, looking just as displeased as his boss.

'It all happened very quickly,' said Juliet. 'There wasn't time to inform everyone.'

'I'm not "everyone", DI Donnelly. I'm the SIO on this case. Not informing me amounts to insubordination.'

'It was Boxing Day, resources were stretched, and we realized that we had to act quickly. Rather than waste time informing everybody, I made the decision to strike while the iron was hot.'

'Again, DI Donnelly, I am not "everybody" – I am the SIO. It was your duty to keep me informed.'

'Would you have done anything differently, DI Kemp? If so, please tell me. Because it seems to me that what I did resulted in the release of the kidnap victim and the arrest of three kidnappers.'

'That's not the point.'

'Oh, really? The successful outcome of the case that you were in charge of isn't the point? Then what is the point?'

'You're deliberately being difficult,' said DI Kemp. 'You know exactly what you did. When you left the cottage at Corsham, you must have known what you planned to do.'

'Once it became clear that the kidnappers had fled before we arrived, Lulu and I decided they probably hadn't gone too far, so we started checking local Airbnbs that were supposed to be empty.'

DI Kemp sneered at Lulu. 'I might have known the crazy cat lady would be involved.'

'There's no need to be offensive, DI Kemp,' said Lulu. 'I was only trying to help.'

DI Kemp opened his mouth to snap at her, but then he took a deep breath and forced a smile. 'I apologize, Mrs Lewis. That was uncalled for.'

'I understand your strength of feeling about this,' said Lulu. 'But really, all's well that ends well. We, the team, have got the two girls back to their parents and have the kidnappers – three of them, anyway – in custody. And as SIO, you'll get the credit.'

'It's not about the credit, it's about . . .' Kemp tailed off, leaving the sentence unfinished. 'Yes, the important thing now is to complete the interviews and get them remanded. I think it best if DI Donnelly and I conduct the interviews. You and DC Arnold can watch from the observation room.'

'Do you want to be good cop, or should I?' asked Juliet brightly.

Kemp's eyes narrowed as he tried to work out whether she was making a joke. Eventually he decided that she was, and he smiled thinly. 'Let's play it by ear, shall we?'

'I'll show you to the observation room, Mrs Lewis,' said Arnold. He led her through a door and up a flight of stairs, then along a corridor with rooms either side. He pushed one open to reveal a group of six padded chairs facing a row of six flat screens. 'Take a pew,' he said.

Lulu sat down and Conrad dropped onto the seat next to her as Arnold closed the door and went over to the screens. Each was labelled with a room number and a camera number, showing two cameras per room. He switched on the two screens for interview room number one and sat down next to Lulu. 'Let the show begin,' he said. 'Would you like popcorn or a soft drink?'

'Actually, a water would be nice,' said Lulu.

'I was joking, but not a problem,' said DC Arnold, and he left the room.

'He seems nervous,' said Conrad. 'More nervous than the last time we saw him.'

'How is his aura?'

'Funny you should ask,' said Conrad. 'There's quite a bit of dark red today, which is a sign of frustration or trauma. I'd say he's under a lot of stress.'

'And what about DI Kemp?'

'The same,' said Conrad.

'And me?'

Conrad chuckled. 'There's more gold in your aura than I've seen for a while.'

'Oh, gold is good.'

'Gold is very good,' said Conrad. 'It suggests self-assuredness. And confidence.'

'Hmm, I'm not sure how confident I feel at the moment,' said Lulu. She was looking at the two screens that DC Arnold had switched on. The one on the right showed a table with four chairs, and a door behind it. The other screen showed a view from the door side, with a glass block window set high in the wall.

As Lulu watched, the door opened and a uniformed officer led Jordan Mitchell in, steering him to one of the chairs facing the door. Mitchell was wearing a blue sweatshirt, black jeans and gleaming white Nikes. Behind them came a bearded man in a sharp blue suit, carrying a bulging leather briefcase. He sat down next to Mitchell and began whispering in his ear. The uniformed officer left the room.

DC Arnold returned with a plastic bottle of water, which he gave to Lulu. He nodded at the screens as he sat down. 'That's Ahmad Chaudhry, one of the duty solicitors. We often see him in Trowbridge. He's not up to much. Not that there's much that can be done; they really were caught bang to rights.'

On screen, the door opened again and DI Kemp and Juliet walked in. Juliet was carrying a small black holdall. They sat down opposite Chaudhry and Mitchell, introduced themselves, and confirmed that the interview was being videoed.

'You were arrested yesterday afternoon at an address in Marshfield, along with Steven Chorley and Rob Ballantine, for the abduction of Olivia Balfour and Poppy Novak,' said DI Kemp. 'The police found Poppy Novak in one of the bedrooms. Do you have anything to say about that?'

'No comment,' said Mitchell. He folded his arms and stared at a spot on the wall.

'Prior to your arrest, your car was found parked outside a cottage in Corsham. Poppy Novak and Olivia Balfour were both held as prisoners in the basement of the cottage. Do you have anything to say about that?'

'No comment,' said Mitchell sullenly.

DC Arnold turned to look at Lulu. 'He's not going to say anything,' he said. 'He's been through this before. He'll just go "no comment" until we give up.'

Lulu continued to watch the screens. 'Let's see, shall we?'

Juliet took a pair of blue latex gloves from her pocket and put them on.

Mitchell frowned, clearly wondering what she was doing.

'The thing is, Jordan, you know how this works,' said DI Kemp. 'You can play the "no comment" game 'til the cows come home, but the only thing that will help you is if you cooperate. Your solicitor is only doing his job by telling you to not say anything. Generally that's the right advice, but in this case he's not doing you any favours.'

Ahmad Chaudhry raised his hand. 'You're not in a position to criticize me for the advice I give to my client, DI Kemp. I have his best interests at heart.'

'No offence intended, Mr Chaudhry. But your client needs to know that with all the evidence we have against him, his guilt isn't in question. We have his car at the Corsham cottage where the two little girls were held.'

'My client tells me that his car was stolen several days ago from outside his house.'

'In which case, he could have reported the theft to the police at the time, and we all know that he didn't. We have

315

a forensics team at the house where he kept Olivia Balfour and Poppy Novak, and we are confident that Mr Mitchell's DNA and fingerprints will be everywhere. He left in such a hurry that he neglected to clean up after himself.'

Juliet unzipped the holdall and took out an evidence bag containing a phone. Lulu realized it was probably Mitchell's.

'Your client also needs to be aware that we have Mr Chorley here, and that we have conclusive forensic evidence against him. We have his DNA at the Balfour kidnap scene.'

'On a cat's claws, I gather,' said the solicitor.

'DNA is DNA. And Mr Chorley has scratches on his face that can only have come from a cat's claws. Here's the thing, Mr Chaudhry. We only need one of the two of them to cooperate. The best advice you can give your client would be to tell us everything he knows before Mr Chorley starts talking.'

'Again, inspector, it is not your place to tell me what advice to give my client.'

'This is a nice phone, Mr Mitchell,' said Juliet, holding out the evidence bag. 'An iPhone 15, is it?'

'Sixteen. And it's an iPhone Pro Max.'

Juliet carefully opened the bag and took it out.

'What are you doing, inspector?' asked DI Kemp.

Juliet ignored him. 'I don't suppose you'd give me your PIN code, would you?' she asked Mitchell.

Mitchell snorted with derision and sat back, folding his arms. 'No comment,' he said.

Juliet leaned forward and held the phone up with the screen towards Mitchell. His face fell as he realized what she was doing. 'Oi, you can't do that,' he said.

Juliet looked at the phone. 'Isn't facial recognition amazing?' she said. 'So helpful.'

Mitchell looked at his solicitor. 'She can't do that, can she?'

Chaudhry wrinkled his nose. 'I'm afraid she can, yes. The phone is evidence.'

'I've got rights, haven't I? Rights to privacy? Human rights?'

'I see you haven't stored any numbers in your phone's memory,' said Juliet. 'So you're using a throwaway SIM card, I suppose? Very clever.' She checked the settings and nodded. 'And you've turned your GPS off, which is sensible.'

'This is a liberty!' said Mitchell. 'You can't do this!'

Juliet ignored him. 'Let's have a look at your recent calls, shall we? Oh, you've had several from the same number? Is that a burner phone, I wonder? Oh, look at that. That number called you just an hour before we arrived at the cottage in Corsham. I wonder if that was the person who tipped you off that we were coming?'

Mitchell glared at her. 'No comment,' he said.

Juliet smiled brightly. 'Let's see if they'll speak to me,' she said. She pressed the call button and looked over at DI Kemp. 'This should be interesting,' she said.

'Clever girl,' said Lulu. She turned to look at Arnold. 'She's right, isn't she? This is going to be interesting.'

DC Arnold was staring at the screens. The colour had drained from his face. He flinched as a phone burst into life within the room where they sat. Then he cursed under his breath.

Lulu smiled at him. 'I think you should answer that, DC Arnold,' she said. 'Don't you?'

DC Arnold swore again, and looked at the door.

'You're in a police station. You're on CCTV. Where would you run to?' asked Lulu quietly.

DC Arnold slumped in his chair, then reached into his coat pocket and took out a cheap Samsung phone. He stared at the screen and shook his head slowly.

Lulu reached over and took the still-ringing phone from his shaking hand. She answered the call, put the phone to her ear and smiled. 'Yes, it's me.' Her smile widened. 'Yes, lovely to hear your voice too.'

Juliet turned towards the camera so that she was looking directly at Lulu and DC Arnold. The detective's lower lip trembled as Juliet mouthed, 'Gotcha!'

37

They were in the same interview room where Jordan Mitchell had been questioned by DI Kemp and Juliet, but this time it was DC Arnold who was in the hot seat, faced by Lulu and Juliet. Conrad sat on Lulu's lap, staring at Arnold with his emerald-green eyes.

'Does that cat go everywhere with you?' asked DC Arnold.

'He does,' said Lulu. 'Yes.'

'If he hadn't scratched Steve, you'd never have caught us. You were lucky.'

Lulu smiled. 'Oh, I'm not sure how big a part luck played in all this,' she said. She couldn't tell him that it was Conrad's super-sensitive nose that had led them to the cottage in Corsham, much as she wanted to.

Juliet nodded at DC Arnold. 'Max, you have refused the services of a solicitor, but I need to remind you again that you can have a solicitor if you want one, and that if you cannot afford one, one will be provided for you.'

DC Arnold shook his head. 'I know my rights, and I know how much shit I'm in. At this point I want to minimize the damage, that's all.' He drew a deep breath and let it out. 'It's a fair cop, as they say.' He looked up at the camera that was pointing at him.

DI Kemp was in the observation room, watching. Beside him was his superior, a gruff superintendent whose brow appeared to be knitted into a permanent frown. Superintendent

Pemberton had been well pleased that the case had been solved and Olivia and Poppy had been returned to their parents. He was less pleased to learn that one of his detectives had been involved in the kidnappings. He had driven straight over from Trowbridge, not at all happy at having his morning disrupted.

DI Kemp had wanted to carry out the interrogation of Arnold, but the superintendent had insisted that Juliet do it. The superintendent had spoken to the chief constables of Wiltshire, Avon and Somerset, and Gloucestershire, telling them that DI Donnelly was taking over as head of the tri-force investigation team.

'You can minimize the damage by telling us who planned all this,' said Juliet to DC Arnold.

'Guilty as charged,' said DC Arnold, raising his hand. 'That was me.'

'You recruited Mitchell, Chorley and Ballantine?'

DC Arnold nodded. 'They all needed money.' He forced a smile. 'Who doesn't, these days?'

'And the idea of abducting Poppy Novak and sending threatening letters to wealthy parents was yours?'

'Yeah.' He snorted. 'This is going to sound crazy, but I was trying to write a crime novel and I came up with the kidnapping idea.'

'You wanted to be a writer?' asked Lulu.

'I wanted to make money,' said DC Arnold. 'Have you any idea how much a house costs in Trowbridge these days? The average is three hundred thousand. A semi-detached in Chippenham costs half a million. How can I ever afford that? You know what a constable gets? I started on less than thirty grand, and after seven years on the job I'll still be on less than fifty. And who knows what house prices will be like then?' He shook his head. 'The world's gone crazy. I'm living in a shitty bedsit and rich landlords are paying over the odds to buy Airbnbs that they can fill with tourists. I ask you, is that fair?'

'Sounds like you made the wrong career choice,' said Lulu.

'It was the right career. I wanted to help people, I wanted to make a difference. But then I realized that the job was all about ticking boxes and the public hated us, pretty much.'

'So you decided that kidnapping children was the route to a better life?' said Juliet.

'Like I said, it started out as the plot of a book. But the more I researched it, the more I realized it was the perfect crime. Nobody got hurt, the people we targeted could afford it, it was almost a victimless crime.'

'Max, you terrified two little girls. And the fact that the people you extorted money from could afford it doesn't make it any less of a crime.'

'The girls were never in any danger, and we made them aware of that.'

'You still kidnapped two little girls.'

'Yes. Kidnapped is the word. They weren't assaulted, they weren't raped, they weren't murdered. We kept them in a nice warm basement and fed them and gave them books and magazines to read. Was that so bad, in the grand scheme of things?'

'Yes, Max,' said Lulu. 'It was bad. Do you have any idea of what you put the Balfours through? And the Novaks? Do you know how they suffered?'

'Of course he doesn't,' said Juliet. 'He doesn't have children. How could he understand?'

'All's well that ends well,' said DC Arnold. 'They've got

their kids back. Who knows, maybe now they'll appreciate them more.'

'You know you're facing life in prison, right?' said Juliet.

'Well, you say that, but am I? Am I really? I didn't kidnap anybody. That was Steve and Jordan and Rob. I never kept anyone prisoner. I never abducted anybody. I didn't even drive the van. Steve and Jordan took all the pictures and sent out the letters. Rob is the one who fed the girls and let them use the toilet. I never went near them. So really, you'd be charging me with conspiracy to kidnap rather than actual kidnapping.'

'They carry the same statutory maximum sentence,' said Juliet. 'Life imprisonment.'

'Yes, that's true. But the average custodial sentence for kidnapping is five years, nine months. So out in less than three. But I'm sure there's room for negotiation, isn't there? You've got three of the gang, but there's a fourth out there. You'd prefer a clean sweep, wouldn't you?'

'Oh, you mean Ronnie Walker?' Juliet grinned when she saw DC Arnold's jaw drop. 'His DNA was all over the cottage,' she said. 'We'll get him sooner rather than later. Ronnie has learning difficulties and ADHD, as you know. He's hardly a criminal mastermind. And I'm not sure that you've got much to make a deal with. Jordan Mitchell has already started to talk, and once we've got Ronnie, I expect he'll be a regular chatterbox. There's only one thing you've got that's worth anything, Max, and that's the money.'

DC Arnold leaned back and smiled. 'Ah yes, the money.'

'Fifty thousand pounds from the Elliotts and two hundred and fifty thousand pounds from the Balfours,' said Lulu.

'Coincidentally, just about what you'd need to buy a house in Trowbridge. And no need to share it with anyone else.'

'Every cloud has a silver lining, they say.'

'They do indeed,' said Lulu.

'You were wrong about the wallets being wiped on the thumb drives,' he said. 'Your cryptocurrency expert may not be such an expert after all.'

Lulu smiled. Arnold clearly hadn't realized that her account of Kirsty's advice had been a ruse, and she didn't intend to enlighten him.

'Max, if you were to return the Bitcoin wallets, I think we could persuade the CPS to agree to a lighter sentence,' said Juliet.

'How light?' asked DC Arnold.

'I don't know. I'd have to speak to them. Perhaps a four-year custodial sentence, which means you'd be out in two.'

DC Arnold rubbed his chin thoughtfully. 'So I'd give you three hundred thousand pounds and you'd give me what, a year? Twelve lousy months? Better I serve the full three years and keep the money. That's almost treble my salary, isn't it?'

Juliet looked at Lulu, and Lulu shrugged. It was hard to fault his maths.

38

Two uniformed constables took DC Arnold back to a holding cell. The detective held his head high and sneered at DI Kemp and Superintendent Pemberton as he passed them.

'I'm not seeing much remorse there,' said the superintendent. 'How did you not realize what was going on, Simon?'

'He was a good bag carrier, sir,' said DI Kemp. 'He never put a foot wrong. I had no idea.'

'Makes us look like bloody idiots,' said the superintendent. 'We let a fox into the henhouse.' He nodded at Juliet. 'Good work, inspector.'

'Thank you, sir. But most of the hard work was done by Lulu.'

The superintendent turned to Lulu. 'I'm told you were a superintendent with the Met,' he said.

'A long time ago, yes.'

'And you're a consultant now?'

'Not really. I'm a family friend of the Balfours – I'm godmother to Amanda Balfour, Olivia's mother.'

'Well, we were lucky to have your input.' The superintendent wrinkled his nose. 'I do have one question for you.'

'Okay.'

'How do you get your cat to stay on your shoulders like that?'

Lulu laughed. 'Practice,' she said.

'I'm more of a dog person myself. I have a golden retriever

at home.' He forced a smile. 'Not seen much of her over the past few days.' He gestured towards the holding cell. 'Personally, I think Arnold is being optimistic with his "six years, out in three". I'll have a word with the CPS. It seems to me that we can charge him with misconduct in public office, which has a fourteen-year maximum sentence plus an unlimited fine. Let's see how cocky he is when that charge lands.'

'That wouldn't help us get any closer to locating the hard drives, sir,' said Juliet.

'Do you have any thoughts on that?'

'Does DC Arnold have family in the area?' asked Lulu.

'His grandparents live just outside Trowbridge,' said DI Kemp.

'How far from Corsham?'

'Half an hour's drive.' Kemp's eyes widened. 'He said he was going to see them on Christmas Day, after we left the cottage in Corsham. We went back to the police station and he said he wanted to drop off Christmas presents for his grandparents, so I said okay. He was gone for a couple of hours.'

Juliet looked at Lulu. 'Worth a try?'

Lulu nodded. 'Definitely.'

39

DC Arnold's grandparents lived in a semi-detached house in the south of Trowbridge. The front garden had been paved over with space left for a monkey puzzle tree to grow. There was a gleaming red SUV parked beside the tree, and two wheelie bins stood nearby.

Juliet parked in the road and they approached the door. Lulu rang the bell. The door was opened by an elderly man who peered at them through thick-lensed spectacles. He was wearing a burgundy sweater and green corduroy trousers and holding an unlit pipe in his left hand.

'Mr Arnold?' said Juliet.

The man frowned. 'Yes?'

Juliet held out her warrant card. 'Inspector Juliet Donnelly,' she said. 'Can we come in and have a word?'

'Has something happened?'

'We'd like to talk to you about your grandson, Max.'

Mr Arnold smiled and nodded. 'He's a policeman, too. A detective.'

'Yes, we know,' said Juliet. 'Can we come in?'

Mr Arnold looked at Lulu, then began to blink furiously. 'Is that a cat? On your shoulders?'

'It is, yes,' said Lulu.

'I thought it was a fur collar.'

'Oh, I'd never wear a fur collar,' said Lulu. 'Fur belongs on animals.'

'It does, doesn't it.' He held the door open for them. 'Please, come in.'

They moved into the hall. There was a string festooned with Christmas cards along one wall and a dark wood coat rack covered with heavy coats by the door.

'My wife is in the sitting room,' said Mr Arnold.

Lulu and Juliet headed towards the sound of a television. Mrs Arnold was sitting on a flower-print sofa, knitting and watching a film. It was *The Dam Busters*, Lulu realized. There was an artificial Christmas tree near the window, covered with baubles and flashing fairy lights.

'Laura, these ladies are from the police. They wanted a word about Max.'

Mrs Arnold reached for the remote and turned off the television. It looked like a new model, Lulu thought, and it dominated the room. 'I like your car, Mr Arnold,' said Lulu. 'It's electric, right?'

Mr Arnold nodded. 'It's an MG. The name is English, but the cars are made in China now.'

'Must have cost a lot.'

'It wasn't cheap. But I needed a new car, and we both agreed the MG was the one to get.'

'Did you come into some money?'

'Sort of. Laura and I have taken out what they call an equity release loan. Basically, we used the house to get a loan. We treated ourselves to the car, a holiday in Vietnam and the television.'

'Well, that's nice,' said Lulu. 'Sounds like a great idea. Enjoy it while you can, right?'

'That's it, exactly,' said Mrs Arnold. 'You understand, but not everybody does.'

'What do you mean?' asked Lulu.

'Max was really unhappy when he found out. He accused us of squandering his inheritance, which was a bit rich. I mean, it's our money, isn't it?'

'Of course it is.'

'I think he thought he'd be getting this house when we eventually shuffled off this mortal coil,' said Mr Arnold. 'We got into quite an argument about it.'

'I'm sorry to hear that,' said Lulu.

'Oh, water under the bridge,' said Mrs Arnold. 'He got over it eventually. He hasn't mentioned it for a while. And he was here on Christmas Day – he popped over to say hello.'

'With presents?' said Lulu.

'Oh no. Just came round for a cup of tea. He said he was in the area and wanted to wish us a merry Christmas. That was nice of him.'

'Did he give you anything to look after?' asked Juliet. 'An envelope or something?'

Mr Arnold shook his head. 'No, nothing. Look, I don't mean to be rude, but what is this about? Has something happened?'

Before Juliet could reply, Conrad began to scratch at the door. 'I'm sorry, I think he wants to go out,' said Lulu. 'Could we possibly use your back garden?'

'Of course you can,' said Mrs Arnold.

'He's very tidy and he'll clean up after himself,' said Lulu.

Mrs Arnold laughed. 'I'm sure he will,' she said. 'Don't worry about it.'

Lulu smiled at Juliet. 'I'll take Conrad out while you explain the reason for our visit,' she said.

'No problem,' said Juliet.

Lulu headed out into the hall and along to the kitchen. The kitchen units and appliances all appeared to be new and the marble floor glistened as they walked over to the door. Lulu opened it and followed Conrad out into the garden, then closed the door behind them.

'I know what you're thinking,' said Conrad. 'He won't have hidden the thumb drives inside the house. There would always be a risk that his grandparents might stumble on them. And three years is a long time. If anything should happen to them and the house was sold, well, the thumb drives would be gone for good.'

'But the garden would always be here.'

Conrad nodded. 'No matter who was living here, he could always visit at night, sneak through the hedge and get them.'

'So what are you thinking – he dug a hole and buried them?'

'Exactly. They're small, right? It'd be the easiest thing in the world to pop out and dig a hole. Look over there, there's a spade and fork by the shed.'

Lulu looked over at a wooden shed in the far corner of the garden. Leaning against it were a green-handled spade and a matching fork. 'Okay,' she said. 'But the Arnolds are clearly proud of their garden. Wouldn't they notice a new hole?'

'He could have lifted some of the turf and hidden them underneath.'

Lulu sighed. 'What do we need to do? Go over the garden with a metal detector?'

Conrad looked around. 'I don't think so, no. He wouldn't do it anywhere that would be overlooked by the house, just

329

in case his grandparents looked out of a window and saw what he was doing. Then there's the neighbours. He couldn't risk any of them seeing him. Could you walk around a bit and see if you can find a spot that isn't overlooked?'

'Of course,' said Lulu. She walked to the end of the garden and turned to look around. It was overlooked from the houses on either side. 'Not here, obviously,' she said. She came slowly back towards the house. At the halfway point she could no longer see the windows of the neighbouring homes, but could still be clearly seen from any of the Arnolds' back windows. To her right was the garden shed; behind it was a rockery with chunks of granite and limestone interspersed with ferns, heathers and succulents. Lulu moved towards it. The closer she got to the rockery, the less she could be seen from the house. Eventually, the shed shielded her from all the windows.

'What do you think?' Lulu asked, looking down at the rockery.

'I think it's the perfect place,' Conrad said. He jumped down onto the edge of the rockery for a closer look. 'Yes, perfect. And no need for a spade or fork.'

'There are a lot of rocks here,' said Lulu.

Conrad jutted his chin up. 'Have you forgotten about my super-sensitive sense of smell?'

Lulu smiled. 'Of course I haven't.'

Conrad began moving between the chunks of stone, sniffing carefully, his tail pointing straight up. He paid particular attention to a large lump of greenish granite, but then shook his head and snorted softly before moving towards the centre of the rockery. He moved his head from side to side, his whiskers twitching. Then his legs stiffened as he approached a jagged piece of beige limestone. He sniffed

330

it top and bottom, then moved back and looked up at Lulu. 'He touched this,' he said.

'Are you sure?' She put up her hands. 'Sorry, of course you are.'

'The thing is, I can't lift the rock, obviously.'

'No opposable thumbs?'

Conrad jumped down from the rockery to the grass. 'Exactly,' he said.

'Allow me.' Lulu knelt down and lifted the rock with both hands. It weighed several kilos and she grunted as she moved it.

'Be careful of your back,' warned Conrad.

'I am,' said Lulu. She put the rock down on the tiled border. The soil underneath the rock was smooth and appeared undisturbed. 'Are you sure about this?' she asked.

'Oh ye of little faith,' said Conrad. He jumped up on the rockery and began clawing at the soil, scattering dirt everywhere.

Lulu stood up and stepped back. 'I can do that,' she said, but Conrad continued to dig.

Soil flew up into the air and scattered onto the lawn with a sound like rain. Conrad was tireless, his ears pricked up and his tail aloft as he worked his front paws. One inch down. Two. Three. His head began to disappear into the hole as he continued to dig. Suddenly he stopped. 'Aha!' he said triumphantly, backing out of the hole.

Lulu peered into the hole. She saw something blue in the soil. She reached down and pulled it out. It was a rolled-up blue latex glove, police issue. Unwrapping it, she saw that there were two hard objects inside, and she fished them out. They were thumb drives, one black and one white.

L T Shearer

'Who's a clever cat, then?' said Conrad.
Lulu smiled and nodded. 'You are,' she said.
'And don't you forget it.'
'I won't,' said Lulu. 'Ever.'

40

Lulu eased back on the throttle and moved *The Lark* to the side to make sure that the approaching boat had plenty of room. Like Lulu, the woman holding the tiller was wrapped up against the winter cold, with a red, green and yellow bobble hat that had a definite Christmas feel and a buttoned-up duffel coat. Lulu waved and the woman waved back as the two narrowboats passed with just a couple of feet between them.

'Happy day before New Year's Eve!' called the woman, in what sounded like a Birmingham accent. Her boat was called the *Over the Hull*, which was quite clever.

'Happy day before New Year's Eve!' Lulu called back.

'That isn't really a thing, is it?' said Conrad, who was sitting on the rear deck seat, keeping out of the wind.

Lulu smiled. 'No, you're quite right. She was just being friendly.'

Amanda and Donald had asked Lulu – and Conrad – to stay longer, but Lulu felt that they needed time alone to get over what had happened. Olivia was often close to tears and never let her mother out of her sight. It was clear that the family needed time to heal, and that healing would be easier if it was just the three of them.

'I still can't understand why that man Arnold did what he did,' said Conrad.

'Money,' said Lulu. 'Plain and simple. He didn't think he had enough, not to live the life he wanted. He probably assumed that one day he'd inherit money from his grand-parents, but then he realized that they were spending all their money now. Those equity release loan schemes are all well and good, but the downside is that the people who take them out usually don't have much to leave to their relatives.'

'But what he did was truly awful,' said Conrad. 'He terror-ized those two little girls and put their parents through hell.'

'He did, yes. But I don't think he ever meant to physically hurt them.'

'He wasn't with the girls all the time, though, was he? He had those other men do his dirty work, and Ballantine and Mitchell had both been in prison. I mean, Mitchell pushed a glass into someone's face. That's really violent behaviour.'

'Oh, I'm not defending him, Conrad. He deserves to be in prison for a long time. And prisons aren't nice places for men who have hurt children.'

'Are prisons nice places for anyone?'

'Not really,' said Lulu.

'So why would he take the risk of being sent there?'

'I think he was blinded by the money,' said Lulu. 'And he clearly always thought he was the smartest person in the room. He probably never even imagined that he'd get caught.'

Conrad chuckled. 'He reckoned without you and me, didn't he?'

'He did.'

'And Donald got his money back.'

'Yes, he did. All of it. And so did the Elliotts. And it looks as if the Novaks are selling their story to one of the tabloids, so at least they'll be getting something out of it.'

'It's an ill wind that blows nobody good,' said Conrad.

'Yes, it is,' said Lulu.

334

'And where will we go now? Back to London?'

'I thought we might cruise for a while. There are several thousand miles of canals and navigable rivers in the UK and we've only seen a fraction of them.'

'That sounds like fun.'

'It is, when you're sharing the journey with the right partner.'

'You say the sweetest things,' said Conrad.

'So do you,' said Lulu. 'I couldn't ask for a better companion.'

'Right back at you,' said Conrad.

The Cat Who Caught a Killer

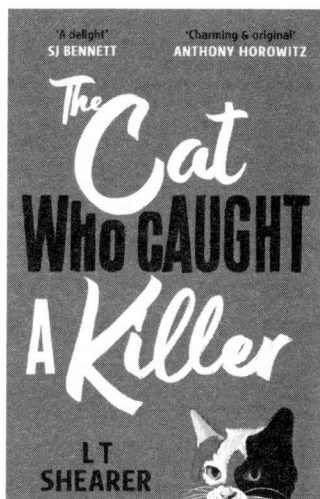

Meet Conrad. Conrad is a cat. You've never met a detective like him before.

Neither has Lulu Lewis, until he walks into her life one summer's day. In mourning after the recent death of her husband, the former police detective had expected a gentle retirement, quietly enjoying life on her new canal boat, *The Lark*, and visiting her mother-in-law in a nearby care home.

But when her mother-in-law dies suddenly in suspicious circumstances, Lulu senses foul play and resolves to find out what really happened. And a remarkable cat named Conrad will be with her every step of the way . . .

Out now!

The Cat Who Solved Three Murders

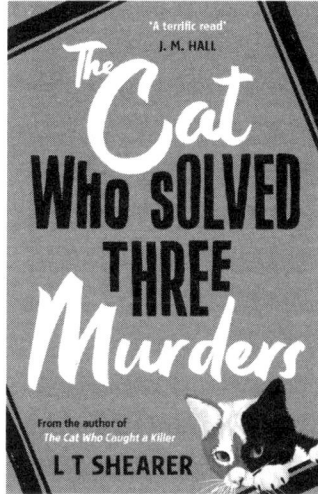

Retired police detective Lulu Lewis's life changed for ever when she met a street cat named Conrad. There's something very special about Conrad, but it's a secret she has to keep to herself.

When Lulu takes her narrowboat to Oxford, she is planning nothing more stressful than attending a friend's birthday party. And drinking a few glasses of Chardonnay.

But a brutal murder and a daring art theft mean her plans are shattered – instead, she and Conrad find themselves on the trail of a killer.

A killer who may well strike again . . .

Out now!

The Cat Who Cracked a Cold Case

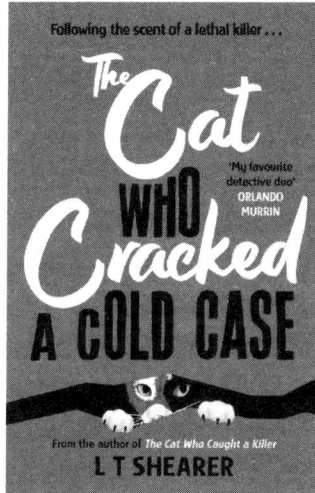

The life of Lulu Lewis, a retired police detective, took an unforgettable turn when Conrad first introduced himself to her. Unforgettable because:
a) Conrad is a special cat;
b) he told her this himself.
Yes, that's right, he can talk.

Visiting an old friend in Manchester, the pair stumble across a chilling news report about a trail of bodies found across the city that echoes a string of cold-case murders from Lulu's past in London.

Joining forces with the local police, the pair must use every ounce of their intuition in order to find a connection between the seemingly random killings – and track down a ruthless murderer . . .

Out now!

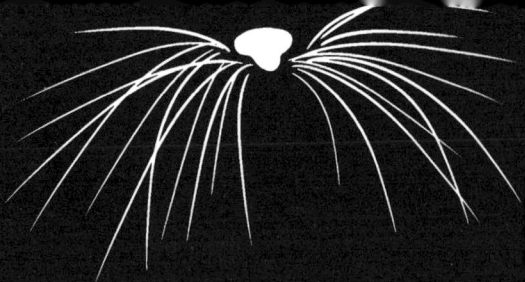

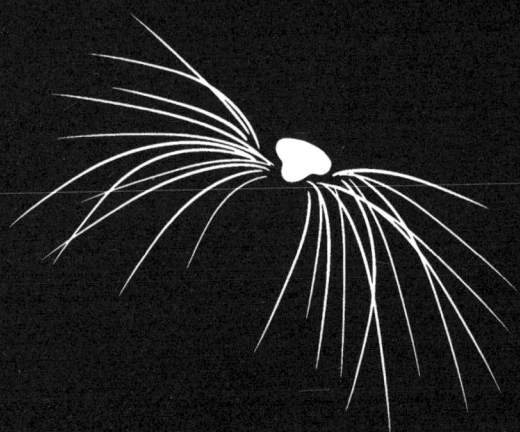

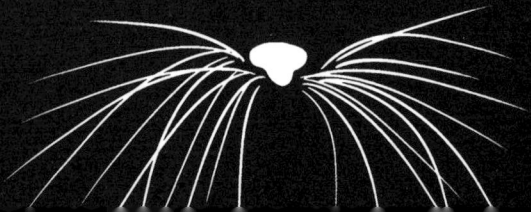